FALL OF NIGHT

ALSO BY JONATHAN MABERRY

NOVELS

Code Zero

Extinction Machine

Assassin's Code

King of Plagues

The Dragon Factory

Patient Zero

Joe Ledger: Special Ops

Dead of Night

The Wolfman

The Nightsiders: The Orphan Army

Deadlands: Ghostwalkers

Watch Over Me

Fire & Ash

Flesh & Bone

Dust & Decay

Rot & Ruin

Bad Moon Rising

Dead Man's Song

Ghost Road Blues

V-Wars (editor)

V-Wars: Blood and Fire (editor)

Out of Tune (editor)

NONFICTION

Wanted Undead or Alive

They Bite

Zombie CSU

The Cryptopedia

Vampire Universe

Vampire Slayer's Field Guide to the
Undead (as Shane MacDougall)

Ultimate Jujutsu

Ultimate Sparring

The Martial Arts Student Logbook

Judo and You

GRAPHIC NOVELS

Marvel Universe vs. Wolverine

Marvel Universe vs. The Punisher

Marvel Universe vs. The Avengers

Captain America: Hail Hydra

Klaws of the Panther

Doomwar

Black Panther: Power

Marvel Zombies Return

Rot & Ruin

V-Wars: The Court of the
Crimson Queen

Bad Blood

FALL
OF
NIGHT

JONATHAN MABERRY

 St. Martin's Griffin ⚑ New York

FALL OF NIGHT. Copyright © 2014 by Jonathan Maberry. All rights reserved. Printed in the United States of America. For information, address St. Martin's Press, 175 Fifth Avenue, New York, N.Y. 10010.

www.stmartins.com

The Library of Congress Cataloging-in-Publication Data is available upon request.

ISBN 978-1-250-03494-6 (trade paperback)
ISBN 978-1-250-03495-3 (e-book)

St. Martin's Griffin books may be purchased for educational, business, or promotional use. For information on bulk purchases, please contact Macmillan Corporate and Premium Sales Department at 1-800-221-7945, extension 5442, or write specialmarkets@macmillan.com.

First Edition: September 2014

10 9 8 7 6 5 4 3 2 1

THIS ONE IS FOR SAM WEST-MENSCH.

AND, AS ALWAYS, FOR SARA JO.

ACKNOWLEDGMENTS

A number of good people provided invaluable information, advice, and assistance during the research and writing of this novel. In no particular order they are: Michael Sicilia, public affairs manager with the California Homeland Security Exercise and Evaluation Program; Detective Joe McKinney, San Antonio PD; parasitologist Carl Zimmer; ethnobotanist Dr. Wade Davis; comparative physiologist Mike Harris; Dr. John Cmar, instructor of medicine at The Johns Hopkins University School of Medicine and an infectious disease specialist at Sinai Hospital of Baltimore, Maryland; the guys at First Night Productions—Louis Ozawa Changchien, Heath Cullens, and Paul Grellong; Dr. Richard Tardell, specialist in emergency medicine; comedians Jeremy Essig and Tom Segura; and screenwriter/director Eric Red. Special thanks to George Romero for inventing the genre and to John Skipp and Craig Spector for ensuring that "zombie literature" would endure. Thanks, as always, to my literary agents, Sara Crowe and Harvey Klinger; my film agent, Jon Cassir of CAA; my editor, Michael Homler, and all the good folks at St. Martin's Griffin; and my social media guru, Don Lafferty.

And a hearty, meaty thanks to the winners of the I Need to Be a Zombie contest: Jake DeGroot, Lydia Rose, Ross Cruickshank, Albert Godown, Missy Lan Goodnight, Amanda Snuffer, John Langan, Rob Meyer, Dustin Lee Frye, Patrick Freivald, Mike Chrusciel, and Deborah Varas. Rest in pieces.

PART ONE

CONTAINMENT

But I've a rendezvous with Death
At midnight in some flaming town.

—Alan Seeger, "I Have a Rendezvous with Death"

CHAPTER ONE
DOLL FACTORY ROAD
STEBBINS COUNTY, PENNSYLVANIA

"This is Billy Trout, reporting live from the apocalypse . . ."

The car sat in the middle of the road with the radio playing at full blast.

All four doors were open.

The windows were cracked and there was one small red handprint on the glass.

The voice on the radio was saying that this was the end of the world.

There was no one in the car, no one in the streets. No one in any of the houses or stores. There wasn't a single living soul there to hear the reporter's message.

It didn't matter, though.

They already knew.

CHAPTER TWO
STEBBINS LITTLE SCHOOL
STEBBINS, PENNSYLVANIA

Stebbins County police officer JT Hammond pushed on the crashbar and the door opened. There were bodies outside in the school parking lot. Scores of them, crumpled and broken.

JT looked around for movement and saw none. "It's clear."

He stepped outside and held the door as the line of infected people shambled out.

Adults and children.

Billy Trout and JT's partner, Desdemona Fox, came last, each of them holding a small child in their arms.

The National Guardsmen popped several flares on the far side of the parking lot to attract the masses of living dead. On that side of the lot, behind the chain-link fence, all of the Guard trucks sent up a continuous wail with their sirens. The dead shuffled that way, drawn by light and noise.

One of the victims, a man who had been bitten by what had been his own wife and children, stared glassily at the stiffly moving bodies. Then he raised a weak arm and pointed to the soldiers.

"Are they coming to help us?" he asked.

"They're coming," said Dez, hating herself for the implied lie. She told the wounded to sit down by the wall. Some of them immediately fell asleep; others stared with empty eyes at the glowing flares high in the sky.

For a moment it left Dez, JT, and Trout as the only ones standing, each of them holding a dying child. The tableau was horrific and surreal. They stared at each other, frozen into this moment because the next was too horrible to contemplate. Then they saw movement.

JT peered into the shadows. "They're coming."

"The Guard?" asked Dez, a last flicker of hope in her eyes.

"No," he said.

They heard the moans. For whatever reason, pulled by some other aspect of their hunger, a few of the dead had not followed the flares and the sirens, and now they staggered toward the living standing by the open door. More of them rounded the corner of the building. Perhaps drawn by a more powerful force.

The smell of fresh meat.

"We have to go," said Trout.

"And right now," agreed JT. He kissed the little boy on the cheek and set him down on the ground between two sleeping infected. Trout sighed brokenly and did the same. Dez Fox clung to the little girl in her arms.

"There's more of them," said Trout.

"Dez, come on . . ." murmured JT.

But Dez turned away as if protecting the little girl she held from him. "Please, Hoss . . . ?"

"Dez."

"I can't!"

"Give her to me, honey," JT said gently. "I'll take care of her. Don't worry."

It took everything Dez had left to allow JT to take the sleeping girl from her arms. She shook her head, hating him, hating the world, hating everything.

"Better get inside," JT warned. Some of the zombies were very close now. Twenty paces.

Trout ran to the door. "Dez, JT, come on. We have to go. We can't leave this open or they'll get inside."

Dez reluctantly moved toward the door, backing away from the child she had to abandon. Trout reached and took her hand, and when she returned his squeeze it was crushingly painful. He pulled her toward the door as the first of the dead stepped into the pale glow thrown by the emergency light.

"JT, come on, let's go!" Trout yelled.

The big cop did not move. He held the little girl so gently, stroking her hair and murmuring to her.

"JT!" cried Dez. "We have to close the door!"

He smiled at her. "Yeah," he said, "you do."

They waited for him to come, but he stayed where he was.

"JT?" Dez asked in a small, frightened voice. "What's wrong?"

JT kissed the little girl's forehead and set her down with the others. Then he straightened and showed her his wrist. It was criss-crossed with glass cuts from the helicopter attack.

"What?" she asked.

He pushed his sleeve up.

That was when she saw it. A semicircular line of bruised punctures.

Dez whimpered something. A question. "How?"

"Upstairs, when those bastards tackled us. One of them got me . . . I didn't see which one. Doesn't matter. What's done is done."

Then the full realization hit Dez. *"NO!"*

It was all Trout could do to hold her back. She struggled wildly and even punched him. The blow rocked him, but he did not let go. He would never let go. Never.

"No!" Dez yelled. "You can't!"

The dead were closing in on JT. He unslung the shotgun. Across the parking lot the last flares were fading and the trucks turned off their sirens, one by one.

"Go on, honey," JT said.

"No goddamn way, Hoss," she growled, fighting with Trout, hitting him, hurting him. "We stand together and we fucking well go down together."

"Not this time," JT said, and he was smiling.

Trout could see it even if Dez could not, that JT was at peace with this.

"No! No! No!" Dez kept repeating.

"I'm going to keep these bastards away from those kids as long as I can," said JT. "I need you to go inside. I need you to tell the National Guard to do what they have to do, but make sure they do it right. They got to wipe 'em all out. All of them."

What he meant was as clear as it was horrible.

"JT—don't leave me!"

He shook his head. "I won't ever leave you, kid. Not in any way that matters. Now . . . go on. There are eight hundred people inside the school, Dez. There are children inside that building who need you. You can't leave them."

And there it was.

Dez sagged against Trout and he pulled her inside and held her tight as the door swung shut with a clang.

They heard the first blasts of the shotgun. Trout didn't hear the next one because Dez was screaming.

JT stood with his back to the line of bite victims, holding the shotgun by its double pistol grips, firing, pumping, firing. There was almost no need to aim. There were so many and they were so close. He emptied the gun and used it as a club to kill as many as he could before his arms began to ache. Then he dropped the gun and pulled his Glock. He had one full magazine left.

He debated using the bullets on the wounded, but then he heard the whine of the helicopters' rotors change, intensify, draw closer; and he knew what would happen next. He just had to keep the monsters away from the children until then. Soon . . . soon it would all be over, and it would happen fast.

He took the gun in both hands and fired.

And fired.

And fired.

Inside the school building, huddled together on the floor, Desdemona Fox and Billy Trout held each other as bullets hammered like cold rain on the walls. It seemed to go on forever. Pain and noise and death seemed to be the only things that mattered anymore.

And then . . . silence.

Plaster dust drifted down on them as the roar of the helicopters' rotors dwindled to faintness and then was gone.

"It's over," Trout whispered. He stroked Dez's hair and kissed her head and wept with her. "I won't ever leave you, Dez. Never."

Dez slowly raised her head. Her face was dirty and streaked with tears, and her eyes were filled with grief and hurt. She raised trembling fingers to his face. She touched his cheeks, his ear, his mouth.

"I know," she said.

Dez wrapped her arms around Trout with crushing force. He allowed it, gathering her even closer. They clung to one another and sobbed hard enough to shatter the whole ugly world.

CHAPTER THREE
STEBBINS LITTLE SCHOOL
STEBBINS, PENNSYLVANIA

The gunship hung in the air like a monstrous insect. Except for the heavy beat of the rotors there was no sound, inside or out. Sergeant Hap Rollins, the door-gunner, crouched behind the M134 minigun, mouth acrid with the gun smoke he'd swallowed, his ears ringing with remembered thunder. Thousands of shell casings rolled around his feet, eddying like a brass tide as the Black Hawk and its crew waited.

Waited.

Rollins removed his hands from the minigun's handles but his skin and bones still quivered from the vibrations of firing four thousand rounds per minute in a steady flow down into the parking lot. He reached up to his face and with clumsy fingers pushed his goggles up onto his forehead. His eyes burned from the smoke, but as he blinked he could feel wetness on his lashes. It wasn't sweat and he knew it. Rollins wiped at his eyes with the backs of his trembling hands.

Below was a scene conjured in hell itself.

The parking lot of the elementary school was littered with the dead.

A few of them whole, most of them destroyed, torn apart by the relentless plunging fire from Rollins's Black Hawk and the other gunships.

But what drew Rollins's eyes and pulled tears from them was the figure that lay twisted into a scarecrow sprawl by the back door. It was a tall black man. Or it had been. A man dressed in the uniform of a police officer.

A man who had been infected; a man no one and no science could save.

But he hadn't turned yet. That was clear to Rollins and probably to everyone. The man had come out of the school leading a staggering line of sick and injured people.

All infected, all dying. None of them dead yet.

Another cop, a woman, had tried to pull him back inside. Rollins could tell from her body language that she was screaming and fighting to pull the male officer to safety. However another man, a white man, dragged her away and forced her inside the school.

Two of the uninfected getting clear.

Leaving the others outside.

Leaving them to die.

The cop had stood his ground and as the zombies closed around him, he fired and fired and fired. It was the most heroic thing Hap Rollins had ever seen in twelve years as a combat vet.

The man had to know that there was no hope.

None.

So why did he fight?

The answer huddled behind him against the now closed door to the Stebbins Little School. A little girl. Other little kids.

The cop fought like a wild man to keep them safe from the monsters. To make sure that their last memory was not of being consumed. To protect them from that while he waited for the big black insects in the sky to end it all with bullets.

Rollins had been in the best position to fire on the black cop.

And the kids.

The orders came.

The killing began.

The dying began.

And the tears.

Now the infected were dead. All of them. The dying and the risen dead. All of them littered on the pavement and splashed against the walls of the school. Against the building designated as the town emergency shelter.

Rollins was not a deeply educated man, but he understood the concepts of irony and farce.

And tragedy.

He wanted to look away from the torn body of the cop and the smaller rag doll figure of the little girl. Wanted to.

Couldn't.

On some level Sergeant Rollins felt that it would have been a sinful thing to do. Disrespectful.

Then the helicopter began moving, rising and turning, pulling him away from the evidence of such hurt and harm. As it went, Hap Rollins hung his head and prayed to a God he was absolutely certain had turned His back on this world.

CHAPTER FOUR
PENNSYLVANIA NATIONAL GUARD FIELD COMMAND POST INSIDE STEBBINS COUNTY

Major General Simeon Zetter watched the live feeds on the screens of four laptops set side by side on the big table. Around him the other officers under his command watched in utter silence. No one spoke. All Zetter could hear was the tinny sound of helicopter rotors from the laptop speakers and the labored exhalations of the men and women around him. Everyone was panting as if they'd all run up a steep hill even though all they had done was watch.

The voice of a Black Hawk pilot suddenly cut through the stillness.

"Zero movement," he said. "Spotters observe zero movement on all sides of the target."

The target was the school.

On the screen, four M1117 armored security vehicles entered through the main gate as machine gunners behind the fence kept watch. The M1117s split and each one began rolling along one side of the school. The vehicles bounced over ragged pieces of the dead.

"Confirmed," said the same voice. "Zero movement."

Zetter heard several of the officers let out deep sighs.

He reached for a microphone and gave a string of orders for his people to expand the ground search using the modified Desert Patrol Vehicles. Lines of these dune buggy–like, two-man vehicles vanished into the surrounding woods and neighborhoods, going where the heavier and clumsier Humvees couldn't.

Then Zetter sat back and let out his own sigh. He got to his feet and turned to the gathered officers, all of whom fell silent.

"This is a tragic and terrible day in American history," he said. "We have all been asked to make hard decisions and to carry them out with professionalism and efficiency."

The officers nodded.

"You are all aware of the political delicacy of what has happened today."

More nods, but now they were careful. There were three huge elephants in the room with them, and nobody wanted to talk about any of them except the infection. That was safe ground because it was why they were there. The president and the governor of Pennsylvania had mobilized the Guard to stop the spread of an old Cold War bioweapon that had been released accidentally by a former Soviet scientist. That was, by strict military parlance, a clusterfuck. And the pathogen's virulence was such that it spread throughout the town, infecting virtually everyone. Killing them. And then in a twist of mad science that even Zetter found hard to accept, it brought the dead back as aggressive disease vectors. The risen dead, driven by the genetically engineered parasites that made up the substance of the pathogen, attacked like sharks—mindless, endlessly hungry, and vicious.

That resulted in the second elephant in the room, the one each of them knew would haunt their lives and taint the military here on the ground and the administration in Washington. Acting under orders to sterilize the town in order to stop the spread of the infection, Zetter's command predecessor, Lieutenant Colonel Macklin Dietrich, had ordered the town's emergency shelter—the Stebbins Little School—to be destroyed. It was filled with people, many of who were infected. Every officer understood the necessity for that kill order; most of them even agreed with it.

However, a reporter, Billy Trout from Regional Satellite News, was inside the school. Inside, but connected to the outside world via a live news feed. As the gunships opened up on the building, Trout made an impassioned plea to the world to save the uninfected children. The plea hit every single news service. The media and public outcry was immediate and massive.

Massive.

And that directly led to the ugliest part of this—at least for the officers in that command center. The reporter's plea was broadcast to the troops outside the building via the school's public address system.

The result?

One by one the soldiers at the fence stood up and refused to follow orders. They would not kill the children.

It was mutiny, and one officer—a young lieutenant—tried to nip it in the bud, but he was overwhelmed and, eventually, outranked as a more senior officer—Captain Rice—went to stand with the mutineers.

The president had immediately ordered General Zetter to relieve Dietrich of his post and assume overall command of the situation. Every officer there knew that it was unfair to put the blame on

Dietrich, just as it was unfair that the public and the media would demonize them for their actions in Stebbins County.

Actions that, had they not been taken, would have opened the door to a massive and perhaps unstoppable pandemic.

That was the biggest elephant in the room, and nobody there dared talk about it.

Now, another chapter had been completed. Zetter had contacted the reporter and two police officers inside the school and made them a deal. If they sent out every infected person then the school would be spared.

It was a bad deal and everyone—inside and outside the school—hated it.

But it would play well in the media. As well as something like this could play.

Zetter looked at each of his officers and read variations on this story in each pair of eyes. He grunted softly and nodded.

"You all have your assignments," he said. "Let's finish the cleanup so we can all go home."

The officers stood to attention—crisply, silently, and with absolutely no trace of expression or emotion on their faces. Zetter couldn't blame them for not wanting to show anything to him. He was the hatchet man for the administration, and that administration would be looking for more scapegoats to sacrifice on the altar of public outrage. It was how the politics of warfare worked, and it was how that worked probably going back to Alexander the Great.

When he was alone, Zetter sat down and sagged into his chair, feeling all of his years and more that he hadn't earned. He knew that once this was over he was as done as Dietrich. Done and gone.

He wasn't even sure he minded.

Not after a day like today.

He reached for his phone and punched in the number that direct-dialed the White House Situation Room.

The chief of staff, Sylvia Ruddy, answered the phone and then put it on speaker.

"Mr. President," said General Zetter, "we have contained the outbreak. It's over."

CHAPTER FIVE
GOOD-NITES MOTOR COURT
FAYETTE COUNTY, PENNSYLVANIA

Dr. Herman Volker parked his car in one of the vacant slips outside of the small motel. He turned off the engine and sat for nearly ten minutes watching the rain hammer down on the windshield. The sluicing water blurred the glass and transformed the neon sign above the office into an impressionist painting. All pinks and greens.

He took a handkerchief from his pocket and wiped his eyes, blew his nose, and then tossed it onto the seat.

Then he opened the door and stepped into the downpour. He wore trousers, a dress shirt, tennis shoes, and a blue sweater, and he looked like the tired, defeated, sad old man that he was. His feet barely lifted from the ground as he shuffled toward the door, pulled it open, and went inside. He carried no suitcase or overnight bag. The only thing he brought with him was his wallet, and it took him a long time to organize his thoughts well enough to fill out the information sheet given to him by the bored night clerk. He paid for the room with his credit card, took the key, and walked outside again. His room was on the same strip where he'd parked.

Volker used the keycard to open the door, went inside, closed the door.

He sat down on the edge of the bed and stared at the ugly painting on the wall. An artless mess that was supposed to remind people of Joan Miró, but didn't. Not in any way that lifted the soul.

The doctor stared at the painting for a long time.

CHAPTER SIX
STEBBINS LITTLE SCHOOL
STEBBINS, PENNSYLVANIA

At first they could only sit there, huddled against the wall, locked in each other's arms, beaten mute by horror, wrapped in their cloak of shared grief.

Time was fractured and each second seemed to expand and stretch, refusing to end, refusing to pass.

Dez kept repeating JT's name.

Over and over.

Was it a plea or a prayer? Trout couldn't tell.

Then suddenly Trout felt a change in Dez. It was a subtle thing, but it was there. One moment she was empty of everything except her pain, and then he felt her body change. Her muscles tensed. No, that was wrong. It was more like they somehow remembered their strength. She straightened in his arms and her clutching hands gripped him and pushed him slowly but inexorably back. He resisted for a moment, then let her create that distance between them. A necessary distance for her, he was sure of it. And in that space Dez Fox reclaimed the personal power stolen from her by disease pathogens, guns, and betrayal.

There was a final moment of intimate contact, when their faces were inches apart. Dez was flushed, her face puffy from weeping, her eyes red and filled with pain. Then he saw the blue of those eyes become cold and hard. And unforgiving.

Her full lips compressed into a tight line with just a hint of a snarl. Trout knew that look, and he was fully aware of how dangerous she was when her mouth wore that shape and her eyes were filled with that much ice. So, he eased back, releasing his embrace, shifting his body toward the wall and away from her.

There was one heartbreaking moment, though, where he saw that she was aware of his allowance and acceptance of her power, and how he withheld his own. Dez gave him a single, tiny nod of shared awareness.

Then she got to her feet. It took effort and it took time, but when she was standing Dez towered over him, and he sat there in her shadow, looking up at her.

"We have to make sure the kids are okay," she said in a voice from which all emotion had been banished. Trout wondered what it cost her to affect that much control.

"Yes," he said.

"And we have to search the building again."

"Okay."

She began to turn.

"Dez—" he began but she held up a hand.

"No," she said. Then she began climbing the stairs.

No.

Trout wondered if she thought he was going to say something about JT's sacrifice. Something encouraging about how the kids inside were safe. Or something more personal. Something about what he felt.

He knew that what he'd planned to say was that he'd do whatever she needed him to do, to help however he could.

But he wondered if those were the words that would have actually come out of his mouth. Dez hadn't thought so.

Maybe, he thought as he got heavily to his feet, she was right.

"Damn," he said aloud.

He patted his pockets and realized that the satellite phone Goat had given him was somewhere upstairs. He needed to get it. To tell Goat what just happened. To have Goat tell the world.

This is Billy Trout reporting live from the apocalypse.

There was more truth to tell. More of the story he needed everyone to know.

Maybe it would help.

Trout was past knowing that, or anything, for certain.

Aching in body and heart, Billy Trout lumbered up the stairs after Dez.

CHAPTER SEVEN
TUNNEL HILL ROAD
STEBBINS COUNTY, PENNSYLVANIA

Corporal Lonnie Silk was sure he was dying.

He could feel the warmth leave him, running in lines inside his trousers, down his legs, pooling in his shoes.

The bleeding wasn't as bad now, but he didn't think that was a good thing. As his daddy used to say, you can't pour coffee from an empty cup.

And he felt so empty.

Of blood.

Of breath.

Of everything. Like God was rolling up the whole world to throw it in the crapper.

It was like that.

The rainswept street was all harsh whites and blacks in the stark illumination thrown by the headlights of abandoned cars and businesses with all the lights turned on but nobody there. The glow gave everything a harsh look, like crime scene photos in old newspapers. No soft edges, even with the rain.

Lonnie knew that he was a dead man. Would be a dead man soon. The captain had told everyone in his platoon about the infection. About how it worked. About what it did.

About how there was nothing anyone could do.

Nothing except die.

And how fucked up was that? How crazy? How impossible?

His legs needed to stop moving, and he collapsed against the corner of a burned-out store at the corner of Tunnel Hill and Doll Factory Road. Across the street was the hulking mannequin factory that had given the road its name. The windows were smashed out, the parking lot littered with the blackened shells of cars and bodies. A car stood alone in the middle of the intersection, its radio playing.

He moved on, stumbling down the long blocks, splashing through puddles. Some were filled with dirty rainwater; some were viscous pools of dark red.

There were so many bodies. All of them sprawled in a sea of black blood. Thousands of shell casings stood like tiny islands. Weak sunshine and dying firelight gleamed on the metal and winked on the rippling surface of that dark lake. No wind stirred the surface, though. Lonnie knew that for sure, and it was one of the things that made dying feel worse, more deeply terrifying.

The black blood was alive with worms. Tiny, white, threadlike. So small that they looked like thin slices carved from grains of rice. But there were so many of them.

From where he stood, Lonnie couldn't see the worms, but he knew they were there. The worms were everywhere.

Everywhere.

He could feel them.

On him.

In him.

Wriggling through the ragged lips of the bite on his arm. Twisting and writhing inside the lines of blood that ran crookedly down his body.

He tried not to look at the wound. He could not bear to see the things that moved inside it, around it.

He could feel that wound, though. And even that was wrong.

The bite was deep. Skin and muscle were torn. It should hurt.

It should be screaming at him with the voices of all those torn nerve endings.

Instead it was nearly silent.

Cold.

Distant.

As if the skin around that bite was no longer connected to him. No longer belonged to him. As if it was on him but not of him.

Cold emptiness ran outward from the wound, tunneling through his body like threads of ice. Every minute he felt more of the cold and less of the warmth he needed to feel. With every step he knew that his desperate heart, his pounding heart, was pumping that infection throughout his body. Cold blossomed like small, ugly flowers all over him. Taking him away, stealing his awareness so that he wasn't even sure he could feel himself dying.

Would he slip away completely and not be aware of it?

The captain had said something about that. And that guy on the radio, the reporter trapped inside the Stebbins Little School. What was his name? Billy Trout? He'd said something scary. Something that was crazy wrong.

That the self—the consciousness, the personality, the everything—of the victim didn't die with the body. Instead it would be there. Hovering, floating, aware but no longer in control of the meat and bone that had been its home.

"Please," said Lonnie, asking of the day. Of the moment. Of anyone or anything that could listen. "Please . . ."

He did not want to die like this. He didn't want to become something sick and twisted. He didn't want to be a ghost haunting that stolen home of flesh and blood.

Above him, somewhere up there, hidden by the buildings, he could hear helicopters. Black Hawks. Vipers. Apaches.

And way above them, the growl of jets carrying fuel-air bombs, waiting to turn the whole place, the whole town, into hot ash.

Forty minutes ago Lonnie Silk would have screamed and run at the thought of that fiery response to the plague.

Now he looked to the heavens, and prayed for it.

It was better to burn on earth than be damned here. Hell here, heaven later?

"Please," he said to the sounds of salvation that flew in formation above the storm clouds. "Please."

But there was no one and nothing to help him.

Lonnie turned and headed along a side street toward the edge of town.

Trying to go home.

CHAPTER EIGHT
OFFICE OF THE NATIONAL SECURITY ADVISOR
THE WHITE HOUSE, WASHINGTON, D.C.

Scott Blair, the national security advisor, wanted a drink so bad his skin ached. He was not normally a drinking man. A few martinis at a State Department dinner, a beer after eighteen holes. But now he wanted to crawl into a closet with a bottle of bourbon and chug the entire thing.

Instead he opened a drawer, removed a bottle of Tums E-X, shook ten of them into his palm, and them shoved the entire handful into his mouth.

Everything was spinning. His head, the room, the media, and maybe the world.

The actual world.

All because of a tiny shithole town in an inbred part of Pennsylvania no one gave a damn about. Not in any strategic sense.

The devil is off the chain.

That was how it started. For Blair and for everyone.

The director of Central Intelligence called the president to forward an urgent message from a nonentity named Oscar Price, a CIA handler whose only job it was to babysit retired Soviet defectors. How hard could it be to keep tabs on a bunch of old men? Instead, one of Price's charges, Dr. Herman Volker, a former Cold War scientist, had taken an old and classified bit of science and turned it into what could only be described as a "doomsday weapon."

Doomsday.

There was a time in Blair's life when that concept was a ludicrous abstraction. A scenario to be considered with no more reality than something cooked up by a Dungeons & Dragons games master.

Except now this wasn't a role-playing game for nerds. It was the most important issue to ever cross Blair's desk. Perhaps the most important issue to ever cross the desk to fall under the umbrella of "national security."

A doomsday weapon. Conceived by devious minds, funded by a

desperate government, constructed in covert labs, and then brought to America by a defector who was long past the point of relevance.

And given a name that was far too appropriate.

Lucifer.

Blair wondered if that kind of name was too close to actually tempting fate. It felt like a challenge. Or an invitation.

All Price had to do was keep the old prick out of trouble until old age or the grace of a just God killed the son of a bitch.

But then that message came in.

The devil was off the chain.

That was how it started. A flurry of phone calls, teams of investigators put into the field, and the machinery of control and containment put into play. Except that nothing was controlled, and Blair did not share the president's confidence in General Zetter that this thing was contained.

His desk was littered with intelligence reports. The latest on the storm. Satellite pictures and thermal scans of Stebbins County. Casualty estimates. And projections of how bad this could get if even a single infected person made it past the Q-zone. This wasn't swine flu or bird flu or any other damn flu. It was a genetically engineered bioweapon driven by parasitic urges that were a million times more immediate and aggressive than those of a virus, though equally as encompassing and indifferent to suffering. Every infected person became a violent vector. Everyone exposed to the black blood was likely to become infected, even if they were not bitten. The larvae in the infected blood clung to the skin and would find an opening. Any opening. A scratch would do it.

There were response protocols. Of course there were. Politics floated on a sea of paper, so there were reports for everything. There were reams of notes on the Lucifer program. Tens of thousands of pages. And right now virologists and microbiologists and parasitologists at the Centers for Disease Control, the National Biodefense Analysis and Countermeasures Center, and over a dozen bioweapons labs were poring over those protocols and the accompanying scientific research records. The protocols prepared after Volker's defection were very specific. Coldly alarming, detailing in precise terms the consequences of inaction or insufficient action.

There was, in fact, only one possible outcome of a Lucifer outbreak.

Doomsday was no longer an abstraction.

Blair made a series of phone calls to get the latest on the hunt for Volker. With each call his heart sank lower in his chest.

The bastard had vanished. He'd walked out of his house, got in his car, and disappeared from the face of the earth, taking with him the greatest hopes of understanding his variation of the pathogen. Lucifer 113, the version loose in Stebbins, did not precisely match the profiles of the old Cold War version. It was much faster, much more aggressive, and the reanimation of the "dead" victims took place in seconds.

Seconds.

It would mean that in any confrontation with a group of infected, the newly bitten victim would become an aggressive vector—a combatant, in a twisted way—while the fight still raged. Apart from the obvious tactical disadvantages, that scenario created a devastating psychological component. When soldiers would be required to suddenly fire upon their fellow soldiers, doubt and hesitation would be born. And many more would die.

It was a nightmare.

It was surreal.

His secretary tapped on the door, poked her head in, and waggled a sheaf of papers at him. "Mr. Blair? The speechwriters have a draft of POTUS's address. They want you to take a look at it."

"Good, let me see it."

She crossed to his desk and handed him the speech. "This is unusual. Asking for your input on a speech."

"'Usual' was last week, Cindy." He bent over the speech.

But Cindy lingered. "Sir . . . the word is that they stopped this thing. That's true, right? I mean, this is just winding down now?"

Blair raised his head and looked at her for a long time, saying nothing. She finally retreated from him and fled. He wished he had something comforting to say to Cindy. However, he liked the woman and didn't want to lie to her.

Blair read through the speech, making disgusted sounds at the end of nearly every paragraph. The speech—written by well-intentioned people who lacked a clear perspective on the problem—took the wrong tack, focusing on a response to Billy Trout's impassioned and ill-considered Internet tirade. Blair felt the president needed to go in a radically different direction. And not only in terms of the speech. General Zetter in Pennsylvania kept trying to convince the president that the devil was *back* on the leash, that the situation was contained. Which, as Blair viewed it, was a criminally distorted view of the facts. He grabbed a red pencil and began hastily redrafting it.

CHAPTER NINE
STEBBINS LITTLE SCHOOL
STEBBINS, PENNSYLVANIA

Billy Trout went to the auditorium to find his camera. It lay on its side among the debris. Less than an hour ago the big multipane windows that lined the east wall had been obliterated by machine-gun fire as attack helicopters fired on the school.

Trout looked at the damage and shivered.

Tens of thousands of rounds had torn the window frames apart, showering the big hall with millions of fragments of glittering glass and jagged wood. The bullets had carved away at the bricks, leaving a gaping maw through which cold winds blew the relentless rain.

The kids were all gone now, moved to other rooms so their wounds could be tended to. It was a freak of happenstance—the only real luck Trout could remember in that long, bad day—that none of these kids had been shot. He couldn't even work out a scenario that explained it. A quirk of physics, a bizarre collision of angle, the storm winds, uncertain targeting, the slanted floor with its rows of seats, and who knew what else.

But the kids were alive.

Not okay, not all right. Merely alive.

Trout skirted the main floor, which was nothing but bullet-pocked detritus, and made his way to the stage, where he'd left his camera and satellite phone. They were beaded with rain, but when he tested them they still worked.

Another stroke of luck, and it made him wonder about the perversity of whatever gods there were that small luck was afforded them while on the whole the fortunes of Stebbins County seemed to have gone bad in the worst possible way.

Shaking his head, he took his gear backstage and found a small office with a desk. Trout cleaned the camera lens, wiped off every last trace of moisture, and set the camera's tripod on the desk. He tested the mike and the signal.

Then he called Goat to make sure that this message would go out as smoothly as the others. The satellite phone was routed directly to Goat's Skype account.

The phone rang and rang.

Goat never answered.

Trout checked all of the connections. Everything seemed to be in order.

He called again.

Nothing, just the meaningless ring with no answer.

Screw it, he thought. He'd record an update anyway and send it to Goat. Maybe his friend was ordering a refill at that nice, warm, safe goddamn Starbucks. Or he was in the nice, warm, safe bathroom taking a leak.

"I am going to let Dez kick your bony ass," Trout promised as he clipped on his lavaliere mike. He hit the record button and set himself in front of the camera.

"This is Billy Trout, reporting live from the apocalypse," he began, then shook his head. "I know how that must sound. If you're anywhere but here it's probably pretentious and corny. But not from where I'm sitting. Right now I'm in a small office near where the military fired on six hundred children a few minutes ago. Since then we've reached a kind of détente with the National Guard. They offered us a deal. We had to gather all of the sick and wounded people—anyone who showed any signs of infection from Lucifer 113—and we had to take them outside. That's right, out where the monsters are. And we had to leave them there. Men and women, and children." He paused and wiped his eyes with his sleeve. "Children. I . . . still can't believe that we did it. Does that make me a war criminal, too? Did I help staunch the spread of a deadly pathogen or did I participate in a heinous act of brutality. I honestly don't know. I don't know."

The camera kept recording, but Trout had to take a moment to collect himself.

"One of the people who went out there was a good man. A good friend. A Stebbins County police officer named JT Hammond. I want to tell you about him. I want you all to know about him. About how decent and kind he was; how strong he was. How courageous he was."

Trout then told the camera about what JT did, about how he was infected and how he made a stand with the children. By the time he was done, tears were streaming down his face and there was a tremolo in his voice.

He sniffed and collected himself.

"And now what, America? We have eight hundred people in this building. Two hundred adults, the rest kids ranging from kindergarten through middle school. We have a few guns and some ammunition. Probably not enough. This place is the town's emergency shelter, so we have food, water, cots and blankets, first-aid equipment, and other basic necessities. Enough to provide for three hundred people for two weeks. Yeah, stop for a moment and do the math."

He had to control his anger because rage wanted to make him say the wrong things and Trout needed to get this right.

"I don't know if this message will ever get out. I don't know if the government is now coming clear about Lucifer 113 or not. All I know is that this plague is immoral and illegal and it's killing people. I know how and why it was created. The man who invented this gave me all the science. The question now, I suppose, is what happens next. With us here in the Stebbins Little School. With what's left of the Town of Stebbins and, really, all of Stebbins County. And with this monster that they've let loose. You tell me, folks . . . what now?"

He sighed, reached over and switched off the camera, then punched the buttons to send it to Goat. Technically, Goat should have been streaming it straight out to the Net, but Trout wasn't sure.

He tried calling him again and once more got nothing. He thumped the phone down in frustration.

And that's when he saw her standing there.

Dez.

She was pale and ghostly in the shadowy hallway, her blond hair hanging in rattails, her uniform torn and dirty, her blue eyes filled with pain and tears.

But her mouth.

Despite everything, Dez was smiling.

"Thank you," she said so softly that he almost didn't hear her.

"For what? I don't know if that even got out."

Dez shook her head and stepped into the room. "I heard what you said about him. About JT."

"I . . ." Trout began, then said simply, "He was my friend, too."

Dez reached for him and he took her into his arms. They kissed for a long time. It was hot and wrong and her lips tasted of tears. But he absolutely did not want to let her go.

Then she leaned back and looked at him, studying his face with eyes that were filled with questions.

"I'm sorry," she said.

He did not dare ask for what. There was so much wreckage behind them. Years of trying to make a relationship work, and years of failure. Sometimes spectacular failures.

Like the last time.

For now, he didn't care what she was sorry for, or if it really related to him at all. He nodded and kissed her again.

Then, after a long, sweet, oddly gentle time, Dez pushed him back, turned, and walked away.

Once she was gone, Trout leaned against the doorframe and stared at the empty hallway.

"I love you," he said to the shadows. "And I'm pretty damn sorry, too."

CHAPTER TEN
THE SITUATION ROOM
THE WHITE HOUSE, WASHINGTON, D.C.

No one spoke while Billy Trout talked about the slaughter of the infected, the devil's bargain made with General Zetter, and the death of JT Hammond. When it was over, the president rubbed his hands over his face.

"Well, that should pretty much bury all of us," he said.

"Actually," said Scott Blair, "we're the only people who have seen that video. The only ones who ever will."

The president stared at him. "What?"

Blair cleared his throat. "We shut down the cell and landlines and are doing focused jamming operations on satellite phone service. Our guerrilla newsman isn't talking to anyone anymore."

"Did I authorize that?"

Blair spread his hands. "I believe it falls under the umbrella of national security, sir."

The chief of staff, Sylvia Ruddy, leaned close to the president. "We'd better run this past the attorney general. We may be on thin constitutional ice here."

"National security," repeated Blair very slowly, focusing it on Ruddy so even she could grasp the concept.

"Cutting Trout off could backfire on us," said Ruddy. "The public already thinks we're killing citizens—"

"We *are*," said the president.

"—but a blackout would heighten paranoia and throw gasoline on the public outcry."

"Let it," said Blair. "We've already been vilified. That damage is done and when the president addresses the nation we'll be able to manage a great deal of what the public perceives. Without Trout being able to release fresh messages his veracity will collapse. We'll make sure that happens. What we have to do now is manage the official information we need to release regarding Stebbins and regain the public's trust."

"There's no trust left," said Ruddy. "Trout pretty much killed it with his first 'live from the apocalypse' speech. And he has Dietrich on tape making threats."

"Trust is fickle, Sylvia," said Blair dismissively. "We're in a crisis. We need control not friendly smiles."

Ruddy leaned close to the president again. "A blackout now would drive the last nail into your credibility."

The president drummed his fingers very slowly, one fingertip at a time, on the table. His presidency already teetered on the edge, and he doubted there was enough spin control left in the world to repair the damage done. If that was the case, then all he had left was his legacy. So, how did he want to be remembered?

He cleared his throat and glanced at Scott. "It's my understanding that Trout was using a satellite to get his messages out."

"Yes, sir."

"To whom? Was he streaming directly to the Net or—"

"We believe he had outside help. Someone on the other side of the Q-zone. Whoever that person is, he's very clever, and it's likely he has either background as a hacker or has hacker friends."

"What are we doing to find this person?"

Blair smiled. "Every agency in the alphabet is looking. We *will* find him. Or them."

"And what about Dr. Volker? Trout mentioned that the doctor gave him the research notes."

"Yes, sir. Dr. Volker confirmed that when he spoke with Oscar Price, his CIA handler. He put everything on a set of flash drives and gave them to Trout."

"Jesus," said Ruddy.

"As protocol blunders go," said Blair, "it boggles the mind. Naturally we are looking for Dr. Volker. Forensics teams are tearing apart his office at the prison where he worked and his home."

"Where is he?" asked the president. "Can't we find the man?"

"We are looking, Mr. President. Every possible resource is in play."

"Will we find him?"

"I have no doubt we'll find him," said Blair. "However, we should consider the obvious alternative."

"Which is?"

"Getting those drives from Billy Trout," said Blair. "By any means necessary."

CHAPTER ELEVEN
BORDENTOWN STARBUCKS ON ROUTE 653
BORDENTOWN, PENNSYLVANIA

Goat looked through the windows at the storm. The night sky was still black but the rain had slowed to a gentle drizzle. From where he sat he could see the lines of red taillights and white headlights on the highway. He wondered how many of those travelers knew what was happening?

Probably all of them by now.

The story was everywhere. It was the only story on the news right now, and Goat suspected that half of those oncoming headlights were reporters trying to get to Stebbins while the story was still breaking. He had already seen ABC, CBS, and CNN vans come through.

He trolled the online real-time news. FOX was the first to pull the word "zombie" out of the info dump of the Volker interview.

Zombie Plague in Pennsylvania.

Goat snorted. It sounded like an *SNL* skit.

Wasn't funny at all.

He looked down at the clock on his laptop. Ten minutes to one in the morning. It wasn't even twenty-four hours since this thing started. It felt like a year. The night had been so goddamn long.

As soon he'd gotten to the Starbucks, the first thing Goat did was to download the files from the flash drives Volker had given Billy and emailed the contents to himself at several accounts. He copied the email to Trout and their editor, Murray Klein. He wanted to send the stuff directly to the other media. *Huffington Post*, *Daily Beast*, *Rolling Stone*, all the others. But Billy had suggested holding off on that. It was their only hole card in case the feds tried something.

Which they would inevitably do, mused Goat. He wondered what he would do if he was in their place. Would he kill to make the situation go away, to hide the blame. Would that protect the public and prevent a panic? Goat wasn't sure. Ethical issues like that seemed clear until you were standing up close, then all perspective became skewed. He hoped he would have the moral courage to do the right thing, but that opened a door to concepts of "greater good" and what that might actually mean.

It was so hard to think it through and come up with a workable plan.

The president was scheduled to speak soon. Originally the word was that POTUS would address the nation at three thirty in the morning, but the speech was moved up to one thirty. On any other day that alone would be highly weird for a presidential address. A lot of people here on the East Coast would be asleep; the West Coast would be in the last hour of prime time. However Goat didn't think anyone but the most abjectly stupid, indifferent, or uninformed would be sleeping or watching sitcoms. And it wasn't just the nation watching this story. The Net proved that the whole world was watching.

A couple of hours ago most of the world—hell, most of the state—had never heard of Stebbins. Now Goat knew that it would become a part of the common language. You'd be able to say "Stebbins" the way you said "the Towers" or the "Boston Marathon" and everyone would know what you meant.

Stories like this changed the world. If not in fact then in perception, by gouging a marker into a page of history. Days like this, events like this, were hinge-points on which history turned.

This story was about to blow up even bigger. The president and everyone in his circle had one chance to win this thing back and that was to own it, take the bullet, and while they were still in office do what they could to prevent further spread of Lucifer 113. Essentially, they could save the world without filtering that through their own political self-interest.

Goat didn't believe in Bigfoot or the Easter Bunny, either, so he figured that wouldn't be the way the White House would play it. It made him wonder where the line was between cynicism and clarity of vision.

Goat sipped his coffee and smiled at what was about to happen. Despite all of the pain and loss, and the deaths of so many people he knew, there was a dark and dirty part of Goat's mind that murmured disappointment that things didn't go completely south at the Stebbins Little School. Billy's previous speech, which Goat had streamed live to all of the news services, had made it impossible for POTUS to allow the National Guard to destroy the school and sterilize the town with fuel-air bombs. From here on, the story would roll forward on wheels greased by the political blood of everyone whose head would roll, and on the public outpouring of grief over the thousands who'd died from the infection. But the story was becoming past tense. The kids at the school, now rescued, would become a symbol, a talking point, a voting influence at the next election. On the other hand, a couple of hundred kids being shot to death and then burned on national TV—that story would keep going, keep running, keep shouting for everyone to pay attention and react. And he, Goat, would be the conduit for that story to get out to the world. He was already part of the story, but if they wiped Stebbins off the map, then he would be the story. The only survivor. The fearless cameraman who'd gotten the truth out, getting footage while the world burned around him.

He would be the most famous journalist on earth. Immediately and irrevocably.

Had the story gone that way, gone that far.

Now it looked like it would break in a different way. There were already posts claiming that the Stebbins thing was another Internet hoax, that Billy Trout was a liar, that he was some kind of grandstanding fruitcake, and even that he was a cyber-terrorist.

Goat wondered how much of that was genuine disbelief or White House spin doctoring. Maybe a fifty-fifty split? Either way, this was brewing into a mother of a story. He murmured the words "impeachment" and "Pulitzer," and he liked how each of them tasted on his tongue.

But then he felt a flash of guilt. He hated that he thought about this thing. That he *wanted* it, on some level. He'd wanted it then and he wanted it now. And there was a flicker of remorse nibbling at his soul that he knew he would always secretly regret the way it had played out.

Goat opened Skype and punched in the number for Billy's satellite phone. But a message window popped up: NO SIGNAL.

He tried it again, making sure he got the number right.

Same message.

"Oh, shit . . ." he murmured.

The last message from Billy said they were going to take the infected outside. Since then . . . nothing. What was going on? Had they gotten to him? Had the helicopters come back?

Goat's fears said *yes*, but his gut told him *no*. There was something wrong, but he didn't think Billy was dead.

Not yet.

He was, however, absolutely positive that the government was screwing around. That it was responsible for this silence.

Cursing under his breath, Goat turned toward the counter to ask the barista if the router was down. Headlights flashed in his eyes as a car pulled into the lot. Goat flicked a glance through the window. A metallic green Nissan Cube. Ugly. Same make and color as the one he'd seen parked in front of the house of Homer Gibbon's old Aunt Selma. It made him think of that, and how it all started.

Then his mind ground to a halt as the driver's door opened and a man got out.

A tall man. Bare-chested despite the cold.

A grinning man, with a tattoo of a black eye on each flat pectoral.

This.

Was.

Impossible.

Goat wanted to scream but he suddenly had no voice at all. He wanted to run, but he was frozen in place.

The man walked the few steps between car and door in an awkward fashion, as if his knees and hip joints were unusually stiff.

Goat's fingers were on the keyboard. Almost without thinking, his fingers moved, tapping keys as the bare-chested man pulled open the door and stepped into the Starbucks. The few remaining customers turned to look at him. The barista glanced up from the caramel macchiato she was making. She saw the bare chest and the tattoos. She saw the caked blood and the wicked smile.

The man stood blocking the door. Grinning with bloody teeth.

Goat's fingers typed eight words.

The barista screamed.

He loaded the address of the press and media listserv into the address bar.

The customers screamed.

Goat hit Send.

Then he, too, screamed.

In Bordentown. Homer Gibbon.
Quarantine failed.
It's here . . .

CHAPTER TWELVE
COMMUNICATIONS COMMAND POST #2
STEBBINS COUNTY, PENNSYLVANIA

"It's working, sir," said the radio specialist.

The captain in charge of communications for the National Guard detail on the eastern edge of Stebbins County was a small, fussy-looking man with the face of a geek. Even with the uniform he didn't look like a soldier; and in his own heart he wasn't. He was an electronics nerd who joined the Army to get free training and to play with more interesting toys than he could afford working at Best Buy.

The unit in which he sat cost more than thirty million dollars, and it was his.

More or less his.

The captain leaned over the specialist's shoulder and looked at the gauges, dials, and meters, then down at the digital readout on the computer monitor. It was arcane to anyone who didn't live and breathe electronics. To him it was a language he understood better than English. A language that was precise, without ambiguity.

The information on all those meters told him that no communication signal was getting into or out of Stebbins except those on very precisely fixed channels. The blackout was immediate and complete. Stebbins County went dark, taking with it the border towns of

Portersville, Allegheny Falls, St. Johns, and Bordentown. All landlines, cell towers, and Wi-Fi were silent. No cell phone, no landline, and no damn satellite uplink.

Everything was being jammed.

He smiled.

"Good," he said, as he reached for the phone to tell Scott Blair that Billy Trout wasn't reaching anyone.

Not anymore.

And neither was anyone else.

PART TWO

BROKEN DOLLS

*It is dangerous to be right in matters on which
the established authorities are wrong.*

—Voltaire, *The Age of Louis XIV*

CHAPTER THIRTEEN
STEBBINS LITTLE SCHOOL
STEBBINS, PENNSYLVANIA

Trout tried Goat a dozen more times and hit the same wall every time. Then he went looking for Dez and couldn't find her. Disturbed and depressed, he drifted back to where the kids had been gathered. It was uncomfortably subdued for the number of young kids there.

"Coffee?"

Billy Trout turned to see one of the younger teachers, Jenny DeGroot, holding a tray on which were a dozen paper cups. Steam rose and clouded the petite woman's glasses and put a flush on her cheeks. Trout fished for her name.

"Thanks, Jenny," he said and took a cup.

She nodded and he stepped out of the way as she entered the big classroom. He hadn't liked the glazed look in Jenny's eyes. Too much shock, not enough hope. Way too much fear. It made him wonder what was in his own eyes.

He sipped the coffee and winced. Not because it was hot but because it tasted exactly like reconstituted horse urine. Possibly the worst coffee he'd ever tasted, and he'd worked in a newsroom for twenty years. He caught Jenny watching him from across the room and Trout hefted the cup in a salute and pretended to smile in appreciation of the taste.

A second sip only confirmed the bad news from the first taste. Horse urine with just a hint of hog feces. Maybe not as tasty as that.

He drank it anyway, standing in the doorway to the art room. The classrooms on this floor had been separated by partitions, but they'd all been pushed aside to create a space nearly as big as the auditorium. Even so, it was crowded. JT had estimated eight hundred survivors, but Billy had done his own count. The math was both more and less encouraging. There were eight hundred and forty-three people here. But that was all there was left of the population of Stebbins and its surrounding villages. Eight hundred and forty-three alive.

More than seven thousand dead.

Or whatever passed for dead now that the world didn't make sense anymore.

"Infected," he told himself. It was a much safer word than "zombie."

He sipped the bad coffee.

Inside the combined classroom, hundreds of children were huddled into groups, their bodies wrapped in blankets or coats. The surviving teachers and other random adults—school staff, a few parents, and stray survivors—sat with them, trying to give comfort when there was no comfort left to give.

Everyone in that room, Trout knew, was in shock. Some were in denial. Some were completely broken. Across the room, by the teacher's desk, a man in a business suit sat holding a little girl and rocked back and forth. Trout knew him. Gerry Dunphries. The little girl, though, was the youngest of the Gilchrist kids. Trout had no idea where Gerry's daughter was. She attended this school, but she wasn't here in the room.

She had to have been at the school, though. Or on one of the buses.

That thought, that knowledge, was dreadful.

He watched Gerry rock back and forth with the girl. His eyes were nearly unblinking and he kept murmuring the same snatch of song over and over again. A piece of a lullaby. Something old, but something that was as broken as he was. Only a piece of song, the lyrics mangled and mostly forgotten, the tune stretched thin by repetition, like a piece of old cassette tape that had been played so long the emulsion was wearing off.

Trout wondered if the girl heard any of it. Neither of her parents was here. Nor were her two brothers. Her eyes were fixed and focused, looking out at the world, but—he was absolutely sure—seeing and hearing none of it.

Broken, both of them.

Like so many others.

Even before the military had opened fire on them, these kids and the adults were teetering on the edge. The infected had attacked the buses, had dragged hundreds of kids out and torn the life from them. Parents and teachers had fought to protect their children, but as they succumbed to bites, they became the very things they'd tried to stop. They had become the monsters that preyed upon the children.

Trout prayed to God that no trace of the original personality was left in any of the living dead, though he knew that his prayer was a hopeless one. Yesterday he and Goat had interviewed Dr. Herman Volker, the former Cold War scientist—now working as a prison doctor—who had created the Lucifer 113 pathogen. Volker had told him that his latest version had been intended as a way of punishing convicted serial murderers. Volker's sister and her children had been savagely killed by such a monster in East Berlin, long before the Wall fell. Volker had spent years working as a Soviet scientist— ostensibly serving the State but actually developing his ultimate revenge. The pathogen, based on genetically altered parasites and a witch's brew of chemicals, kept the consciousness alive even after the body died. It was Volker's desire that any prisoner executed for mass murder be conscious of his fate even while his body rotted in the grave. It was a horrible punishment, though had it only been used on its intended subjects—in this case the serial killer Homer Gibbon—Trout might have privately wished Volker all the success he could get.

But that's not what happened.

Gibbon was infected with the pathogen during his execution by lethal injection, but instead of going immediately into a numbered grave on the prison grounds, a previously unknown relative had come to claim his body. Aunt Selma. Many years ago Selma had helped her heroin-addicted sister take the infant Homer to a shelter. At the time Selma considered taking the baby and raising him herself, even though she was the madam of a whorehouse. She did not, however, and instead Homer went into the system, going from one foster family to another. Some of those families cared for him, but others abused him. The abuse happened too soon, too early in Homer's life to give him any chance of normalcy. In that meat grinder of a system, a true monster was born. Homer earned his conviction and his sentence, and no one was going to mourn him.

Except Aunt Selma. Driven by regret, by the last spark of her conscience, she claimed his body with the intention of burying him on the family farm where he might have some rest after a life in hell.

But the pathogen was already at work. Homer's mind was alive in the dying body.

And the parasites that made up the substance of Lucifer 113 were alive, too.

Alive and hungry.

They kept his mind alive, they woke him up, and they awakened in him a hunger that was unlike anything nature could ever have created.

Trout was only now putting the pieces together of what happened here in Stebbins. He knew from Dez Fox that Doc Hartnup, the town's mortician, had been killed along with Doc's cleaning lady. Both of them reanimated, though, and from what Dez said, the first victims of Homer Gibbon did not demonstrate any awareness of self or recognition of other people. They were mindless monsters.

Zombies, to use Dr. Volker's word.

And yet the doctor had insisted that the pathogen kept the consciousness alive, that in each of those zombies was a kind of helpless passenger. Aware of what his or her hijacked body was doing but totally unable to exert control. All it could do was feel the flesh rot and witness what the body did.

It was the most horrible thing Trout had ever heard.

And it was loose in Stebbins County.

It had consumed the town of Stebbins.

As he stood there looking at the traumatized man holding the traumatized little girl, he wondered what had broken each of them. Was it simply the shocking deaths of the people they loved? Certainly that would be enough.

Or was it worse?

Had they looked into the dead eyes of their own family members—wife, children, siblings, parents—and somehow saw the screaming ghost of the people they knew. Trapped like victims behind the windows of a burning building.

Had they seen that?

Billy Trout prayed that was not the case.

He knew that if—God forbid—anything happened to Dez, if she

was infected and became one of those things, and if he looked into her beautiful blue eyes and saw the person he loved there, trapped in the body of the monster she became . . .

He didn't know how to even think about that without screaming.

But he knew what he would do if such a thing happened.

He wouldn't run. And he certainly wouldn't—couldn't—take the headshot that would bring her down.

No, Trout was absolutely sure he would simply drop whatever weapon he held, that he would stop fighting, that he would let her take him.

Slowly, slowly, Trout backed out of the doorway and turned away. He wandered down the empty hall, careful not to step in any of the pools of disease-blackened blood, mindful of the tiny larva that wriggled in the mess. He kicked shell-casings away with shuffling feet.

When he reached the end of the hall he stopped and leaned against the wall. The satellite phone hung from his belt and he removed it and once more punched in the number for Gregory "Goat" Weinman. The phone rang.

And rang.

Goat did not pick up.

From down the hall, through the open doorway to the art room, Trout could hear sobs and the eerie echo of a broken man singing a broken lullaby to a broken little girl.

Billy Trout leaned his back against the wall and closed his eyes and tried to think of a way out of this.

CHAPTER FOURTEEN
THE OVAL OFFICE
THE WHITE HOUSE, WASHINGTON, D.C.

Scott Blair was admitted to the Oval Office and was pleased to find himself alone with the president.

"You made your changes?" asked the president, holding a hand out for the speech.

"I did, Mr. President." He handed over the papers and waited while the president read through it. Then POTUS removed his glasses and sat back in his chair to appraise him.

"This is what you want me to say?"

"This is what I think needs to be said."

"What about the Trout video?"

"Our people are tearing it to pieces online. By morning it won't be any part of the official story."

"What about the popular story?"

"We'll manage it and we'll weather it."

The president smiled. "You're beginning to sound like Sylvia."

God forbid, thought Blair, but managed a bland smile. "We have to protect the administration if we're going to win this."

"We *beat* this, Scott. Not sure why everyone else thinks so and you don't."

Because I don't have my head up my ass, he almost said, but managed to think it through first. Instead he said, "I know you and Simeon Zetter are friends, and I know you trust him . . ."

"Implicitly."

"Understood. I, however, do not trust anyone implicitly. It's my job not to make assumptions."

"Are you saying that's what I'm doing?"

"I'm saying that's what everyone is doing, Mr. President. We are all in shock because of this, and we are all cognizant of the implications of last night's events. Heads will roll here in Washington, even with the spin control we're using. Heads will have to roll. Dietrich will take the most heat, but everyone knows that a soldier follows orders. Unless we intend to crucify him as a rogue who exceeded all authority including a presidential order—which would put him in jail—then we'll have to hang others out to dry. That's a political fact."

The president shifted uncomfortably in his seat, but he did not disagree.

"But all of that is secondary, Mr. President. I can't stress enough how strongly I believe that this matter *is not over*."

"General Zetter is in Stebbins, Scott. You're not."

Neither are you, you officious moron, thought Blair.

"Sir," Blair began slowly, but the president cut him off.

"I'm not ordering another attack on Stebbins."

"I understand that, sir, but to put it quite simply, Simeon Zetter is nearing the end of his career, and even though he was formidable in the field once upon a time, I think now he's become more of a politician than a soldier. He is supporting you and your presidency. I don't know that I entirely trust his assessment of the situation in Stebbins, because we have to accept the *possibility* that he is wrong about containment, we must—absolutely must—get Dr. Volker's research notes."

"I thought you said we'd find Volker."

"We will, but we haven't yet, and every minute we spend looking is time *not* spent preparing for contingencies."

The president considered, nodded. "Did you have something in mind?"

"Yes. Trout has that research on Volker's flash drives. Sir, I would like to—"

"Stop right there, Scott. I know what you want to do. You want the Guard to storm the school and take those drives away from Trout. I won't do that. What I have done is order General Zetter to obtain the drives. This he will do. End of discussion."

Blair wondered if he could throttle the president before the Secret Service could stop him.

"Now . . . is there something *else* you'd like to discuss, Scott?" asked the president.

"Yes, sir," said Blair tiredly, "but it concerns General Zetter. If . . . I may speak candidly—?"

The president steepled his fingers. "Go ahead," he said guardedly.

"I think we need an independent assessment of the state of things in Stebbins County. We need unbiased eyes on the defenses, the deployment of resources. We need someone who has experience in ultra-high profile biohazardous situations—which, by the way, no one under Zetter's command has. We need a diagnostician, not a general practitioner."

The president pursed his lips, considering the point. "Do you have someone in mind?"

"Yes," said Blair, "there's a man we both trust, and he's already in the area."

"Who?"

Blair gave him the name. "I think you'll agree that he's well-suited for this particular assignment. He's also available and close. I could have him and a small team inside the Q-zone in twenty minutes."

The president gave him a calculating smile. "He just happened to be in the neighborhood?"

"No, sir. I called him yesterday and told him I needed him in the on-deck circle. Just in case."

"And he's there to observe, assess, and report only, is that correct?"

"Yes, sir."

"Nothing else?"

"No, sir."

"I would take it amiss, Scott, if I found out that your pet shooter was there to do an end-run around Simeon Zetter. It would pain me to learn that he and his team put so much as a foot inside the Stebbins Little School. You understand me when I say that? We're clear?"

"As glass, Mr. President."

They studied each other, both wearing small smiles, both watching the other with cold eyes.

"Very well, Scott," said the president. "Send him in."

"Thank you, Mr. President."

"Scott," said the president with a gentler smile, "take a breath. This is over. We won. We saved the country, and you played your part. Be proud."

"Yes, sir, I am," lied Blair.

CHAPTER FIFTEEN
THE OVAL OFFICE
THE WHITE HOUSE, WASHINGTON, D.C.

Sylvia Ruddy, the president's chief of staff, came in as Blair left.

"Scott looks like he's about to explode," she observed. "Is he still trying to nuke Pennsylvania?"

"Fire bomb," corrected the president, "but no. Not at the moment, anyway." He told her about the flash drives.

"He wanted to send a team after Trout?"

"I nixed the idea."

"Good."

"However, I am letting him send a team in to do an independent evaluation of the integrity of the Q-zone."

Ruddy made a face. "Simeon won't like it."

"Simeon works for me. He doesn't have to like it. Besides, I actually do want to know. Scott's right about one thing—we have to make sure we don't spike the ball before we're in the end zone. I want to believe this is over, but quite frankly, Sylvia, I'm scared out of my mind."

"So is everyone," she countered, "but don't let Scott drive you crazy. He's such an alarmist. He was an alarmist when he was the national security director and he's an alarmist now. Maybe more so now. I told you that when you appointed him."

"Maybe, but he's been right more than he's been wrong."

"Sure. But when he's wrong he's all the way wrong. And he's wrong on this. He's overreacting to a situation that now requires careful handling and a great deal of subtlety."

"I know."

"And yet you gave him permission to release the hounds?"

"Hardly that. Scott will do what he's told," the president said firmly. "He may have his issues, but he's still one of us."

He handed her Blair's amended speech. As she read it her face went white and then dark red. "This isn't a speech," she snapped, "this is you begging to be impeached and indicted."

"I don't see it that way."

"No, *Scott* doesn't see it that way. He doesn't have to worry about reelection."

"There are more important things than winning another four years."

"Are there?" she asked.

CHAPTER SIXTEEN
STEBBINS LITTLE SCHOOL
STEBBINS, PENNSYLVANIA

"Oh, God—there's another one!"

Billy Trout wheeled around but had no time to get out of the way as half a dozen people came running straight at him. The lead man was one of the teachers and he simply shoved Trout, and as Trout tried to take a step to catch his balance his back flared and his right leg buckled. He collapsed to the floor and half the people running down the hall tripped over him and went sprawling.

It was like a bad comedy routine, except no one was laughing. Most of the people had weapons. Guns, makeshift clubs, and fire axes. Everyone was ragged and dirty, streaked with grime, wild with panic.

Trout scrambled painfully to his feet and grabbed the sleeve of the closest man—Bowers, the art teacher. "What's happening?" he demanded.

Bowers was a frail, frightened man with eyes that jumped and twitched. "Down in the gym," he gasped. "I think it's Mr. Maines."

Trout didn't know who Mr. Maines was. A parent of one of the children? A teacher? A refugee trapped in the school?

"Is he infected?"

Bowers's face, already pale, turned a sickly white. His eyes were jumpy with shock. "They said . . . they said he bit one of the kids."

It felt exactly like being punched over the heart. Trout wanted to sag back against the wall, slide down, bury his face in his hands, and weep. He wanted this to end, to go away, to not be real.

"Show me," he said.

Trout heard himself say the words, felt his body launch into motion, felt his pulse quicken, but he did not want to see this. Not more pain. Not another kid.

No way he wanted to see another infected kid. Another hurt kid.

Another lost kid.

But he heard himself growl as he snatched up a fire axe dropped by one of the men who had fallen.

"Hey!" said the man, grabbing for it, but Billy ignored him and kept the axe.

At first he followed Bowers.

Soon, though, he simply followed the screams.

Billy Trout ran down two flights of stairs. Each step shot an arrow of pain into his back. Earlier, when he and Desdemona Fox had fought their way across the parking lot to the school, Billy had picked up a heavy bag filled with guns and ammunition. He grabbed it the wrong way, though, and something had exploded in his lower back. The pain was awful but it was also useful. It made him grind his teeth on it, to bite down on it to say fuck it to agony and everything else. Fuck it to his rage at what was happening, to his terror, and to his grief.

His fists were locked around the handle of the fire axe as he ran, but already he could feel fear sweat loosen his grip. Rage, he was discovering, was not a constant. It wasn't armor that he could wear until this was all over.

If it was ever going to be over.

The screams echoed upward from the basement, bouncing off the walls of the fire tower.

Another one.

That's what Bowers had said. That's what he was running to see.

Another one.

God.

Another of the dead. And another child with a bite.

The small knot of teachers and other survivors lagged behind him, their determination to reach the source of the screams diminishing with every step. Trout couldn't fault them. Not one bit. After all, what in their lives had ever prepared them for something like this?

They reached the basement and burst from the stairwell into the gymnasium. A big, damp empty space that Trout remembered from humiliating dodgeball games when he was in the fifth grade. That had been his hell year, before the growth spurt that would give him the length of bone and quality of muscle he'd later use in high school baseball and track. The gym was linked to his memories of being a weird, shy, strange little boy who didn't have many friends. Dez Fox had been his first real friend. When two older boys tried to pants Billy here in the gym, Dez had beat the shit out of them.

He'd been in love with her ever since.

"In there," gasped Bowers, pointing.

Only a few lights were on, pale cones of yellow that did little to push back the immense darkness. The screams were constant. High and thin. They tore through an open office door at the far end.

Please, begged Trout. Not another kid. Please, please . . .

The axe was heavy and he knew he'd have to use it on Mr. Maines—whoever he was. There was no Plan B for dealing with those who were so far gone that they had crossed over into—

Into what?

Even now Trout had a hard time calling it what he knew it was.

These people were infected.

These people were also dead.

Technically, dead.

Essentially, dead.

And yet they moved around, some of them shambling, some running awkwardly, all of them chasing, hunting, grabbing, biting.

Eating.

The dead consuming the living.

Zombies.

It was madness and Billy Trout's orderly mind rebelled at it. Death was death and the dead don't do this. Can't do this.

The screams told him otherwise.

Despite the pain in his body and the agony in his soul, Trout ran faster.

He was six steps from the gaping doorway when sudden light and noise exploded within.

The deafening blast of a gun. The eye-hurting flash of shot after shot.

Trout skidded to a sloppy halt, lost his footing in something wet, fell, slid all the way to the mouth of the open door.

There was one last blast, one last flash.

The screams stopped.

Trout lay there on the floor. He could hear Bowers somewhere behind him. Panting, mumbling something. Maybe a prayer. Maybe he'd simply gone fucking nuts. Billy wanted to.

Something moved inside the office.

A shifting of the shadows, the scuff of a shoe.

And then a figure staggered out. Lumbering, uncertain, sagging sideways against the frame, clothes torn and streaked with blood, eyes dark and dead.

Trout looked up into the face.

"Dez . . . ?" he whispered.

Those dead eyes shifted toward him.

Tears broke and fell down her dirty cheeks. The slack expression of shock disintegrated into horror and shame and grief.

"Oh . . . Billy . . ."

She sank down to her knees, the gun still held in one hand, but that hand was slack at her side, as if forgotten or disowned.

Trout scrambled to his knees and gathered her in his arms as the first terrible sobs detonated within her. In the bad light Trout could see the leg of a man—Mr. Maines—and the sprawled form of a child, lying tangled together in a pool of black blood. The smell of gun smoke burned in the air.

He wanted to push her away, he wanted to turn away from what she'd just done, what she'd had to do. But he loved this woman.

And this—all of this—was their world now.

So he held her close as she wept.

As they both wept.

"It's okay," he lied. "It's all going to be okay."

Except they both knew that it wasn't.

CHAPTER SEVENTEEN
WHAT THE FINKE THINKS
WTLK LIVE TALK RADIO
PITTSBURGH, PENNSYLVANIA

"You're listening to Gavin Finke and this is *What the Finke Thinks*, coming to you live from Pittsburgh. It's the middle of the night but I don't think anyone within the sound of my voice is sleeping. The eyes of the world are on the town of Stebbins down in Stebbins County, right on the Pennsylvania-Maryland line. And why? Well, my friends, that depends on whom you ask. We all know that Stebbins was ground zero for Superstorm Zelda—a real b-i-t-c-h of a storm that picked up a lot of water from the Three Rivers and dropped it on the Mason Dixon Line.

"Sure, that's how it started, but then the cow patties hit the windmill, let me tell you. First there were unconfirmed reports of a double homicide in Stebbins. But within minutes there were all sorts of wild rumors about a riot at a funeral home. But buckle up, kids, 'cause it was a fast slide down the crapper from there. The governor released a statement saying that there was an outbreak of a new kind of virus in Stebbins. Then the Internet went—"

Gavin Finke took a long drag of his cigarette and winked at his engineer.

"I tell you, folks, I don't know what to believe. Tell the Finke what you think is happening on this dark and stormy night."

He gave the call-in number and before he'd even finished the board lit up like a Christmas tree.

CHAPTER EIGHTEEN
THE OFFICE OF THE NATIONAL SECURITY ADVISOR
THE WHITE HOUSE, WASHINGTON, D.C.

After Scott Blair left the president he hurried to his office. He blew past three of his aides, growled at his secretary to hold his calls until further notice, and closed his door. As soon as he was alone he took his cell phone from his pocket, punched in a five-digit code to activate a scrambler, and ground his teeth while he waited through five rings before the call was answered.

"How'd it go?" asked the man at the other end.

Blair snorted. "How do you think it went?"

"Jesus," said the man at the other end. "Did you show him the math? Did he see the projection numbers if this thing breaks the Q-zone?"

"I did, but for all intents and purposes that broadcast from the school cut his balls off. He's almost afraid to act."

There was a pause. "Which means what?"

"I gave him an alternative suggestion."

"Which is?"

"You, Sam," said Blair. "I told him I wanted to send you in."

There was a brief silence at the other end of the line. "Go in and do what?"

"Find out exactly what's happening in Stebbins. You and a small team. I want to know how bad things are there. However, you are not to report to General Zetter. He and everyone here in Washington is acting like the Super Bowl is over and we're all doing postgame chatter."

"How's that make sense? Surely they read the same report you forwarded to me. This pathogen isn't a suitcase nuke. You can't defuse it and sit back for a victory cigar."

"Preaching to the choir, Sam."

"So . . . what the hell's happening? Why the shift from 'move heaven and earth to win this' to whatever the heck you'd call this shit? Is it that broadcast?"

"Mostly. That was like being hit by a cruise missile. It cut everyone's balls off. There are people here who think that the attack on the school could be used to do more than bring down the president. They're afraid it's done permanent harm to the structure of government as we know it."

"I watched the president on TV. He did a pretty solid job of pissing on that video. Don't know if you watched the commentary afterward, but CNN, FOX, and even MSNBC are edging away from belief that Trout's video was the real deal."

"I know, but once the storm's over and the press actually gets into Stebbins, some of what Trout said is going to be verified. The school looks like it was fired on by machine guns. We can't change that."

"Unless you blow it up."

"Hiding the body after a murder isn't the same as removing doubt about the crime." Blair blew out is cheeks. "No, Sam, this is doing political damage, there's no doubt about it."

"But . . . ?"

"But who the fuck cares?" growled Blair. "How did we ever allow ourselves to get to the point where careers and political agendas matter this much? We are facing a doomsday scenario and they're acting like it's the midterm elections. Doomsday, Sam. It's not even an abstract concept. It's right there, and we're handling it all wrong."

"And you want me to go in and—what? Take photos of the Gates of Hell to prove they're opening?"

"Pretty much."

"Jesus."

"I need irrefutable proof that we're not on top of this so I can force the president to respond the way we should have responded from the jump. Can you do that?"

"I can try.

"Sam . . ."

"I'll do it," Sam amended.

"How soon can you be on the ground there?"

"Almost right away. I have some assets I can put into play. I . . . well, I kind of figured this was coming and I tapped some friends who were in the area."

"You're already there?"

"Not inside the Q-zone, but close," said Sam. "We're at a motel just outside. Me and four people I can trust."

"I . . ."

"I anticipated this, Scott. Don't act so surprised. If I was off my game we wouldn't be having this call."

"I knew I could rely on you."

"Yeah, yeah, if the world doesn't end, buy me a beer."

"I'll buy you a brewery."

"Deal. Now," said Sam, "if we're done with the bullshit, Scott . . . tell me why I'm *really* taking a squad of first-team shooters into the Q-zone."

CHAPTER NINETEEN
FARMLANDS SUPER MOTEL
BORDENTOWN, PENNSYLVANIA

Sam put down his cell phone and took a long breath, held it until everything inside his mind and body felt steady, then let it out with slow control. Both aspects of the job Scott Blair wanted him to do—the official and unofficial mission—were going to be a real bitch. Although Sam had run with a SpecOps team for a long time, that was years ago. He hadn't fired a shot in anger in a decade.

His technical skills were still there. On the rifle range he was still one of the two or three top snipers in the U.S. military. But was he still fit and sharp enough to lead men into a situation like this? Had he have lost a step getting to first base?

Possibly.

More important, could he do what Blair wanted him to do? Would he do it? Sam certainly agreed with the NSA advisor's logic and even, to a degree, with the plan. But it was ugly and it was risky.

There were a lot of ways it could go wrong and very few ways it could all work out right.

He took a second calming breath.

And a third.

Then he called the four members of his team waiting in rooms here at the motel. They were all seasoned Special Operatives. None of them were active military. Like Sam, they had retired to contract work, but also like him their only employer had been Uncle Sam. Different groups within the government, and sometimes the agendas didn't quite mesh, but since they were freelancers they could pick and choose their jobs. None of them ever wanted to follow an order they didn't like or couldn't square with their consciences. That adherence to a specific ethical code had earned the team the sobriquet of The Boy Scouts. Nice nickname but far from the truth. People in Special Ops never felt entirely comfortable in, say, a confessional. Certainly not Sam.

Sam caught his reflection in the mirror bolted to the back of the motel room's door. The man he saw looked small, old, and guilty even though he hadn't yet done anything except take a call from an old friend. But then he thought about what was at stake. He thought about his family back in California. His dad, his stepmom, his brother, and his infant half-brother. They were three thousand miles away from this, but with something like Lucifer 113 distance wasn't a guarantee of safety. All it did was buy some time.

Time before what?

Before the inevitable or something that might already be over.

There was no way to know. No way to be certain.

Except to gather his team, saddle up, and cross the Q-zone into Stebbins County. The one place on earth that no one in their right mind wanted to go.

"The fuck are you doing?" he asked himself.

His reflection looked pale and sickly and it offered no reply.

Then Captain Sam Imura stood up, reached for his gear bag, slung his sniper rifle over his shoulder, and headed out to war.

CHAPTER TWENTY

BORDENTOWN STARBUCKS ON ROUTE 653
BORDENTOWN, PENNSYLVANIA

"Please . . ." he begged. "Don't . . . please . . ."

Goat was crammed into a cleft formed by his overturned table, a couple of chairs, the wall, and a tourist who sat bleeding and weeping. He huddled into his niche, arms wrapped around his head, knees drawn up tight as if the bones of his limbs offered some real protection for what was happening. The air in the Starbucks was filled with screams and prayers.

And laughter.

Low, thick. Wet.

"Please," Goat whimpered. He thought desperately about Volker's information, uploaded to his email accounts but not sent. Not shared.

And with sudden screaming clarity he realized that he and Billy had made a serious mistake. That information should have gone out. Goat's instinct had been to send it, but he hadn't. It was in attachments. It was just sitting there. As useless as he was.

God . . .

Despite the carnage around him, Goat cut a sly, frightened look at his laptop, which lay on the floor not five feet away. How long would it take to locate the email and forward it to the listservs of reporters to which he belonged. How long?

Five seconds?

Less.

That's all the time it would take to maybe save the whole fucking world.

A handful of seconds.

Goat felt himself begin to move, shifting away from his worthless hiding place, edging toward the laptop.

Then the laughter stopped.

"Hey," said a voice, "I know you."

The world seemed to freeze around Goat and for a terrible moment even the screams seemed muted as if those words had flipped a switch on everything. Goat didn't look up, though, too frightened to risk acknowledging anything.

"Yeah," continued the voice, "I seen you somewhere, ain't I?"

Goat held his breath, refused to move.

Then pain exploded in his thigh as something hit him with jarring force. A cry burst past the self-enforced stricture in his throat, and he rocked sideways, suddenly whipping his arms out like defensive stabilizers. Despite his need not to see this man, Goat's eyes opened and there he was. Standing right there, looming over him, bare-chested, ugly, covered in glistening red, eyes dark and wild, smiling mouth full of promise.

"Fucking-A, I knew I knew you," said Homer Gibbon. "You were there when they killed me."

Behind Gibbon and all around him was pain and horror.

People were broken.

Broken.

Arms shattered, mouths gaping to reveal broken teeth, handfuls of hair torn out from customers who had tried to run but were one step too slow. Everyone was bloody. Every single person.

Some of them lay sprawled, dead or dying.

But even as he thought that, Goat knew he was wrong.

Dying maybe. Dead?

Not really.

Death, as Goat had known it his whole life until yesterday, was no longer a fixed point in reality. It was no longer a doorway that, once entered, could not be passed again. All of that had changed.

Because of Dr. Volker.

Because of something called Lucifer 113.

And because of this man.

This monster.

Homer Gibbon.

When Goat didn't answer, Homer kicked him again. Same spot, only harder.

Gibbon wore no shoes but he knew how to kick. And from the laugh that bubbled out of him, he enjoyed it. The way some kids like kicking cats. A small cruelty that spoke with disturbing eloquence about this man. Even if Goat had not known what kind of monster Homer was, even if Goat had not sat through weeks of testimony by clinical psychologists and forensics experts at this man's trial, he would have deduced important truths about him from that kick and its accompanying laugh.

"I asked you a question, boy," said Homer, his voice colored by an accent that sounded southern but was pure rural Pennsylvania. "Want to see what happens if I have to ask you again."

"Y-yes . . ." stammered Goat.

"Yes, what?"

"Yes, I was there."

Homer kicked him again. Even harder. Goat screamed in pain and tried to turn away to protect the spot on his leg that now burned as if scalded.

"You was there when what?" demanded Homer.

"Yes," said Goat in a small, fractured voice, "I was there when they killed you. At the prison. At the execution. I was there."

Homer nodded in satisfaction. "What's that make you? Some kind of news reporter?"

Behind Homer one of the wounded people was crawling toward the door. Her shirt was torn, revealing a bra with little blue flowers on it. Most of her right shoulder looked like raw hamburger. Goat hadn't witnessed the attack specifically on her, but he recognized the bite. Even from ten feet away Goat could see a thick black goo mixed in with the blood, and in that goo tiny threadlike worms wriggled. Dark lines ran crookedly from the torn flesh, delineating the pattern of her veins and blood vessels. Even though the bite had just happened a few minutes ago, the infection was spreading at incredible speed.

So fast, thought Goat, it's happening so fast.

It was nothing Mother Nature could ever have created. Nothing natural could spread infection at that rate. Lucifer 113 had been genetically engineered to be a perfect rapid-onset bioweapon, and the modified parasites took hold inside the bloodstream with all the deadly speed of a neurotoxin.

Homer turned, following Goat's line of sight, and again there was the low, wet laughter.

"Fuck yeah," he said. "That's right. That bitch is one of mine now."

"One of yours?" asked Goat weakly.

Homer turned back and then squatted down in front of Goat, arms dangling off the tops of his knees like a gorilla. "You gonna lay there and tell me you don't know what's happening? You're a reporter and you want to tell me you don't know what I done in Stebbins? You going to fuck with me like that?"

"N-no . . ."

Homer reached out and patted Goat on the cheek. Three pats, each one harder so that the last one was a full slap that rocked the reporter back against the table. It was not as hard as the kicks had been, but hard enough, and Goat's head banged off the wooden table. He twisted sideways, once more curling into a fetal ball, collapsing against the side of the badly injured customer who'd been sitting there weeping and bleeding.

It was then that Goat realized two very bad things.

The first was that the man was no longer weeping. Or breathing for that matter.

And second was that his eyes were open.

Wide open.

Staring right at Goat.

Black mucus ran from between the man's slack lips. There was nothing in his eyes. No pain, no confusion over the way in which everything had suddenly gone wrong for him, no spark of anything. The eyes saw Goat, though; that much was certain.

The dead man opened his mouth to show his teeth.

Behind Goat Homer Gibbon chuckled.

"Look who woke up hungry," he said.

He was still chuckling when the dead customer lunged at Goat, grabbed him by the shirt and hair, and pulled him toward those blood-streaked teeth.

CHAPTER TWENTY-ONE
STEBBINS LITTLE SCHOOL
STEBBINS, PENNSYLVANIA

Desdemona Fox pushed herself back from Billy. The movement was abrupt, as if she'd suddenly reached the limit of the grief she allowed herself, though Trout knew it was more than that. People were watching. Civilians. And Dez was the only person of any authority left, even if that authority no longer carried any official weight. There was, after all, no Stebbins County Police Department anymore. All of the other officers and even all of the support staff were as dead as the mayor, the town selectmen, the director of public works, and the chief of the fire department. There was, in fact, nothing left of Stebbins except the small knot of people here and the real estate on which they stood.

Even so, Dez had to play her part. She knew, as he did, that her badge and gun, her uniform and the personal power everyone knew she had, formed the rails in a frail fence between order and chaos. If she lost it, then these people would likely lose it, too. And if that happened, then none of the children upstairs had a chance.

Not one chance.

Dez kept her face averted while she went through the mechanical process of removing the magazine from her Glock and thumbing in fresh rounds to replace those she'd fired. She did not bother to pick up her spent brass. Everyone stood mute as they watched this, and when she slapped the magazine back into place they all flinched. The face Dez showed them as she holstered her gun was composed, hard, uncompromising, and totally closed. If anyone noticed the drying tear tracks on her face they dared not mention them.

Dez nodded to two men who stood slightly apart from the group. "Bob, you and Luke get some of those big plastic trash bags from the kitchen. We have to wrap the bodies and get them out of here."

The men stared at her and then past her to the room where the killing had been done. They didn't move.

"Now," she snapped, and they flinched again.

Bob opened his mouth, maybe to protest or maybe to ask a question, but then he caught the look in Dez's eyes and answered with a curt nod. He tapped Luke on the arm and they turned and hurried across the gym floor.

Dez appraised the rest of the group.

"Listen to me," she said in a quiet, dangerous tone. "The rest of you are going to search this place. Again. I don't know who searched down here, but because some assfuck didn't look in a closet or a closed office another kid's dead. You hear me? Someone killed that kid and I'm not talking about the dead son of a bitch who bit him. For now I don't give a shit who searched down here. But we need to search this whole building again and that means every nook and fucking cranny. You hear me? And if another kid gets hurt because one of you jerkoffs didn't do your job, then God help you because when I get done with you there won't be enough left to feed to the fucking zombies. Anyone think I'm joking, anyone has anything to say about that, say it now and I'll shove it down your throat with your teeth. This isn't a debate. Now move!"

They scattered like scared birds. As they moved away, Trout saw that their eyes were now filled with a different kind of fear. Not of the dead but of the living. Of her. Everyone in town knew Dez Fox. Most of the people in Stebbins didn't like her, and Trout knew that a lot of them wouldn't piss on her if she was on fire, but no one could say that she wasn't a good cop. There were a lot of stories floating around town about how Dez treated wife beaters and child abusers. None of those stories were exaggerations, Trout knew.

Add to that the things she'd done here in the school. She and JT, her partner. Partner, mentor, best friend. Father figure.

JT was outside, his body infected by a bite and torn by heavy-caliber machine-gun bullets. He'd sacrificed himself to help clear the school of the infected, and he'd gone down fighting to keep the infected children from being mauled by the dead before the military could use their guns to end all pain for them.

Trout wrestled with that, understanding on one level that the slaughter was necessary and even merciful in a twisted way, but on all other levels it was perverse. No matter from which angle it was viewed, the innocents were the victims.

Now the last surviving children of Stebbins County were here in this building. No more of them should have died.

The men hurried away, splitting into two-person teams, not saying anything until they were in the stairwell on the far side of the cavernous gym. All of them were bigger than Dez. Most of them were tough, hardened farmers and factory workers, some were even combat veterans. No one said a damn word to Dez Fox.

Dez stood there and watched them go. Trout saw that her whole body was trembling. Rage and pain.

He wanted to take her into his arms again.

That would probably earn him an ass-kicking, too.

So instead he said, "Dez—what do you want me to do? How can I help?"

It took a long time before she reacted, as if she was off in some distant place and there was so much distance to travel to get back to where he was. Her head turned slowly until she faced him, but even then there was no immediate recognition in her eyes.

She said, "What?"

"How can I help?" he repeated gently.

"I . . ." she began, but faltered. She shook her head, then without another word, Dez crossed the big empty room and vanished into shadows.

Billy Trout stood watching the emptiness of the open doorway to the stairwell.

"Shit," he said softly.

He found a chair and dragged it over to a spot near where the child and the dead Mr. Maines lay. He didn't want to see them, but he felt it was important to stay with them until Bob and Luke returned with their makeshift body bags. When he tried to understand this self-imposed vigil he found no useful answers. No insights.

He checked his sat phone to see if there was anything from Goat, but got no signal down here in the basement. It made him wonder how the story was spreading. Was it time to do another broadcast.

This is Billy Trout, reporting live from the apocalypse.

That was what he'd said. It hadn't sounded silly at the time. He meant it to be shocking. Now it sounded strange to Billy. It was less than one hour since the military attacked the school.

And yet it felt like forever. Like he and Dez and the others had always been here; like this was one of those nightmares he sometimes had where he felt trapped in a twisted funhouse experience that never ended.

Reporting live from the apocalypse.

Shock tactics or straight reporting?

The line seemed badly blurred right now.

Goat had told him that the whole thing had gone viral, but Trout didn't know what that actually meant in terms of the survival of the people here and the handling of the outbreak. Was it all over?

Was his part in it over?

Trout was a career reporter, even though that career had dumped him back into his hometown of Stebbins. A one-stoplight dirt stain on the Pennsylvania map. Rarely had he gotten so much as a whiff of a significant story. Even his coverage of the execution of convicted serial murderer Homer Gibbon was not star-making. There were too many better-known reporters there. At best the pieces he filed for Regional Satellite News were folded into stories by bigger—and very likely better—journalists around the country.

But now he was the story, and that was a paradigm shift so radical it stripped all the gears.

He sat on the rickety folding chair, staring at the shadows, listening to the sounds of an old building settling into its own grave. He could still feel the dried tear tracks on his own cheeks. Somewhere, beyond the walls of the school, out there in the black night, he could hear the heavy drone of helicopters, the menacing *throp-throp-throp* of their blades.

"Ah, Dez . . ." he said softly. He thought about what this was doing to her. Hurting her, aging her.

Desdemona Fox was the most beautiful woman in the world to Trout. Tall, fit, powerful, blond, with great bones and every curve on his personal must-have list. Curves he knew more intimately than anyone. Granted he was far from the only person—or even the most recent person—to have explored that landscape, but he was the one who loved them and loved her. Not in that order.

They'd been an item more times than he could count, and they'd both logged mileage in breaking each other's heart. The last time had been a doozy. He'd proposed marriage and the next day he walked in on her with a biker. That was her reply to the proposal. Classic Dez. Why cross a bridge when you could burn it?

Since then, she'd been a raging bitch to him. And, to hear others tell it, she'd been a raging bitch to the whole world. Even more viciously defensive than normal, which was saying quite a lot. There was, however, a corresponding increase in her efficiency as a police officer. She wrote more tickets, arrested more drunks, broke up more bar fights, and kicked more ass than before, all of it with a nasty fuck-you smile on her pretty lips.

Then the devil came to Stebbins County.

Even now Billy found it hard to reconcile the fact that his town was being destroyed by something conceived half a world away during the Cold War. It was spy movie stuff. It was horror movie stuff.

He wondered what the death toll was here in town. Seven thousand people had lived here. Were all of them dead now?

Was that even possible?

Add to that the kids bused in from neighboring districts and the parents who had come to get them out of the path of the storm. What was that—another thousand, maybe two?

Someone else's madness had brought wholesale death to town.

Except in Stebbins County "death" wasn't death anymore.

He put his face in his hands. Not to weep, but to try and hide.

CHAPTER TWENTY-TWO
WHAT THE FINKE THINKS
WTLK LIVE TALK RADIO
PITTSBURGH, PENNSYLVANIA

Gavin muted the mike and hit the intercom. "How are we on calls?"

"We have them lined up from here to next year," said Gavin's producer, happy with this kind of call-in volume. "Sending you a hot one now."

Gavin Finke punched a button to take the call. "And we're on with Brenda from Harrisburg."

"Hi, Gavin, longtime listener, first-time caller."

"Glad you picked up the phone, Brenda. So, tell me, what do *you* think is happening in Stebbins County?"

"Zombies," she said.

"Come again?"

"Zombies."

"You're saying 'zombies.'"

"Yes. Zombies."

"In Stebbins County.

"Oh, yes. They're all over Stebbins County."

"Zombies?"

"Zombies."

"Oooo-kay, this a new one even for *What the Finke Thinks*. Tell me, Brenda, what makes you think there are zombies at large in western Pennsylvania?"

"My nephew told me."

"Your nephew? And does he see zombies on any kind of regular basis?"

"Oh, no. He's a soldier. He's with the National—"

"Sorry, Brenda, I have to cut you off," said Gavin. "I'm being told we are going to have a statement from the president of the United States. Going live to Washington . . ."

CHAPTER TWENTY-THREE
THE OVAL OFFICE
THE WHITE HOUSE, WASHINGTON, D.C.

"Mr. President?" said the cameraman. "We're on in five, four . . ."

He finger-counted down the rest of the way and then pointed to the commander in chief, who sat at his desk, neat and tidy and severe.

"Hello, everybody," said the president, his voice deep and sober. "There are two issues confronting us this evening. The first is the major storm that has developed in western Pennsylvania. This storm, now being called Superstorm Zelda, has exceeded the predictions made by the National Weather Service. The severity and duration of the storm has caught everyone by surprise. However, I just received a full briefing from our emergency response teams, including FEMA, and agencies that are going to be helpful in the response and recovery efforts—the Department of Energy, the Department of Transportation, the Department of Homeland Security, and the Department of Health and Human Services."

Behind the teleprompter, Scott Blair nodded. He'd helped write this announcement, using his typical hands-on approach. The president had raised objections about much of the content, but in the end had been persuaded to handle things a certain way. In the way that Blair and the Joint Chiefs all agreed was the only way to keep the train on the rails.

"Obviously," continued the president, reading it verbatim, "everybody is aware at this point that this is going to be a big and powerful storm, and that it is far from over. What were originally estimated to be a line of smaller cells moving behind the main storm front have taken an unfortunate turn and are strengthening. However, all across the region, I think everybody is now able to make appropriate preparations and everyone is taking appropriate actions. I've spoken to the governors of Pennsylvania, Maryland, Ohio, and West Virginia. They have issued emergency declarations. Those have been turned around quickly here in the White House. We have prepositioned assets so that FEMA personnel are working closely with state and local governments. We're making sure that food and water and emergency generation is available for those communities that are going to be hardest hit. But because of the nature of this storm, we are certain that this is going to be a slow-moving process through a wide swath of the country, and millions of people are going to be affected."

Beside Blair, Sylvia Ruddy stood with her arms folded tightly across her chest, wearing what the French would call a mouth of disapproval. Blair disliked her because she was far more concerned about party politics and the president's legacy than she was about actual national security.

"So the most important message that I have for the public right now," said POTUS, "is please listen to what your state and local officials are saying. When they tell you to evacuate, you need to evacuate. Do not delay. Don't pause; don't question the instructions that are being given, because this is a serious storm and it could potentially have fatal consequences if people haven't acted quickly.

The president paused and gave the camera a two-second beat of unblinking intensity. "But keep in mind that for folks who are not following instructions, if you are not evacuating when you've been asked to evacuate, you're putting first responders in danger. We're going to have to have search-and-rescue teams in and around multiple states all at the same time. And although we've got the Department of Defense all positioned, if the public is not following instructions, that makes it more dangerous for people and it means that we could have fatalities that could have been avoided.

Transportation is going to be tied up for a long time. And probably the most significant impact for a lot of people, in addition to flooding, is going to be getting power back on. We anticipate that there are going to be a lot of trees down, a lot of water. And despite the fact that the power companies are working very closely with their various state officials and local officials to make sure they are bringing in as many assets as possible and getting those ready in preparation for the storm, the fact is that a lot of these emergency crews are not going to be able to get into position to start restoring power until some of these winds have died down. And because of the nature of this storm, that may take several days. So the public should anticipate that there's going to be a lot of power outages, and it may take time for that power to get back on."

Blair glanced at his own copy of the prepared message. The groundwork was established, but the real game was about to begin.

Don't fuck it up, thought Blair, knowing the president's tendency to go off script.

"Now we come to the second matter before us this evening," said the president in a voice that changed from firm control to something approaching cold steel. "Many of you are already aware of reports of an outbreak of a new kind of flu virus. This outbreak was first reported in Stebbins, a small town on the border of Pennsylvania and Maryland. There has been some wild speculation in the press as to the nature and severity of this disease, and that speculation has sparked a rash of irresponsible and inaccurate posts on social media. Much of the information being shared about this outbreak is false, and some persons have posted faked videos and audio files purporting to be from reporters in that town."

The president paused for effect, and Blair believed that everyone in the country paused with him, taking the same deep breath, holding it in their chests, waiting for the heavy punch that follows the tentative jab.

"Those reports are false," said the president with real edge in his voice, "and they pose a serious threat to the efforts of FEMA and the Centers for Disease Control. Reports like that are the worst kind of Internet manipulation, and investigations are currently under way to determine if these posts are an attempt to deliberately disrupt our ability to provide effective emergency response. I can assure you that the substance of these posts are false and I will promise you that the persons responsible will be found and prosecuted as cyber-terrorists. It is abhorrent when a misguided or malicious few attempt to exploit a catastrophic event in order to further their own agendas, especially if that goal is at the expense of the American people. We will not allow them to succeed, and we will protect the people of this great nation."

Good—nailed it, word for fucking word, thought Blair, and he wanted to fist-pump, but didn't.

The president almost glared at the camera. "Last point I'll make, though—this is going to be a difficult storm, but the great thing about America is when we go through tough times like this we all pull together. We look out for our friends. We look out for our neighbors. And we set aside whatever issues we may have otherwise to make sure that we respond appropriately and with swiftness. And that's exactly what I anticipate is going to happen here.

"So I want to thank all the federal teams, state and local teams that are in place. I'm confident that we're ready. But I think the public needs to prepare for the fact that this is going to take a long time for us to clean up. The good news is we will clean up and we will get through this. Thank you. God bless you and God bless the United States of America."

The camera lingered on the president's face for a moment, then cut to a place card of the presidential seal.

"And we're out," said the cameraman.

The president sagged back and closed his eyes. He looked as exhausted as Blair felt. It was nearly an hour into a new day and they'd been at this since early yesterday. Blair knew that there was little chance any of them would get a moment's rest any time soon. They were all wired with caffeine and whatever prescription stimulants they each had in pockets or handbags.

Even so, Blair smiled and nodded to himself, well pleased with the statement that had just gone out. He leaned toward Sylvia Ruddy. "That was letter perfect."

The chief of staff swiveled her head like a praying mantis and glared at him with absolute hatred in her eyes.

"We're all going to hell for this," she said.

CHAPTER TWENTY-FOUR
OVER STEBBINS COUNTY

Sergeant Hap Rollins crouched over the minigun and peered through the slanting rain at the endless rows of stalked corn eddying like waves beneath the rotor wash.

"Anything?"

The voice in his headphones was the pilot, Sully. It was maybe the fortieth time he'd asked the question since they'd come out to the farm country. Rollins wished Sully would shut the hell up. If he saw something he'd say so, and Rollins didn't see shit. Nothing human, anyway. Bunch of cows lying down to try and get out of the wind and a few horses running free from an overrun farm. The farmhouse and outbuildings had already been destroyed by rockets. Thirty or forty times they flew over dead bodies lying on the road or on lawns or in the middle of fields. Dead bodies. Not walking dead.

Rollins was still processing that distinction.

The officers wanted them to use the word "infected," but most of the guys were calling them zombies. A word from old Bela Lugosi movies. A word from comic books and horror novels.

Zombies.

Rollins didn't like the word, didn't like the way the word fit inside his head. It had too many sharp edges. It nicked the walls of his worldview. And it didn't do anything good for his faith. Rollins was a Catholic and the only dead that were supposed to be walking around were the ones Jesus raised, like that little girl he said was only sleeping. Lazarus, too. And JC himself.

Only saints and saviors were supposed to be walking around if they were dead. Those were the rules, and Rollins didn't remember reading anything about infected ordinary dead people getting up and walking around biting people.

That wasn't death, no matter what the mission intel said.

That was something else. Something bad, sure, but dead people don't do what these people were doing.

Even though Rollins believed in Jesus and God, he wasn't as sure about the concept of the Devil. He knew he was supposed to believe that, and even though he could imagine a place where sinners went—his ex-wife and her boyfriend came to mind—a guy with hooves and horns directing traffic for lost souls was hard for a grown man to accept.

He wiped raindrops from his goggles and leaned out to look down the rows of corn.

Nothing.

"We're good," he said into his mike, and he had to repeat it over the constant crackle of interference. Some of the guys said the communications team was operating jammers in the area. Collins could believe it. He'd tried to call home to check on his parents, who lived in Pittsburgh, but there was no signal on his cell. That had been a couple of hours ago. So, jammers? Sure, he could buy that. "Let's go check out the other field," he yelled into the mike. "Looks like a pear grove. Come in low on the west side and we'll see if there's anything under the trees."

"Roger that," confirmed the pilot, his voice fuzzy and distorted.

The Black Hawk lifted away from the waving corn and began a shallow climbing circle. They were working with nineteen other helos, quartering and searching the vast farmlands that filled this corner of the county. It was a crazy job and Rollins, like everyone else, knew that it was pretty damn close to a fool's errand. There were three hundred farms here, ranging from little postage-stamp herb gardens to the fruit and vegetable groves that stretched for miles. There were fifty teams in various ground vehicles and a couple of hundred two-man patrols. And with all of that it seemed like an absurdly impossible task to Rollins.

Even so, there was plenty of radio chatter from the ground and the other Black Hawks saying that they were finding spots to clean out. Infected trapped inside locked cars. A whole bunch of them trapped inside the Weis supermarket after downed trees knocked out the power. Some strays wandering through fields.

Like that.

The infection was out there, and the Q-zone seemed to be holding, but Rollins had his doubts.

His buddy Dave, who was a lot more Catholic than Rollins was, had confided to him that he was really scared by all this. Religious scared, not just regular scared. Dave couldn't understand why God allowed something like this. The dead to rise.

Rollins told him, "This ain't God, man, it's science. This is weird science shit."

"It's the dead rising, man . . ."

"Nah. Just sick people acting dead. Like in that old movie, the one in London—*Twenty-eight Days Later*. It's only a disease."

"No, man," said Dave, lapsing into a confidential whisper, "I think this is what they talked about in the Book of Revelation. The End Times."

Rollins started to grin at that, but the look on Dave's face killed that expression before it was born.

"C'mon man," Rollins said mildly, "it's just like that anthrax thing. It's a disease and that's all it is. Don't mess your head up by thinking bad thoughts."

But Dave wasn't convinced and Rollins didn't at all like the look in Dave's eyes. No, sir, he did not like that look at all. Kind of wild. Maybe a little crazy.

He wondered how Dave was getting along. He was out working a checkpoint with their drinking buddy Tito Rodriguez. Out on the Q-zone line.

The pilot came out of his turn and slowed as he dropped down almost to the level of the road. The rotor wash blew into the field and raised the skirts on the pear trees. Muddy water swirled upward, but Rollins had a clear-enough view under the front four or five rows. He saw slender tree trunks and between those . . .

"Shit," he said suddenly. "Got one."

There was a man there. Dressed in farmer's clothes that hung in torn rags from his burly shoulders. His eyes and mouth were black, and as the helo edged sideways toward him, the man snarled and reached for a man crouched in the open doorway.

Rollins took a small breath, let it out wrapped around a small prayer to Mary, and pulled the trigger. The captain said to go for a headshot, but that didn't much matter when you fired a minigun. The heavy-caliber bullets tore the infected apart, splattering him to the wind. The parts that fell no longer seemed to belong to something that had once been human, and the rain pressed the red detritus down into the mud.

"Got the sumbitch," said the pilot, sounding happy about it.

The feelings within Rollins were far less certain.

"Anything else?" asked the pilot.

"No," said Rollins, though he wasn't as sure as he sounded.

The helicopter drifted along the farm road, blowing back the boughs of the trees, tearing half-grown pears from the branches, looking for more things to kill.

As it flew, Rollins remembered the look in Dave's eyes when he said that he thought this was maybe the End Times. Rollins mouthed the words of the prayer to Mary.

Holy Mary Mother of God, pray for us sinners now and at the hour of our death.

Hoping that he was just being ridiculous.

Hoping.

And praying.

CHAPTER TWENTY-FIVE
OPERATIONAL COMMAND POST
INSIDE STEBBINS COUNTY

A young lieutenant knocked and entered the general's trailer just as Colonel Dietrich left.

"Sir," said the young office to Zetter, "we're still getting reports," he said, holding out a clipboard wrapped in plastic.

Zetter took it, shook off the raindrops, and studied the data. Six patrol helicopters had encountered infected, two of them within a mile of the Q-zone. Sixteen ground patrols had also located and eliminated the walking dead. In all cases the infected were eliminated without any of his people taking injury. No additional loss of life was reported.

"And there's this," added the aide, handing over a second report. The general took it, and as he read he felt his heart sink. He turned away in case his feelings showed on his face.

Zetter stood there, considering the information in the second report. He sighed, read the rest of it, sighed again.

"Damn," he said to himself.

During the ground search, his teams had encountered twenty-three people who displayed no signs of bites or other injuries, and who did not appear to be in any way infected. Five men, seven women, eleven children. Two of the children were babes in arms.

The report was written in the way that such reports had to be written.

All potential risks were removed with dispatch.

Removed with dispatch.

They didn't even use the word "eliminated."

Removed.

"Is there a reply, sir?" asked the aide.

"Just . . . proceed with the operation as directed," said Zetter.

"Yes, sir."

The aide left.

General Zetter sat heavily in his chair and stared bleakly at the report.

"Goddamn it," he breathed.

He considered calling this in to the White House.

In the end, he did not. There was nothing new to report except that the cleanup was proceeding as anticipated. Proceeding, in fact, at something close to the best-case scenario outlined in the National Biodefense Analysis and Countermeasures Center protocols.

"We're winning this," he told himself. "We're winning."

CHAPTER TWENTY-SIX
THE SITUATION ROOM
THE WHITE HOUSE, WASHINGTON, D.C.

The president met with his advisors for an update and learned that nothing new was happening. That should have been comforting, but wasn't. He shooed them all out and told the Secret Service agents to make sure he wasn't disturbed for ten minutes. They nodded like silent robots and pulled the door shut.

The president dug into his pocket for a pack of Winstons and the gold lighter given to him as a gift when he agreed to visit a NASCAR event in Georgia. He kissed one out of the pack, popped the lighter, leaned into the flame, inhaled all the way down to the bottom of his feet, and sank back into his leather chair. He held the smoke inside, enjoying the way the menthol changed from cold to hot in his lungs, and then blew a long stream of blue smoke at the ceiling.

On the big TV screen there were half a dozen windows showing various views of General Zetter's efforts to clean up Stebbins County. Gunships filled the rainy skies. Armored personnel carriers were laden with guns of kinds he couldn't name, some of which he'd never seen. The president was a lawyer and career politician and had never served. Not that it mattered, because many of his predecessors hadn't either. Not everyone could be JFK.

He tried to understand the military, though, and felt he had a good grasp of its philosophies. He knew the big-budget technology, of course, the drones and missile programs, the fleets and the last jet fighters. All of those were big-ticket items that were constantly in the press. As he watched a line of soldiers in hazmat suits deploy from the back of a troop transport, he made a mental note to become more familiar with their gear, with the things they had to carry into fights like this.

He took another drag, wishing for a moment that he was back in college and hitting a blunt instead. That was a long time ago, and he hadn't gotten high since junior year.

Now seemed like a good time.

Maybe it would take the edge off.

Or maybe not. He remembered the paranoia that sometimes accompanied the high, and he sure as hell didn't need any more of that.

As he lifted the cigarette to his lips again he studied his hand. It was shaking.

Had it done that during the meeting?

He wasn't sure.

Was it relief that the crisis was over—at least everything except the spin control—or was it something else?

Was Scott Blair right? Were the generals right? Except for Zetter they all agreed with Blair.

So what did that mean?

The president punched a button on the table.

"Yes, Mr. President?" asked his secretary.

"Doris, get General Zetter on the line. Private call."

"Right away, Mr. President."

It was just that. In less than a minute Zetter was on the line.

"General," said the president curtly, "are you alone and is this a secure line?"

"Yes to both, sir," said Zetter. The connection was still weak and static-filled because of the high-intensity jammers.

"Good. I'm alone as well, Simeon, so this is just the two of us. What I want is the bottom line. No politicizing, no padding or fluff. I want to know the absolute truth about where we stand in Stebbins County."

There was a very small pause at the other end of the call. "We're in good shape, Mr. President," said Zetter. "However, with the storm strengthening we could use more men."

"Have there been any fresh sightings?"

Another pause, a little longer this time. "There are scattered sightings, sir, but each encounter has been satisfactorily resolved."

"How's the line holding?"

"We're confident that the Q-zone is absolutely solid," Zetter said . "There have been no incidents at any of the checkpoints, and we have satellite and helicopter surveillance as well as roaming patrols and spotter planes. A mouse with a head cold couldn't get out of Stebbins."

"Simeon," said the president, "I need you to be absolutely sure about this."

"I am, sir." Another hesitation. "However, we could really use the extra troops. National Guard, Reservists, or regular Army. Any or all. The more boots we have on the ground the tighter the lock and the quicker we can put a button on this whole matter."

"Very well. Send your requests to Sylvia Ruddy and I'll sign the order and make the necessary calls right away."

"Thank you, Mr. President."

"Of course. And Simeon—?"

"Sir?"

"I appreciate you stepping in to take control of this situation."

"Doing my job, sir."

"I know that Mack Dietrich is your friend. If there was time to have someone else ask him to stand down I would have made that call."

"He's a professional soldier, sir. He understands, as do I."

But there had been one last little hesitation before Zetter said that.

The president took a long drag, considering the implications of that pause. He exhaled slowly.

"Simeon, there's another matter that you need to be aware of."

He told Zetter about the flash drives believed to be in Billy Trout's possession.

"That's a wrinkle," Zetter said slowly, clearly unhappy with the news.

"It is."

"Do you want me to *iron out* that wrinkle?"

"Gently. You have a relationship with the police officer in the school? Desdemona Fox?"

"We spoke. It wasn't, as you can imagine, a comfortable conversation for either of us."

"Will she talk to you again?"

"I believe so."

"Good. Do so, and ask her—and I mean that, Simeon, *ask* her for the drives."

"I could send some of my people into the school to have that conversation, Mr. President."

"In front of eight hundred witnesses? Do you think that's the best move?"

"No, sir."

"No," agreed the president. "If, as you say, the situation is under control, then there is no immediate need to escalate an already tense situation."

A pause. "Very well, sir."

"Let's repair bridges, not burn them."

"Of course, Mr. President."

"Though . . ." the president said, drawing it out with feigned casualness, "have some people on standby. Just in case. Always good to be prepared for eventualities."

"I agree, sir."

"Thank you, General. Keep me apprised."

And disconnected the call.

He sat in silence, looking through the smoke at the images on the screen, eyes narrowed, brain working, hands still trembling.

CHAPTER TWENTY-SEVEN
WHAT THE FINKE THINKS
WTLK LIVE TALK RADIO
PITTSBURGH, PENNSYLVANIA

"We have Merry from Philadelphia. Go ahead, Merry, you're on the air. What do you think is happening in Stebbins County?"

"It's not aliens," said the caller.

"Glad to hear you say that."

"It's definitely not aliens."

"So you say. Want to tell the listeners what you think is going on?"

"It's the Chinese."

"Chinese Americans?"

"No, the *Chinese* Chinese. The government of China, Gavin."

"In rural Pennsylvania?"

"That's where it starts. It starts off the radar. It starts right in the heartland. The Chinese already own America."

Gavin signaled the producer for more coffee. This was going to be a long night.

"Tell me how they're planning to do that, Merry."

"It's the Asian bird flu. That's what's killing people. The Chinese have sent agents over here to release their flu, and you know we don't have anything that can stop it."

"Why's that, Merry?"

" 'Cause it's Asian."

The coffee arrived and Gavin took the flask from his briefcase and added two fingers of Early Times.

Definitely a long night ahead.

CHAPTER TWENTY-EIGHT
STEBBINS LITTLE SCHOOL
STEBBINS, PENNSYLVANIA

Dez Fox ghosted through the empty halls of the Stebbins Little School. Her Glock was in its holster, her hands empty of everything except promise, her heart heavy with shame and grief. Every once in a while she paused and cocked her head to listen to the old building. Even the silence was not silent. With buildings this old there was always some sound. The faint hum of the battery-operated clock mounted high on the wall, its glass face covered by a heavy wire grille. The creak of timber and stone as the building settled. The faint banshee whistle of wind clawing its way in through broken windows upstairs. The muffled sound of children weeping beyond classroom doors at the other end of the hall.

No new shouts, though.

No screams and gunfire.

She was positive, though, that she could hear the discordant pounding of her own heart.

Without warning the walkie-talkie clipped to her hip squawked. The sound tore a cry of alarm from her.

"*Officer Desdemona Fox, please respond,*" said a voice clouded by harsh static. "*Officer Des—*"

Dez snatched up the device and keyed it. "This is Fox."

The voice said, "Officer Fox, please hold the line."

"Is this some kind of trick?" asked JT, but Dez didn't reply.

Another voice spoke, one she hadn't heard before. "Officer Fox?"

"This is Fox. Who's this?"

"This is Major General Zetter."

"Glad you remembered that we're alive, General."

"Is Mr. Trout with you?"

"No."

"Can you put him on the line?"

"What is this about, General? If you're thinking of trying to change our deal, then you can shove that right up your—"

"It's my understanding that Mr. Trout is in possession of a set of flash drives belonging to Dr. Herman Volker. Are you aware of this?"

"Yes," Dez said carefully, though she knew that Billy didn't have the flash drives. Goat did. But Dez didn't want to say so to Zetter, and definitely not without talking to Billy first.

"Are you aware of what's on those drives?" asked the general.

"Abso-fucking-lutely."

"We would very much like to get our hands on that information, Officer Fox."

"I bet you would. And I bet that one minute after you got them you'd shove a Hellfire missile up our asses. No thanks."

"This isn't a trick, Officer Fox."

"Uh huh. And the check's in the mail, I'll call you in the morning, and I won't come in your mouth."

"Officer Fox—"

"Do you really expect us to believe anything you say?"

"You have been given assurance on behalf of the president of the United States that no further attacks would be made on the school as long as you followed the safety protocols."

"Right. Tell that to the Sioux."

"What?"

"As much as it causes me physical pain to say this out loud to another . . . what I assume is another Republican, our government doesn't have a great track record for keeping its promises with people who have something they want."

"Kennedy Democrat," said Zetter.

"What?"

"I'm a Democrat. It may surprise you that there are plenty of us in the military, Miss Fox."

"Whatever. You get what I'm saying? You know there's not a lot of trust going on here."

"I suppose that's an unfortunate truth. But given that I was no more involved in making treaties with the Indians than I was behind the attack on the school, how about we avoid making assumptions that might confuse the situation? And it was I who ordered our troops to stop firing on the school."

"Oh, blow me, Zetter. Billy Trout's broadcast hit the news services and the president's nuts crawled up inside his chest cavity. That's what happened. He told you to stop trying to kill us only because it would look really fucking bad at the next elections. If you're going to try and pretend otherwise then this conversation is over."

Zetter took a moment with that. "Fair enough," he said. "We don't see things from exactly the same perspective, but I take your point."

"Which leaves us where, General?"

"In the middle of a grave national crisis. Everything else aside, all *bullshit* aside, Officer Fox, the infection is still out there. Contained for the moment but still out there, still a major threat. You know that this is a bioweapon, one designed by Cold War scientists and then redesigned by Dr. Volker. If we stand any chance of eradicating it, then we need to have his research notes."

"Why the fuck are you bothering us about this? Go ask Volker for them."

"If that was a possibility, Officer, we wouldn't be having this conversation."

"Meaning what?"

"Meaning that right now we can't locate Dr. Volker."

Dez felt the floor tilt under her. She staggered into one of the classrooms, checked that it was empty, leaned against the wall and slid down to the floor.

"Officer Fox—?"

"Didn't he . . . didn't he leave any records?"

"None that we have so far been able to find," said Zetter.

"How the hell are you idiots allowed to run a country? I should have voted for a clown college. They'd at least have a reason for being this stupid."

"I don't want to debate politics, Officer Fox. We need what's on Mr. Trout's flash drives."

A thousand thoughts raced through Dez's head. None of them were good. Most were way across the line into paranoia, but she felt justified in thinking every one of them.

"Tell you what, General," she said, "how about you do this? How about you airlift us the hell out of here? Take us to Pittsburgh or Philly or somewhere other than where people are eating each other. How about you do that and then we can talk about the flash drives."

"You know we can't risk that. You have to understand that."

"Sure. Have a nice day, General. Thanks for calling."

"Wait!"

"What?" she barked.

"We *can't* take you out. You have to understand that. We don't know enough about this disease to guarantee that it's safe to bring you out. Until we look at Dr. Volker's research notes we don't know all the ways in which this thing can be communicated. We have concerns that anyone coming into close contact with the skin or blood of one of the infected might be at risk. We don't know if someone can carry the infection without developing obvious symptoms. There are a lot of things we don't know and until we do, we need to keep you in isolation. Surely you can appreciate the severity of this, surely you can understand the necessity of—"

"Okay, okay, yeah, I get it. Fuck."

"So letting us have the flash drives is the quickest and surest way to help us understand this enough so that we *can* get you out of there."

"I get the logic, General, but pardon me if I don't trust your motives worth a wet shit."

The general sighed. "Is there something else I can do for you that would encourage you to do the right thing here?"

"Fuck you."

"Officer Fox, I—"

"No, General, fuck you. In fact, fuck you and that asshole in the White House, and fuck everyone else who had a hand in this. Fuck all of you. *All* of you. Am I making myself clear? Is any of that getting through? You deserve to burn in hell."

General Zetter's response caught her totally off guard. He said, "I know."

A sob broke in Dez's chest. She squeezed her eyes shut as tightly as she could, wincing at the effort not to see anything, even her own thoughts.

"You killed him," she said.

"Who?" asked Zetter sharply, clearly alarmed. "Is Mr. Trout—"

"Not him, you douchebag. You killed JT."

"Who is that, Officer Fox? Was that a friend of yours?"

"Patrol Sergeant JT Hammond, Stebbins Police. A good man. A family man. A decent person who only ever cared about other people. You maniacs killed him."

Zetter said, "Was he the officer who went outside with the other infected?"

"Yes." It hurt Dez to say that one word.

"I . . . he . . ." Zetter cleared his throat. "I saw what happened to him. I saw what he did. He protected the children from the infected. Officer Hammond died a hero."

Dez banged the back of head against the wall. "JT was murdered and you bastards killed him. And now you want us to spread our legs and let you fuck us."

"That's not how it is, Officer."

"Yeah," she said. "It is."

Neither of them spoke again for several burning seconds.

Then Zetter said, "We *need* those flash drives."

"If you try to take them, General, I'll burn them. You can come in here with guns blazing and you won't find shit. But I can promise that every single thing you do will be streamed live to the Net. The world's watching, General."

"Officer Fox," said the general, "be careful not to overplay your hand. You might not have as many good cards as you think. I'm trying to work something out we can both live with—and I do mean *live*—don't make fools out of both of us, and don't make martyrs out of the children in that school."

Dez almost told him to eat shit, but she kept her tongue. What he'd just said chilled her, filling her mind with awful possibilities.

"Look," she said, "Volker gave the flash drives to Billy. It's his call. I'll talk to him and get back to you."

"Very well, Officer Fox, I apprec—"

She switched off the walkie-talkie.

Moving slowly, like someone awakening after surgery, she got to her feet, closed the door, crossed to the teacher's desk, pulled out the chair, and crawled into the footwell. It was a tight, dark space that smelled of shoe polish, crayons, and old coffee. Dez pulled her knees up to her chest, wrapped her arms around her shins, and laid her head down. Sobs shuddered through her whole body and tears steamed hot and thick down her face.

"Oh, God," she wept. "JT."

The shakes began then.

Dez crammed a fist into her mouth to block the scream that tried to tear its way out of her throat.

CHAPTER TWENTY-NINE
THE OVAL OFFICE
THE WHITE HOUSE, WASHINGTON, D.C.

The president returned to his office and there received an endless flow of advisors, including generals of different wattage; planners from FEMA; senators from Pennsylvania, Maryland, West Virginia, and Ohio; scientific advisors; the senior members of his staff; and Scott Blair. Over and over again, Scott Blair.

His desk began piling up with reports on everything from estimated casualties—the current guess was more than nine thousand—to letters from heads of state expressing sympathy and offering assistance. The offers were rote lip service that carried as little actual weight as people at a funeral suggesting the bereaved call on them if there's anything they can do. Most people wouldn't want to take that call, and that was doubly so in global politics. Besides, the quickest way for his administration to look even weaker than it was would be to ask for help from another country.

However, that was secondary.

When he was alone for a few minutes, the document that caught and held the president's attention was the estimated loss of life. He read the numbers, then closed his eyes and winced as if each digit gouged a fishing hook under his skin.

Nine thousand people.

Three times as many people than died in the fall of the Twin Towers.

Nearly twice as many as died during the Iraq War; more than twice the number of Americans killed in Afghanistan.

Nine thousand. All in one day, on American soil.

On his watch.

During 9/11 he'd been a junior senator from a midwestern state, and he'd been at home when the tragedy happened. He met with dozens of groups of citizens, from a few dozen at a Rotary Club to tens of thousands at a memorial service in a baseball stadium. He saw something in each one of them, something that connected them, one to another, while also binding them to that moment in time. It was a pervasive, shared wound that would never really heal. The scar itself would hurt, and it would continue to hurt for years, possibly for the lifetime of each person who'd lived through that terrible day. Even now, so many years later, if you mentioned the Towers or 9/11, there was a flicker behind the eyes. Not exactly pain, but a memory of pain, an awareness of that scar gouged into the national soul.

Now this.

Nine thousand people dead. Not from a foreign enemy or fanatics prosecuting a radical ideology, but from within the U.S. government. Illegal bioweapons research. Military action against civilians.

It wouldn't matter that the research was initiated before his presidency and conducted without his knowledge. He would still be blamed.

It didn't matter that the Colonel Dietrich's attack on Stebbins and the school were desperate measures to prevent the pathogen from spreading and killing millions. If your dog gets out of the yard and bites people, you get no sympathy. You're still to blame.

Which meant that in the eyes of the public he was the villain of this piece.

It would destroy him. His career, his credibility, and his legacy.

The only chance he had, the only way he could imagine to save some shred of his presidency, would be to prove that Volker acted alone and without sanction, that the man was mentally unstable, and that all actions taken were the only ones left.

All of which was true.

But none of which could be proved.

Without the flash drives.

As the night wore on, he began to regret Blair's suggestion that they label Billy Trout as an anarchist hacker and cyber-terrorist. That was useful in the heat of the crisis, but if this thing was truly over, then the truth about Trout would come out and he'd become the hero opposing the big, bad villain in the White House.

"Shit," he muttered. He decided that it was Scott Blair's problem to fix.

His intercom buzzed. "Mr. President, the secretary of state is here."

The president rubbed his eyes and sighed. "Okay. Send him in."

He listened to that aide, and others, and still others; hearing what they said, interacting, pretending to give his full attention, while all the time waiting for General Zetter's call. Waiting to be told that the drives had been obtained.

Waiting for a lifeline.

Then he got a call from Scott Blair.

"Mr. President," said Blair, "the FBI have located Dr. Volker . . ."

CHAPTER THIRTY
GOOD-NITES MOTOR COURT
FAYETTE COUNTY, PENNSYLVANIA

The two FBI agents who parked in front of the motel were named Smith and Jones. Actual names, and the pairing was done by random chance rather than due to some supervisory sense of humor. Adam Smith and Miriam Jones were both of average height, average build, early thirties, with good hair and off-the-rack suits. They carried the same model handgun, wore identical wires behind their ears, and worked out at the same gym.

And they liked each other.

Smith privately thought that Jones was a closet liberal who was probably using the job as a way to leverage herself into the much higher-paying world of corporate security. Jones thought that Smith was a semiliterate mouth-breathing Hawk who yearned for the chance to shoot someone.

They were both entirely correct about the other.

Neither ever expressed their opinions to anyone, and certainly not to their partners. On the job they were clinically precise, appropriately efficient, and entirely humorless.

Smith nodded to one of the units whose door opened to the parking lot. A Toyota Rav4 was parked outside.

"Credit card trace says Volker booked that room," he said.

Jones consulted her iPhone. "Tags match."

As one they looked from Volker's car to the one parked next to it, a Crown Victoria nearly identical to theirs. There were no other cars in that part of the lot. Sodium vapor lamps painted the falling downpour a chemical orange. Winds blew the rain across the lot in serpentine waves.

They got out of their car and Jones placed a hand on the hood of Volker's Toyota.

"Cold," she said. Neither of them wore hats or used umbrellas, and they were immediately soaked. Neither of them cared.

Smith felt the hood of the Crown Vic. "Warm."

"Federal tags," said Jones.

Smith cocked an eyebrow. "CIA?"

"They weren't scheduled for this pickup," said Jones, frowning his disapproval. "Not that I heard."

The agents unbuttoned their jackets to facilitate reaching their guns, crossed to the motel unit's door, and knocked. It was opened almost at once by a man dressed in a business suit very much like the one Smith wore. He had an ID wallet open to show them his credentials.

"Saunders," he said.

"What are you doing here?" demanded Jones.

"Volker's one of ours."

"We know that," said Smith. "But we were assigned to pick him up. The Agency doesn't have jurisdiction here."

Saunders was a tired-looking man in his fifties. Probably a former field agent relegated to scut work on the downslope of his career track. "Moot now," he said, and he stepped back to open the door.

Smith and Jones gave him hard looks as they entered the motel room of the man who had created Lucifer 113.

They stopped just inside the door.

There were two other men in the room. One was Saunders's partner, a gap-toothed and freckle-faced young man who looked like Alfred E. Newman, except he wasn't wearing a goofy smile. Instead he was staring up at the second man.

Dr. Volker's shoes swung slowly back and forth ten inches above the carpeted floor. His arms and legs were slack, head tilted to one side, eyes wide, and tongue bulging from between his parted lips. A length of heavy-duty orange extension cord was affixed to the neck of the ceiling fan and cinched tight around Volker's throat.

A handwritten note was affixed to his chest with a safety pin.

I gave my research notes to the reporter, Mr. Trout.
This is all my fault.
I hope there is a hell so that
I may burn in it for all eternity.

"Ah, shit," said Smith.

"Fuck," said Jones.

"Yeah," said Saunders.

CHAPTER THIRTY-ONE
WHAT THE FINKE THINKS
WTLK LIVE TALK RADIO
PITTSBURGH, PENNSYLVANIA

Gavin Finke's producer and engineer were screening a huge number of calls and putting them in queue.

"Okay," said Gavin, "we have Ron from Fayette County. Thanks for calling."

"Hey, Gavin, big fan of the show. Been listening for years."

"Thanks, my man. So tell me, what do you think is happening in Stebbins?"

"It's all a big government cover-up," said Ron. "I heard they were testing some kind of bioweapon on the people in Stebbins County and it got out of control."

"That's quite a claim, Ron. What makes you think that?"

"It was on the Internet."

"And if it's on the Net it has to be real?"

"Well . . . no, but I saw a video by a reporter from Stebbins. Billy Trout. You know the guy, he does that *Fishing for News with Billy Trout* thing. Did all those stories about Homer Gibbon all the way up to the execution and all. He's a real reporter."

"Not sure there are any *real* reporters anymore, Ron, but sure, Billy Trout's a friend of the show. We had him on with the Yardley Yeti story."

"I heard that show. I think that was a *chupacabra* and—"

"Keeping on point here. Why do you think Billy has his finger on the pulse of a government conspiracy?"

"Well, c'mon, man . . . why else would they have tried to kill him?"

CHAPTER THIRTY-TWO
CHECKPOINT #43
STEBBINS COUNTY LINE

The young sergeant stepped into the muddy road and made that air-slapping gesture that meant to slow down and stop.

Without turning to the captain, the driver said, "We good here, boss?"

"I got this," said Imura. "Put on your poker faces and don't say shit."

The four members of his team—three men and a woman—said nothing, but they each removed credentials from their pockets and held them on their laps. The sergeant was a thin Latino with a precisely trimmed mustache and absolutely no air of authority. New to his stripes, thought Imura.

"Identification, please," said the sergeant. He wore a white combat hazmat suit over which were gun and equipment belts. His protective hood was pulled off, though, and hung behind ears that stood out at right angles to his head. The sergeant looked cold, wet, far too young, and completely terrified. The rain had slowed to a steady, depressing drizzle and the two small all-weather camp lanterns set on either side of the road did little to push back the darkness. Lightning flashed behind the trees but the thunder was miles off.

Another storm was coming, though. The National Weather Service was calling for nearly five inches of rain over the next sixteen hours. The levees were going to fail, no doubt about it. And that would be proof that God or the Devil was using Stebbins as a urinal. Just like Scott thought.

The sergeant studied the ID, then handed it back and went through the process with everyone in the car. The credentials said that Sam Imura was a captain, which was true, but it identified the others as lieutenants, which they were not. All four of Imura's group had once been sergeants of significant rank, from the former master sergeant at the wheel to the gunnery sergeant seated directly behind Imura. Sergeant was the most common rank among shooters in U.S. Special Forces. Each of them was certainly sharper, more knowledgeable, and more competent than most officers of any rank, and Sam Imura knew that was no exaggeration. But staying as an enlisted man kept them out of military politics. A nice, safe, sane place to be.

None of them, however, currently held rank in the United States military. Nor did Captain Imura. They were all officially retired, though because they were private contractors working for the government, their ranks clung to them like comfortable clothes.

The sergeant glanced at the other man working the roadblock. He was an even less authoritative slice of local white bread, stood on the far side of a sawhorse barrier that would provide no real defense against a determined intrusion. He held an M16 at port arms and tried to look like G.I. Joe because there was a Humvee filled with officers.

Imura accepted his ID case back. "How are you doing out here, Sergeant?"

"All quiet and secure, sir."

An answer that meant nothing.

The young man gave the "officers" a crisp salute, which was returned in the casual manner used by career officers. Nice theater.

Imura said, "This should be a four-man post, Sergeant. Where are your other men?"

The young sergeant took a moment on that. "Sir, we're pretty thin on the ground. As far as I know there are two men on every road." He paused as if uncertain he should have said that. "They have four-man teams on some of the bigger roads."

That last part sounded like a lie to Imura. He figured there were only two men on every road. Maybe fewer on some. Between main road, side roads, farm roads, fire access roads, and walking paths, there were ninety-seven ways to leave the town of Stebbins by wheeled vehicle. That was a minimum of one hundred and ninety-four men per shift. Figure twelve-hour shifts and that's roughly four hundred men just working roadblocks. That didn't cover supervisory personnel, reconnaissance, the men needed for reinforcing the levees, the men guarding the survivors at the Little School, and patrols hunting down stray infected.

It also didn't really address all of the ways out of Stebbins on foot.

And the infected don't drive, he thought.

There was no point in discussing this further with someone at the sergeant's pay grade.

"Stay sharp, Sergeant," he said. "It's going to be a long night."

The white boy picked up the sawhorse and walked it to the side of the road. The Humvee began rolling through the mud into the town of Stebbins.

Imura caught the driver looking in the rearview mirror. "What?" he asked.

When alone, there was always a speak-up and speak-plain policy with Imura's team.

The driver, whose name was Alex Foster but who was known on the job as Boxer, said, "You realize that if anything really comes out of the woods those two kids are a late-night snack." It wasn't a question.

"Can't all be that bad," said Rachel Bloom, combat call sign Gypsy. She was second in command of the Boy Scouts. A tough woman with five full tours under her belt, running special operations in Iraq and Afghanistan, and many more since signing with Sam.

The man seated behind Boxer, DeNeille Shoopman, known as Shortstop, said what they were all thinking. He was a pragmatic man who preferred maintaining a big-picture view of everything. "It only takes one hole."

"These infected sonsabitches aren't armed," said Bud Hollister—Moonshiner, the rowdy former biker-turned-soldier. "You see the footage from the school? They walked right into the bullets and didn't give much of a wet shit."

"Headshots put 'em down," observed Shortstop.

"Yeah?" Moonshiner snorted. "And how many soldiers do you know who can reliably get a headshot in a combat situation? In the dark? In the rain? In a running firefight? Please."

No one answered. Everyone cursed quietly. Gypsy and Shortstop turned to look back at the small glow of lantern light that was quickly being consumed by darkness and distance.

CHAPTER THIRTY-THREE
OFFICE OF THE NATIONAL SECURITY ADVISOR
THE WHITE HOUSE, WASHINGTON, D.C.

Scott Blair put down the phone and sat there staring at it. Wanting to smash it. Wanting to burn his office down just so the damn thing wouldn't ring again.

Dr. Herman Volker was dead.

God almighty.

CHAPTER THIRTY-FOUR
BORDENTOWN STARBUCKS ON ROUTE 653
BORDENTOWN, PENNSYLVANIA

A bloody hand shot out and clamped around the throat of the zombie a split second before those teeth could snap shut on Goat's flesh.

"Hold on a minute, slick," said Homer Gibbon. He was smiling and there was a crooked playfulness in his voice. "I'm trying to have a conversation here."

The zombie tried to pull free. It clawed at Homer with its finger-nails and squirmed around, attempting to bite the wrist of the hand that held it. Goat shrank back from it, and then he saw the look in Homer's face. There was no trace of fear. Nothing. The man squat-ted there, his face and body covered with fresh blood, maggots wrig-gling in open wounds in his skin, and yet his mouth wore a smile of curious wonder like that of a child watching a butterfly. Homer's eyes were filled with dark lights.

"I know you," he said softly, directed his words to the struggling zombie. "I see you with the Black Eye, yes I do. I see all the way into your soul. Do you believe me?"

The creature writhed and snapped, but he was helpless in Homer's powerful grip.

"The Red Mouth has whispered to you, hasn't it? You understand its secrets now, don't you, boy? Yes . . . I can see that you do. And that Red Mouth is screaming so loud inside your head that you have to do something. You have to let it speak through you. You have to feed it because it's so goddamn hungry, tell me if I'm lying."

The zombie did not respond, though Goat turned to look at it, to seek for something in its eyes. Was there something there? Was there a flicker of something deep in those dark wells?

They say that the eyes are the windows of the soul. Goat had heard that a million times. If so, then these windows looked into a landscape that had suddenly become blighted, like the floodplains of Mississippi and Louisiana after the levees failed. Like Japan after the tsunami. There was wreckage that proved that life had once ex-isted there, but the life itself was gone.

Or . . . was it?

"Yes, you've heard the Red Mouth speak and you've listened, haven't you, boy? You listened real good and you took it all to heart. That's nice. That's real nice."

For the briefest of moments, as Homer spoke to the infected in his slow, rhythmic backwoods voice, Goat thought he saw a shadow move behind the zombie's eyes. Was it the mind of the dead leav-ing a deserted house? Or was it something else? A lingering trace of the man Homer had killed? A ghost haunting the body it once owned.

Whatever was happening, it was horrible from every angle. A life destroyed. A monster created. And a soul . . .

What?

Lost?

Trapped?

Goat's mind rebelled at placing too precise a label on it.

The zombie pounded at Homer's hand with soft, clumsy fists.

Without turning to Goat, Homer spoke to him, "I done this, you know."

"What?"

"I done this. This plague thing. It ain't no bioweapon like they're saying on the radio. It was me that done this. The Black Eye opened in my mind and now I speak with the voice of the Red Mouth. Used to be I was a slave of the Red Mouth, or at least I thought I was, but after I died and woke up in that body bag . . . ? Well, hell, I knew. I realized that all this time the Black Eye was my own mind's eye, and the Red Mouth is my mouth. You understand what I mean by that, son?"

Goat didn't know how to answer that question. It seemed like there was a thin tightrope between possible answers and that rope was covered in slippery grease. He clamped his mouth shut and shook his head.

"Go on, son," said Homer, clearly understanding Goat's reluctance. "Don't be shy. I won't bite."

There was a beat after that last phrase came out and then Homer realized what he'd said and what it meant, and he burst out laughing.

The zombie pounded on his arm, tore at the flesh of the hand holding him. Black saliva dribbled from the corners of his mouth.

Suddenly Homer got to his feet and dragged the zombie upright. It was a display of enormous strength because the struggling infected had to weigh at least two hundred pounds. Homer let go of the creature's throat, grabbed both shoulders, spun him around, and shoved him toward the door. The zombie staggered and tripped over the twitching leg of a barista who was just now returning from some dark place to a world that was darker still. Homer looked down at her and at the man he'd just shoved.

"This is about to get twitchy," he said, though Goat didn't know if he was speaking to himself or not. Then a slow smile began to form on the killer's pale lips and he turned fully toward Goat. That smile was perhaps the most frightening thing Goat had ever seen. Homer once more stabbed a finger at Goat. "You tell stories, right? I mean, that's what reporters do, right?"

Goat nodded. A tiny, frightened nod, but there didn't seem to be any traps built into so simple a question.

The zombie Homer had shoved, spun back around, and he lunged forward. Not at Homer, but to try and barrel past him to get to the only person in the whole place who wasn't dying or dead. Goat.

Without a blink, without a fragment of hesitation, Homer drove an elbow into the zombie's face with such sudden, shocking force that the infected's whole upper torso froze in place while his legs ran up into the air. Then the creature's body canted backward and he fell bonelessly to the floor. The back of his head struck the marble floor and exploded, spraying red and black outward in a starburst pattern. His legs and arms instantly stopped moving and he lay dead. Truly dead.

"Impolite motherfucker," muttered Homer. Then he smiled once more at Goat. "Where was I? Oh yeah, telling stories and shit. During my trial and when they killed me, you were one of those asshole reporters who was there nearly every day. Telling the court's version of my story. Only the thing is it isn't really my story. It isn't the story of the Black Eye and the Red Mouth. No, sir, it is not. It isn't the full story and it sure as shit ain't the right story. And, let's face it, son, I got a story worth telling. Look at me. I mean, seriously, look at fucking me."

Goat couldn't take his eyes off of Homer Gibbon.

The man was huge, powerful, covered in blood, and . . .

And he was a monster.

An actual monster.

Something the world had never seen before.

Dead and yet not dead. Infected with the Lucifer 113 plague and yet still capable of thought—though whether that was "rational" thought was up for debate in Goat's mind. A man who had been the nation's most notorious serial killer—up there with legendary murderers like Ed Gein, Albert Fish, Saint John, and Ted Bundy—and who had been tried, convicted, and executed.

And who was now what, exactly?

Was he a victim of Dr. Volker's insane desire to punish criminals of this kind? Yes.

Was he the brutal and sadistic maniac who slaughtered ___ ___ people and deserved the punishment given him? Absolutely.

Was he patient zero of a new plague, something that, should it be allowed to spread, could become an unstoppable pandemic?

Yes.

God almighty, thought Goat. He felt like fireworks were exploding inside his head. Everything was too bright, too loud, too massively wrong. And all of these thoughts tumbled through his brain in a burning moment.

Homer was still speaking, but his smile had dimmed. "You listening to me, boy? You'd better be 'cause it looks like you're ankle deep in shit right about now. Tell me I'm wrong. No? Nothing? But I got your attention, right? Give me a nod or something, boy."

Goat nodded.

"Good boy," said Homer, his grin returning. A few of the other dead were starting to rise. "We ain't got no time at all, so how about we cut the shit and get to it?"

Goat found himself nodding again, though he had no idea what the "it" was Homer wanted to get to.

The twitching woman rolled over onto hands and knees and began to rise. Homer took two short steps closer and snapped his foot out in a powerful kick that sent her sprawling into the path of two other dead who had managed to get to their feet. The three of them collapsed into a hissing tangle of arms and legs.

Homer snorted, amused by it. But at the same time he seemed momentarily uncertain as he watched his clumsy victims.

"Shi-i-i-i-i-it," he breathed, drawing it out. Then he blinked and turned back to Goat. "Okay, boy, here's the deal. I'm going to get my ass out of here before this becomes a buffet. I don't think these fuckers will hurt me—not with the Black Eye open inside my mind—but they'll definitely go ass-wild on you. You're a bag of bones, but I'll bet there's some tasty meat on you, yes, sir."

Goat felt blood drain from his face.

"But I think I'd rather let you keep sucking air. For a while, anyway. You game with that?"

The sound that escaped Goat's throat might have been a yes, but it sounded like a mouse's squeak.

Homer took it as assent, though, and he nodded. "So, here's the deal. You come with me. You do what reporters do. Interview me, whatever. You do that for me, you tell my story, my side of it, you let the Red Mouth speak through me and you write down every word and then pretty it up some for the newspapers. What do they call it? Edit it? Rewrite it? Whatever. You do that, and you play fair with me while you're doing it, you make sure to tell the whole truth, and you might just walk away from this. How's that sound?"

The dead were getting up now. The three who'd fallen and others. Goat didn't know how many people had been in the Starbucks when Homer came in. Fourteen, give or take? Some of them were hurt but not dead, victims of Homer's rage. Shattered bodies, torn limbs, bitten flesh. No one was whole. No one was uninfected.

Except him.

The moans of the newly resurrected dead filled the store.

"Think quick, son," said Homer. "Big ol' fucking clock ticking right here."

Goat tried to answer, squeaked again, coughed his throat clear and forced out a reply. "You promise you won't hurt me?"

He hated how weak and small and terrified his voice sounded.

And he hated it much more when he saw how his words and his tone changed the grin on Homer's face. The killer licked the blood from his teeth and lips.

"I just said I wouldn't hurt you, boy."

"No," insisted Goat, grabbing whatever thread of a lifeline he could, "listen, listen . . . you want your story told? I mean really told? Told so that it reaches everyone and everyone knows who you really are? That's what you want? Then I can give it to you. I'm the one who broke this story. Me and my friend Billy Trout. I got the story out that no one else could. I know how to make sure it gets out."

Homer narrowed his eyes.

There were sudden screams behind Goat and he turned to see the newly risen dead falling on the dying victims of Homer Gibbon. The infected snarled and growled as they tore into living flesh.

Blood sprayed the walls and the screams were high and piercing and entirely without hope.

"You broke that story?" said Homer slowly.

"Yes. Billy and I."

"I heard that Trout fellow on the news."

"He's still inside the town. In Stebbins. He's at the school."

The screams rose and rose. Goat cringed away from it, edging toward Homer only because he was closer to the door. If he could get Homer to take him outside, then maybe Goat could make a break for it. The highway was right there. He'd take his chances with high-speed traffic in the rain.

Homer was still studying him with narrowed, suspicious eyes.

Then his eyes flicked to what was going on behind Goat.

"Shit," he grumbled, "those are some persistent fuckers."

There was no need for Goat to look. The slap of slow feet on the wet floor told the story.

"Please," begged Goat.

Homer snaked out a hand, caught Goat by the front of his shirt and jerked him forward just as something brushed the nape of Goat's neck. As he stumbled forward, the cameraman craned his head around to see long, red fingers clutching at the air where his head had been a moment ago.

"I need my laptop," Goat said. "And my camera bag."

Homer shrugged. He picked up the MacBook and tossed it to Goat, then snatched the handle of the canvas camera bag out from under a murder victim who was twitching his way back from death. Homer slung the heavy bag on his brawny shoulder and began backing toward the door as the zombies shuffled forward.

"Get your ass in gear," warned Homer as he grabbed Goat again and hauled him away. Goat staggered toward the door and then thrust through it into the rain. He wanted to slam it in Homer's face, but the hydraulic door closer was too strong, Homer came outside and he tried to slam it, too. When it resisted him, he leaned his full weight against it. The dead hit the door with enough slack weight to push it several inches outward again.

"Shit," said Homer, though he did not seem particularly concerned.

He still held Goat with one hand and had the other pressed against the glass. He cut a sharp look at Goat. "Listen to me, boy. We got to make a run for the car or they'll eat your dick sure as God made little green apples. But . . . and I want you to listen real hard to what I have to say now. If I let you go and you try to run, then you better pray that I can't run faster than you, 'cause if I catch you then I'm going to bite your dick off and make you eat it. You believe me when I tell you that?"

Goat did. And he said so.

Homer pushed back against the door. "Then let's go. Car's un-locked. Go!"

He shoved Goat toward the passenger side and held the door long enough for the cameraman to take a few stumbling steps, correct himself, and begin backing toward the car. Goat clutched the laptop to his chest as if it was a shield. Forty feet away the highway was bright with headlights and fast metal. Could he make it? Then he caught Homer watching him; the killer turned to follow Goat's line of sight, then turned back and smiled.

"Call the play, son."

Goat's heart hammered like desperate fists. Tears fell down his hot cheeks. His legs and muscles trembled with adrenaline and terror.

Go, he told himself. Go, go, go!

A sob broke from his chest as he spun around and reached for the door handle of the metallic green Nissan Cube.

CHAPTER THIRTY-FIVE
STEBBINS LITTLE SCHOOL
STEBBINS, PENNSYLVANIA

Billy Trout left the basement gymnasium after the bodies had been taken care of. Because they were forbidden to open the exterior doors to the school, the two corpses in their makeshift body bags were placed in one of the shower stalls. After the others left, Billy lingered and stared down at the silent forms.

He wanted to say something, a prayer or something of importance, but even though he kept calling on God since this whole thing started, his actual faith was as dead as the town. This sort of thing did little to rekindle what had always been a weak flame in him. Even so, he mumbled something, a fragment of the Lord's Prayer, getting some of the words wrong but getting the gist of it out there. For the dead, in case they believed. And . . . in case he was wrong about there being no God. Trout was open to taking any help they could get. He'd have prayed to the Flying Spaghetti Monster if he thought it would earn the people in this school even a small measure of grace.

Then, heavyhearted, he turned away and climbed the stairs to the first floor. He tried again to call Goat, but he still had no signal. Frowning, he went to the second floor and found a room with big windows so there was no chance of interference.

Nothing. The little meter on the satellite phone said that he still had half a charge. Power, but no signal. No contact with Goat, or with anyone.

The explanation for it was obvious to the realist in him, but Trout resisted it nonetheless. He didn't want it to be the case.

"Uh oh . . ." he murmured.

Depressed and frightened, he went downstairs and looked once more into the big classroom. Two of the teachers were handing out little plastic containers of fruit cocktail. Trout thought it was such a bizarre sight. He remembered getting those little cups when he was a kid in this school. It was always a happy moment. They packed a ton of sugar into those cups, and it was nice to see halved maraschino cherries floating among the chunks of peach and pear. Now it seemed incredibly sad. The children took the cups, opened them with clumsy fingers, spooned out the fruit, chewed, swallowed, and all in a ghastly silence.

Trout backed out of the room and went to find Dez.

At first she seemed to be nowhere at all, and he poked his head into every room. Then he caught sight of her heading toward the fire tower at the far end of the hall. He immediately understood where she was heading. He limped down the hall as quickly as he could, hissing whenever the pain shot down the back of his leg. The heavy fire tower door creaked as he opened it, and for a moment he listened to the sounds from below. Soft footfalls fading into silence. He descended slowly and silently, and finally paused on the stone steps and saw her there, standing with her palms on the steel door, shoulders slumped, head bowed.

On the other side of that door was what was left of the infected from the school.

And JT. He was out there, too.

"Damn," breathed Trout. His voice was soft but in the utter stillness of the fire tower it carried and Dez suddenly stiffened. She didn't turn though.

"Billy?"

"Yeah, babe."

There was a beat. "Don't call me that."

"Right. Sorry." Now wasn't the time to test the limits of whatever new connection they'd forged.

He descended the last few steps and moved toward her, mindful to come into her peripheral vision well out of strike range. Experience is a wonderful teacher.

She stared at the closed door as if it were made of glass. "What do you want?"

He almost said that he came looking to see how she was, but Trout preferred his balls still attached to his body. So, instead he said, "They said they'd airdrop some food to us. That's fine, but nobody I talked to knows how to get up on the roof without going outside."

"There's a fire access stairway."

"Right, okay, that's good," he said. "But no one else knew that."

She turned to look at him, but said nothing.

"Once they drop the stuff," Trout continued, "it's got to be inspected, sorted, and distributed. You've seen how people are reacting. They're going to do it wrong. Some of these people are a twitch away from losing it. They might grab stuff or horde stuff. We have to take control of things. We have to make sure we do everything right."

Her eyes searched his face and after a long moment she gave a single nod.

"There's something else," he said. "No, two things. The first is that we have to double—no, triple—check everyone. I mean everyone."

"We did. No one has a bite."

"That's not what I'm saying. The guy who . . . I mean the guy down in the gym. I didn't see a bite on him."

A line formed between her brows. "Of course there was a bite."

"No, there wasn't. I, um, checked. Everywhere. I even had to cut his clothes off just to be sure."

She pushed off from the wall and turned completely to him, her eyes hostile and hot. "The fuck are you trying to say, Billy?"

"That guy didn't die from a bite. Maybe he got infected some other way. Maybe he got some of the black blood in his mouth. When Goat and I interviewed Volker he said something about the infected spitting. So maybe it was that."

"Shit."

"Or maybe it's just enough to get blood on your skin. Everybody's pretty badly dinged up. Maybe the worms in the blood can get into an open wound and . . ."

His voice trailed off. Both of them wore clothes that were caked with dried blood. A lot of that was black blood. Dez began wiping at her clothes—almost absently at first and then she started slapping at her uniform faster and faster until her hands became a hysterical blur.

"*Stop it!*" yelled Trout.

He had to yell it three times before she froze. For a moment Dez's eyes were so wild that the whites showed all around. Crazy eyes. Trout had seen her like that before. Once, naked and wild-eyed, she'd chased him with a shotgun. Not one of their better moments as a couple.

"Dez . . . we wiped ourselves down with Purell, remember? Remember? You damn near did Jell-O shots of the stuff."

The wild look slowly faded, and she gave him a slow nod. She was panting, though. "Right, right . . . sorry. Jeez . . . I'm sorry."

Trout tried to touch her, to give her arm a reassuring squeeze or maybe coax her into a hug, but Dez walked a few paces away, hands on hips, and stared at the wall as she worked on her breathing.

Without turning she asked, "Volker gave you all that research stuff on a couple of flash drives, right?"

"Sure. Goat has them and—"

She half-turned. "Did you think to keep a copy of it?"

Trout shook his head. "There wasn't time for that. Things were already falling apart. I dropped him at the county line and he walked across a field to the Starbucks in Bordentown and I went to my office to get the satellite phone. Things just kept going wrong from then on. Why?"

Dez chewed her lip for a moment, then tapped the walkie-talkie on her hip. "General Zetter called me on the walkie-talkie. They want the drives."

"I bet they do."

"He said that they need the science and research on them. Apparently that ass-pirate Volker did something to the Lucifer disease thing. Changed it somehow. They don't understand what he did and they can't come up with a way of stopping it without Volker's notes."

Trout slumped. "Ahh . . . damn it."

"Zetter thinks you have them."

"How do they even know about them?" mused Trout. "Wait, no, that's my bad . . . I may have mentioned something in my last broadcast."

"That was stupid."

"I was making a point."

"About being stupid?"

"Dez . . ."

"They need that stuff. Zetter didn't go so far as making a direct threat, but with all those guns out there pointed at us, he doesn't really have to. I told him that if he tried to storm the place and take the drives by force I'd destroy them."

"What did you do that for?"

Her eyes shifted away. "I didn't know what else to tell him. And I—"

"You wanted him to think we had something he needed. Okay, I get it. It was—"

"What? 'Stupid'? Are you going to throw that back in my face?"

"No, I'm not," he said with a smile. "I was going to say that it was an understandable stalling tactic."

She grunted. "We need to get in touch with Goat. Maybe he can email stuff to us. There have to be flash drives here. If we can send the stuff we could actually have something to bargain with."

Trout held out the satellite phone. "That was the second thing I wanted to tell you," he said. "I can't get a call through to Goat."

"What?"

"I know."

"Where'd you call from? Maybe there's no reception down in the—"

"I've called from a dozen different, places on the first and second floor. Right by the windows, too. Nothing."

"Shit."

"What I don't get," said Trout, "is why they're bullying us about this. All they have to do is talk to Volker."

"Zetter said they can't find Volker."

"Oh . . . crap."

"So," Dez asked, "what do we do now?"

Trout shook his head. "Geez . . . I really don't know. Keep trying to get in touch with Goat."

"Billy," said Dez, "we could tell them where to find Goat."

"And have them put a bullet in his head?" Trout fired back. "No thanks."

"Would you rather they stormed in here? With all these kids?"

"I'd rather we find a way to get in touch with Goat."

They looked at each other for a few moments, and then off into separate quadrants of the middle distance.

"Can we use the walkie-talkie to call Goat?" asked Trout.

"I don't know. If so, I wouldn't know how," she admitted. Then she tilted her head to one side as if listening to a thought. "Could they be blocking the sat phone somehow? I mean, could they be jamming it or something?"

"Goat could tell you that," said Trout. "He's the techno geek."

"But it's possible, right?"

They thought about the situation for a long time, but neither of them had a solution. Dez's knowledge of electronics didn't extend much beyond downloading Hank Williams Jr. ringtones and watching

YouTube videos. Trout was more savvy, but nowhere close to Goat's level.

"I guess so," Trout said at last. "It's funny, we had a story scheduled about the twenty-first-century army, but I haven't started the research yet. Bad timing."

"Yeah, it blows that the death of our entire town got in the way of your job."

"Bite me, Dez. You know what I mean."

"I know. I was making a joke."

"Hilarious."

She ignored him. "So, where does that leave us other than five miles up shit creek?"

"Not sure what we can do beyond keep trying," he said. "I'll call Goat every minute if I have to."

"Why bother?" she said.

"What?"

Dez walked over to the door that separated her from whatever remained of JT Hammond. "This is all totally fucked," she said. "We're wasting our time. Zetter is going to come in here whether we help him or not. We're completely screwed." She leaned her forehead against the cold metal. "Why don't you go upstairs?"

"Why don't you?"

"To do what? Count how many people we're going to get killed?"

He walked over and stood a few feet away. "Dez, a few minutes ago you just gave a pretty good speech about searching the building and taking responsibility. That was good. It helped. You got this group of refugees in motion."

"They searched the building. It's clear. Mission accomplished. Now leave me alone."

"That's not what I mean," said Trout. "I'm trying to say that somebody needs to step up and be in charge of this mess."

"Did you hear anything I said? They're going to fucking kill us."

"Maybe they will," said Trout, "and maybe they won't. Maybe I'll get in touch with Goat. Maybe they'll find Volker. Maybe this whole thing is over. We don't know what's happening or going to happen, Dez. All we *do* know is there are six hundred people upstairs and every single one of them is lost and scared. They need someone to look to so they know how to deal, how to act. They need an anchor. They need you."

"The principal can handle all that stuff."

"No," said Trout. "Mrs. Madison doesn't have the power and she doesn't have the authority."

"She's the *principal*."

"Of what? An elementary school? C'mon, Dez, are you trying to tell me that she has the goods to bring this whole place under control and keep everybody in line? Some of the people here aren't even from the school. They aren't parents or staff. They're survivors who came here because it's the town's emergency shelter. What do they care if a grade school principal gives them an order?"

Dez barked out a harsh laugh. "And you think they'll listen to me? Are you high or stupid? I'm only a small-town cop." Dez looked at him and her eyes were haunted. "And let's face it, Billy, cops didn't exactly save the day. There wasn't a lot of protecting and serving going on. Or have you forgotten that the entire Stebbins Police Department is dead?"

Trout slapped his palm flat on the door six inches from her head. It was as loud as a pistol shot and Dez jerked backward.

"Now you fucking well listen to me, Desdemona Abigail Fox," Trout growled. "I know you're hurting because of JT. I know what losing him means to you."

"No you don't—"

"The hell I don't. I lost a lot of friends, too. Everyone I work with except Goat. All of my close friends except for you. And *as* for you, I know you a lot better than you ever gave me credit for. Maybe I know you better than JT did. Go ahead and punch me if that offends you, because—"

She did punch him.

It was very fast and very hard and it felt like being shot in the chest. Trout staggered four paces back and then fell hard on his ass. He sat there, legs splayed, gulping for air like a trout on a riverbank.

"God*damn* it, you crazy bitch," he wheezed when he could finally speak. It wasn't the first time she'd ever punched him, but it was harder than he'd ever been hit by anyone in his life.

Dez loomed over him. "*You don't talk about JT.*"

Trout struggled up off the cold concrete. "I wasn't talking about JT," he roared. "I was talking about me and you."

"What do you want from me, anyway?" she demanded, getting up in his face.

He thought, fuck it, and got up in hers.

"I want you to step up, Dez. I want you—I *need* you—to stop being Dez Fox the injured crazy person and be Officer Dez Fox the cop. Yeah, okay, the rest of the Stebbins cops are dead, and that sucks. And, yeah, you have no real authority left. Yeah, life sucks, too, and everyone we know is dead. Yeah, yeah, yeah to all of that. But I just came from a roomful of terrified children. Children, Dez. *Hundreds* of them. Children who are probably going to die unless we put on our big-girl panties and take charge. And by we I pretty much mean you. Hit me again if it'll make you feel better. Kick my ass and stomp me if that's what it takes, but then put your big-girl panties on and go do what you know you have to do."

For a long handful of silent seconds Trout was absolutely positive that Dez was going to pistol-whip him. He could see the desire to do that in her eyes. Her lips compressed and he heard the creak of her knuckles as her hands balled into fists.

Then Dez abruptly took a step back. The action looked like it hurt, like it physically tore her away from the moment. She glanced wildly around as if looking for a doorway that would open onto a different world. Maybe the world of two days ago, when everything made some kind of sense; or a world where there was no Stebbins County, no Billy, no JT, no Lucifer 113, and no zombies.

She exhaled a long, deep, ragged breath.

"Fuck you, Billy." She said it in a whisper.

"Yeah," he agreed. "Fuck me."

Then Dez nodded. Not to Trout. Maybe to herself. A single, curt bob of her head.

Without another word Dez turned and climbed the steps as heavily as if mounting the stairs to the guillotine.

Trout watched her go.

When he was alone, he leaned against the wall and he, too, exhaled. His chest really hurt. Oddly, his back felt a little better, as if falling had knocked something back into place.

"Why, thank you, Billy Trout, for that crucial sanity check," he said aloud in a bad approximation of Dez's voice, then switched to his own. "Oh, you're quite welcome, Officer Psychopath. Anything for a friend."

Then he pushed off the wall, rubbed his aching chest, and limped up the steps after her.

CHAPTER THIRTY-SIX
WHAT THE FINKE THINKS
WTLK LIVE TALK RADIO
PITTSBURGH, PENNSYLVANIA

"We have Borden on five."

"Borden? Is that a first or last name?" asked Gavin.

The producer spread his hands. "It's all he gave us. Coming to you now."

Gavin took the call. "We have Borden from Bordentown. Thanks for calling in."

"Yeah, okay, I listen to this show all the time and you talk about a lot of really weird stuff but I saw something tonight that's weirder than anything you ever talked about."

The man had a thick Kentucky accent and Gavin figured he was right out of one of those deep woods hollers. A good old boy's good old boy.

"I'm all ears, Mr. Borden."

"It ain't 'mister.' Just Borden."

"Fair enough."

"I'm a trucker—"

"You shock me."

"—and I'm doing a run from Chicago straight through to Balti-more and I pulled off the interstate to get me a cup of coffee. One of them Starbucks places."

"I've heard of them."

"And as I'm walking out I see this car pull up. And who do you reckon I saw getting out of that car just as bold as you please?"

"I don't think I'd want to hazard a guess."

"It was Mr. Homer Gibbons."

"Wait, the serial killer?"

"The very same."

"Excuse me, Borden," said Gavin, "but it's my understanding that Homer Gibbons was executed at Rockview Prison two days ago."

"That's what I'm saying. They kilt that boy deader'n dead and there he was getting out of one of those little Nissan thingamabobs. The Cube. Bare-chested, barefooted, bold as you damn please."

"Homer Gibbon."

"Yessiree bob."

"Alive?"

"Well, sir, to be fair, he didn't look all that hot. I think they must have messed him up some when they kilt him."

Gavin looked at the producer, who was laughing silently on the other side of the glass. Gavin grinned and gave him a thumbs-up.

"Tell me exactly what happened, Borden. This is absolutely fascinating."

CHAPTER THIRTY-SEVEN
IN STEBBINS COUNTY
STEBBINS, PENNSYLVANIA

Lonnie Silk did not understand the hunger.

He was too hurt, too tired, too sick to even think about food, and yet it was all he could think about. With every staggering step he took, the need for something to eat turned like a knife in his stomach. It was worse than any hunger he'd ever felt. It was so much bigger than the pain of his wounds. So much more important than the disease that he knew was at work in his blood and flesh.

He was so hungry that he wanted to scream.

Or maybe he had screamed. Lonnie couldn't quite remember. If he had, then the storm winds had blown it away.

He sagged against a wooden post at the corner of a big rail fence that bordered a field of swaying corn.

Corn.

He looked at it. He'd eaten raw corn before. Everyone who grew up in farm country had tried it.

Before he knew he was doing it, Lonnie climbed up onto the rail fence, leaned over, let himself fall into the mud on the other side. He landed hard and pain flared in every damaged inch of him.

It didn't matter.

He was too hungry to let it matter.

Lonnie tried to get up. Couldn't.

So he crawled to the nearest stalk, grabbed it, pulled it down, tore the ear from the stalk, ripped the green leaves away, and bit savagely at the kernels.

And immediately spit them out.

He flung the corn away, disgusted by it. This isn't what his hunger wanted.

Needed.

Craved.

Lonnie cried out in frustration, and this time he heard his voice. It was not an articulate cry. There were no words. Instead it was just an expression of need.

Of hunger.

Lonnie looked wildly around as if expecting to see plates of food right there. Needing to see food.

Drool ran from the corners of his mouth and Lonnie dared not wipe it away; if he did, then he'd see what was in that spittle. What white, wriggling things were there.

Things that were also hungry.

So hungry.

He moaned again, and wept at the sound of his own voice.

Lonnie grabbed the slats of the fence and slowly, painfully pulled himself up. Then, holding on to the rail, he began walking again. He didn't know where, he had no specific destination. He wasn't even sure where home was anymore.

Down this road?

Or farther along the road he'd been on?

He didn't know, couldn't tell. Didn't really care.

He went the way his weak legs could go, using the fence to stay upright. Following his moans. Following his hunger.

Looking for something to eat.

CHAPTER THIRTY-EIGHT
TOWN OF STEBBINS
ONE MILE INSIDE THE Q-ZONE

Sam Imura told Boxer to pull onto a side road, and the Boy Scouts climbed out of the vehicle. Moonshiner hefted out a big duffel bag, zipped it open, and began handing out heavy-duty protective garments. These were not the standard white hazmat suits but were instead SARATOGA HAMMER Suits. They were permeable chemical warfare protective overgarments with composite filter fabric based on highly activated and hard carbon spheres fixed onto textile carrier fabrics. Sam had rolled into action on dozens of occasions wearing a HAMMER Suit. They were tough but light enough to permit agile movement during unarmed and armed combat.

"Hoods?" asked Shortstop.

"Not unless we know we're heading into close-combat," said Sam. "It's a serum-transfer pathogen. No airborne components."

"Shit," said Boxer.

"You don't want these fuckers to French kiss you, brother," said Moonshiner.

"Be a lot more action than I've been getting lately."

They all laughed. Sam turned to them and when they saw the look on his face the laughter faded.

"What?" asked Moonshiner.

"Let's understand something right from the jump," Sam said. "The infected are designated hostiles and we react and respond the way professional soldiers should while in combat. But . . . these are people. We don't disrespect them. If we have to pull a trigger then it's a mercy kill not a booyah moment, feel me?"

The others took a moment, then nodded.

Moonshiner said, "Sorry, boss . . ."

"No," said Sam, "it's cool. None of you have ever been in this kind of fight before. There are no rules except the ones we make. So let's make rules we can live with when we're done."

"Yeah, I'm down with that," agreed Moonshiner.

Gypsy, however, cocked her head and appraised Sam. "Boss . . . you said that none of us have ever been in this kind of fight. Have you? I mean, I thought this was all new shit."

Sam gave her a weary smile. "The team I used to run with dealt with something a lot like this. Different pathogen, but similar effect."

"Zombies?"

"Close enough for government work," said Sam.

"What happened?"

Sam adjusted the fittings on his HAMMER Suit. "Bad things."

They climbed back into their Hummer. No one spoke at all for nearly a mile.

Shortstop finally broke the silence. "Boss, they've got jammers running, right?"

"Yes. Nothing's getting through except one channel reserved for the Guard."

"What about us?" Shortstop tapped the small earbud he wore. "What about the team channel?"

Sam jerked a thumb over his shoulder. "We have a booster in the back, tuned to provide a dedicated channel for this mission. Good news is that we'll have a clear signal. Bad news is that the effective range is about one mile."

"That kind of blows," said Moonshiner.

"Yes, it does," said Sam. "So consider it an intimate conversation between friends."

"Makes me all tingly," muttered Gypsy.

Then Boxer tapped the steering wheel to get their attention and pointed to something at the extreme range of the headlights. "We got movement, boss."

Imura saw it. A pale shape, vague and indistinct more than a hundred yards away. "Get off the road."

Boxer killed the lights and pulled off the road, climbing the verge into a field. A tractor sat cold and quiet in the rain, and beside it was a huge flatbed piled high with harvested vegetables. The humid air was thick with the smell of onions and dirt.

Gypsy leaned between the seat backs and handed a pair of night vision goggles to Imura. He put them on and adjusted the settings, then opened the top hatch of the Humvee and leaned on the big machine gun to steady his line of sight. There were no streetlights this far into farm country, and the sky was utterly black. Then, as he turned on the night vision goggles, the landscape was transformed into a thousand shades of sickly green and ghostly gray.

Because of the new position of the Humvee it took almost a full minute before the thing that Boxer saw came into sight.

"Looks like a group of people. Three of them. Just them. Don't see anyone else." He didn't whisper because the sibilant "S" sounds carried, and instead he spoke quietly. "Civilians. Two men and a kid."

"Are they infected?" asked Boxer.

Sam slid back down into his seat, pulling the hatch closed. "Can't tell."

Moonshiner pulled on a second pair of goggles. "Let me go take a closer look."

"Roger that. Gypsy, go with him."

They opened the doors and got out. The dome light of the Humvee had been disabled. Gypsy put on her night vision goggles, then drew small arms and began moving down toward the side of the road. It is impossible to move with total silence through ankle-deep mud; however, the sound of the rain masked most of the noise. Moving without haste hid the rest. Moonshiner was on point with Gypsy behind and to his right, mindful to keep him out of her line of fire.

The three figures were a hundred yards away. Both men were dressed in work clothes that were pasted to their bodies by rainwater. The child wore jeans but no shirt. No one carried an umbrella. No one seemed to give much of a damn about the cold rain.

"Uh oh," said Gypsy very softly.

An old slatted wooden fence ran along part of the road and angled up to create a property line with the next farm. Moonshiner angled that way and he and Gypsy squatted down by the corner post. While Moonshiner kept his pistol aimed at the three figures, Gypsy tapped her earbud.

"You seeing this, Ronin?"

Ronin—Sam Imura—said, "Rain's too heavy. What are you seeing?"

She told him. "You want us to let them pass or take them down?"

"Hold your position," he said. "I'm coming out."

A few seconds later the rest of the team converged on the corner post.

The lead figure was the oldest. Maybe forty-five. A tall man with a black beard.

"See any bites?" asked Boxer.

"Negative," said Moonshiner.

"We can front them to make sure," said Shortstop. "See if they're responsive to verbal commands."

"Let's try it," said Sam. He stood up and began walking slowly toward the road, his pistol down at his side. Shortstop followed in his wake. The others fanned out to cover the road from several points.

Come on, thought Sam, happy ending here.

Sam stepped into plain view. "U.S. Army," he announced in a clear voice. "We're here to help, however I need you to stop right there. Raise your hands and allow us to check you for signs of infection."

At first it seemed that the three figures would walk past him without taking note of him. But then Sam realized that with the heavy rain they may not have heard him. He tried it again, repeating what he'd said.

Be cool, now, he thought. Let's everyone be cool and be friends.

The bearded man peered at him for a moment, his eyes dark in a pale face. Then he smiled at Sam, showing big white bucked teeth.

Only it wasn't a smile.

"Sir," said Sam with flagging optimism, "I need you to—"

And those teeth parted as the lips curled back from them. With a howl of aching hunger the man came rushing at Sam Imura, pale hands reaching, pale teeth snapping at the air. Behind him the younger man and the boy immediately rushed after him.

CHAPTER THIRTY-NINE
STEBBINS LITTLE SCHOOL
STEBBINS, PENNSYLVANIA

Dez tagged six adults to stay with the kids and stand watch and ordered everyone else down to the gymnasium. Not asked, ordered.

Trout knew the six she picked—middle-aged farm owners. Fathers and mothers. The kind of steady people that you could count on.

Everyone went. Even Gerry, the dazed man who had been singing to the little girl. One of the women in the group held his hand, though Trout didn't recognize her. It was a comfort gesture, he supposed; nothing even remotely romantic in it. Human contact.

The stick-thin principal, Mrs. Madison, walked with Dez with Trout following behind. They were the two most powerful women left in Stebbins and they were as different as two people could possibly get. Mrs. Madison was tiny, older, highly educated, very cultured and mannered, and the exact opposite of what Trout would consider a "physical" person. He couldn't even imagine her going to the bathroom.

Dez, on the other hand, was raw and powerful in a way that was entirely different from male power. She was never mannish, and could even be feminine—or so Trout remembered with an aching fondness—but she was neither delicate nor mannered. If anyone had the sheer lack of personal survival skills to suggest that Dez was a member of a "weaker sex," Trout knew that what was left of that sorry individual would regret the ill-chosen and archaic sentiment for what remained of his life. Dez was a boozy redneck country girl who would be equally at home in a Mississippi trucker bar or a Kentucky holler. She exuded a feral power in exactly the same way the big hunting cats do. Quick to anger, glacially slow to forgive. And yet, Trout loved her and respected her even though at times he felt like they were from entirely different branches of the evolutionary tree.

When everyone was downstairs, the group formed a loose circle around Dez and Mrs. Madison. Trout did a quick head count. One hundred and eight-two, plus the two upstairs. More women than men by a two-to-one ratio.

Mrs. Madison took point and raised her hand for silence. Trout remembered her doing it the exact same way when she was his fourth-grade teacher. So, apparently, did most of the people here. An uneasy, expectant silence fell over the group.

"Thank you," said the principal. "Officer Fox would like to say a few things. She and I have already discussed these matters and we are of a mind. I believe that what she has to say and the things she will suggest are what's best for everyone concerned. Officer Fox?"

Mrs. Madison stepped aside and turned to face Dez, and Trout recognized it as a tactic used by speakers who are practiced at validating another speaker through their own visible attention. It worked, too, because Trout saw the focus of the entire crowd zero in on Dez. He suppressed a smile, appreciating the way that was handled.

Dez, however, was no public speaker. She glared at the crowd with open suspicion and hostility, and Trout prayed she wasn't going to use more threats and bullying to get things done.

She surprised him, however.

"Okay, listen up," she said in a neutral tone, "here's the situation as we know it. We finished our sweep of the building and there's no one else left inside who has any bites or any sign of infection."

The crowd nodded. They'd all been part of that search. Even so, it was good to hear it said.

"We have to face some realities here," Dez continued. "First, we have to stay inside the building. The National Guard made that clear and I don't think they're going to cut us any slack. So, for all intents and purposes we're stuck on an island in the middle of the ocean. The good news is that we have our own generator and enough fuel for five days. Because this is the town's emergency shelter, we have blankets, flashlights, batteries, first-aid kits, water, and a lot of food. Enough for maybe a week with the number of people we have.

When we get low, the Guard says they'll drop more on the roof. So we're good for now, and this thing will all be over by then."

"Over?" asked Jenny DeGroot, one of the teachers. That one word was heavy with meaning and implications.

"You know what I mean, Jenny," said Dez. "They'll get us out of here and then we can all . . ." She paused, fishing for the way to say it. "So we can all take care of what needs to be taken care of."

Most of them said nothing and just looked at her; a few—the ones Trout thought were the steadiest among them—nodded. Grief was tomorrow's problem. Today's agenda was all about survival.

"Now, the first thing we really need to talk about," said Dez, her mouth, eyes, and voice hardened, "is rationing. We are going to share everything. I'm going to put a few people in charge of inventory, someone else will be in charge of allotment, and some others will take care of cooking and food prep. No one else touches any food unless it's on their own plate. No one hoards anything. Not food, not anything. If the supplies do get low, then the kids eat first and we eat second. Does anyone have a problem with that?"

Trout scanned the crowd. If anyone had a problem with it, no one said so. He even thought he saw some relief on their faces, and Trout could understand that. A plan was evidence of structure, and structure was stability. It was something they could react to.

"Good," she said. "Next is the generator. The town's power is out, so the generator is all we have. I don't want to use it anymore than we have to. If we turn it off during the day we can stretch it out for longer than a week if we have to. That means that we eat the stuff in the cafeteria freezers first. After that it's Spam and canned beans, unless they drop us some McRib sandwiches."

That got a few small smiles. It was a dent, and Trout was relieved to see Dez attempting humor. It meant that she was on sounder emotional ground herself.

"Now we come to the real issue," continued Dez. "Security. We need to secure this building. If the Guard is wrong and there are more of those—things—out there, then we need to make sure they don't get inside. Partly because we don't want to turn this place into a Denny's for dead motherfuckers."

No one laughed at what was an intensely lame joke. Dez colored a little but plunged on.

"And if the Guard think that our security has been compromised then they're going to finish what they started."

She cut an inquiring look at Trout, who mouthed the words, *Go for it.*

"And there's more," said Dez gravely. "We all know that the military wants to sterilize all of Stebbins, which means wiping out everyone and everything. Right now the only thing stopping them is the broadcasts Billy made. That . . . and one other thing. They think Billy has some information that might help them fight this disease or whatever it is."

The people turned to Trout, and many of them moved back from him like he was infected.

"Does he?" asked Mrs. Madison.

"No," said Trout, and he briefly explained about Volker, the flash drives, and Goat.

"As long as they think he has the stuff, we're probably safe," said Dez. "But there's also a chance they could kick down the doors and come in here to take it."

A murmur of dismay rippled through the crowd.

"Wouldn't they leave us alone if they thought we didn't have it?" asked Jenny. "Wasn't that the deal? We stay in here and they leave us alone?"

"That was the deal," said Dez. "Sure. But right now I'm not feeling too filled with the spirit of trust and belief."

One of the farmers asked, "So what do we do? Looks like we're in deep cow shit no matter how this thing goes."

Dez nodded. "We do the only thing we can do. We fortify this place and do whatever it takes to protect the children, and everyone else in this building. It's as simple as that."

"That's all well and good," said Jenny, "but nailing boards over the windows isn't going to stop those helicopters."

"I don't think they'll use the helicopters again."

"Why not? We can't fight them."

"No," Dez agreed, "but if they use heavy weapons then they

can't guarantee they won't kill Billy and destroy those flash drives." She shook her head. "If they come in here, it's going to be with regular men and guns, and we can stop them."

The farmer looked uncomfortable with that. "I don't want to get into a firefight with our own troops."

"Neither do I," said Dez. "You think I'm nuts? I'm not saying we start a war, but we have to be ready to defend this building if they try something. I mean . . . what choice do we really have?"

No one had a good answer to that. Trout wanted to punch a wall because the situation was so frustrating and awkward. Nothing was a clear choice. Nothing really made sense to him. All trust in the system was gone.

One of the parents cleared his throat. "Okay, so . . . um, how do we do that? Secure the place, I mean? Do we, like, barricade the doors and stuff?"

Daz managed an encouraging smile.

"That's a start," she said.

CHAPTER FORTY
TOWN OF STEBBINS
ONE MILE INSIDE THE Q-ZONE

The three infected left the road and came splashing and slogging through the mud toward Sam Imura. Each of them ran differently. The boy's gait was erratic, like a stroke victim trying to run. The younger man barely shuffled along, his limbs stiff and awkward. But the older man ran with an almost normal gait. Fast and with clear determination.

"Ahh, shit," said Boxer's voice in Sam's earbud.

"Boss?" asked Moonshiner.

"I got this," said Sam, and he could hear the sadness in his own voice. He raised his pistol and sighted along the black length of the Trinity sound suppressor. He slipped his finger inside the trigger guard and squeezed.

A black dot appeared an inch above the right eyebrow of the

bearded man, and his head snapped back. Sam used a .22 automatic. The bullet punched in through the front of the skull but it lacked the force for a through-and-through. Instead the lead bounced around inside the man's skull and destroyed the brain. The efficient mechanics of the infected man's gait were destroyed in a microsecond. His legs and arms stopped pumping and instead they flopped uselessly, like a puppet whose strings had all been cut. He fell badly, landed on his face, and did not move.

The younger man was three paces behind him and only with the third of those running steps did he try to move around the obstacle. As if it took that long for whatever drove its brain to identify the obstruction and attempt a course correction. It was too little and too late, and his foot struck the dead man's outflung leg. The younger man pitched forward, hit hard, and slid five feet through the mud.

Sam Imura ignored him for a moment and watched the boy. He was maybe eleven or twelve. A good-looking kid in a hayseed kind of way. Probably would have been a farmer when he grew up. Probably liked sports and girls and his folks. Probably a pretty good kid.

Sam shot him.

The boy fell and stopped being anything. Not a boy, not a monster. He was meat that would cool in the relentless rain.

Something ignited in Sam's chest. He'd been in firefights before with other kinds of infected. He'd had to pull the trigger on what the military shrinks called a mercy killing and what his commanding officers filed away as a righteous shoot. However Sam knew full well that when any sane person pulls a trigger on a child—even an infected one—there was no mercy in the action. And it was in no way righteous. It was an act that made him feel complicit in a process of deception and abuse that was as old as warfare. Once, when a fellow operative made a crude joke about such kills as "collateral damage," Sam took him outside and attempted to beat some conscience into the sonofabitch. The lesson hadn't worked, it didn't change the asshole and it hadn't made Sam feel any better. Though it felt good at the time.

His shrink had a field day with that.

Now, standing in the rain and watching the boy fall, Sam thought about the pathogen. Lucifer 113. Named for a fallen angel.

He wondered how far he was falling. How far he had yet to fall.

The third infected was struggling to his knees. Sam almost shot him.

He didn't.

It wasn't a matter of mercy, even now.

He tapped his earbud. "Converge on me. I need a spit hood and flex cuffs."

The man crawled like an arthritic toward Sam, and as he did so he uttered a low, terrible moan. Was it hunger? Or was it something else? Sam thought he could hear desperation in that moan. Like a person trapped in a burning building.

The rest of the Boy Scouts swarmed in, coming at the infected man from four points. Moonshiner, the biggest of the team, swept the man's hands off the muddy ground and as the young man collapsed, the big man dropped his knee onto his back. He caught the back of the dead man's neck and forced the pale face into the mud, keeping it there despite all of the struggling. Sam observed those struggles. There was no art to them, no plan. It was pure reaction.

Gypsy pulled a spit hood over the man's head and the others bound his wrists with plastic flexcuffs.

"What do we do with him?" asked Gypsy. "Leave him here?"

"Pop him," suggested Moonshiner.

"No," Boxer said quickly. "What if the doctors can do something for him?"

Shortstop shook his head. "Intel I read says that this disease is a one-way ticket. No one comes back."

"That's theory," insisted Boxer. "We don't know that. It's not like this thing's ever been field tested."

Moonshiner made a dismissive sound. "Kid, look at this fucker. He's cold. I'll bet his body temp is already down five, six degrees. Take his pulse if you want to. Check for pupillary dilation. Do whatever you need to do, but he's not sick, Boxer, he's dead."

But Boxer shook his head. "Seen a lot of dead, man, and he doesn't look dead to me."

"Okay, then deadish. Deadlike. Pick whatever word you want to use. Make something up. Point is, this stuff's already eating his brain. What do you think the docs could do for him? Build him a cage with an exercise wheel?"

"It's not—"

"No," said Sam, cutting him off, "it's not fair and it's not right and it's damn well not normal. But it is what's happening. The assholes who invented this took the concept of death and broke it. Doesn't mean what it used to and we have to accept that. No matter how it looks, this man is dead. He's also infected and dangerous."

"Okay," said Gypsy, "so what's the call?"

"We have a to-do list and one item on it is to determine if all of the infected are at the same level of coordination, aggression, and mobile speed."

"We saw some variety right here," said Gypsy. "All three of these cats were different."

"Yeah," agreed Shortstop, "but why?"

"I'll take all theories," said Sam.

They thought about it as they watched the bound infected struggle.

"Damage," said Moonshiner after a few moments. "That could be some of it. Head trauma, joint damage, even other infected gnawing on their tendons."

"Jesus," breathed Boxer.

"It makes sense," insisted Moonshiner. "They're all injured, right? So, think about any group of ordinary people who are injured in a battle or an explosion. You get all kinds of different mobility."

"Makes sense," agreed Gypsy. "These are all going to be walking wounded."

"That covers coordination," said Sam. "What about speed?"

Boxer said, "Maybe . . . rigor mortis?"

They looked at him.

"C'mon," he said, "think about it. If these things are really supposed to be dead, and only some of them are functioning because of those parasites, then wouldn't the rest of them do what pretty much all dead bodies do?"

Gypsy glanced around. "How fast does rigor set in? Three to four hours, something like that? Up to that point the infected— actually, can we call them zombies? Infected makes them seem like sick people."

"And what?" asked Shortstop. "'Zombies' is easier?"

She shrugged. "It's not as real."

They all got that. Everyone nodded.

"So, these zombies start stiffening up within a couple of hours, so that'll account for different rates of movement right there. Freshies move more like real people, stiffies kind of stagger, like we saw on the video feeds we watched."

Shortstop nodded. "Rigor hits maximum stiffness in something like ten, twelve hours, right? Makes me wonder if there are any zombies out there who can't move at all. Or can't move worth a damn. Standing there, or maybe lying in a field somewhere 'cause they can't move."

"Okay," said Boxer, playing devil's advocate, "but nobody's reported a bunch of human scarecrows. These things are walking."

"But not well," observed Shortstop. "General Zetter's report talked about a lot of the infected moving in a slow, shuffling manner. I think that's full rigor right there."

"What about when the rigor wears off," asked Boxer. "It does that. Wears off."

"Sure, but in like four, five days after death," said Gypsy.

"Even so, how will they be able to move then? Will they get fast again?"

Sam said, "We don't know. There hasn't been that much time yet. The first infection was early yesterday, so we're not even one full day into this thing."

The bounded infected continued to struggle.

"So . . ." drawled Shortstop, "what do we do with Sparky here? Do we take him back so they can study him? Is that what they want?"

"No," said Sam. "The Guard can get as many samples as they want. We're on the lookout for anything out of the ordinary. And yes, I realize how that just sounded. Zombies and all."

Everyone grinned at him.

"Point is that if we go on the basis that there are zombies and that a combination of injuries and the onset of rigor will explain most of how they walk and act, then what we look for is something that doesn't fit that model. A mutation, maybe."

"Why?" asked Moonshiner.

"Because we're hoping this disease isn't as perfect as everyone thinks it is," said Sam. When the others looked blank, he explained. "A mutation, should one even exist, is more likely to tell the scientists something about the stability of Dr. Volker's variation of the Lucifer plague. If mutations are possible and—better yet—reproducible, then that opens a door for introducing other mutations that could disrupt the function of the parasite."

Boxer said, "Wow, I actually understood that."

They stood for a moment longer, all of them in a loose circle around the writhing dead man.

"Again," said Shortstop, "what do we do with Sparky here? Strap him to the hood like a six-point buck?"

"No," said Sam. "We leave him."

"Like that?" asked Boxer, pointing to the cuffs and spit hood. "It doesn't seem right."

Gypsy shrugged. "It's not like he's suffering, man."

Moonshiner leaned close and whispered, "He's dead, Jim."

Boxer shoved him away. "Yeah, yeah, very funny."

"Leave him," repeated Sam.

Nobody moved, though. They glanced around, at the rainswept road, at the body that lay struggling at their feet, and back the way they'd come.

"Boss," said Shortstop, "if these three kept walking down the road they'd have come right up to the checkpoint we passed."

"Uh huh," agreed Sam.

"Three of these fuckers against those two kids back there?"

"Uh huh."

"You think those kids would have stopped them?"

"What do you think?" Sam said, making it an open question.

They looked down at the infected. The man continued to writhe and fight against the restraints. His jaws snapped at the material of the spit hood. Gypsy made a disgusted noise. Moonshiner's grunt was dismissive. But it was Shortstop who answered the question.

"Not a chance in hell, boss," he said. "Not one chance in hell."

Together the Boy Scouts walked up the slope to the Humvee. The big Browning .50 mounted on the roof looked ominous. Waiting.

Hungry.

CHAPTER FORTY-ONE

STEBBINS LITTLE SCHOOL
STEBBINS, PENNSYLVANIA

"Ground-floor windows are a priority," said Dez.

"All of the windows are security glass," said Mrs. Madison, "with wire mesh in each pane."

"Won't stop a bullet," said a farmer.

"So we block the windows," said Dez. "Look, this school is built like a blockhouse. There aren't all that many windows anyway, not on the first floor."

"Twenty-two," said Mrs. Madison, and Trout felt like kicking her.

"Twenty-two, okay," conceded Dez. "So we lock them and cover them with paper or cloth so no one can see in. Then we stack stuff in front of them. Cans with marbles or pieces of metal, anything that will make a lot of noise if the window is forced. We'll post people in the halls and if anyone hears those cans falling over then they shout out and we all come running."

Several people nodded, and Trout felt the first splinter of encouragement.

"All of the classroom doors open out," said Jenny DeGroot. "We can get benches from the gym or other stuff and put them in the halls. If we hear someone breaking in, we can wedge the benches crossways so the doors won't open out."

"Great idea," said Dez, jumping on it.

And suddenly everyone was throwing ideas out. Some were poorly thought out, just things to say from people who needed to be part of a solution—any kind of solution; but there were some good ones, too.

"There are tools and hammers and nails and all that stuff in the janitor's office," said one of the teachers.

Someone cleared their throat loudly and the crowd turned toward one of the farmers, a young man with old eyes. Trout fished for his name. Uriah Piper.

Piper shook his head and said, "There's a better way to secure the doors."

"Okay, Uriah," said Dez, "what have you got?"

"Well, first," he said, speaking in the slow way some farmers do, "we don't need every door to even open. Once we secure the windows, we can seal off a bunch of the rooms. We can set those noise-making cans you mentioned, but otherwise make sure those doors won't even open."

"How?"

"Easiest and fastest way would be to nail a piece of wood along the bottom of the door. Nail it, or better yet, screw it right into the floor, and position it so that it also attaches to the wall right there at the bottom, and maybe again at the top. Or we could erect a brace at an angle to the floor and toe-nail it in, then nail another piece to the floor behind that. Take a battering ram to open a door like that, and even then it wouldn't be easy. You'd have to tear the whole door apart to get through, and I don't think even soldiers can do that without us knowing about it."

"Are you a carpenter?" asked Clark, one of the teachers, his tone filled with skepticism.

"No, sir, I'm a dairy farmer, as I believe you know."

"Then how do you know that will work?"

Piper gave him a small, cool half-smile. "You live in farm country, Mr. Clark. How do you *not* know that would work?"

That coaxed a few chuckles from the crowd.

"Okay, okay, you're right," interrupted Dez, clapping Piper on the shoulder. "It'll work and it conserves our supplies. Uriah, you're in charge of securing the doors and windows. Everyone else helps you. Set up work parties and get going."

She glanced around, saw some nods, a few blank stares, and Clark's doubt-filled scowl. Dez locked her eyes on him.

"We're not going to have a problem, are we?" she asked.

Trout wondered how long Clark could meet that uncompromising blue-eyed stare. As it turns out, the teacher lowered his eyes after maybe a full second. Trout was pleased that Dez wasn't so small that she nodded to herself to acknowledge the victory. Clark wasn't a bad guy or an asshole. He was scared and confused and defiance or resistance was probably the only way he knew to try and find solid ground or a scrap of personal power. Dez apparently knew that, too.

"Okay, then let's get started," said Dez. "I want this all done an hour ago."

The group started to break up, but then Gerry Dunphries, the man who'd sung the fractured lullaby, grabbed Dez's arm. "Wait, wait, hold on, let's not go crazy here."

Everyone paused, looking at him. His eyes were wide and wild and Trout was sure the man was a very short step away from screaming.

"Hold on for what, Gerry?" asked Dez.

"We're acting like this is all really happening," he said. "And it's not. It can't be. None of this is really happening. I mean, come on, people going crazy and . . . eating each other. That's not happening. That's not what's really going on."

Mrs. Madison took a step toward him and in a gentle voice asked, "Well, Mr. Dunphries, what do you think is happening?"

"It's something in the water," he said. "I mean, that's obvious, isn't it? It's happened before. Like when they put LSD in the New York subways. They did that at the Chelsea Hotel, too. And in France back in the 1950s, the CIA did it in France, they put psychedelic mold in bread and freaked all those people. It was in, in, wait a minute, in . . . yes, in Pont-Saint-Esprit. And remember what Jim Jones did at Jonestown with the Kool-Aid. That's what this really is. They're doing something to us. They're messing with our brain chemistry. This isn't really happening. It's something in the water. Maybe they seeded the clouds and that's why it started happening when it started raining. Nobody's really killing each other. My wife didn't kill anyone. My kids are fine. Tracy and Sophie are just fine, and don't you dare try and tell me different. They're fine, but they're probably freaking out, too, and we have to get out of here, not lock ourselves up. We have to get out and—"

And Dez Fox spun him around and slapped him across the face.

It was, after all, what you do with hysterical people. Trout had seen it a thousand times in movies and on TV. You slap the crazy out of them and knock some sense into them with a big opened-hand wallop across the chops.

The sound was as loud as a gunshot. Gerry Dunphries spun in nearly a full circle and caromed into Clark, who tried to catch him and failed. Gerry crashed to the floor, his face blossoming with a bright red handprint.

Dez loomed over him, hand raised for a second blow, her mouth starting to form words that Trout knew would be some variation of the "cowboy up" speech.

But Gerry screamed.

He scuttled away from her, tears breaking from his eyes, his mouth trembling as terrified sobs tore their way out him. He crawled all the way to the wall and huddled there, hunched and cowering, arms raised against the next blow. Against the next inevitable hurt.

The moment ground to a halt.

Everyone froze into a tableau that came close to breaking Trout's heart. Dez was caught in a role for which she was totally ill-suited—that of a bully terrorizing a helpless person. The other people looked shocked but there was guilt there, too; everyone was complicit in this moment. If the slap had worked—and Trout doubted that it ever did outside of Hollywood or a bad novel—then they would have tacitly supported what Dez did. Instead they were bystanders to injury and there was no way to step back onto the ledge.

"I . . ." began Dez, but even that small a thing, a single tentative word, made Gerry flinch again. He buried his head under his arms and wept brokenly. Dez turned right and left as if looking for the doorway back to a minute ago. She spotted Trout. "Billy, I . . ."

Trout moved past her and knelt in front of Gerry, who instantly shied away. But Trout made very soft, very slow shushing sounds. He sat down on the floor next to Gerry, wrapped his arms around the man, and pulled him close, rocking him the way the man had rocked the little girl. Trout fought to find the words of that old nursery rhyme. Found some of it. Sang it quietly, leaning over Gerry to comfort the man with the warmth of another body.

"Come along," said Mrs. Madison in a hushed voice. "We have work to do."

One by one everyone left until only Dez lingered, looking wretched and guilty and confused. Trout met her eyes. He gave her as much of a smile as he could muster, then a small nod. He mouthed the words "It's okay."

Near to breaking herself, Dez Fox backed away until she reached the far end of the gymnasium, then she turned and fled.

"It's okay, Gerry," Trout said to the sobbing man. "It's all going to be okay," he lied.

CHAPTER FORTY-TWO
THE OVAL OFFICE
THE WHITE HOUSE, WASHINGTON, D.C.

Scott Blair had a hard time keeping himself from committing a federal crime. He wanted to punch the president in the mouth.

No, he wanted to do more than that. He wanted to beat some sense into the man.

"Mr. President," he said with as much control as he had left, "the intelligence we are getting from Captain Imura clearly contradicts the reports being filed by General Zetter. The situation in Stebbins is far from stable and—"

"And we have ten thousand additional troops inbound," said the president. "We have another five on standby. The NBACC field team has arrived and they are making their assessment and, frankly Scott, I think they are in a better position to assess this kind of threat than a former special operator."

"I couldn't disagree more strongly," insisted Blair. "Sam Imura is one of the most experienced people we have, with the except of Captain Ledger who is, unfortunately, out of country and out of reach."

"Captain Imura is retired from active field work," said Sylvia Ruddy. "He's been out of the field, in fact, for years."

"So what? I'd still trust his judgment more than anyone else on the ground in Pennsylvania."

"That's not your call to make," said Ruddy.

Blair stiffened. "Mr. President, may I speak with you privately?"

The president scowled. "All right, that's enough. I don't want you two throwing rocks. This isn't the time or place."

Ruddy folded her arms and said nothing.

"Please, Mr. President," said Blair, not budging. "Two minutes."

"This is ridiculous," said Ruddy, but the president held up his hand.

"If you don't mind, Sylvia?" said the president.

She stared at him as if he'd kicked her. Then she turned on her heel and stalked about, slamming the door behind her. The president sighed.

"That's going to cost me."

Blair shifted to stand between the president and the closed door, forcing himself into the line of sight. The president sat back in his chair and gestured for him to speak.

"Two minutes, Scott."

"Permission to speak candidly?"

"You keep asking that."

"I keep needing to."

They regarded each other, then the president nodded. "Go ahead."

Blair leaned his fists on the edge of the desk. "What the fuck are you doing?"

"What?"

"This isn't like you," said Blair, his voice low and even. "This isn't even close to you. Yesterday you were in command, you were the voice of reason while all hell broke loose. Now you're fumbling at the edges of this thing. Wait, hear me out. You said I could speak my mind and this may be the last chance I have."

"Don't worry, I'm not planning on firing you."

"Christ, who cares about that? How can you still think that this is about politics or anything but a crisis? Sam Imura knows biohazardous threats better than anyone currently on U.S. soil. Anyone. He trained most of the people in the NBACC teams. He wrote their field response protocols. While Simeon Zetter was playing hide-and-seek with the Taliban, Imura was hunting—and bagging—world-class bioterrorists and he did so for four different people who sat in the chair on which you are currently resting your ass."

The president didn't respond, but his face grew steadily redder.

"Sam said that the checkpoints along the Q-zone aren't adequate.

There are a couple of thousand local and state police itching to be a part of this. I know that we pulled them because we didn't want to deal with the complications of jurisdiction and we were afraid of how they'd react if they found out our ground forces had to terminate infected police officers inside Stebbins. That's yesterday's news and it does not matter. What matters now is getting armed, trained men and women to reinforce that Q-zone while there is still time. The National Guard reinforcements won't cross into Stebbins sooner than two hours. We can put a thousand police officers on that line in twenty minutes."

"And we'd lose all control of the situation in terms of media and—"

"—and that doesn't matter."

The president shook his head. "Scott, while I commend you on your passion, I simply do not agree that we are in danger of losing control of the situation. I've known Simeon Zetter too long and too well to doubt his word."

"So have I, and it's not his word that I doubt. It's his ability to properly assess this kind of situation."

The president spread his hands. "I'm not convinced, Scott. Sorry."

Blair really wanted to hit him.

He wanted to kill him.

He took a breath and said, "Will you at least do this much? I have a scientist in my office, a Dr. McReady. She's possibly the best virologist we have and she wants to talk to you. She has some things to tell you about Lucifer that you don't know. And she would like you to open a dialogue with Dr. Price at Zabriske Point."

"Who at where? I don't know that person."

"That," said Blair, "is the point. Price is the man who knows more about the Lucifer project than anyone."

"And Zabriske Point?"

"It's a bioweapons research laboratory in Death Valley."

"Since when do we have a lab there?"

"We've always had one there."

"You knew about this and I didn't?"

Blair offered a chilly smile. "Yes, sir. It's my job to know about such places. Just as it's my job to advise you when the national security is in genuine peril."

The president's eyes were hooded as he considered that.

"Okay, Scott. Go fetch your mad scientist."

CHAPTER FORTY-THREE
ROUTE 653
BORDENTOWN, PENNSYLVANIA

Goat squeezed himself against the passenger door, long legs pulled up, arms wrapped around them, trying once again to hide behind his own limbs. Once again failing to accomplish an impossible task.

Beside him, Homer Gibbon steered the Cube from lane to lane. Windshield wipers slapped back and forth. On the radio Townes Van Zandt was singing about how he was "waitin' around to die." Homer had the volume so loud that it hurt Goat's head and made his eyes twitch. Homer sang along, knowing every word.

When the song ended and a softer outlaw song by Willie Nelson started playing, Homer turned the volume down. Outside the rain was so heavy that the wipers were doing almost nothing. Homer never slowed down, though. He cruised at a steady seventy.

Goat found himself praying for an accident. He was willing to take his chances in a head-on collision. He eyed the wheel, wondering if he dared grab it and spin them into the oncoming headlights.

Maybe.

Maybe.

As if he could read Goat's mind, Homer said, "Don't be thinking bad thoughts, son."

Goat squeezed his eyes shut and shook his head.

The killer beside him chuckled.

They drove.

Then Homer said, "Tell me about yourself, boy. What kind of reporter are you?"

When Goat could trust that his voice wouldn't squeak, he said, "I . . . I'm a cameraman."

"What—you ain't even a reporter?" Homer's mouth hardened. "The fuck?"

"No, I'm a reporter, but I mostly do camerawork. And video editing. And social media."

"Social media? What's that shit?"

"Twitter, Facebook, stuff like that."

Homer grunted. "What's that have to do with news?"

"Everything," said Goat. He realized that this was a chance to reinforce his usefulness. "The Internet is a lot more important than anything when it comes to getting the news out there. Most people get their news from the Net."

"Yeah, I've seen Yahoo News. But that ain't that Twitter shit."

"No, but a lot of people take URLs—Web address links—from sources like Yahoo News and other services, and they post them on Twitter and other social media platforms. Other people repost the links. Sometimes a news story only reaches a lot of people because of posts on social media. Everyone tweets these days. Even the president."

"'Tweets.' Now ain't that masculine as all shit?" Homer let loose a big horse laugh. "That's hilarious. Look at me, Homer fucking Gibbon, public enemy number one, tweeting. That's funny as balls."

Goat shifted his position, still defensive but easing the stricture in his muscles. "It would get your story out," he said. "To the biggest number of people. Millions. All over the world."

Homer shot him a look. "For real?"

"Absolutely." Goat paused. "That's how we got this story out. Billy Trout sent me news feeds from town and I posted them all over the Net so they'd go—"

He chopped off that last word, not daring to say it.

But Homer reached over and jabbed him with a finger. "They'd go . . . what?"

"Um . . . there's an, um, expression that, um . . ."

"Fucking say it, boy."

Goat took a breath and said it in a rush. "When social media is used to break a story and it spreads really fast, it's call 'going viral.'"

It took Homer a moment to process that, and then he began laughing.

He was laughing so hard that he drove right off the road and slammed into a tree.

CHAPTER FORTY-FOUR
STEBBINS LITTLE SCHOOL
STEBBINS, PENNSYLVANIA

When Gerry Dunphries could walk again, Trout took him back to the big classroom and turned him over to Mrs. Madison. The principal wrapped a blanket around Gerry's shoulders and led him away.

Billy Trout looked at the children. Despite the sound of hammering and people shouting as they worked in teams to fortify the school, some of the kids were actually sleeping. It amazed him. As exhausted as he was, he was absolutely certain that he could not fall asleep. Not now and maybe never again. Too much possibility of things waiting for him in the dark shadows behind closed eyelids.

There was still no word from Goat, and with every passing minute Trout grew more convinced that it somehow meant that everyone in the school had slid from the frying pan directly into the fire.

Just for the hell of it he tried the satellite phone once more.

Nothing.

"Fuck," he said, then immediately apologized, though none of the kids seemed to have heard or reacted. He spent a few minutes wandering around checking on the kids, tucking blankets more securely around them, studying their faces to fix them in his mind, pulling names out of the air for as many of them as he could. He saw one face, a black-haired chubby little girl with a beautiful face who slept with her arms wrapped around a small pillow, holding it to her chest as if it was a trusted teddy bear. Trout realized that he knew this girl very well but hadn't seen her in the crowd before. He'd been to her first birthday party, to her christening. To at least five barbecues at her aunt's house. Her name was Belle, and she was the only niece of Marcia Sloane, the woman who had handled phones and done research for Regional Satellite News. Marcia was a curvy retro-Goth woman, north of forty but always possessed of a timeless sexual appeal that was a legend throughout Stebbins County. Fiercely intelligent, saucy, and the very best of company under any circumstances.

That realization brought with it the memory of the last time he'd seen Marcia. It was yesterday afternoon while Trout was coming back to Stebbins after interviewing Dr. Volker. By then the outbreak had cut all the way across the town. His last image of Marcia was her pale, torn, snarling face as it vanished below the level of his car's hood while the Explorer ground her into the mud. That had been the start of it for him, the point at which the wild story he'd gotten from Dr. Volker became the irrefutable reality of Billy Trout's life.

"I'm sorry," he murmured, uncertain whether he was saying it to the girl, for all she'd lost, or to her aunt for what he'd done to her. Or to everyone, for what they were enduring and what lay ahead.

More deeply saddened than ever, Trout turned and drifted back into the hallway. He caught sight of Dez and called out to her. She turned and began walking toward him. They met at the hall's mid-point, by a 4H trophy case filled with photos of kids with their awards for best piglet, biggest sow, largest pumpkin. Brightest future.

"Is . . . is Gerry okay?" she asked tentatively.

"He was in bad shape to begin with, Dez. I don't think this did him any extra harm."

"You're a bad fucking liar, Billy."

"With the very best intentions."

Dez considered him for a moment. "Guess you do. And I guess I don't burn up a lot of calories giving you credit for it."

They looked at the trophies and listened to the hammering. Echoing down from the second floor they heard Uriah Piper and the teacher, Clark, yelling at each other.

"Billy?"

"Yeah?"

"What happens if we can't get in touch with Goat?"

"We will."

"No, what if we can't. What if something's happened to him? I mean . . . if the stuff on those flash drives is that important . . ."

"I don't think it matters," said Trout.

"Why not?"

"When I interviewed Dr. Volker yesterday, he seemed to be pretty sure that Lucifer 113 was unstoppable. If there was a cure, or even notes about a possible treatment on those drives, I'm pretty sure he'd have told me."

"Then why'd he give them to you at all?"

"So someone would have a record."

She turned. "A record of what?"

Trout didn't want to answer the question.

"Of what, Billy?"

He could see the ghost of his own reflection in the glass of the trophy case. "A record of how it all ended."

"How *what* all ended?" she demanded, and then she got it. She grabbed his arm and squeezed it hard enough to hurt. "Jesus Christ, are you saying that Volker thought this was going to *spread*? I mean, really spread? Like a pandemic and shit?"

"That's what he was afraid of. He thought Homer Gibbon would go right into the ground, buried in a numbered grave behind the prison. Volker planned it that way. The parasites that drive the plague would consume him and then die off for lack of food. It would have ended right there. But when Homer's aunt claimed his body that changed the dynamic. What should have been some kind of sick punishment for a serial killer became something that kicked open the door to an outbreak."

Dez's eyes were as wide as saucers.

CHAPTER FORTY-FIVE
ROUTE 653
BORDENTOWN STARBUCKS

They had no names.

Not anymore.

There were names on cards and licenses in wallets and purses, but those things no longer related to the things that moved and milled inside the coffee shop. Even the faces no longer matched the pictures on the cards. On the driver's licenses and university IDs, none of the faces was missing flesh, none of the smiles showed broken teeth. None of the clothes were torn and splashed with blood. These figures weren't those people anymore.

The feeding was done, the hungers shifting from the flesh at hand to the potential of fresher meat elsewhere. The parasitic urges that drove them lost interest when it could no longer detect the signs of life. Breath and rushing blood and a beating heart. Genetic manipulation had ensured this, built it into the organic imperatives that drove these things. Just as the brain chemistry and nerve conduction was repatterned to kill and infect, to feast quickly but not completely, to spread the disease.

That was the only goal.

That was everything.

Though the body ached for food. The minimalized brain moaned in desperation for it, even though there was meat right there. But there was not enough intelligence left even for frustration at the collision of immediate need and driving force.

They bumped into each other without rancor or argument. It happened. They lost balance, recovered, moved on, either toward another collision or toward the door. Eventually it was all toward the door. Toward the movement outside. Lights in the rain. The stink of gasoline fumes, and beneath that was the smell of living meat.

One by one they collided with the heavy glass door, rebounded, hit it again until it open, stepping into the teeth of the storm with their own teeth bared. Unaware of the stinging rain or the hands of wind that tried to push them back. They moved toward the parked cars, sniffed the air, found only trace scents—old scents—but nothing alive. They staggered on through the small parking lot, spreading out, some heading toward the line of red taillights, others toward the line of white oncoming lights.

The first of them that stepped onto the highway was a man with a green apron and a matching billed cap. He had no fingers. They'd all been bitten off. Some by Homer Gibbon, though this man had no idea who that was. He had no thought at all, about Homer or anyone, anything, except the hunger. He stepped off the grassy verge and walked directly into the hazy dark gap between two bright head-lights of a UPS tractor trailer going seventy miles an hour.

The impact smashed him into the air and hurled him thirty feet away. It exploded him. Parts of him were flung all the way over the truck. One arm struck the window of a blue Subaru hard enough to crack the glass. The rest of him was pulped beneath the semi's wheels as the UPS truck tried to brake.

There was a moment when the truck seemed to defy gravity, to rise like a balloon as mass and momentum and the storm-slick road conjured bad magic in the night. The semi slewed sideways and the trailer hunched up and over it, snapping cables and tearing metal. The two cars behind it, the CNN van, and the Walmart truck be-hind it punched one-two-three into the twisting truck and into each other. The storm was too violent for that kind of road speed. Every-one knew it, and everyone drove that fast regardless. The storm and the plague killed them for it.

The air above the eastbound lane was filled with a scream of metal and the popping of safety glass, the hiss of tires that were find-ing no genuine purchase on the wet roads, and the whump-crunch of vehicle hitting vehicle.

Thirty yards away the same vehicular gavotte was imitated on the westbound lane as three of the infected walked into the traffic. Cars and trucks slammed each other into accordion shapes. Other vehicles tried to swerve but there was nowhere to go in that kind of traffic.

On another night when there was no storm and no major crisis, the roads would have been far less crowded. There would have been no rubberneckers, no press, no emergency vehicles, no troop trans-ports, and no cars filled with family and friends trying to get to their missing loved ones in Stebbins.

Cars spun and danced, lifting from the asphalt as big trucks hit them. Airbags popped like firecrackers. Seat belts restrained and they broke and they cut into flesh. The last of the bloody figures from Starbucks moved onto the highway and were crushed by the colliding cars.

Then the symphony of impacts faded out, replaced by the blare of horns and the rising chorus of screams.

For a short time—a precious short time—the infected were unable to attack, each of them defeated by the metal things they had tried to attack to get at the soft food within. The victims of Homer Gibbon's attacks were crippled and mangled, every last one of them.

It would be nearly six minutes before the first ambulances arrived, filled with EMTs who would see hurt people in the wreckage. Badly hurt and yet somehow still alive. Still moving. The EMTs would work shoulder to shoulder with ordinary civilians, survivors of the wrecks or people who'd been able to stop their cars and rushed forward to help. The EMTs and the civilians would work like heroes to pull the mangled people from the wrecks. To triage them, to stabilize them. To save them. Driven by professional responsibility, they would do everything they could to preserve the lives of the suffering wounded.

All of this happened less than one mile outside of the Stebbins Q-zone.

CHAPTER FORTY-SIX
CHECKPOINT #43
STEBBINS COUNTY LINE

Lonnie Silk saw the soldiers up ahead and his heart lifted in his chest.

They wore the same kind of combat hazmat suit he did, but their's were intact, and they still had weapons. Both of the soldiers had they hoods off, though. Lonnie recognized them. The sergeant, anyway. Rodriguez. Lonnie couldn't remember his first name. The other guy was a stranger. Some white kid.

It was the best thing he could see.

Someone he knew.

More important, soldiers. People who could help him.

Lonnie raised his hand, took as deep a breath as his aching lungs could manage, and called out to them.

Except that's not what happened.

It took Lonnie a few seconds to realize that what he thought he did and what he actually did were slanting downhill in different ways.

It wasn't one hand that he raised. Both hands came up. Not in a signaling gesture. Not a wave at all. His hands came up and reached toward the two soldiers as if, even from this distance, he could touch them.

No.

Not touch.

Grab.

Grab?

Was that right? Lonnie struggled to understand it. His fingers splayed open and then clutched shut as if trying to grab the image out of the air.

Why?

To do what?

He could feel his lungs expand as he drew in the air for his yell, but the ache was gone. There was pain, but it was different. A totally new kind of discomfort that felt oddly distant. It was like feeling someone else's pain, though that was totally nuts. Impossible.

The most confusing thing for Lonnie was how his words sounded as they issued from his throat.

They weren't words at all.

He didn't hear his voice call Rodriguez's name. He didn't hear words at all.

The sound was so strange. So weird.

So wrong.

It was a long, sustained sound of complaint. Of need.

Of . . .

Of.

Oh God.

Of hunger.

He tried to stop that sound from coming out of him. He tried to pull down his reaching hands.

He tried.

Lonnie Silk tried.

The infection within him did not allow his voice or his hands to obey.

The soldiers stood there, looking the wrong way, looking past the sawhorse barrier to the road on the other side of the Q-zone. As if they needed to see that. As if that road was important.

Idiots.

Fucking dumbass idiots.

Lonnie screamed at Rodriguez.

But the scream was another moan.

Deep and plaintive and filled with a different kind of pain than Lonnie felt. Not the pain of bites and torn flesh and damaged muscle. This was the ache of pure hunger.

The winds and rain tried to tear the moan out of the air, and for a moment Lonnie thought that the soldiers wouldn't hear it.

Then the white kid turned.

Turned, stared, let his mouth drop open, and then he screamed.

"Tito! Jesus Christ—Tito!"

Tito Rodriguez, that was his name. He spun around, bringing his gun up. He stared, too. He screamed, too.

They both fired.

Lonnie Silk heard the first bullets burn through the air around him and then vanish into the storm. Then he felt his body—what had once been his body—shudder and tremble as something hit him in the chest, the stomach. The thigh.

There was pain, but only of a kind. So far away, so small, so . . .

Meaningless.

His mouth opened and the moan was louder now, rising above the howl of the storm.

Rodriguez and the white kid kept firing.

No! cried Lonnie in a voice that had absolutely no volume. His cries were unwanted in that stolen throat. No one heard them at all. Not the soldiers, not the infection, not the storm.

But it was all Lonnie had. He had no control over his body as it lumbered through the mud and into the hail of bullets. The two soldiers were fucking idiots. They fired wildly, forgetting all of their training, all of the captain's warnings. They tried to bully him down with round after round to his body. Wasting ammunition. Wasting seconds as Lonnie closed from fifteen feet to ten to five to . . .

Suddenly Lonnie's left eye went dark and as an aftereffect he felt the thudding impact of the bullet that hit him.

He thought that would be it. A headshot. That's what the captain told them all. Hit the infected in the head and they go down.

Aim for the head.

Don't you get it, you stupid fucks, he tried to scream. I'm one of them. I'm infected! I'm . . .

Aim for the fucking head.

Please . . . oh, God, please, aim for the head. The head. Shoot the head. Shoot me in my head.

Except that one of these assholes had aimed for his head. Had hit his head. Had blown out one of his goddamn eyes.

And yet Lonnie watched his hands grab at the white kid. Saw the kid's face come suddenly very close as the hands pulled and his own broken, bleeding head lunged forward.

Felt the tough, rubbery resistance of skin beneath his . . .

His teeth.

Jesus Christ.

Skin between his teeth.

Lonnie felt the skin compress. Become taut.

Collapse.

Tear.

Rupture.

And then the blood.

The liquid heat of blood against his lips, on his cheeks.

In his mouth.

Please, God, just fucking kill me!

And then he felt another impact. This time over his right eye. He felt it for all of one moment, and then a vast, featureless black mouth opened in the world and Lonnie Silk fell into it. As he vanished into the darkness, he thought he heard Tito Rodriguez calling his name. But soon it wasn't his name anymore. And the darkness was everything.

CHAPTER FORTY-SEVEN
ZABRISKE POINT BIOLOGICAL EVALUATION
AND PRODUCTION STATION
DEATH VALLEY, CALIFORNIA

Dr. Dick Price was the director of research applications for a facility buried deep in a billion-dollar laboratory. The lab was located in a place Price personally felt was the most aptly named spot on earth: Death Valley. There was no way to get to his lab except by helicopter, and when the birds were out of the coop he and his staff felt like they'd been abandoned on the dark side of the moon.

Team members had to go through ten kinds of security screening including incredibly thorough background checks and psychological evaluations that felt like personality rape. The few who passed those tests then had to put their names to a stack of waivers and nondisclosure agreements, and one frightening document which, for all intents and purposes, signed away their constitutional rights.

Once someone arrived at Z-point, as it was familiarly known, the government owned them. Body and, as Price saw it, soul.

Everyone on the science team knew that the place was illegal as hell. Even the support staff—cooks, guards, cleaners, and janitors—suspected as much. A word to a journalist could bring the place down and likely have several members of Congress and the Department of Defense thrown into jail, but the wording of those documents would land the whistle-blower in an adjoining cell.

It was criminal but necessary. At least as far as Price and his masters at the DOD were concerned. The international agreements and bans on certain kinds of biological warfare were nice in their way, but Price didn't believe for a moment that any of the signatory nations was truly abiding by those rules. It didn't make a lot of sense to do so, not as he saw it. There were terrorist groups who knew how to grow viruses, and plenty of nations—North Korea, Iran, and China sprang to mind—that were definitely cultivating the next generation of weaponized pathogens. The CIA had proof, but politics and the subtle chess game of brinksmanship kept that information below the surface. It was leverage in all kinds of discussions, and as long as the bad guys screwed around with their bugs and bombs, the State Department and the CIA had some dials they could turn. Blackmail was far more important and useful than public disclosure.

On the other hand, knowing that your enemy was designing microscopic monsters was in itself a tacit mandate to do the same. Maybe not for attack—not even Price thought that America was crazy enough to release the kind of bioweapon that teams like Z-point developed—but in order to build a good shield you have to be able to study the sword it needs to stop. That's what the people at Z-point did. They made monsters in order to study them and—ideally—craft response protocols, sera, antitoxins, and other prophylactic measures.

For these reasons and others, Dick Price believed that he was prepared for the conversation he was about to have with the president of the United States. He'd had two similar conversations with a previous president during a bioweapon attack at the Liberty Bell Center in Philadelphia more than a dozen years ago and then when a group of domestic terrorists created weaponized and communicable versions of genetic diseases including Tay-Sachs and sickle cell. Those had been difficult conversations, especially the first one, since the sitting president of any given administration is never advised about the existence of Zabriske Point or similar stations until he needed to know. Plausible deniability was such a useful thing.

"We're just about ready," said his aide.

Price sat at his desk with a large laptop open and the encryption conference software up and running.

He adjusted his tie, sipped some water, took a calming breath, and nodded to the aide.

The screen display changed from a placeholder of the presidential seal to the face of the commander in chief. Two people sat on either side of the president—Scott Blair, the national security advisor, and a young and very intense-looking black woman Price knew by reputation only, Dr. Monica McReady, a rising superstar in the epidemiology world. A woman, he reminded himself, who had been mentioned several times as perhaps a better fit for the directorship of Z-point than he was.

Shit, he thought. That's just swell.

He could feel sweat begin to form along his spine.

"Dr. Price?" said the president.

"Yes, Mr. President. Despite the circumstances it is a pleasure to meet you, even virtually."

The president gave a tiny nod. There was a brief round of introductions, but it was done fast and without the usual courtesies.

"Have you been brought up to speed on the situation developing in western Pennsylvania?"

"I have, Mr. President."

"Am I to understand that you are familiar with Lucifer 113?" There was both frost and anger in the president's tone.

"Yes, sir. Very familiar."

"In what way are you familiar?"

Price paused. "Well, Mr. President, as you know we—"

"No, Dr. Price, I don't know. Until twenty minutes ago I had never heard your name or the name of your facility. While I am aware of the requirements of security and confidentiality, I am distressed to learn that we are continuing work on a bioweapon of such devastating potential that one of my predecessors felt compelled to use an executive order to terminate all work on it. Are you aware of that order, Dr. Price?"

Price said nothing, and against his will his eyes flicked toward the national security advisor.

"Mr. President, I . . ." began Price, but his words faltered.

The president shook his head. "When this matter is resolved," he said coldly, "there will be a full investigation. Make no mistake. However I think it's fair to say that heads will roll at a higher pay grade than yours."

Blair looked at the fingers of his folded hands and Price saw something flicker on his face. Was it irritation? Was it cynical humor? Whatever it was flicked on and off his mouth in a microsecond and the president did not see it.

Price said, "I . . . um . . . I mean, thank you."

"But hear me on this, Doctor," interrupted the president, "a new executive order is forthcoming and that will be enforced. Failure to comply will be met with the harshest possible penalties."

"I understand, sir."

The president studied him for a long two-count. "Do you, Dr. Price?"

"I believe I do, Mr. President."

"Then let's get down to it. Samples of the pathogen are being sent to you by military courier. Even though you already have the original pathogen there, we now know that Dr. Herman Volker used a modified version. Volker said as much to his CIA handler when he called to alert us about what he'd done."

"What about Dr. Volker? If the release of Lucifer was an accident, then surely he'd be eager to help us—"

"Herman Volker is dead," the president said flatly.

"What?" gasped Price. "Was he infected?"

"He hung himself."

"Oh no. That's horrible."

"Dr. Price, let's not waste time weeping over a man responsible for the deaths of thousands of American citizens."

Price straightened and cleared his face of expression. "Of course not, sir. It's just that he could have helped us. Remodeling a weaponized pathogen is tricky work, and even though it can result in something as apparently unstoppable as Lucifer, there are often chinks in the armor, so to speak."

"What kind of chinks?"

"Intentional vulnerabilities left by the designers so that they are not as vulnerable to the pathogen as, say, their enemies. Or, in some cases, design flaws that can be exploited to create a counteragent or some prophylactic measure."

The president brightened. "Are you sure?"

"Sure? No, sir."

"What will make you sure?"

Price considered. "One of two things offer the best chance of that. The first will be an examination of the Lucifer 113 samples being sent to us. We'll learn a lot by comparing it to the most recent version of Lucifer that we have."

"That's going to take time, though," suggested the president.

"We can work pretty fast when—"

"Skip the sales pitch. What's the other chance?"

"Looking at Volker's research notes. Do we know where they are?"

"There are no records in his office at the prison where he worked. The hard drives have been completely wiped and degaussed."

"Everything?" asked Price, aghast that any scientist would do that to his own work. "He kept no backups?"

"He did," said the president. "All of his research was copied to a set of flash drives."

"That's terrif—"

"Which we do not have."

Price had to bite back a curse. "Is anything being done to obtain those drives?"

"Of course," said the president. "However, since we have no guarantee of that happening right away, we need to move forward with what we have. Is there anything you can tell me about Lucifer based on what you've so far been told about the current crisis?"

Price nodded. "I believe so, sir. I reviewed some field reports from a doctor attached to the National Guard. If the reports are accurate then there are marked differences between the current strain and the samples we were initially given here."

"What differences?"

"Well, the rate of infection appears to have been greatly accelerated. Possibly by a factor of ten. The original Lucifer samples we have been working with here have a much longer gestation period. This was a problem the Soviets recognized that essentially limited practical application of the weapon because there was too great a lag time between introduction and a full-blown outbreak. Now that appears to occur in minutes. That's rather exciting."

"Doctor," warned the president, his voice low and slow, "be very careful in your choice of words."

"I—I'm sorry," stammered Price. "I meant from a scientific perspective."

"I know what you meant."

The president's eyes were hostile. So, Price noted, were those of Dr. McReady. Price composed his own features to show contrition.

"Yes, sir," he said. "My apologies."

McReady bent close and whispered something to the president, who looked unhappy, but he nodded.

"Doctor," said the president to Price, "how active has your research been on the Lucifer pathogen?"

You bitch, thought Price. Aloud he said, "We, um, have continued to study it in order to prepare a response protocol in the event of the weapon being deployed as, um, it currently has been . . ."

"What is the status on that research?"

Price licked his lips. "We have developed several advanced strains of the pathogen."

"And where are you with response protocols?"

Again Price tried not to look at Scott Blair. "We've made some progress." He leaned slightly on the word "some."

"Describe that progress, Doctor," ordered the president.

"Sir, before I do, I need to explain what Lucifer is. It's more than just a weaponized disease. Lucifer was built using select combinations of disease pathogens and parasites. Those parasites have undergone extensive transgenic modification. Toxoplasma gondii is a key element, as is the larva of the green jewel wasp. The toxoplasma is a key element in artificially induced schizophrenia, a disease that heightens fear and increased psychological distress. This is the keystone of the uncontrollable aggression of the infected. Their brains have—to put it in layman's terms—been rewired to react as if they are constantly under attack. This triggers our most basic survival instincts, feeding each infected a modified cocktail of adrenaline, dopamine, and other elements. At the same time, the genetically modified lancet flukes Dicrocoelium dendriticum and Euhaplorchis californiensis combine to regulate that aggressive response behavior into a predictable pattern. Specifically a pattern that includes seeking uninfected prey, attacking it, and infecting it. Remember, sir, this was developed by Soviet scientists during the Cold War as a self-cleaning weapon. Once introduced to, say, a base or station, the disease would spread like wildfire and ultimately there would be no uninfected survivors. The infected would be unable to manage any organized defense, even to the point of being unable to aim and fire a gun. An armed infiltration team could then enter the base and eliminate the infected and thereafter secure any physical assets like computers, equipment, and so on."

The president nodded. "If there's more, Doctor, let's hear it."

"The central element of the entire Lucifer program was the

transgenically rebuilt green jewel wasp, a parasite that normally targets cockroaches. The wasp's venom blocks the neurotransmitter octopamine in the target, and from that point on, all movements of the host are controlled by the imperative biological needs of the wasp. Those needs are, of course, reproduction. With the combination of the toxoplasma, the wasp, and the flukes, the host has essentially become an organic robot whose sole operational software requires that it attack, bite, feed, and then seek other prey."

The president looked sick, but his mouth was a hard, flat line. "About the feeding," he said, his voice thicker than it had been, "field reports indicate that the infected stop feeding on their victims after a while. Why don't they consume the entire body?"

"They can't and won't," said Price. "That's a design requirement. If the infected lingered to consume their victims, there would be no new vectors, and it would stall the overall rate of infection. Mind you, they do need to feed, but only for the raw protein to feed the parasites as they spread throughout the bloodstream and infuse the mucus membranes. The hyperaccelerated life cycle of the parasites expends a great deal of energy. They need fresh protein to make more larva so that every single drop of saliva is crammed with millions of eggs ready to hatch. But of equal importance to the infected is the need to spread the disease. That far outweighs their need to continue feeding."

McReady spoke aloud for the first time. "If I may, Mr. President? Dr. Price," she said, "what triggers the host to stop feeding on their victims? What's the biological off switch? We're hoping that there may be something there we can use as a prophylactic measure."

Price shook his head in grudging approval of the question. "It's partly a reaction to nerve conduction but it's mostly triggered by blood pressure. The normal intensity of blood pressure sparks aggression and appetite, but as it diminishes through injury and subsequent blood loss, it sends a signal to the parasite that the target is no longer a viable food source. That's the off switch, Dr. McReady, and God only knows how long it took the Soviet's to crack that, especially with the crudity of genetics during the Cold War."

"Doctor, when you're done congratulating madmen," the president said drily, "perhaps you can tell us about what your team has developed as a countermeasure. Can we kill the parasites?"

Price cleared his throat. "We, um, were never able to actually kill the parasites, Mr. President. Not the way you mean, not with a vaccine or anything of that nature. Not in an active vector. By the time the victim has become a host the parasites have spread throughout his body; however, this corresponds to a dramatic drop in circulation. The host is very nearly dead in clinical terms, with minimal brain function, respiration, circulation, and nerve conduction in play—just enough to allow it to continue acting as an aggressive vector. The Soviets did their work very well, however, and they designed it so that there was not enough circulation in play to transmit any kind of parasite-specific toxin throughout the host. Only destruction of the host stops it, and by that I mean either isolation long enough for the larvae to die off—say five, six weeks—or, more practically, incineration of all infected tissues."

The president closed his eyes for a moment. "Dear God," he murmured.

However, McReady said, "Wait a minute, Doctor," she snapped. "You said that you were working on a countermeasure. Short of headshots, did you actually come up with anything?"

"We . . . um . . ." hedged Price. Then he took a breath and said it. "We found that the only possible or practical response was along the lines of fighting fire with fire."

"Which means what?" growled the president.

"We created a different parasite," he said. "One that is genetically designed to attack and consume the larva of the green jewel wasp. We're in the earliest stages of testing it. But . . . I think it might work."

The president suddenly looked at something off screen and Price heard someone that he couldn't see say something. Price couldn't hear most of the words, but he saw the way in which those words affected the president. Anger and concern were replaced by shock and then a twisted mask of what appeared to Price to be absolute horror. The same horror was mirrored on the faces of Blair and McReady.

"Oh my God . . ." breathed McReady as she covered her mouth with her hands.

Panic flared in the eyes of Scott Blair.

The two words Price did hear hit him like punches to the face.

"...*quarantine failed*..."

If he heard more, his mind was momentarily unable to process it.

CHAPTER FORTY-EIGHT
STEBBINS LITTLE SCHOOL
STEBBINS, PENNSYLVANIA

Dez and Billy sat on opposite sides of a teacher's desk in an empty room. Dez had swept all of the items from the desk and had covered it with rifles, handguns, and boxes of shells.

"This is what we have," she said. "Not counting the pieces I gave to Piper and a few of the others. Three rifles with fifty rounds each. Two shotguns, but only forty-four shells left. Three Glocks and nine magazines, all full, and this piece of shit thirty-eight." She nudged a Ruger LCR revolver. "I don't know why I even brought it. But there's a box of hollow-points for it, so it's not entirely like giving a blow job."

Trout smiled thinly. "Didn't Sirhan Sirhan kill Bobby Kennedy with a twenty-two?"

"What's your point?"

"Thirty-eight's a bigger gun."

"It's not the caliber that matters, Billy. It has a five-round cylinder." She patted the Glock 22 Gen4 holstered at her hip. "Extended magazine with seventeen rounds. Which would you rather have if the shit comes down again?"

"I can't hit a barn with a baseball, Dez, so I'm not sure it would matter."

Dez leaned across the desk and pushed one of the shotguns toward him. "It's Korean, but don't hold that against it. Daewoo USAS-12. Gas operated with selective fire. Very nice in close-combat situations, which is pretty much the definition of life as we know it. I have a ten-round detachable box magazine or a twenty-round drum magazine, take your pick. Fires twelve-gauge."

He hefted it and winced. "Shit, this thing is heavy."

"Thirteen pounds fully loaded," she said. "Don't be a pussy."

"I have a bad back."

"Really? I thought maybe you had menstrual cramps."

"Dez . . ."

She grinned at him, and it was the first time he'd seen an unguarded smile on her face in a long time. "I'm just messing with you."

He grinned back.

Dez picked up a pistol that didn't look like it could fire anything. There was no barrel.

"What's that, a Taser?"

"Close. Nova SP-5. Five-shot stun gun."

"Bulky."

"Yeah," she agreed and she affixed the holster to her belt.

"What's the point? I thought only headshots bring them down."

Dez snorted. "How many human assholes have we dealt with so far?" she asked. "Much as I'd love to pop a cap in some of them—and the name General Zetter comes to mind—I don't think that would go over well."

"And you think Tasing him would?"

"They don't execute you for making a dickhead general piss his pants."

Outside the storm battered at the building. Dez walked over to one of the windows and looked down at the parking lot. On one side of the lot the National Guard had set up their camp, and there were all kinds of vehicles and portable structures down there, all of it turned gray by the rain. However, at the other end of the lot were big yellow school buses. Lots of them. Some from Stebbins and at least twice as many from surrounding regions. Buses that had brought the kids here to the emergency shelter.

Trout joined her and looked out.

Some of the buses had burned. Others were wrecks, torn apart by gunfire. The dead had attacked while the kids were being off-loaded. Thousands had died, but there were fewer than a hundred bodies. The rest had walked off. Trout wondered how many of them had been killed along with JT.

"They could clean out those buses," said Dez. "They could hose them out and put some heavy-grade clear plastic over the windows."

"To what end?"

"To get us out of here. There are places they can take us. Places where they could quarantine us but where'd we all get better food and medical attention."

"Maybe they will," he said. "Maybe in the morning."

She just shook her head. He studied her profile, and then he saw her sudden frown. He followed her gaze and saw that something was happening down there. People were suddenly running everywhere, soldiers scrambled to climb into troop transports, and beyond the fence the big vanes of a dozen helicopters were beginning to turn.

"What is it? Are they coming for us?"

"No," said Dez, "I think . . . this is something else."

As they watched, the soldiers dragged boxes toward the armored personnel carriers.

"It looks like they're leaving," said Trout. "Why do you think? Because of the storm?"

Dez shook her head.

"Maybe," Trout began, "maybe it's over. Maybe they've stopped this thing and they're standing down."

Dez turned to him and gave him a brief, harsh look. "Does it look like anything's over, Billy? Is that what it looks like to you?"

Trout hesitated before answering. His statement had been on the stupid side of hopeful and they both knew it. The troops below did not move like people whose long, dark night was over. There was none of the postcrisis malaise in anything they did. There was none of the laughter that comes at the end of great tension. Every movement down there was fast, but not everyone moved with the smooth and practiced ease of professional soldiers.

"They're definitely leaving."

"Yeah," agreed Dez. "And in a big damn hurry."

Trout saw people collide into each other. He saw them drop things. He saw people running for transports only half-dressed. There was only one word that appropriately described what he and Dez were seeing.

Panic.

PART THREE

COLLATERAL DAMAGE

*Pale death with impartial tread beats at the poor man's
cottage and the palaces of kings.*

—Horace, *Odes*

CHAPTER FORTY-NINE
WHAT THE FINKE THINKS
WTLK LIVE TALK RADIO
PITTSBURGH, PENNSYLVANIA

"If you're just joining us, folks, it has become a wild, wild night in western Pennsylvania. There are unconfirmed reports of military activity in the vicinity of Stebbins County. That is correct, you heard me when I said it. Military activity. So, what does the Finke think about that? Well, we know that the National Guard is on call for flood control and disaster aid, and FEMA has also announced its presence. The president of the United States made a rather vague statement earlier in which he talked about natural disasters and cyber-terrorism. Every word of that speech has already been dissected by the brain trusts on MSNBC and FOX, both of whom need a GPS and Sherpas to find a clue. FOX is talking about zombies. MSNBC is spouting some socialist claptrap about military helicopters firing at a school in order to stifle the live broadcasts of some whack job who claims to be reporting live from the apocalypse . . . and unfortunately that whack job is a longtime friend of the show, Billy Trout of Regional Satellite News. We tried to contact Billy to get him to tell us his side of the story—or to find out what he's smoking—but it looks like Superstorm Zelda has knocked out more than the lights. There's no cell reception at all in or out of Stebbins County and large parts of Fayette County."

Gavin paused to light a cigarette.

"So, again you ask me, what does the Finke think?"

He laughed.

"For once, my friends, the ol' Gav has to admit that I don't have a clue. Not tonight. This one has me stumped. So, help Uncle Gavin out and call in to tell me what *you* think is happening on this dark and stormy night."

Once more all the call lights lit up.

Gavin Finke took a long drag, blew smoke into the air, and took the next call.

CHAPTER FIFTY
THE SITUATION ROOM
THE WHITE HOUSE, WASHINGTON, D.C.

"How bad is it?"

The president fired the question off as he hurried into the Situation Room. It was the tenth time he'd asked the question, but so far no one had been able to give him a definitive answer. Even now each of the faces that looked up from the table gave mixed signals—doubt, anger, frustration, determination, and naked fear.

"Sir," said Scott Blair as he came to intercept the president, "here's what we know. The—"

"I was told there was an attack on one of our checkpoints."

"There was," said Blair, "and we lost a soldier, but the other man on that post eliminated the infected and, ah, resolved the resulting infection."

It took the president a beat to understand what that meant. He blanched. "Jesus Christ."

"The checkpoint has been reinforced and all checkpoints are on high alert," said Blair, but he was shaking his head as he said it. "The problem, however, is elsewhere."

A map of Stebbins County filled one window on the big plasma screen. A red dot glowed beside one of the major highways.

"There was an attack at a Starbucks on Route 653."

"How many casualties?"

"It doesn't matter," said Blair.

"How the Christ can it not—?"

"Sir, the victims of that attack were able to leave the Starbucks and they wandered into traffic. Their presence resulted in multicar pileups. Both directions." Blair pointed to a second screen, which showed an aerial view of a terrible traffic accident and what appeared to be a riot. Helicopter spotlights ranged over the crumpled wrecks of dozens of cars and trucks. Bodies lay in the road, some of them clearly crushed under or between the vehicles. The president walked numbly over to the screen to study the scene more closely. The pileups completely blocked the highway in both directions and even spilled over into the Starbucks parking lot, which was positioned on a wide spot in the median. Behind the roadblocks, lines of cars stretched for miles in bumper-to-bumper traffic, headlights on, windshield wipers slashing back and forth. And everywhere— everywhere—running between the cars, crawling over the wrecks, moving along the lines of stopped cars, filling the median, were people.

Fighting.

Struggling.

Rolling over and over in the mud or on the slick streets.

Punching and kicking.

Biting.

Biting.

Biting.

The president tried to say something. His mouth worked, but there was no breath in his lungs, no air in the room.

No words.

General Zetter's voice croaked from the speakers. "Mr. President . . . my God, Mr. President. Permission to engage. Permission to engage."

He said it over and over again as on the screen hundreds—no, thousands—of people fought, and screamed, and died.

And came back.

To kill.

To eat.

To . . .

Scott Blair touched the president's arm. Lightly, almost gently. A gesture of pleading.

"Mr. President," he said in a ragged whisper, "give the order."

The president looked at him with eyes that were filled with so much confusion that it was clear the man teetered on the edge of collapse.

"Mr. President . . . please."

"Congress," muttered the president. "I need to inform them. I need approval for this. I can't . . . I can't . . . the nation . . ."

"There isn't time, Mr. President. If we don't act now there won't be a nation to save."

The president's staring eyes blinked, blinked again, and then suddenly filled with a measure of understanding.

"Do it," he whispered.

It was the loudest sound in the room.

Blair wheeled around. "General Zetter, the president has authorized you to go weapons hot. Engage the enemy with all resources."

"Acknowledged," said Zetter breathlessly, "going weapons hot."

The guns on the helicopters opened up and instantly the screams of the dying were drowned out by the heavy growl of machine guns. The running figures began juddering and dancing as the rounds punched into them. Other helicopters—Apaches and Black Hawks—moved down out of the storm, flying awkwardly in the high winds. The pilots kept as much distance from each other as they could, but this was worst-case scenario for any pilot. High winds, heavy rain, enemies who looked like civilians, and no clear set of targets.

"Some of the pilots are not engaging," said one of the officers in the room.

"General Zetter," growled Blair, "half of your pilots have not engaged."

There was the sound of arguing and shouting from the speakers and they heard Zetter yell, "There are no civilians, goddamn it. This is a target-rich environment. Fire at will. Anything moving is designated an enemy combatant."

Even with that some of the pilots repeated requests to verify those orders. Finally the president himself had to yell into the mike, repeating the same words Zetter had used.

Blair thought about how clinical and detached those words were. Target-rich environment.

Enemy combatants.

No civilians.

Zetter was, finally, with the program. Finally getting it right, but it was still so insanely wrong.

On the screen, one by one the helicopters began to fire on the crowds.

General Armistad Burroughs growled, "All pilots, you are cleared to deploy all weapons. Deploy all rockets, all missiles."

Once more there was a lag in obeying those orders.

Once more the president had to repeat the orders.

And once more the helicopters obeyed, one by one, slowly at first, and then with the kind of wild aggression Blair knew was only born from panic and despair.

The helicopters rained fire down on the road. Rockets struck pockets of shambling dead and exploded like parodies of big-budget movie special effects. In the movies, though, people flew away from explosions, pulled by wires or digitally added as computer graphics. Here, the people burst apart in ragged pieces that lacked art or style. And though real explosions are always less dynamic than movie special effects, they were far more horrible in their understated destruction.

Automobile gas tanks exploded one after the other, lifting the tail ends of Toyotas and Fords and Coopers and Hyundais with equal indifference and efficiency. Chain guns stitched endless lines of holes along pavements, through automobile skin, and through flesh and bone. The living and the living dead crumpled under the cudgel blows of rapid-fire lead. The living died and stayed down. The dead, those with no traumatic damage to their brains or brain stems, rose again; less whole, less human-looking, but infinitely more monstrous. The living tried to hide from the dead and from the rain of fire; the dead were indifferent to it, walking or running or crawling after the fresh meat, stopping only when the spark of life was blown from their central nervous systems.

Blair and the president stood together, their eyes open and mouths slack at the hell unfolding on the screen.

Then Blair forced his mouth to speak. He turned to the Air Force general. "General Susco, where are we with the fuel-air bombs?"

"We have four MQ-1C Gray Eagle drones fitted out and on deck. We can have them in the air in—"

"ETA?" interrupted Blair. "What's the flight time?"

Susco didn't even pause. "Twenty-two minutes and change and that includes launch time."

"Shit."

"And we have four A-10 Thunderbolt II's from the 104th Fighter Squadron at the Warfield Air National Guard Base in Maryland. Fires are lit and all they need is the word."

Blair again touched the president. "Sir, we have to order them in *now*."

The president's entire attention was locked on the screen.

Blair wanted to punch him. He had never in his entire life wanted to beat anyone as badly or as brutally as he did this man. Before he even knew he was going to do it, he grabbed the president's sleeve, spun him around, and backhanded him across the mouth. Blair was not a big man but there was so much rage, so much fear in every ounce of his body that the blow sent the president crashing sideways against the edge of the big table. Blood burst from torn lips.

And a split second later Blair was on the floor, his body exploding from sudden agony in his back and the after-impression of a Secret Service agent kidney-punching him. He was slammed to the carpet with a knee on his cheek and a pistol barrel screwed into his ear. Someone clicked cuffs onto his wrist, cinching them painfully tight.

"No . . . *no*!" bellowed someone, and through the pain Blair realized that it was the president's voice. From the corner of his eye, past the knee of the Secret Service agent kneeling on his face, Blair could see an agent and General Burroughs helping the president to his feet. Blood streamed down onto the president's chest, staining his white shirt, dripping onto his shoes. "Leave him alone, goddamn it. Let him up. I am ordering you to uncuff him and let him up. Christ, someone get me a cloth."

The agents hauled Blair roughly to his feet and took the cuffs off, but they weren't gentle with either task. He stood there, legs weak and trembling, his right hand beginning to swell from where his knuckles clipped the president's cheek. The president gave him a look of savage intensity, but for the first time since the crisis began there was that old spark in POTUS's eyes. That old fire. The fuck-you blaze that had won him the primaries and enabled him to bully his way through brutal debates and a nail-biter of an election. The fires that had allowed this man to play hardball with Iran and North Korea, to refuse to be bent over a barrel by the Chinese.

This was his president.

The president pointed a finger at General Susco. "Scramble the jets. Launch the drones. *Stop* this."

The general began shouting orders into a phone.

Blair sagged with relief and fatigue.

But then the president grabbed a fistful of his necktie and pulled Blair so close they were breathing the same air. Secret Service men closed in on both sides but the president growled them back. He tightened his hold on Blair and in the coldest, most dangerous voice Blair had ever heard the president use, said, "Call Sam Imura and tell him to get me those flash drives. *Now.*"

CHAPTER FIFTY-ONE
STEBBINS LITTLE SCHOOL
STEBBINS, PENNSYLVANIA

"This does not look good," said Trout. Beside him, Dez simply shook her head.

They stared out the window, stunned, mystified, and deeply frightened by what they saw. The soldiers were scrambling to get into their gear and climb into vehicles. The roads leading away from the school were choked with Humvees and Strykers and an assortment of smaller and lighter armored vehicles. Then one of the big eight-wheeled M1135 Stryker Nuclear, Biological, Chemical Reconnaissance Vehicles rumbled through the gates, the decks crowded with armed men in hazmat suits. Its fifteen-ton mass made the windows rattle.

"Damn, it looks like they're all going," said Dez.

She snatched up the walkie-talkie and tried to raise General Zetter, but all she got was static. Trout tried the sat phone, and it was as dead as it had been all night.

"Something really bad's happening," muttered Dez.

Then the whole building seemed to rumble and they craned their necks to look up. A phalanx of helicopters flew over. Black Hawks and Apaches.

Trout counted thirty of them before the rain obscured his vision.

They were not coming to attack the school. They were not headed toward the center of Stebbins. They were all headed northwest.

Toward Bordentown.

Toward the edge of the Q-zone.

"Oh shit," said Dez.

CHAPTER FIFTY-TWO
TOWN OF STEBBINS
TWO MILES INSIDE THE Q-ZONE

Boxer turned off the farm roads and drove along the stretch of Mason Street, heading toward the center of Stebbins. According to the GPS, they needed to turn onto Doll Factory Road, and then veer off of that to follow a secondary road to the Stebbins Little School. The rain slowed to a desultory drizzle for a few minutes, but the thunder was closer and louder, and the lightning flashed like artillery fire.

"What's that?" asked Gypsy, leaning forward from the backseat to point at something on the road ahead.

Boxer slowed as they approached a pair of wrecked cars that were little more than burned-out shells. The blacktop around the vehicles was littered with shell casings. Sam Imura rolled down his window to get a better look. A hunting rifle lay on the hood of one car. Beside it, its shape slowly distorting to pulp in the rain, was a box of .30-30 cartridges. A second gun, a military M4, lay sideways across the yellow line down the center of the two-lane. Near it was a Pittsburgh Pirates ball cap, and a dozen feet away was a blue wool women's sweater.

"No bodies," murmured Shortstop.

No one commented on that.

"Keep going," said Sam, and Boxer gave the wrecks a wide berth.

They passed other cars, and once they saw a big eighteen-wheel Peterbilt that had gone off the highway and smashed its way through the young maples that grew wild beside the road, until it crashed itself to silence against a massive old oak. The driver's door stood open, the cab empty.

And that was the pattern of it. Wrecked cars and trucks with open doors and broken windows, houses and buildings with doors standing ajar, and miscellaneous debris, but no trace at all of the people of the destroyed little town.

No living people.

Several times they found bodies sprawled haphazardly on the road, on the verge, on porch steps, in parking lots. Every single one of them showed evidence of traumatic injury to their heads. A few lay with their heads hacked off.

"Somebody put up a hell of a fight," said Boxer.

"Doesn't look like they won."

They reached a deserted gas station and made the turn onto Doll Factory.

And stopped before they went two blocks.

Slowly, all five of them got out of the Humvee and stood looking at the monstrous thing before them.

A Stryker armored combat vehicle sat at an angle in the middle of the street. It was a brute. Eight feet wide and twenty-two feet long, sitting on eight fat tires, with a big Browning .50 caliber machine gun mounted on the top—the same model as the one mounted on the deck of their Humvee. Thousands of empty brass shell casings littered the top of the vehicle and their curved sides peeked out from puddles. At least three hundred bodies clogged the street, many of them civilians, but there were uniforms of local and state police and even some soldiers.

Dead.

All dead.

Sam had seen the Browning in action, had fired one himself. He could easily—too easily—visualize the moment of slaughter as the living dead shambled into the storm of lead.

But what puzzled Sam was how the soldiers lost this fight.

The Stryker was abandoned here in the rain, the gun silent.

How many of the dead had the Guardsmen faced? Had it been overwhelming odds? Had they run out of ammunition? Or had they been caught in one of those terrifying moments when a gun jams or reloading takes one second too long?

He would probably never know, but looking at the scene sent a chill up Sam's spine. It felt like the icy breath exhaled against trembling flesh during a moment of precognition. Or, perhaps it was an icy touch not of revelation but of realization as he saw, here on this battle-ground street, what was coming. Soldiers were more than a match for the dead in any kind of fair fight. Even five to one, ten to one.

But there were at very least seven thousand infected in Stebbins, and possibly many more.

When a crowd attacks, the front ranks take the bullets so the ranks behind them can advance. Given sufficient numbers the defenders simply run out of time or ammunition or both, and the wave passes over them. It was something used on battlefields ever since armies went to war. The foot soldiers of Alexander and Napoleon knew it, the riders of Genghis Khan and Santa Ana, and the marching lines of the Romans and the Confederate boys in butternut brown. Cannon fodder. A forlorn hope.

Only here it was no more planned or orchestrated than the thousands of worker ants that die when the entire nest goes to war, or the millions that fall when locusts swarm. In the end, all that matters is that the main host survives. The hive.

This was what Sam was seeing, he was positive. This was the real terror of this infection. The parasitic impulse to procreate through infection and to sustain itself through feeding was matched with a ferocious aggression that had no parallel in nature because it was not natural. Volker had made this, building it on the bones of Cold War bioweapons madness.

He heard the shallow breathing of the rest of his team, but realized he was holding his own breath. Sam let it out slowly.

"We are so fucked," said Moonshiner.

No one disputed him.

They heard the crunch of glass and they all wheeled around at the same time, bringing their guns up. Across the street was a diner with a gaping hole where a big picture window should be. The entire frame, and all of the building, was covered by so many bullet holes that it looked like polka dots, except there was nothing fun or festive here. The rifle-mounted flashlights of the five soldiers painted the front of the store in pale yellow light.

A figure moved in the gloom just inside the diner.

"Inside the store," called Sam. "United States Special Forces. I need you to step out of the building with your hands raised. If you have a weapon I need to you drop it now."

The figure came out of the shadows and into the glare of the overlapping flashlight beams.

It was a man.

He wore only ragged boxer shorts. The rest of his clothes were gone. Much of his flesh was as well.

He raised his hands toward the five people standing near the Humvee.

It tried to moan, but there was not enough of its face left for that. No jaw, no tongue. Just a gaping red horror below the stumps of its broken upper teeth.

"I got this," said Shortstop and he fired a single round, the report crisp in the wet air. The zombie's head snapped back and it fell into the store. But then it seemed to hover there, not quite hitting the ground, and for a bizarre moment Sam thought that it was somehow fighting for its balance even though it was bent so far backward. Then the body shuddered and tumbled to one side as something else came into view.

Another of the infected.

This one was crawling, and its humped body was what kept the first one from hitting the floor. The dead thing's face was smeared with red and its mouth still worked, still chewed on some piece of something that dangled from between its lips.

The creature looked at them and bared its teeth.

Sam heard Boxer gag.

Not because of the horrible thing on the floor or what it was clearly eating.

He gagged because the zombie was dressed in the woodland camouflage of the Pennsylvania National Guard.

It was a soldier.

Behind it, other shapes moved in the gloom of the diner. And these figures sent up the moan that the first zombie could not. A haunting, wretched cry for something to staunch the dreadful hungers that drove them. They began moving through the shattered window frame.

So many of them.

So many soldiers among them, their battle dress uniforms torn, helmets lost or askew, bodies opened by teeth and nails, souls lost, eyes vacant. Black blood dribbled from their mouths.

"Oh, fuck me," breathed Boxer. "Fuck me, fuck me."

"Keep it steady, kid," said Moonshiner.

A scuff of a clumsy foot made them turn and they saw more of the infected coming out of the open doors of the bank, the feed store, the craft shop, and the county assessor's office.

Fifty at least.

"I thought General Zetter said they had this shit under control," growled Gypsy.

"Fuck me," said Boxer.

"This is some evil shit right here," agreed Moonshiner.

"Stand or fight, boss? And I'm really okay with hauling ass," said Shortstop, but for once even his pragmatic cool seemed to be crumbling away.

"There's so many of them," said Boxer, and as he said it more of them rounded the corner of the next block. There were children mixed in with the adults. Their faces and limbs turned worm-white from blood loss, mouths black as bottomless holes.

All of them torn. All of them ragged.

That's how it stuck in Sam's mind, and somehow he knew that's how it would always be.

The Ragged People.

As if they were all members of some secret fraternity, bound together in death. Or from some far country where the sun never shines and all there will ever be is the hunger.

"Boss?" urged Gypsy.

"No," said Sam, turning. "Everyone back in the Hummer. This isn't what they sent us to do."

They held their weapons out and ready as they climbed in. The Humvee was armor plated and had reinforced glass windows, but Sam did not feel even a little safe as he shot the lock on his door. He knew the others didn't either.

"Get us out of here, Boxer," he said with a calm he did not feel, but the younger soldier was already putting the car in gear.

He backed up and circled the Stryker, then stamped on the brakes as more of the pale figures moved through the downpour.

"Shit," he said and spun the wheel.

"This is turning into a crowd scene," said Moonshiner.

Despite everything he knew about the situation and everything they'd done so far this night, Sam hated the idea of opening fire on these ragged people. It felt like abuse to him. Like bullying.

But there were so damn many of them.

The flash drives, he told himself. *Get the flash drives or this is the whole world*.

All he had to say aloud was, "Shortstop."

The man rolled open the top hatch of the Humvee and stood up into the fierce rain. He whipped the cover off the big Browning, yanked the bolt back, and began firing. The heavy bullets tore into a knot of zombies, knocking them backward with massive foot-pounds of impact, bursting apart joints, ripping loose connective tissue, splashing the Stryker and the other infected with black blood. Four of the creatures went down. Then another five.

"Go, go, *go!*" yelled Sam, and Boxer hit the gas again. The Humvee rolled over the fallen infected, heavy tires crunching bones. Shortstop pivoted and fired at the zombies closing in on the right. Twenty of them.

"Stop Sunday driving," he bellowed. "Move this fucking thing."

The Humvee kept rolling forward, but it was difficult to climb over the human debris while avoiding all of the wrecked and abandoned cars. The dead began closing like a fist around the vehicle.

"Little help up here," called Shortstop. "This shit's getting weird."

"Windows," ordered Sam, and except for Boxer, the others lowered their windows and stuck gun barrels into the rain. A moment later the inside of the truck was filled with ear-splitting thunder. Shell casings hit the ceiling and bounced off each other and stung like wasps where they hit bare flesh.

"Shortstop," roared Sam, "grenade."

Shortstop stopped firing, plucked a green ball from his rig and pulled the pin.

"Frag out!" he cried as he flung it into the midst of the dead closing on the front of the Humvee. He ducked down a split second before the grenade exploded. Everything in the blast radius was torn to ragged pieces and at the edges of the blast the concussion knocked the zombies off balance, leaving a rough opening that was clouded with blood-red mist.

Sam punched Boxer on the shoulder. "Punch it."

Boxer gave it all the gas it would take and the Humvee leapt forward, smashing through the crippled dead, crushing others. Behind him the main mass of the infected closed like the waters of the Red Sea. They collided with one another in their desperate race to get to the living flesh. Gypsy and Moonshiner leaned out of the windows and fired back at them, shooting at legs to shatter thighbones and drop the pursuers into the path of the rest of them. Shortstop climbed back up and turned the Browning in a circle, not needing to aim. There were targets everywhere.

The Humvee shot through the bloody opening and there was clear street beyond it. Boxer kept his foot on the pedal all the way down to the floor and with every second the horde of the dead dropped behind. One by one the guns stopped firing, and after a full minute Sam touched Boxer on the shoulder.

"Okay, kid, ease it down."

Boxer dropped the speed from seventy to fifty to forty and kept it there. They passed other zombies, but by the time the infected could turn and target them, the Humvee was past. No one fired at them.

Everyone sagged back, exhaling balls of burning air, their hands trembling with adrenaline and shock.

"Reload," snapped Sam. "Do it now."

They did it, and the orderliness of that action helped steady each of them. Not completely, but enough so they could reclaim themselves. Enough so they could dare look in each others' eyes.

They drove on, no one speaking. There was nothing that needed to be said.

Then a soft purring buzz broke the silence. And Sam lunged for his satellite phone.

"Sir," he said as soon as the connection was made, "Stebbins is not under control. There is extreme activity and—"

"Sam, to hell with that," Blair snapped. "The Q-zone is compromised. I repeat, the devil is off the chain. The president has ordered the Air Force in. Drop everything else and get to the school. Get those flash drives. Do it now."

"How bad is it?"

Blair paused for a shattered moment. "It's bad, Sam. Volker is dead. We're going to have to go big on this to try and stop the spread—but we *need those drives*. You are authorized to use all means and measures to secure them."

Sam felt his throat tighten.

"Understood, sir," he said. But the line was already dead.

The members of the Boy Scouts exchanged looks.

Then Boxer kicked down on the gas, the tires spun on the wet ground until smoke curled up behind the Humvee, and then they were rolling fast, gaining speed, heading toward the Stebbins Little School.

CHAPTER FIFTY-THREE
THE SITUATION ROOM
THE WHITE HOUSE, WASHINGTON, D.C.

The president was surrounded by ghouls.

Every face of every person at the table looked like a death mask: pale, devoid of hope, sunken, and hollow-eyed.

On the screens the glowing icons that represented the jets were streaking toward Bordentown. Other dots indicated the movement of General Zetter's National Guard forces and the reinforcements that had been ordered in to help hold the quarantine line. With that line broken, the troops were being deployed in a wide circle around the Starbucks.

The president took a long drink of water, but it did nothing to soothe his dry, raw throat. He set the glass down with a clunk that seemed absurdly loud in a room that was unusually quiet.

"What are our options?" he asked of the people around the table. The people whose job it was to always have answers.

General Amistad Burroughs said, "The jets will—"

"No," interrupted the president. "I want to know what we need to do afterward. After the bombs."

Sylvia Ruddy shared a look with Scott Blair. She said, "You'll have to address the nation again."

"And say what?" asked the president. Ruddy flinched. "No, I want you to tell me, what can I possibly say that will help the country understand this."

"Sir, I—"

The president picked up a sheet of paper and shook it at her, at everyone. Everyone had a copy of the same report in front of them. None of them had touched the report after first reading it. The papers lay on the table, unwanted, feared, despised.

"These are casualty estimates. In just under five minutes we are going to kill thousands of American citizens. Thousands more are already dead. And we don't yet know if this is the end of it. So, tell me . . . what exactly is it I'm supposed to tell the nation?"

The dead faces stared at him and said nothing.

CHAPTER FIFTY-FOUR
STEBBINS LITTLE SCHOOL
STEBBINS, PENNSYLVANIA

The last of the military vehicles rumbled out of the parking lot, leaving behind a scene of disorder and desolation.

"Now what?" asked Trout.

Dez nibbled thoughtfully on her lip. "If they're really gone . . ."

"What?" he prompted.

"I can think of only three reasons they'd leave," she said, ticking them off on her fingers. "It's over and they've been told to stand down."

"Is that likely?"

"No. They left too fast and left too much shit behind. They were told to drop and run. Question is whether they're running from or running to."

"Huh?"

"That's choice two and tree. So, the second option is that there's another problem. Maybe they found a bunch more of these zombies. Or, more likely, there's a problem at the quarantine line."

"What's the third option?"

She gave him a flat stare. "Getting out of the line of fire."

For emphasis she pointed up to the ceiling. Trout followed her finger as if they could both see a jet loaded with fuel-air bombs screaming its way across the skies of Stebbins County.

"Well," Trout said slowly, "shit."

"Yeah."

"But . . . the flash drives . . . they want those. They won't blow us up if they think we have them."

"Surc. Unless they found Dr. Volker, in which case when this is over you are going to be one inconvenient motherfucker, Billy. Same goes for me and anyone you may have talked to in here. Which is everyone."

Even after everything that happened, Trout was aghast at the thought of such cold-blooded murder. He kept shaking his head, but he wasn't sure he actually disagreed.

"We have a window, Billy," said Dez as she turned, hurried to the desk and began shoving the guns and ammunition back into the duffel bag. "We need to get the fuck out of here while there's still a *here* to get out of."

"What are you doing?" asked Trout.

She nodded to the windows. "Neither of us believe this is over, right? Not with the way they left. And maybe they're not going to bomb us, but where does that leave us?"

"In a nice, safe building that we're reinforcing," he said. "With lots of food and supplies."

"For a week, Billy. Now, think it through. If this is as big a disaster as Zetter said, as big as what Volker told you, then are you telling me that we might *only* be stuck here for a week?"

"No, but they said they'd airdrop supplies to us."

"You want me to punch some stupid off of you?"

He rubbed his chest. "No thanks. What am I missing?"

"If the Guard had to run out of here like their dicks were on fire, then this thing is spreading. Which also means that there are so many of those dead fuckers out there that they had to take everyone including the cook. Does that sound like anything's under control?"

"No," he admitted sheepishly.

"No," she agreed. "It sounds like big trouble. So, go big picture for a minute. Pull back and look at it. If you're General Zetter and things are going to shit, do you give a crap about, as I said, inconvenient people trapped in a school, or do you go fight the fight?"

"You go fight the fight."

"Right, now look at it from where we stand. Sure, we have a secure building and, yes, I think we could hold it against a million of those things."

"Exactly."

"Until we run out of bullets and bread. Until there's no more gas for the generator, no more fresh water, and no more cans of Spam. Tell me, Billy, what happens then? And before you say something stupid like 'but they'll come for us by then,' take a moment and think about how long people waited after Katrina. Weeks, in some cases. And that was without a bunch of dead sonsabitches trying to eat everyone."

Trout used her words as a lens to stare into the future, and the things he saw were ugly and wrong.

"Jesus," he murmured.

"We've got our window. No one's watching us and, for the moment, no living dead assholes are trying to bite us. I say we load all our supplies and all of us into those buses. We have more than enough of them. We load up and we get the hell out of Dodge."

"And go where?"

She shrugged. "Pittsburgh's nice this time of year. So's Harrisburg. So's Philly." Then she paused. "Actually, if things are really hitting the fan, there's Sapphire Distributors in Fayette."

"What's that?"

Dez smiled. "A food distribution warehouse. Big-ass brick building. No windows on the ground floor, truck bays where we can backup the buses, its own generator with probably a lot more fuel than we have here, plus enough food to replenish a dozen full supermarkets. We could survive there for months."

"How do you know about it?"

Dez's eyes slid away for a moment and she focused on packing the bag.

"Dez—?"

"I, um, dated a guy who works there. Head of security."

"Who? Do I know him?"

"Maybe."

"Who, Dez?"

"It doesn't matter, damn it."

Trout sighed. "What makes you think your *boyfriend* would even let you in?"

Dez colored.

"Dez?"

"He's, um . . . still sweet on me."

"Jesus H. Christ in a clown car."

Dez glared at him. "Give me a better idea, then."

Trout picked up a box of bullets, looked at the label without reading it, and shoved it into the bag.

"Is anything with you ever simple?" he muttered. "I mean *ever*?"

CHAPTER FIFTY-FIVE
ROUTE 653
BORDENTOWN, PENNSYLVANIA

Patrick Freivald knew that he was crazy to be out on a motorcycle in the middle of one of the worst storms in Pennsylvania history. Crazy and maybe a little suicidal. The problem was that his car—his nice, warm, dry car—was parked outside of his nice, warm, dry house way the hell up in the Finger Lakes region, on the far side of Canandaigua Lake, and that was a hell of a lot of miles from here.

He'd hit the road after a very good but very long couple of days bartering and dealing at Monster Madness, a small pop culture convention in Friendsville, Maryland. Patrick had traded some old Aurora monster model kits, including an absolutely pristine *Forgotten Prisoner* for some newer stuff, including the Vampirella, which was a new limited edition based on a Frank Frazetta painting. He'd made enough profit off the Aurora model to stock up on a bunch of lower-end but still cool PVC statues of classic Universal monsters. All of that was in UPS boxes on their way home, and like a lot of the conventioneers, he'd waited out the storm yesterday and hit the road when they said the worst of it was over.

The weatherman was dead wrong.

Big surprise.

He'd barely hit the Pennsylvania state line before the rains started again. Not the sluggish end-of-the-storm showers, but a real downpour. So bad a lot of cars were pulling off the road. Good for them, they could sit there and listen to Howard Stern on Sirius and stay dry. Can't do that on a hog.

Outrunning the storm wasn't going to happen, Patrick could tell that much without having to listen to the news. There was lightning so thick and frequent it looked like a neon forest stretched all the way to the horizon. To every horizon. Going back was for shit, too.

His only real option was to motor through until he hit the first town with a cheap motel. With a storm like this even a roach motel would be good. If it got any heavier, a barn out here in the sticks would be just fine.

Patrick wasn't crazy enough to listen to an iPad while driving his bike, but he didn't need the weatherman to tell him there was a storm. Everyone knew about Superstorm Zelda, Sandy's country cousin. As the miles fell away, though, he began wishing he could hear a traffic report. Ahead of him he could see the double rows of red taillights thickening from a sparse few into tightly packed lines that vanished into the distant rainy darkness. Road speed, already down to forty because of the rain, was slowing more and more until he was barely making enough headway to balance his bike.

"Shit," he muttered as the line of cars finally ground to a complete stop. Right out in the big dark, smack dab in the middle of nowhere. The last sign he remembered seeing was for a twenty-four-hour Starbucks in someplace called Bordentown. He'd never heard of the town, and at that moment didn't give a crap if it was a nice tourist spot or not. A coffee shop open all night was like a gift from God.

He roll-walked his Italian motorcycle out of his lane and saw that the shoulder was clear ahead. He gunned the bike and began moving again. The winds tried to knock him sideways into the line of stalled cars, but Patrick leaned forward to cut the resistance and kept moving. He cut quick looks at the people in the cars. Some of them ignored him, some flipped him off for doing what they hadn't yet dared.

The first thing that troubled Patrick was the sudden sound of a helicopter overhead. With the helmet and the roar of the Moto Guzzi's burly engine he couldn't hear most sounds, but this was a roar, and he risked a look up as a big damn chopper flew right above him. It was huge, one of those bulky military machines, with stubby wings laden with what looked like missiles.

Missiles?

He was so surprised that he almost rear-ended a Civic that cut onto the shoulder right in front of him. The chopper moved slowly above him, heading farther up the road. The rotor wash took the rain and wind and churned them into a fresh and more intense miniature storm. Patrick had to really fight to keep from having those winds knock him down.

The second thing that bothered Patrick was how low the chopper was flying. It could not have been more than a hundred feet above the tops of the cars. Patrick had never even seen a news helicopter fly that low, especially in winds like this.

That's when Patrick saw beams of light sweeping down from the storm clouds. Massive, bright searchlights. Intensely bright, but for a moment they did not appear to belong to anything. It was like a scene from that old movie *Close Encounters*, and for a brief, irrational moment Patrick thought that's what he was seeing. UFOs. Aliens.

Then the helicopter above him switched on its light, and Patrick understood.

The stormy sky was filled with helicopters.

No.

That wasn't exactly right.

The sky was filled with *military* helicopters.

CHAPTER FIFTY-SIX
ROUTE 653
BORDENTOWN, PENNSYLVANIA

Goat Weinman was pretty sure he was dead.

So why was he moving?

He tried to open his eyes but either the world was totally without light or he was blind.

Am I dead? He wondered.

Panic detonated in his mind as everything Volker had said about the Lucifer pathogen came sweeping back. When a person is infected, the physical body dies but the mind, the consciousness, lingers, trapped inside hijacked flesh, floating, observing, able to see and feel, connected to every nerve ending but totally unable to do anything.

Trapped.

Was that what was happening?

Was his body now a . . . a . . .

"Oh, God!" he cried out. "I'm one of them . . . please, God, no don't—"

Then a voice said, "Wake the fuck up."

That was immediately followed by a hard slap across his face and Goat felt himself reeling and then slamming into some hard. Metal. He began to fall and thrust his hands out to stop himself.

He.

Thrust.

His.

Hands.

He did it. Not some parasitic impulse over which he had no control.

Goat grabbed on to what had to be the fender of a car and he crouched there, sore, his face stinging, terror and doubt screaming at each other in his head. He could feel his hands on the wet metal of the car. He flexed his fingers and they obeyed.

He wasn't dead. He wasn't one of them.

Then he felt the wetness on his face. Not the rain. Something heavier, thicker. On his forehead. In his . . .

Eyes.

Suddenly he was pawing at his eyes and immediately there was faint light. Bad light, but there. He wasn't blind after all. Not blind or dead. There was something in his eyes. He tilted his face to the rain and rubbed at his eyes until he could see. There was something black on his fingers.

Until the lighting flashed and then he saw that his black fingers were red.

Slick, glistening red.

It was blood. His eyes had been pasted shut with dried blood that was now washing away in the rain. And there in front of him, crumpled against a tree, was the ruin of a metallic green Nissan Cube.

And that's when it all came back to him. Homer. Starbucks. The accident.

He turned sharply to see Homer Gibbon standing behind him. The killer stood there in the howling wind and pouring rain, bare-chested, wide-legged, with a monstrous grin of red delight on his face as the lightning burned the sky behind him.

"Don't you go die on me," he said with a wicked chuckle. "Not until I want you to."

Traffic splashed by on both sides of the median, but the Cube was almost invisible in the copse of trees into which it had plowed. Goat looked at the car. It was totaled. Smoke curled up from the wheel wells and one tire had exploded.

"Never liked that faggoty little piece of shit," grumbled Homer. "Now we need to shop for something better." He pointed a finger at Goat. "Stay."

He said it the way people do to dogs. Homer chuckled to himself and began walking toward the highway.

Goat stayed.

Then Goat realized that for some reason the traffic was completely stalled over there. Cars and trucks sat bumper to bumper under the pounding rain. The line stretched all the way to the west, far out of sight. On the other side of the road there was nothing. He tried to make sense of it, but his head was too sore and none of his thoughts worked the way they should.

You have a concussion, he told himself, but he couldn't remember hitting his head. Could an airbag concuss a person? He thought he should know the answer to that, but couldn't find it in the messy closets of his brain.

Homer was almost to the line of stalled cars now.

Run, jackass!

Goat tried to run. He had that much pride, that much clarity of thought left. But when he took his first step toward the opposite side of the highway, his left leg buckled and he went down hard into the mud. Like an old tape player slowly catching up to speed, Goat's mind replayed the events of the crash. He remembered seeing the tree suddenly filling the view beyond the windshield, and then the windshield itself bursting inward in ten thousands pieces of gummed safety glass. He remembered the white balloon of the airbag and the numb shock as the dashboard seemed to reach in toward his knees, hitting one, missing the other.

Then blood and darkness and nothing.

He propped himself up on his elbows, spitting bloody water and mud from his mouth. How long had he been unconscious in the car? Long enough for the blood to dry to dense mud in his eyes.

For a moment—just a moment—Goat wished that the crash had been a little harder. Or that the blocky little Cube had been built with less care for the safety of its passengers.

It is a weird and dreadful thing to realize that death was far more desirable than being alive. Goat had never suffered through depression, never rode the Prozac and lithium highway. Never held a razor next to his wrists and wondered if the pain of the cut was worse than the pain of the next hour or next day. Never looked into the future and saw a world where he was absent. He was in love with life. With living it. With women and sex. With film and the complexities of filmmaking. With the tides and currents of social media. With being him.

But now . . .

Behind him he heard Homer calling out to the people in the cars. "L'il help! L'il help now."

Goat thought he heard a car door open. Then a man's voice asked if Homer was hurt, if everyone was okay.

And then screams.

Such high, shrill, awful screams.

Goat closed his eyes and stared into the future and prayed, begged, pleaded for him not to be any part of what was happening or what was to come.

Like all of his prayers over the last twenty-four hours, it went unanswered.

And then suddenly the sky seemed to open and against all sanity and logic the morning sun rose in the middle of the night. Goat gaped at it, at the gorgeous, impossibly huge burning eye of morning.

"Oh . . . my . . . God . . ." he breathed and despite all of his life-long agnosticism and cynical disapproval of organized religion, he believed that he beheld the fiery glory of a god revealing himself to His people at the moment of their greatest need.

He began to cry. He covered his head with his hands and wept, apologizing for everything he had ever done wrong, promising—swearing—that he would be a better man, that he would hone the grace of this moment. A part of his bruised mind could hear the shrill, hysterical note in his voice, but he didn't care.

He was saved.

This is what people believed would happen. In the dark night of the soul. At the end of all hope.

The night became brighter and brighter and Goat looked up, truly expecting to see angels with fiery swords. Believing it in that moment.

A second sun rose above the horizon.

And a third.

Goat said, "Oh my God," again. It meant something entirely different now.

This was not the rising of the sun any more than it was the shield of God's protection to keep harm from His children.

They were fireballs rising from over the darkened hills.

"What—?" Goat asked the fire and the night and, perhaps, God.

His answer came in the form of a streak of light that arced across the sky and vanished behind the hill. Another ball of fire rose up, veined with red and black, expanding as it fought its way upward against the rain. Goat turned, following the backtrail of the streak and saw something massive and powerful tearing through the sky.

"God," he said once more.

But it wasn't what he meant.

The A-10 Thunderbolt II screamed through the storm above him. Others flew in a wide formation and they, too, spoke in voices of fire and thunder.

Goat's brain, concussed and confused, now understood the difference between heaven come to earth and hell on earth.

CHAPTER FIFTY-SEVEN
ROUTE 653
BORDENTOWN, PENNSYLVANIA

Patrick Freivald slowed his bike, suddenly unsure of how badly he needed to get to Starbucks and get out of the rain.

The sky was filled with dozens of helicopters. Their searchlights cut back and forth to illuminate something on the far side of the hill three hundred yards ahead; and all around the helicopters there were smaller flashes as the beams struck illusionary sparks from the falling rain.

As he slowed and the roar of his motorcycle eased down, he could hear sounds from up ahead. The heavy beat of rotors, the blare of horns. And something else, something staccato and deep. For a moment Patrick through it was the base rhythm of some techno music played at incredible volume, or a drum solo by someone gone totally apeshit.

It was neither, and as he slowed to a stop, he heard it much more clearly; and it was at that moment that he realized the flickering lights in the sky were not searchlights reflecting on raindrops.

They were muzzle flashes.

Above him there was a sharp hiss, loud as a fire hose, and something streaked over the tops of the cars toward the hill a few thousand yards away. It left a trail of smoke that was quickly torn apart by the rain. Then the whole night turned to day as an immense cloud of yellow and orange light rose up over the hill. The deep-chested boom of an explosion rolled along the blacktop, rocking the cars and knocking Patrick to the side. He nearly crashed his bike but pushed his weight against it and fought it back upright; and he did that without thought because his mind was numb from what he was seeing.

A fireball rose into the air, defying the rains to extinguish it.

Patrick said, "Oh my—"

But the rest was struck from his mouth as a second explosion sent a competing fireball up into the night. And a third.

A fourth.

Soon all of the helicopters were firing missiles and rockets. And guns.

People began getting out of their cars. Despite the rain, despite the insanity of all of this. Patrick could hear them yelling. And screaming.

There was movement near the top of the hill and for a moment it looked like roaches boiling out of a sewer drain, but then he realized it was people—hundreds of people—their clothes dark and shiny with water, running from the helicopter attack. Running along the road, moving between the cars, climbing over them, and . . .

And . . .

Patrick stared, not sure of what he was seeing. He raised his visor and peered through the slanting rain. Some of the people seemed to be fighting with each other. Wrestling, falling to the ground, bending each other backward over the hoods of cars.

"What the fuck . . . ?" he said.

The tide of violence swept along the row of stalled cars. Coming his way.

Coming fast.

He had no idea what was happening. A riot of some kind. People going nuts.

Either way, he wanted no part of it.

Patrick cut a look across the wide median and for the first time took note that it was empty, and he tried to recall if he'd seen a single car come that way since this began.

He was sure he hadn't. Not one.

What the hell was happening over that hill?

The helicopters kept firing. Fireballs raced each other into the air. People were trying to turn their cars, and some of them managed to squeeze out of the press and U-turn on the shoulder. They blared their horns and there were dozens of fender benders as the panic to escape the moment overcame everything else.

CHAPTER FIFTY-EIGHT
ROUTE 653
BORDENTOWN, PENNSYLVANIA

A wall of superheated gas came rolling down the highway, flattened wet grass, knocking people down, setting off the car alarms of those stopped vehicles their owners had turned off, bending the trees, turning the rain to steam.

It hit Goat as he struggled to his feet and flung him against the wrecked Cube. He hit hard, cracking the back of his head, his elbows, the middle of his back. His skin suddenly felt like it was covered with ants as the heat leached moisture from his flesh. Goat felt hot wind blowing into his screaming mouth and down his throat.

He collapsed on his knees, aware on some distant level that new pain exploded in his injured knee but not immediately able to care, then as the fiery shockwave passed he sagged over into mud that was no longer wet and cold.

Goat lay there, flash-burned and stunned, gasping for air in a world that no longer seemed to have any. Then . . .

Pulled into the vacuum created by the shockwave, fresh air buffeted him. He dragged in lungfuls of rainy air, sucking it down like a gasping fish returned to the healing waters of the stream.

People were screaming.

Screaming.

Horns blared and Goat heard gunshots. Spaced, erratic. Hunting rifles, he thought.

A moment later, the air above him was churned to pieces by the beat of helicopter blades, and a split second later heavier guns opened up. Goat wriggled painfully toward the back of the wrecked car and looked past the rear wheel to see something that made no immediate sense.

Five big military helicopters swayed in the air, their pilots fighting the harsh winds as door gunners fired miniguns at the lines of parked cars.

People were running in wild panic between the cars, racing out into the farm fields on the far side of the road, tearing cross the median toward the empty westbound lanes. Some had managed to get their cars going and were peeling out of the traffic jam, but most vehicles were too tightly packed. The driver of a Jeep Patriot rammed his vehicle forward, threw it into reverse and rammed backward, and went forward again, crushing bumpers until he'd forced open a hole big enough for him to turn off the road. But the car was blind, the headlights smashed, the grill punched in. It limped down the shoulder but stalled within a dozen yards. And everywhere Goat looked the panicking people were fighting.

Except that wasn't what it was, and after staring for several long moments he understood what was happening. The firebombing. The attacks on the people in the cars. The violence unfolding before him.

He spoke a name.

Not Homer's name.

He said, *"Lucifer."*

Then headlights burned his eyes as a huge Escalade came tearing through the storm. The SUV slewed to a sideways stop, showering Goat with fresh mud and rainwater. The driver's door swung open and a figure climbed out. Huge and powerful, but moving stiffly as if every muscle was cramped.

Goat said his name now.

"Homer."

"The fuck you doing down there, boy?" laughed the killer. His face and chest glistened with bright, fresh blood. "Nap time's over. We gots to go."

He jerked open the Cube's doors, grabbed Goat's camera bag, laptop, and recorder, put them into the Escalade, then bent and grabbed Goat by the belt and hauled him out of the mud with a huge sucking sound. Homer stood Goat on his feet and gave him a shove toward the passenger door.

"Get in." He had to shout to be heard over the continuous machine-gun fire and all those screams.

Goat obeyed and crawled into the SUV.

He even buckled up for safety.

Homer staggered around and climbed in behind the wheel, grunting with the effort of bending his body. Goat wanted to believe that the killer's stiffness and pain were the result of the accident, but he knew better.

It's rigor mortis, he whispered in his own thoughts, marveling that something as bizarre as that could be the truth.

There was a hiss in the air and then on the road three cars flew up into the air on a fireball.

"Rocket," said Homer as casually as if he was commenting on a breed of dog walking down the street. "Let's get some gone between us and that shit."

He put it in drive and the Escalade lurched forward, wanting to run, but Homer did not race away from the battle. Instead he killed the headlights and angled toward the trees that filled the thirty-yard-wide median. Between explosions and the lightning there was just enough light to steer, and Homer drove with care.

"Don't want to wreck this ride," said the killer. "Always wanted me an Escalade. Never could afford it." He paused, thinking. "Guess the ticket price don't mean shit now."

Goat said nothing. He jammed his good leg against the floor and clutched the dashboard, using his hands to brace himself against unexpected impacts. But the car hit nothing.

No trees, anyway.

Several times Homer had to swerved to avoid running people, and twice he didn't swerve fast enough. The dull thud of meat and bone against metal was horrifying.

"Slow as shit," Homer said as one man went spinning off the left fender, his body twisting in ways it shouldn't.

When the median thinned, Homer angled across the road to

where the line of cars was now thinner. He bullied his way through the traffic and went right off the road again into a farm field.

With every second they were leaving the disaster farther behind. Escaping.

Goat realized that he was watching the single most dangerous man in the world escape.

And he was too frightened to do a thing about it.

CHAPTER FIFTY-NINE
STEBBINS LITTLE SCHOOL
STEBBINS, PENNSYLVANIA

Trout heard the sound and thought it was more thunder. He and Dez whipped around toward the row of windows that faced the north. They saw the light and for a moment they thought it was more lightning.

Then the whole sky lit up and something monstrous rose up from behind the forests and rows of houses. A colossus that towered like a fire god from some pagan dream of Ragnarok, a titan of flame who reared above the town and raised a burning sword with such fury that the storm itself recoiled in terror.

Dez said, "What the—"

She got no further as a wall of furnace-hot air blew across the treetops, setting them ablaze, tearing the smaller ones down, shattering thousands of windows, whipping debris into the air and igniting it.

The reinforced windows of the school bowed inward, the glass fracturing into tens of thousands of tiny silver lines but the fragments held fast by the wire mesh. Tongues of flame licked in through those windows that were open, setting fire to curtains and shelves of books, and American flags on wooden poles.

Trout screamed as he fell backward, steam rising from his clothes. Dez screamed, too, and began slapping at his clothes, swatting out tiny fires that wanted to take hold.

The building shuddered as if it was being pummeled by giants.

And then it was over except for the fading echo of a dragon's roar that rolled away from them into the night.

The space around the school seemed empty, devoid of air, as if they were suddenly on the surface of the moon. Then with a banshee shriek winds whipped out of the east and west with ferocity, attacking the vacuum left by the wave of heat. The winds brought with them the rains. The winds blew long and long and black.

Trout lay on the floor and Dez knelt over him, both of them gasping like runners, their eyes wide with terror, their faces flushed with residual heat.

"Jesus, Mary, and Joseph," whispered Dez, "what was that?"

But they both knew.

In the distance the fireball still curled upward into the night. Silent now, but all the more frightening for its persistent reality.

CHAPTER SIXTY
ROUTE 653
BORDENTOWN, PENNSYLVANIA

Patrick Freivald's mind was going into shock but he felt his body respond to a primal survival drive. Adrenaline slammed into his system and with a growl he wrestled his bike around, pointing the front wheel toward the verge. He gunned the engine and drove off the road. The verge slanted down and he sloshed through muddy water so deep it nearly stalled the engine, but Patrick kept it going, doing it right, steering well, keeping control.

He picked up speed, kicking up a fantail of mud forty feet high as he plowed through the rainy field, looping away from the madness and toward the line of cars that had been behind him. He was aware of other vehicles racing through the field, too, and they were all going so fast that he knew the drivers were in full-bore panic mode. That made them dangerous. A motorcycle in the rain was no match for even the smallest compact.

So he was forced to steer away from the road and deeper into the field, but it was ink-dark out there. His headlight couldn't compete with the storm and rain. Far ahead, at the absolute outside range of his vision, he saw a small side road. A farm road. It was empty.

He thanked God and gunned the engine, racing to reach it and get the hell out of there.

Patrick never saw the big black Escalade that came bucketing across the field, headlights off, the driver pale and grinning; the passenger paler still, his mouth open in a silent scream. Patrick didn't see any of that.

He did, however, feel it.

But only for a moment.

CHAPTER SIXTY-ONE
ROUTE 653
BORDENTOWN, PENNSYLVANIA

There was a grinding crunch and suddenly the Escalade slewed sideways, fishtailing in the mud as Homer fought for control. Goat had a fleeting afterimage of a man and a motorcycle flying through the rain, but the SUV kept turning until it spun in a complete circle. As it came out of the turn, Homer gave it enough gas to reclaim the steering, and the machine lurched and bucked, but finally smoothed out. It shot forward across the field.

"Fucking fender's all for shit, goddamn it," complained Homer.

"We hit . . . we hit . . ." Goat tried to say, but couldn't finish the sentence.

"No, boy, we didn't hit shit. Asshole on the bike hit us. Fuck him."

Goat was trembling so bad that his teeth chattered. Homer cut him a quick look and then laughed.

They drove on.

Homer kept his speed under forty, and often a lot lower, even when he found a farm road and pulled onto it. The road was lined with huge oaks and elms. Homer lowered his window and squinted up through the falling rain.

"Good," he said. "That's real good."

Goat understood what Homer meant. The helicopters were firing on the cars and on the people fighting between them and fleeing from the road. The infection was out and they were trying to keep it contained. But a black SUV driving slowly under the eaves of the trees was invisible in the storm, and with every minute they left the sounds of destruction farther behind. Homer kept driving with great care for nearly ten miles, long past the point where Goat, twisting around in his seat to look, could see the fireballs. All he could hear now was the rain and the wind.

Goat licked his lips, tasting mud and blood, and he dared ask a question.

"Where are we going?"

Homer took his time answering. He found a connecting road and turned onto the blacktop. There were other cars there, some heading to the turn-off to Route 653. Goat wanted to yell at them, to warn them; but that was impossible.

Eventually Homer flicked on his headlights as he brought the Escalade up to fifty-five miles an hour. They crossed the line into Fayette County and found another road that headed north.

"Where are we going?" Goat asked again.

Homer grinned at him with bloody teeth.

"Back to where I was raised," he said.

That confused Goat for a moment. Homer had been born to an addict mother and given up for adoption. He'd been raised in a series of foster homes scattered all over western Pennsylvania.

No, he thought suddenly. *He's going home. To the place where he became a monster. To the foster home where he was first abused by a sadistic man and his wife. To a small apartment in a big city.*

"Pittsburgh . . . ?" said Goat in a small, frightened voice.

Home shot him a look, then grinned again. It was not a man's smile. Maybe not even a zombie's smile. It was the smile of the Black Eye and the Red Mouth. It was the smile of a monster.

Homer Gibbon drove on through the night.

"Home again, home again, jiggity-jig," he sang in a voice that was filled with such dark promise.

CHAPTER SIXTY-TWO
THE Q-ZONE
STEBBINS COUNTY, PENNSYLVANIA

They moved across the quarantine zone alone and in packs. Some of them wore rags that had once been coveralls and jeans of farmers. Some wore ordinary shopkeepers' clothes. A few wore the blood-smeared battle dress uniform of the Pennsylvania National Guard.

There were whites and blacks, some Latinos, a few Asians. There were adults and children. There were men and women.

None of those professional, cultural, racial, or gender identifiers mattered anymore. They were all of a kind now. All of the same species, and they were all unified by a purpose which, though not actually shared, was the same for each of them.

Hunger.

Age didn't matter anymore. They were all as old as they would ever be.

They walked as fast as broken bones and torn tendons would allow them to walk. Some moved with the stick-figure gait of rigor mortis. Others loped along, low and feral and fast.

Most of them were leaving Stebbins County.

Not that they understood or cared where the county line was. They lacked the capacity for that kind of perception. They left because they could not smell food anymore. It had moved.

And so they followed it.

But not all of them.

Some stayed because they could still smell the fully blooded meat of the living. Those were the ones closest to the town's only high ground.

The ones closest to the Stebbins Little School.

CHAPTER SIXTY-THREE
THE SITUATION ROOM
THE WHITE HOUSE, WASHINGTON, D.C.

On the big screen, in ultra-high definition and perfect detail, thousands of people died.

The thermobaric bombs did terrible work.

Someone had the kindness or sanity, or perhaps cowardice, to mute the sound, and so the bombs detonated in ghastly silence. Flashes of light that seemed to halt the storm and repeal the dark rule of night.

The president of the United States watched his orders being carried out with the meticulous precision that is only possible at the highest level of military training. Everything was done exactly right. The jets reached their targets with rapidity, they released their payloads with great accuracy, and the weapons performed exactly according to design requirements and mechanical construction. It all happened without a hitch.

If the president had been a madman, he would have been able to enjoy such a level of craftsmanship and professionalism.

But because he was a sane man, he sat and witnessed and wept.

CHAPTER SIXTY-FOUR
STEBBINS LITTLE SCHOOL
STEBBINS, PENNSYLVANIA

When they could make their trembling legs move, Dez and Trout hurried downstairs. The children were screaming in panic. So were most of the adults. Small fires still burned, threatening to take hold on the old building. Dez beat and shoved and screamed at the teachers and parents, forcing them from shocked inaction into teams that attacked the flames with water, with fire extinguishers, with jackets they held in their hands and snapped at anything smoldering.

Seventy-two people had burns.

Eighteen of them were serious.

Mrs. Madison, whose hair was singed and whose eyes had begun to twitch, organized people into emergency care teams. When the first-aid supplies ran out they used Crisco as an unguent.

Trout limped along the hallways searching for children who had panicked and run during the explosion. He opened every door, looked into closets.

It was almost the same pattern as when they had looked for the infected.

On the ground floor, all the way in the back, he saw a door close as he approached it. He almost called out, but there was something odd about the way it closed. Soft. Almost furtive.

Or perhaps sneaky.

He slowed to a cautious walk and moved to the edge of the door, away from the smoked glass panel, not wishing to throw a shadow on it.

Inside he heard a sound that at first he couldn't understand or identify.

A whispering voice. Male. Low.

And then snuffles.

A child.

No. *Children*.

Trout pressed his ear to the door to try and hear better. That's when he heard the window.

It squeaked and rattled in the frame, and as it did the sound of rain became louder.

Someone inside was opening the window on the ground floor.

Panic flared in his chest and he grabbed the doorknob and turned it.

It only turned halfway and then stopped.

Locked.

"Hey!" Trout yelled, throwing caution away. "Who's in there? What the hell are you doing?"

He pounded his fist on the door.

Inside a child cried out.

"Open the door, goddamn it . . ."

The cry of the child changed. Just like that.

It became a scream and overlaid with it was the low, hungry, unmistakable moan of the living dead.

CHAPTER SIXTY-FIVE
WHAT THE FINKE THINKS
WTLK LIVE TALK RADIO
PITTSBURGH, PENNSYLVANIA

"We have Teddy on the line," said Gavin. "Welcome aboard the crazyboat, Teddy. Tells the Finke what you think."

"Hey, listen man, I got to make this quick."

"Take all the time you need, Teddy."

"No, seriously, I only have a minute, but I needed to get this out. I needed to tell someone what's really going on out here."

"And what is happening out there?"

"This whole thing, all the deaths, the stories about people attacking each other, about people going crazy and killing each other and eating each other? Those aren't stories, man. That's happening. It's happening right now."

"'Eating each other,' Teddy?"

"It's not funny."

"I'm not laughing," said Gavin. "But I also don't understand. Who's eating whom?"

"The people who get this thing, this disease, they die, but then they come back right away. So it's not like they're really dead. They get up and start going crazy. You can't talk to them. They don't react the way people do. They're really out of it. All they want to do is eat people."

"And that's what you say is happening in Stebbins County? People running around eating each other?"

"That's definitely what's happening."

"And how do you know this, Teddy?"

"I'm here, man. I'm right here in Stebbins. My whole unit is here. And we're under orders to hunt the infected down and . . . and shoot them."

Before Gavin could ask for clarification and verification, the line went dead.

The producer grinned through the glass and twirled his finger by his temple. Another loony. Gavin had to agree, but it was loonies that paid the light bill. He punched another button.

"We have Samantha from Evans, Pennsylvania. Hi, Samantha, tell the Finke what you think."

"It's bigfoot . . ." she said.

CHAPTER SIXTY-SIX
STEBBINS LITTLE SCHOOL
STEBBINS, PENNSYLVANIA

Trout tried to kick the door in.

He stepped back, raised his knee to his chest, and snapped out with every ounce of strength he possessed. He knew where and how to kick in a door. He'd witnessed cops do it, written about it in news articles, seen it in movies. His heel hit the wood right beside the doorknob. Angle, placement, and leverage should have torn the lock out of its hinges and slammed the door inward.

There was only a tiny fragment of time for his brain to process a sudden and awful reality.

This door opened out into the hallway.

There was absolutely no way to stop that kick.

His foot hit and the door did not—could not—burst inward. Instead the force of the impact rebounded from the immovable object and shot through his heel, up his shin, and through dozens of muscular transfer points into the nerve clusters in his lower back that were already damaged.

He shrieked in pain and instantly fell onto his back on the hardwood floor, the shock knocking the air out of his lungs.

Beyond the door the screams rose to the ultrasonic, burying the sound of hungry moans.

Trout was absolutely incapable of movement.

Even when he saw the doorknob jiggle and turn. Even when he heard the lock click open. Even when the door began to swing outward.

The edge of the door struck him on the hip, but his sprawled body prevented it from opening beyond a few inches. A small, desperate hand suddenly thrust out through the crack, tiny fingers clawing at the air, trying to grab something. A lifeline, a hope. Anything.

Then the hall was filled with a dreadful roar of rage and horror.

Billy turned his dazed head and saw a demon running out of the shadows toward him. Beautiful and terrible, blue eyes blazing like lasers, teeth bared in an animal snarl.

"D—Dez . . ." he croaked.

She leapt over him and as she landed she planted a foot against his hip and shoved him away with ruthless force. He rolled over, fresh agony spearing through him. Dez tore open the door, grabbed the child—a little black girl with cornrowed hair decorated with pink dragonfly clips—and hauled her out of the room.

The child came staggering into the hall.

Covered in blood.

Trailing blood.

Streaming blood.

The sound that came from Dez Fox was more savage and far less human than anything Trout had heard from the mouths of the infected. It wasn't a sane sound. It was bestial and horrible.

She whipped the door all the way open and ran into the room, and through that open door Trout could see the tableau and understand what had happened. One of the adults had tried to escape through a window, taking several children with him. But the dead had been outside. Without the soldiers to surround the school, the dead had come hunting for food. Three of them were already inside the room. More of them milled beyond the open window. All of them were blackened and burned, their skin cracked from the heat, their hair burned away, their clothes still smoking. The only color Trout could see was the white of their teeth, the milkiness of their dead eyes, and the red blood on the mouths of the zombies inside the school.

Trout saw all of this in a terrible flash. Then the storm outside seemed to enter the school as thunder and lightning tore the room apart. Dez had her gun out and she fired, fired. The booms of the Glock seemed impossibly loud. The muzzle flashes strobed images into Trout's memory. A blackened face flying apart as hollow-point rounds exploded its skull.

Then Dez was moving, shoving her way past children who cringed back, hands clamped to bleeding wounds, voices raised in desperate pleas that Trout knew could never be answered. Not anymore.

Two of the burned infected were down, and the third lunged at Dez from her blindside.

"Watch!" cried Trout, but Dez was already turning, firing, blowing the hungry need from the eyes of the dead thing.

She raced to the window, gun out in front of her in two hands and emptied the rest of the magazine into the faces of the things that were fighting each other to climb inside. They fell backward. Dez swapped out the magazine, letting the empty one fall. She leaned out and began firing again, screaming at them to fall, to die, to fucking die.

And they died.

Feet pounded down the hallway and Trout turned to see a knot of adults racing toward him, guns and clubs in their hands. He saw them reach for the children and even though he hated himself for doing it, even though he knew it would earn him a sentence in hell, he yelled them back.

"They're bitten!" he bellowed. "They're infected."

The adults stumbled to a halt, their fear and uncertainty warring with their basic humanity.

The little black girl with the pink clips had fallen down and she lay still and unmoving on the floor five feet away from Trout. Her wounds no longer bled, and as he stared the blood around the bite marks changed. At first the bright red seemed to fade to a paler pink, but that was an illusion created as thousands of tiny white worms seemed to explode within the mess. The process was so damned fast that it was like watching a movie speeded up. First there dots of white and then they expanded before his eyes before finally bursting open as worms. Then within seconds those new-born worms began seeding the blood with new eggs, which swelled and burst, continuing a cycle that seemed impossible. Except that it was going on, right there, right in front of his eyes. Volker's monster at work.

The worms excreted an oily black substances whose nature Trout could not even guess, and soon the blood became as black as motor oil. Totally polluted, totally corrupted.

Then the little girl's eyes opened.

She and Trout lay five feet apart. A child and a man. Both of them trapped inside a nightmare.

CHAPTER SIXTY-SEVEN
TOWN OF STEBBINS
ONE MILE INSIDE THE Q-ZONE

Back in the Humvee, Sam took the radio booster unit, removed a small cable, and plugged it into his cell phone.

"I thought everything was jammed," said Boxer.

"Special line," explained Sam. "For emergencies. Have to keep the conversation short, though, because it's not all that secure."

Sam punched a number and was not surprised when it was answered halfway through the first ring.

"Are you inside?" asked Scott Blair. The connection was very bad, but workable.

"Affirmative," said Sam, "and I have two things to report. First, there are definitely Zees at large within the area. Does that match your latest intel?"

Boxer mouthed the word "Zees."

Blair said, "On-site command reports that the last Zees are being dealt with."

"That sounds like the bullshit it is, sir," observed Sam. "We found three without even looking. That tells me there are more, and probably a lot more. Between terrain and the storm, no ground search can make reliable claims."

"For what it's worth, even S.Z. agrees," said Blair, careful not to name General Zetter over an open line. "He has requested ten thousand additional units be shipped to his warehouse. ETA two hours."

Ten thousand new troops. Sam whistled. "Not soon enough," he said. "And that brings me to the second thing. The checkpoint we passed was manned by a couple of kids who couldn't keep anyone out of anywhere. S.Z.'s using two-man teams on the roads, and the roving patrols between checkpoints are a joke. They couldn't keep kids out of a candy store. If the whole area hasn't already been breached, then it's a matter of time."

Blair cursed.

"Listen to me," said Sam, "I don't know or care what you have to do to convince the Big Man that the current response is inadequate. Seems to me that everyone is proceeding like this thing is over, but it's not going to take much for this thing to go into the shitter. If it helps any put me on the phone to the president."

"It's worth a try," said Blair. "But now I have something to tell you. H.V. is dead."

It took Sam a second. H.V.

Dr. Herman Volker.

"Ah . . . shit. Tell me he at least left the *accounts*." He leaned on the word.

"That is a negative. Zero accounts."

Sam watched lightning fork in the sky. "Where does that leave us?"

"With a mission change," said Blair. "I need you to scrap the science trip and proceed to the secondary source. It's all riding on that. Do whatever you have to do."

The line went dead and Sam put the phone away. He told the others what Blair had said, and explained that the secondary source of Volker's information was in the possession of Billy Trout.

"Which means we have to infiltrate a school full of scared kids and force this Trout guy to pony up the flash drives?" asked Boxer.

"In a nutshell."

No one looked happy.

"I volunteered for this gig, boss," said Boxer, "but I didn't sign on to kill civilians, and I sure as shit won't cut my way through a bunch of kids."

Sam Imura said nothing. Around them, the storm slapped against the windows of the Humvee and the night seemed to go several shades darker.

Gypsy very quietly said, "If this thing gets out of the Q-zone it's game over for the whole world. That's not trash talk, Boxer. That's not a bad line from a monster movie. That's real shit and it's what we're here to stop. I don't want to hurt anyone but bad guys, either, but if it's a few civilians versus the rest of the fucking world . . . I mean, c'mon, is that even a discussion?"

No one answered that, not even Boxer.

"C'mon," said Sam, "let's go hunting."

CHAPTER SIXTY-EIGHT
STEBBINS LITTLE SCHOOL
STEBBINS, PENNSYLVANIA

Dez Fox knew she was losing it.

Or maybe she had already lost it.

She knew that as certainly as she knew that she should not—should absolutely not—climb out of the window of the Stebbins Little School. All she had to do was close the window. Close it, lock it. Then close and lock the door to that room.

That was all.

Something simple.

A smart and very sane choice.

Which she did not make.

Instead she hooked a leg over the sill, shifted her buttocks onto the ledge, ducked her head out of the dry room and into the rain. Hands reached out of the storm to claw at her. Fingers that were withered to black claws by heat. Soot-stained teeth clacked together as the dead came for her.

Behind her, Billy Trout was screaming her name.

"Fuck you!" she growled.

Dez was never sure if she meant that for Billy or for the dead.

It didn't matter.

Her mind was filled with the immediate images of those children. *Her* children. The little ones under her protection. Bitten. Infected. Doomed.

She jammed the barrel of the Glock against a charred forehead and fired.

Did it again to another infected.

Two of the dead fell back, their suddenly limp bodies collapsing against the other zombies, hampering them, tangling up with them.

Dez jumped down, using the pistol to smash aside the reaching hands. She kicked at wobbly legs, shattering bones, causing jagged splinters of white to rip through the blackened skin. She fired and fired. Every shot was point-blank.

Every bullet hit a face, a forehead, a temple.

Every hollow-point round did what it was manufactured to do. It expanded and exploded through the brain matter. Blowing out the backs of skulls, spattering the other dead with pieces of bone and brain. More than once the bullets, fired from so close, punched through one skull and then struck another.

She fired every round in the magazine. Released it, let it fall, swept another magazine from her belt, slapped it into place. The process was absolutely automatic, as orderly and efficient as the functions of a machine. A robot.

The dead kept coming out of the rain.

Ten of them.

Fifteen.

Thirty.

The gun was heavy in her hands, the recoil sending jolts of pain into her palms and wrists, her trigger finger burning with overuse, her skin tingling with powder burns.

When she had come leaping out of the window Dez had been screaming. A primal war cry, something like a cave woman might have bellowed as predatory animals stalked toward her own mewling children in the dark of a prehistoric night. But as she fired and fired, the scream burned away, leaving only the rasp of her panting breath and the thunder of her gun. She could feel her face lose expression.

It wasn't a calmness settling in her muscles. It was a deadness, a nothingness.

The dead wore no expressions either, and the battle became strangely dreamlike.

Dez dropped an empty magazine and fished for her last one.

And did not find it.

Suddenly the deadness was gone.

Panic returned in a terrible rush as she realized that she had miscounted the number of magazines she'd carried. That she'd used every last bullet.

There were at least a dozen of the dead still on their feet, and four or five more crawling along, trailing broken legs behind them.

She turned toward the school and with a cry of horror realized that somehow she had moved away from it, that she had walked into the schoolyard, leaving the building fifty yards behind her.

She was trapped out in the storm, surrounded by the dead, and there was not even a bullet left to take her own life.

The dead closed around her.

CHAPTER SIXTY-NINE
STEBBINS–FAYETTE COUNTY LINE
EAST OF THE BORDENTOWN STARBUCKS

Ross Cruickshank staggered away from his burning car and ran for the woods. Steam rose from his clothes and he could feel a dangerous heat spreading on his skin. His mind was filled with mad images that were fractured and strange. Pale-faced people with black mouths. Blood-splattered people reeling out of the storm and throwing themselves at the crowd that stood watching in numb horror as helicopters fired on the lines of stopped cars. And then something else.

A screech from above the dark clouds.

Streaks of bright yellow light.

And then fire.

Fire.

Everywhere.

Cars leapt into the air and exploded.

People ran screaming, their hair and clothes ablaze.

People flying apart; each separate piece of them igniting as the heat blooms spread out from the point of impact.

The shimmering wave of hot air moved across the road like an attacking mirage, surreal and deadly.

Ross was at the extreme edge of the blast zone. His car was more than two miles back from the Starbucks on Route 653, and until the blast he stood on the edge of the median, hands cupped around his eyes so he could see through the rain as he tried to make sense of what looked like a soccer riot there on a rural highway in Pennsylvania. The radio had been weird all night, with local news talking about virus outbreaks and rumors of people being killed in Stebbins.

Ross had never heard of Stebbins beyond it being a place on the map between his long drive from an uncle's funeral in Akron to a friend's wedding in Cape May, New Jersey. He'd taken the back roads because the news said the Pennsylvania turnpike was slowed to a crawl, even this late. Because of the storm and because of whatever the hell was happening in wherever the hell Stebbins was.

Then he hit the traffic jam on Route 653, totally blocked in, sitting there for forty minutes before finally getting out of the car to see what he could see. What he saw was the riot.

Or whatever it was.

Then the helicopters.

That made no sense to Ross.

Then the jets and the flashes of bright light.

And now he ran through the rain with steam hissing from his clothes and a mouth filled with hot ash and gritty debris. He coughed and gagged as he ran. He fell several times, dropping knees-first onto the highway, then falling off the asphalt into the rainwater that surged through the brimming run-off ditch. Falling into the cold water was like plunging into a river of knives. Ross screamed hoarsely, his burned throat seemingly filled with razor blades.

He scrambled up the other side and struggled weakly to his feet just as a second streak of fiery light arced out of the clouds and struck the line of stalled cars. Then Ross felt himself flying.

Flying.

He soared through the storm winds, wondering if this was real or a dream.

Ross did not remember landing.

His next conscious perception was pain.

And sickness.

He lay in the dark, legs and arms splayed, face turned to the sky as water filled his mouth. He coughed. Swallowed too much water and then rolled to his side and vomited. The insides of his mouth ached from the superheated air he'd inhaled and there was a burning line of scalded tissue running along the wall into his lungs, and down into his stomach. It hurt. And it itched.

He coughed again and spat something bitter and foul into the mud.

Ross pawed at the dribble on his lips and he thought, just for a strange little moment, that he could feel something wriggle between his fingertips. Something tiny. But the rain washed it away.

The itching in his throat continued.

Sickness sloshed like sewer water in his stomach.

He vomited again. And again, unsure of whether anything was coming up. It was too dark to see and his throat hurt too much to tell.

The darkness took him again.

When he was next aware of things, he was on his feet, walking. It wasn't the median anymore, nor was it farmlands. When the lightning flashed it painted vertical lines all around him. Tree trunks. He was in the woods.

Ross did not know which woods. At night, in the dark, he hadn't seen much of the landscape. This was rural Pennsylvania, though, and it was a green state. Lots of damn forests.

He knew, on some level, that he was in shock, and that he was hurt. Maybe badly hurt. But he didn't seem able to care about it.

He did care about the sickness, though. His stomach felt like it was full of wriggling snakes, and his entire esophagus itched terribly. His skin did, too. He scratched his arms and chest, but it didn't help; the itch was under the skin. Deep and painful.

I got to get home, he thought.

And while he understood what that meant, it felt somehow irrational and stupid. Home was hundreds of miles away from here and he didn't even have a car.

Why didn't he have a car? he wondered, but he couldn't answer that question. It was so hard to think clearly.

The ground began to slant downward and he followed it because it was so much easier than climbing uphill. He staggered along, going in and out of awareness.

Then his foot caught on an exposed root and Ross was falling, falling.

He felt himself hit the ground chest-first, the shock driving the air out of his lungs, and then as he fell face-forward into the mud there was sharp metallic *snap* and a white-hot explosion of pain on both sides of his face. He could feel something like knives punching in through his jaw and cheeks and temples. Broken bits of teeth filled his mouth and he tried to spit them out so he could scream. But he could not scream. Not the way he wanted to, not the way he needed to. The teeth held his jaws shut, locked. Trapped.

Ross Cruickshank lay there in the dark with a heavy-grade steel bear trap locked around his face, the teeth buried deep, a chain anchoring it to the trunk of a tree.

It took nearly an hour for him to die from blood loss, shock, and burns.

It took less than a minute for him to come back.

But all through that night and for all the nights and days to follow, Ross lay facedown in the forest, caught in the jaws of the trap, chained to the tree, unable to rise, unable to hunt, unable to do anything about the awful, gnawing hunger.

All he could do was lay there and moan.

And rot.

EAST OF THE BORDENTOWN STARBUCKS

Deborah Varas drove like hell.

And hell itself seemed to follow.

Mushroom clouds of burning gas billowed into the air, and the trees along both sides of the road burned like candles.

Her husband, Roger, was a silent, twitching hulk in the seat next to her. She tried not to look at him, tried not to smell the cooked meat stink of him. He'd stood between her and the first blast of superheated air. She would remember how it looked as he seemed to rise into the air, arms out to his side as if crucified against the night. And then flew back against her and they both went tumbling and crashing into the watery mud beside the road.

It was the mud that saved them, of that Deborah had no doubt.

If they were, in fact, safe.

It had been a screaming hell to pull him out of the mud and to support him as they staggered toward their car. The doors were still open from when they'd gotten out to see what was wrong, and Deborah pushed him in. She didn't dare pull the seat belt around him. Too much of him looked blistered.

Instead she limped around to the driver's side, got in, slammed her door, cut the wheel, and tore off another car's bumper as she broke out of the line of stopped cars. She hit the gas hard to give the car enough momentum to fly across the drainage ditch. Even then the rear wheels hit the lip and for a moment Deborah thought the car would slide backward into the water. But the muscular front wheels somehow found purchase in the mud and the car lurched forward onto the median. She cut across, weaving around staggering survivors who were all trying to flee the blast, and then she hit the opposite lane, fishtailed around, straightened, and bore down to the west. The speedometer climbed to sixty and then eighty, and after that she stopped looking.

Deborah had no idea what had happened. The stalled cars and then something that looked like a riot, but it was half a mile from where she and Roger stood. It looked, though, as if whatever the commotion was it was coming their way, but then the world seemed to explode. She wondered about that, and whether she should be far more upset than she was. Shock. It was shock.

I'm in shock.

It was a strange thought to have. Like realizing you're drunk. You know it, but can't really take control of body or mouth or anything. Like being a passenger in a hijacked car.

I'm in shock.

She knew it to be true, but she didn't know what to do or how to even react to that truth.

As she drove, she tried to work saliva into her mouth to clear away the awful taste. When the heat wave hit them, she'd taken a mouthful of ash and hot dust. She wasn't badly burned—no worse than eating soup that was too hot—but the ash had a terrible taste. Sour and nasty.

And it itched something terrible.

Then she scolded herself for worrying about that when her husband was in such agony. She had to get him to a doctor. To a hospital.

Deborah fished for her cell phone, but there was no signal. None.

She turned the radio on, but the only station she could find was a conspiracy theory talk show. She switched it off.

Tears ran down her face as she drove.

Three times she saw flashing red and blue police lights, but they were on some other road, parallel to where she was, and far away. Heading toward the blast. And she did not want to go back there for anything. Deborah didn't know if it was some terrorist thing or something equally horrifying, but she wanted no part of it.

In the darkness beside her, Roger moaned and shifted. She touched him as gently as she could, and he didn't hiss or jerk away. Maybe he wasn't as bad as he looked, she thought, praying that she was right.

"Roger?" she asked. "Hold on, baby, we're going to the hospital."

He moaned softly. An inarticulate sound. Like a dreaming person might make.

He pawed for her hand, though, and she let him take it.

"It's okay, honey, we'll get this taken care of."

Roger kissed her hand, and his tenderness, even this deep into the horrors of his own pain came close to breaking her heart. Fresh tears filled her eyes as she spoke soothing words to him. Meaningless words, more a sound of comfort than any promises she knew she could keep. The world beyond the windshield was wet and vast and dark and she had no idea where the closest hospital was.

She drove on, faster than anything that was safe or sane.

Roger put her fingertips in his mouth. Kissed them and . . .

Licked them?

It was such a strange thing. Like he was trying to nurse on her fingers, the way a child would at her breast. God, was he that damaged? Was he that far gone that he was reduced to a childlike state? An infantile state?

"Oh, Roger . . ."

A heartbeat later she screamed as Roger bit down on her fingers.

CHAPTER SEVENTY
STEBBINS LITTLE SCHOOL
STEBBINS, PENNSYLVANIA

Dez Fox knew that she should scream.

A scream would be good. It would punctuate this moment, seal it, send it into eternity.

People were supposed to scream when they died.

Especially when they died like this, trapped inside a nightmare.

Yet when she opened her mouth she said, "JT."

In her ears the name sounded like "Daddy."

It meant the same thing to her.

The dead shuffled forward, stumbling over the sprawled limbs of their dead companions. Some of them tripped and fell, but they got up again, mindless of cracked kneecaps and fractured wrists from their collisions with the unforgiving ground.

Dez backed away, but she knew that she had nowhere to run. There were zombies between her and the school. The lighted window was fifty yards away. It might have been a window on the face of the moon for all that it mattered to her.

She saw figures moving inside. Teachers, parents. Maybe even Billy.

It didn't matter.

"JT," she said.

And as if in answer to her speaking that name she thought she heard his voice.

This isn't done, girl.

"JT . . . ?"

Desdemona, you listen to me. You're a cop and you're a good one, but you're not acting like one now.

"I . . . I can't . . . I don't . . ."

The closest of the infected were a dozen feet away. In four steps they would have her.

Four.

What about the kids, Dez? Asked JT. *What about the little ones?*

The school was a million miles away.

"I let them die."

Damn it, girl, don't give me that crap. It's not your fault some damn fool opened that window.

Three steps. She could smell their burned flesh.

"I let them die, JT. I should have been there. I should have been smarter."

You can't unring that bell, girl, he said sternly, his voice as clear as if he stood right beside her. *You can't undo that. But you can damn well save the rest of them.*

"No . . . I can't . . ."

You can. That's your job. Saving them is why you became a cop. Saving them is what's kept you alive all these years, and you know it.

Two steps.

"JT . . . how can I do this?"

You know how.

"I don't," she said, but even as she said it her hands touched her belt, feeling the things clipped to it. The pouches with the handcuffs. The empty slots for magazines. The pepper spray.

Nothing there.

No help.

The stun gun.

No use against the dead. They didn't react to pain.

Damn it, Dez. Be smarter than that, growled JT.

Stun gun.

The dead were driven by parasites. That's what Billy had told her.

The parasites shut off most of the body's functions except a little respiration, a little blood flow, and the nerves needed for standing, moving, grabbing, biting, swallowing.

Nerves.

Nerves.

Nerve conduction.

The hands touched her sleeves, her shoulders, her breasts, her face.

And then her hand drew the Taser.

Nerve conduction.

She heard JT laugh quietly. *There you go. You're not the fastest, girl, we both know that, but damn if you don't always get there in the end.*

The weapon came free of its holster. The Nova SP-5.

The stun gun had a five-shot magazine.

Open a door and go home, said JT.

She brought the weapon up, activating the laser site. Found a target a yard from her. Fired.

The flachettes whipped through the air and struck the dead flesh high on the chest. The charge surged through the wires and instantly the infected body arched back, all four limbs trembling like a puppet hanging in a stiff wind. The eyes bulged wide and the mouth opened and it tried to scream.

Scream.

Oh God . . . it actually tried to scream.

Two other infected were behind it, pressed against it to try and get to her. The rain and the intensity of the charge flashed from one to the other and the three of them were suddenly falling.

Falling.

Opening a hole in the wall of charred flesh.

Dez released the first cartridge and chambered the second, moving now, running through that hole. She fired again and a woman with no eyes suddenly juddered to a stop and then fell away, a whistling shriek rising from between her burned lips.

The scream was the first human sound any of these monsters had made.

It chilled Dez Fox all the way to the core of her soul.

The screams were so—*normal.* God . . . did that mean the people who had been in those bodies before the infection took over were still in there?

Don't think about it, bellowed JT. *Run. Run!*

She ran.

She released the second cartridge. Fired a third, heard another tearing scream of human pain.

The zombies tried to close in on her, but she smashed into them, driven now by panic as much as need. She elbowed them and jump-kicked them in the stomachs, and rammed them with her shoulders.

Two shots left and twenty yards to go.

The air around here was suddenly split apart by thunder.

Small thunder. Not from the sky but from . . .

Gunfire rippled from the windows of the school.

All of the windows. A dozen barrels cracked. Four of the zombies went down. Two stayed down, two others began instantly to climb back to their feet, their bodies absorbing anything except headshots.

"Dez!" called a voice, and this time it wasn't the ghost of JT Hammond hollering in her fractured mind. It was Billy Trout. "Run! The side door. Go . . . go . . . *go*!"

She saw it then, the staff entrance door stood ajar and five men were clustered there. Piper was among them, a shotgun spitting fire in his hands.

Dez fired her fourth shot and a man she recognized—Albert Thomas, who owned a tattoo parlor on Buckley Road—staggered back, a human cry torn from his dead throat. It sounded like Albert, too. But there was a quality to it, a rising note of panic as if in that one instant the man she knew was able to give voice to all the horrors that had been done to him. And it was then, with perfect and dreadful clarity, that Dez Fox realized the true and full extent of what Dr. Volker had unleashed on humanity.

Lucifer 113 was intended to make Homer Gibbon be aware of every moment, every sensation of what was happening to him as his dead body rotted in a coffin and was consumed by maggots. This was a punishment intended for a serial killer to make him pay for what he had done to the innocent.

And now it was doing that to every single infected person.

They were all in there. Their consciousness trapped in the hijacked bodies. Aware, connected to nerve endings, and totally unable to prevent their stolen flesh from committing unspeakable things.

Only in the moment of intense electric shock from the stun gun were those people able to give voice, to cry out. For mercy. For forgiveness. For release.

As she ran, Dez thought about the effect that bullets had. It ended the unnatural life of the living dead.

Did it also end their torment?

Was a bullet to the brain a kindness?

It was so twisted and perverse a concept that even as she ran she nearly doubled over and vomited.

There was one last zombie between her and the door, but it was in a direct line between her and the men with guns. She had one charge left in her gun. Could she use it, knowing this ugly truth? Could she bear to hear that scream again, knowing that she couldn't then end the suffering of the person trapped inside the dead flesh?

It came at her, mouth wide to bite, hands reaching to grab.

She shot it in the throat, hoping to drop it without the scream.

But it screamed anyway.

It screamed like someone burning in the fires of hell itself.

The infected fell away and then human hands reached for her and pulled her inside the school and then slammed the door shut. Bodies thudded against the outside of the door and down the halls; echoing from the classrooms there was a last volley of gunfire.

Then three spaced shots from the hallway.

Dez knew what those shots meant.

Three shots for three small heads.

Followed by the sound of retching. And weeping.

CHAPTER SEVENTY-ONE
STEBBINS–FAYETTE COUNTY LINE
NORTH OF THE BORDENTOWN STARBUCKS

Dustin Lee Frye was making the slowest getaway he'd ever heard of.

It was driving him crazy.

Four hours ago a friend of his had dropped him at the parking lot of the Woodsman Rest, right off Route 381 in Fayette County.

Dustin had crouched under a dark gray poncho in driving rain waiting for his ex-girlfriend's new boy toy to come to work. The boyfriend, a shovel-jawed goon with little pig eyes, worked the night shift as bartender at the Rest, and that meant he'd be on until two a.m.

At ten minutes to eight, Shovel-jaw roared into the lot in his 1970 Mustang Boss 429. A perfectly restored, mint-condition classic muscle car. The Grabber green skin seemed to glow in the downspill of light from the sodium vapor bulbs arranged around the parking lot. Over two hundred thousand dollars worth of car, bought for the asshole by his daddy, who owned big chunks of logging and pulp all through Pennsylvania and Maryland.

Dustin didn't think it was at all fair that the pea-brained mouthbreather should have his ex-girlfriend *and* one of the sweetest cars in the world. Actually, as Dustin saw it, he could keep the girl. She and Dustin had ended things badly. Harsh language was involved. So was a restraining order. Not the happiest times in his life.

She was elsewhere, probably fretting over what to do about the stretch marks now that Shovel-jaw had knocked her up. *If* the baby was even his. There had been one last bout of makeup sex with Dustin before everything went to shit, so the whole paternity thing was a dice-roll.

The car, though. Dustin didn't want the Neanderthal to have the car.

It wasn't fair.

The car was perfect. From tailpipe to headlights, it was the absolutely perfect car. And assholes should not be allowed to have perfect cars. Dustin was sure there was a law about that somewhere. Or ought to be.

So stealing the car, in Dustin's view, was not so much a matter of committing a crime as it was serving the public welfare.

He waited for Shovel-jaw to park the car in his special extra-wide slot, lock it, give the creamy green hood its usual pat, and go into the hunters' club to mix drinks for the other mouth-breathers. The parking lot was nearly deserted, though, because of Superstorm Zelda. A smarter person, Dustin mused, would have called out and stayed at home. But no one ever called this guy smart. Rich, yes. Obnoxious, to be sure. Smart? Not so much.

Dustin started to get up so he could boost the Mustang, but another car came crunching over the gravel. Two men got out and hurried through the rain to the restaurant. Then another came. And another. Then one of the cars left.

It was like that for hours. Despite everything that was happening in the skies and the world, the damned place was doing bang-up business. Dustin was afraid to leave his hiding spot for a minute, sure that someone would spot him and then there'd be real trouble.

Finally, well after one in the morning, the steady in-and-out flow dwindled and died. There was a protracted stillness and when it seemed apparent that the last drinkers inside were going to take it all the way to the bell, Dustin rose up quickly from his place of concealment beside the Dumpster and drifted around the perimeter of the parking lot to come up behind the Mustang. Dustin had a friend who boosted cars on a regular basis—not professionally, more of a hobby, but he was good at it—who'd lent him a slim-jim and a key gun. Dustin moved to the driver's door, checked the lot again, eased the slim-jim from under the poncho and fed the thin strip of metal down between the glass and the door. Popping the lock was a breeze.

He shucked the poncho and slid behind the wheel, mindful to keep the rain off the leather seats. He chunked the door shut and fed the teeth of the key gun into the ignition.

The engine started at once.

And it started with a very loud, very distinctive growl. All of those horses under the hoods shouting at the storm.

Dustin had no idea if Shovel-jaw heard the car start. He didn't wait to find out. He put the car in gear, spun the wheel, and kicked ten pounds of wet gravel at the back of the restaurant as he peeled out. As soon as he was out of the lot, he turned left and followed a couple of crooked feeder roads until one spilled him out onto 381, where he turned north to catch 653, and from there he planned to turn the car west and drive it until he figured out what tomorrow would look like.

But after he turned onto Route 653 and drove ten miles, crossing out of Fayette and cruising the outer edge of Stebbins County, things started to slide downhill.

First it was the rain.

The sky split apart with thunder and for a moment it seemed as if the clouds themselves were being ignited by the lightning. Flash after flash, boom after boom. It hurt his eyes and rattled the windows. And the rain that fell was so thick that the windshield wipers did exactly nothing. It slowed him to a nervous crawl. All he could make out were the taillights directly in front of him. Those lights rolled forward at barely over twenty miles an hour and it was like that for a long time. The rain did not let up once. Dustin had never seen rain like this before.

Then the car in front of him—an old Camry—slowed more and more.

It finally stopped, and after a long time, the driver shut his engine off.

The rain only began slackening after Dustin had been sitting there for ten more minutes. It was still coming down pretty steadily, but it wasn't wrath of God rain. It wasn't Noah's ark rain.

The Camry up front didn't move, though. The driver simply sat there.

Dustin didn't dare toot his horn or make any kind of fuss. Not while driving a stolen car worth a couple hundred g's. No, sir. That would be monumentally stupid.

So he waited.

And waited.

That's when the thunder started again. And lightning.

Except that's not what it was, and Dustin realized it by slow degrees as balls of yellow light lifted from over the horizon. He watched as the light illuminated the thousands of cars stalled in long lines ahead of him, and in the rearview he could see thousands more dwindling into the distance behind him.

Then he heard the screams and the gunfire. Dustin had seen every war film and action movie ever made. He knew the sound of heavy-caliber machine-gun fire.

"Holy shit," he said aloud.

People were running up the road between the cars. Fleeing whatever the hell was happening. But also . . . fighting?

He leaned forward to peer out at the night.

Not a hundred feet away he saw a woman in a pretty autumn dress dive at a guy in coveralls, slam him against the fender of a Chevy Aveo and . . .

"Holy *shit*!" he cried as he saw blood shoot up from the man's neck like water from a broken fountain.

Two men pulled open the front doors of an Expedition and dove in. Blood splashed the insides of the rear window. A teenager with one arm missing—*just fucking gone*—ran directly at the front of Dustin's car and flung himself onto the hood, denting it, smearing it with blood.

"Holy shit!" screamed Dustin.

He put the car in reverse to get away as the one-armed teenager began pounding on the windshield, but the Mustang shot back only twenty inches before crunching into the front end of a Focus.

"Fuck you!" bellowed Dustin, both at the Focus and the insane teenager. He threw it into drive and rammed forward, crushing the grille against the Camry's rear. Glass exploded and one of Dustin's headlights went blind. Five minutes ago he would have been heartbroken if a road stone tore a fingernail-sized scratch on the Grabber Green hood. Now he rammed forward and back three times, accordianing the bumpers, screaming at the howling thing that still knelt on the hood and pounding one-handed on the glass. Then he had an opening, and he was out. He jerked left out of the lane and onto the shoulder, spilling the bloody teenager off with a bone-jarring crunch. Beside the shoulder was a drop-off that was filled with water and it looked like a death trap to Dustin. Behind him other cars were pulling out and blocking the route for a backing-up escape. A quarter mile ahead there was a wide pull-off. If he could get there, maybe he could find a way to cut across the median. The opposite lane was completely clear. Farther along the road he saw a guy on a motorcycle do exactly that. So Dustin shifted again and hit the gas, sending the big Mustang rocketing forward.

At that moment, there was the biggest explosion yet from over the hill. A massive fireball that seemed to lift the whole road up and drop it. Thousands of people fled from it, screaming and bleeding, chased by waves of heat that set their hair and clothes ablaze. Behind them, mixed in with them, attacking them as they ran were other people. Wild-eyed and bloody, with snapping teeth and grabbing hands. Some of them were on fire, too, but they didn't seem to care about that. All they seemed to want—or seemed capable of wanting—were the people who ran from them.

Heat punched at the Mustang, blackening the green paint, covering the windshield with ash. And in one frozen moment, Dustin could see things in that ash. Tiny threadlike worms that wriggled as the hot wind slapped them against the glass. There were other things hitting the car, too. Pieces of charred meat. Pieces of broken bone and burning swatches of cloth.

Dustin's mind absorbed all of that visual data in a microsecond, and then he drove the gas pedal to the floor and the Boss 429 engine hurled the Mustang at the crowd of living and dead.

By the time he hit the wall of them he was going fifty miles an hour.

Dustin felt himself rising from the seat. He felt the steering wheel hit him in the chest. Saw the windshield coming at him so fast.

So fast.

The fires and explosions, the rockets and bullets, the teeth and hands of the dead—none of that did any harm to Dustin Lee Frye.

In the end, it was the car that killed him.

SOUTH OF THE BORDENTOWN STARBUCKS

Major General Simeon Zetter got slowly out of his command vehicle and watched hell unfold. He and his aides were in the safe zone, outside of the blast area, well beyond the perimeter of violence that the satellites and surveillance helicopters determined enclosed all of the infection.

No one spoke.

No words really fit the moment.

During the drive here from the school, Zetter was absorbing the intel from FEMA, from the White House, and from other sources. Initial estimates of potential civilian casualties were staggering. Four thousand minimum.

Minimum.

More than that were expected.

More than that were likely, perhaps inevitable.

The fireballs from the fuel-air bombs rose like the pillars of hell, seeming to push back the storm. The heat was so intense that it turned the rain to steam.

Behind where he stood, the Black Hawks and Apaches were touching down in the parking lot of an abandoned drive-in movie theater. It had been dangerous bordering on foolhardy to have them in the air at all with a storm of this kind, and they'd lost one crew to a crash. Something he had not yet reported to the president. Now, with these bombs, there would be shockwaves that would endanger all the others.

He heard one of his aides say something to himself, and for a moment Zetter thought it was a prayer. It wasn't. It was the thing that Oppenheimer had said when the first atom bomb was tested.

"I am become Shiva, destroyer of worlds."

And while fuel-air bombs were non-nuclear, the point was eloquent. Zetter felt like striking the man, but hitting someone for speaking the truth was not the way to survive this moment.

In silence, he endured the rebuke implicit in that statement.

Destroyer of worlds.

Destroyer of lives.

So many people.

The outer edge of the heat wave rolled through the night toward them. It had been greatly weakened by distance and did little more than brush past his face and fill his mouth with a bitter taste. Zetter turned and discretely spat into the mud. Some of the others did, too. A few still wore their hazmat masks.

The heat blew past them and for a moment there was a deceptive stillness, a calm that told lies about the night. Then the rains began to fall again, and the storm winds blew, and the sounds of screams echoed through the night. Car horns blared, faint and muted.

"Sir," said another aide, hurrying toward him from the communication truck, "you need to see this."

His voice held a rising note of panic that made Zetter spin around and go running after him, with his other aides in tow. As he ran

Zetter turned and spat again, trying to clear his mouth of the acrid, itchy dust from the shock wave.

He felt sick to his stomach, but he decided that it was the shock, the stress, the horror of it all.

In that, General Zetter was entirely wrong.

ACROSS THE FAYETTE COUNTY LINE, PENNSYLVANIA

They moved across the quarantine zone alone and in packs. In the ragged, bloody, and fire-blackened clothes of farmers and tourists, travelers and news reporters. A few wore National Guard BDUs. They moved together, weeping, crying out in unending pain from bites that had torn through skin and muscle, or from blistered burns that bubbled on skin that had been touched by the hellish heat.

They staggered away from the flaming pit where the Starbucks had been, and away from the blackened shells of their cars. They left behind friends and family members.

Those that could run, did.

The rest limped and shambled and crawled.

Away from the bombs and the bullets and the things that bit.

None of them had a plan, or a direction. They simply fled.

And the dead followed after.

CHAPTER SEVENTY-TWO
STEBBINS LITTLE SCHOOL
STEBBINS, PENNSYLVANIA

Trout and Dez sat in the principal's office. Mrs. Madison had found a blanket and wrapped it around Dez's shoulders, but rainwater dripped from her clothes and pooled on the floor beneath her chair. Trout pulled his chair close and sat with his hand on her knee. He thought she'd object to that, but after a while she squeezed his hand.

Mrs. Madison sat across from her. Uriah Piper and Jenny De-Groot were in the office as well. No one else.

"It was Gerry Dunphries," said Jenny.

Dez looked at her. "What?"

"He was supposed to be helping in the kitchen, cutting open cereal boxes, but when I looked up he was gone. I figured he went to the bathroom, or . . ."

"Or what?" asked Trout.

"Or needed to find a quiet place to cry."

Everyone tried not to look at Dez, but one by one they did, and it made Trout winced.

Mrs. Madison tried to console her, "Please don't think you're in any responsible for what Mr. Dunphries did. He was deeply distraught by everything that's happened and—"

"Fuck him," Dez said quietly.

Mrs. Madison blinked. "Pardon?"

"Fuck Gerry Dunphries and fuck his being 'distraught.'"

"That's—"

"And fuck you for whatever you're about to say," she said. "I don't want to hear it. I don't want to hear any bullshit from anyone. Dunphries opened that window and he got three kids killed. End of story and may he burn in hell."

"That's hardly fair," said Piper.

"It's unrealistic," agreed Mrs. Madison. "Shock can induce many different degrees of psychosis."

"Since when are you a psychologist?" sneered Dez.

"Since I got my MA in psychotherapy and child counseling before you were born."

"Yeah? Well fuck your MA, too."

Mrs. Madison recoiled and her throat flushed pink.

"Dez," Trout said gently, "let's dial it down and—"

"Oh, and most of all fuck you, Billy Trout." She slapped his hand off her knees. "Okay, so Gerry Dunphries was batshit. Lot of that going around. Our town is overrun by zombies and we've just been abandoned by the military. Batshit seems to be the only flavor we have left, so we all better get used to sucking on it. You want to know how batshit crazy *I* am? When I was out there surrounded by all those frigging dead sonsabitches with no ammunition—you know who helped me? You want to know who talked me through it? You know who saved my life? JT motherfucking Hammond. Yeah, my dead partner. My best friend. The man who helped save all of your lives. He had my back and told me what to do and how to get through it just like he always did. How's that for batshit?"

The room was utterly silent.

Dez leaned forward and fixed Mrs. Madison with a steely stare. "You want to know the kicker to that? Even now, even knowing that I'm crazy my ownself, even right here in your office, I can still hear JT's voice. Telling me to stop yelling, telling me to watch my language, telling me to take it out of overdrive. Yeah, I can hear that clear as day."

"Dez . . ." began Trout, but she ignored him.

Dez sat back. "We're all crazy. Fine. If it's the way things are then it's the way things are. I'll be happy to talk to the rest of the adults and explain the facts of life to them. If any of them are too fucked up in the head to be part of how we're going to survive, they have my permission to hang themselves or give themselves a sponge-bath with steak sauce and go outside. But they don't take any of the kids with them, they don't let the kids see it, and they don't let those fucking zombies in here. And if *anyone* does *anything* to endanger the other kids, I will personally shove a gun up their ass and pull the trigger. That is not—I repeat *not*—a joke. Am I making myself crystal fucking clear here or do I need to start kicking some basic survival sense into everyone in this frigging school?"

The silence following her words was heavy and long. Trout looked at the faces of the others, tried to read their eyes and predict what they'd say.

It was Uriah Piper who spoke first. "I won't shoot anyone for being crazy or stupid," he said. "But if you need to do that I'll load your guns for you."

Mrs. Madison gave a slow, grudging nod.

A strange smile formed on Jenny DeGroot's young face. "I'm absolutely with you, Dez."

Dez and everyone else turned to Trout. He cocked an eyebrow, "Honey, if you even need to ask then you really are batshit."

The harsh mask of anger and hurt on Dez's face softened. "Thanks, Billy . . . but if you ever call me honey again I'll kneecap you."

"I'll take my chances."

Piper cleared his throat. "I hate to interrupt a tender moment here . . ."

"Fuck you," Dez and Trout said at the same time.

". . . but I need to get back to securing the building. Looks pretty clear that there are more of those things out there and for whatever reason they seem to be coming here."

Dez started to nod, then abruptly held up a hand. "Wait."

"Wait . . . no . . ."

"What?" asked Trout.

"When I was outside," she began slowly. "The buses . . ."

"What about them?"

She began shaking her head. "We're thinking about this the wrong damn way. Jesus, how could I have been so dumb?"

She stood up, dropping the blanket to the floor and walking to the door. She opened it and looked out through the suite of offices toward the main part of the school. Her gaze roved over everything including the walls and the ceiling. Then she turned and leaned against the frame and shook her head again.

"When this thing started I came here because I knew this was where they were going to take the kids. Town shelter and all that. Okay, fine, it's strong and defensible and we have some supplies. Then we were locked in here by the National Guard. This became our place, you see what I'm saying?"

No one did.

"We thought we were going to ride it out in here. The Guard would airdrop food and supplies and the geniuses at the CDC would cook up a cure or vaccine or something. Then the frigging Guard lit out of here like their asses were on fire. It wasn't an orderly retreat and it wasn't the kind of wrap-up you have after a field deployment has completed its job. No, the way they went tear-assing their way out of here means they were going to a fight, and it was a bigger fight then they anticipated. Armies plan and move with some kind of order. They only bolt and run when the shit has seriously hit the fan. Then there was that explosion. Or maybe it was a series of them. Big fucking airbursts. Not nuclear because we'd all be dying right now if they'd dropped a nuke on Stebbins or Bordentown. No, I think they found a big fucking nest of these things and they tried to sterilize them with fuel-air bombs."

"What are they?" asked Jenny.

"Thermobaric cluster bombs. It's the biggest and most powerful non-nuclear device we have."

"Dear God," murmured Mrs. Madison.

"I see where you're going with this," said Trout. "Can't say I like it."

"I *don't* see," said Jenny.

"Last resort," said Piper, and both Trout and Dez nodded. The farmer explained, "A bomb like that wouldn't be something they'd use if they could contain this with regular tanks and helicopters and such. Scorched earth is what you go for when you're losing a fight."

"Exactly," said Dez.

"I'm still not following," said Jenny. "Does that mean they wiped them out?"

Trout fielded that. "You didn't see the infected who were outside. They were all burned. The bomb may have killed some of them, but it didn't kill all of them. Any of them who weren't in the direct blast zone, any of them who were only burned, are still out there. And after what just happened, I think it's pretty clear they're coming here."

"Here? But *why*? I mean, wasn't this just random? Weren't these infected just whichever ones were in the area?"

"No," said Dez, "they were too badly burned. They're coming here from closer to wherever ground zero was."

"The blast was north and west," said Trout. "Over by Bordentown or near there." He paused. "Which is where the quarantine zone line is."

And where Goat was, he thought, but he didn't say it.

"Okay," said Jenny, "but again—why here? Why the school?"

"Yes," said Mrs. Madison, "surely you're not saying they can smell the children here."

"With the rain?" mused Piper. "Probably not."

"Then why?"

Trout glanced at Dez. "I've wondered this before. I know the infected are supposed to be, for all intents and purposes, brainless. Brain dead. But could there be some trace left? Maybe something the parasite drive can tap into? Genetic memory? There's a precedent in science."

Dez turned haunted eyes away from him. "I don't care what's driving them. I don't care if they are coming here because they remember the school or because they think it's prom night. Fuck it. The point is that they are coming here and if we stay here, then this place is going to stop being a refuge and start being an all you can eat buffet."

She turned back to them and now her eyes were cold and dangerous.

"And I will not let that happen."

Trout said, "What do you have in mind?"

CHAPTER SEVENTY-THREE
THE SITUATION ROOM
THE WHITE HOUSE, WASHINGTON, D.C.

"Talk to me," croaked the president in a voice grown hoarse with yelling and pleading. "Where are we with containment?"

Every eye turned away from him and focused on the big screen and its many smaller windows. The satellite thermal scan still showed hundreds of dots moving in all directions. Smaller windows were ground-level views from military vehicles and some field-troop helmet cams as they engaged the infected. The sounds of gunfire, even muted to a whisper, were dreadful. And there was so much screaming. From the infected who had not yet died, from possibly uninfected civilians running from the blasts and from the dead, and from the soldiers.

"Sir," said General Burroughs, "General Zetter is requesting orders on what to do with uninfected survivors."

Sylvia Ruddy said, "How can we tell if they're uninfected? Do we have a way to triage this?"

"Scott?" asked the president.

Blair felt like he was a passenger on a sinking ship. Like he was the only man to have seen the iceberg but no one had paid attention to his shouts of warning. Now the president wanted answers from him. Solutions.

"Sir," he said slowly, "we do not have the protocols or resources to triage anyone. We don't have the manpower on the ground to detain and monitor large numbers of civilians."

"What are you saying?" demanded the president.

"What I'm saying, sir, is that we cannot afford the luxury of treating anyone as potentially uninfected. We have to respond as if every person coming across those fields is a carrier. Every single one."

The president got to his feet and towered over Blair. "Are you *insane?*"

"No, sir. You asked for my recommendation. That is the only possible course of action."

"I refuse to accept that, goddamn it."

Blair rose as well. "Refusing to accept the truth about Lucifer 113 is what brought us to this point, Mr. President. We have acted timidly and slowly from the beginning and we are fighting an uphill battle."

"Those are survivors?"

Blair pointed a finger at the screen. "*They're already dead!*"

"No," said the president with a stubborn shake of his head. "Simeon Zetter will contain this."

Blair gaped at him, simply unable to speak.

On the screen, with every second that passed, the images told a story that anyone with eyes could understand, but everyone with hearts refused to accept.

Except for Blair.

CHAPTER SEVENTY-FOUR
STEBBINS LITTLE SCHOOL
STEBBINS, PENNSYLVANIA

Dez and Trout called a meeting of as many of the adults as could be spared from guard duty and childcare. Trout suggested that everyone meet them downstairs in the gymnasium.

"Why here?" asked Dez as she and Trout went down to wait for them to gather. "People died down there today."

"Right," he told her. "Where better to make your point about how safe the school *isn't*?"

"You want me to play these people?"

"Of course I do, Dez. Play them and then lead them, because you are the best chance we all have of getting out of here."

Dez studied him for a moment, then gave him a small, wicked smile. "If we ever get ourselves out of this thing, Billy, I'm going to bang your eyes crooked."

"You've done that more than once."

"I ain't saying we're getting back together, but . . . yeah, I think a littler recreational yee-haw might take some of the edge off."

"That's all it'll be?" he said, arching an eyebrow. "Something to settle the nerves?"

"You have a problem with that?"

"Not even a little one."

Dez bent and gave him a quick, wet, delicious kiss. But instead of the quick catch-and-release he expected, she took his face in both hands and looked deeply into his eyes. Her smile faded away completely.

"I—wasn't screwing around back there."

"When?"

"When I said I heard JT talking to me."

He smiled. "Wait . . . you're telling me you're crazy? You? Dez Fox? You shock me, woman. Shock me, I say."

"Fuck you."

"I believe that is what we've been discussing."

She kissed him again.

When she was done he did not feel a single one of his injuries. He was gasping for air when she pushed him back. He was also hard as a rock and he believed that there was never a less sensible or convenient time for an erection in the entire history of sexual congress.

Dez, quick as always, saw the bulge and her smile came right back.

Before she could hit him with a joke, he said, "No, it's not a gun in my pocket. I'm just very damn glad to be here with you."

She reached down and cupped his hardness through the stained cloth of his jeans.

"Careful now," she said, "or you'll make a girl blush."

She gave him a squeeze, then released him and turned quickly away as the gymnasium door opened and people began filing in.

Billy Trout genuinely hoped he had enough time either for a cold shower or to spend five useful minutes banging his head on a brick wall.

CHAPTER SEVENTY-FIVE
ON THE ROAD
PITTSBURGH SUBURBS

"Why are we going to Pittsburgh?" asked Goat, though he thought he knew the answer.

Homer shot him a sly look. "See a few old friends."

Goat knew that he should just keep his mouth shut, but despite all of his fear, the pain in his body, and the absolute strangeness of this experience, there was a part of him that was a still a newsman. Or maybe it was the other aspect, a somewhat older and more precisely defining aspect of who he was—the filmmaker. This was all good drama. It would be great cinema. Cinema verité in real point of fact, because this was the truth. This was real.

It only felt like a nightmare.

He said, "You're going to find your foster parents, aren't you?"

It was the first time Goat saw Homer lose control. It was brief, but it was there. The car swayed and for a moment the look of Homer's face wasn't that of a killer or a monster; it was the lost and desperate look of a child.

Goat knew the story. He'd been in the courtroom during testimony by prison psychiatrists and social workers. After Gibbon's heroin-addicted mother had given him up for adoption, Homer went through one foster home after another. In a couple of them the child had endured horrific sexual and physical abuse. One of those former foster parents was later arrested in connection with the abuse of another child, and investigators found hundreds of photos stored on the man's computer. Photos of him and various girlfriends and drinking buddies, doing things to children—boys and girls ranging in age from five to twelve—that sickened everyone in the courtroom. Billy Trout had gone outside and thrown up in a trash can. Goat tried to look at the poster-board-sized reproductions of those photos as clinically as he could, pretending in his mind that these were movie props; but the bitter and raw truth of them gouged marks on his soul.

The photos were presented as part of Homer's defense, claiming that any crimes he'd committed were direct results of permanent emotional and psychological disfigurement inflicted upon him as a child. Disfigurement. That was the word one psychologist used and it stuck for the duration of the trial, becoming a catchphrase. It was a word Goat had never before heard used in that context, and he could not shake the ugly awareness of all it implied.

The defense was thorough and exhaustive in an attempt to cultivate sympathy through horror, but rather than any sympathetic reaction the effect was to emotionally numb the jury. They disengaged from the evidence, and Goat watched that happen. It's how he would have filmed the scene. As far as he saw it, the defense lost the case more than the prosecution won it, and it did so by an overuse of the most compelling argument.

The expression that flitted across Homer's face now was tied to those memories, and Goat was absolutely sure that in that moment, Homer felt rude hands on him and cringed at the thought of how, once again, his body and his world would be plundered.

When Homer spoke, his voice was quiet, filled with a false calm that was as fragile as spun glass. "There's a couple of people I wouldn't mind saying hello to. People I never got around to thanking."

"Thanking?"

Homer turned to him and the smile that formed on his lips was inhuman, repulsive. Vile.

"For opening the Black Eye and teaching me how to speak with the Red Mouth."

Goat didn't dare reply to that.

Homer gestured to Goat's equipment. "Shouldn't you be taping this shit?"

"Yes," said Goat quickly, realizing that this was gold and that it was his lifeline. He unzipped his bag, removed the camera, plugged it into his laptop and adjusted the settings. He turned the dome light on because otherwise it was far too dark, but the yellow light chased only some of the shadows away. There still seemed to be too many bits of darkness hiding in the cab, waiting to pounce.

Goat found some small steadying comfort in the process of handling the tools of his trade. It returned to him a measure of personal power.

"Okay, we're good to go."

"What do you want me to do?"

"I'll do a quick introduction and then you could just talk," suggested Goat. "Tell your side of it."

"My 'side'?"

"Tell the truth as you see it. Or would you rather I ask questions?"

"I don't know. Set it up and let's see what happens. But don't say where we are, okay?"

"No problem."

He hit Record, then turned the camera on himself, gave his name and his affiliation with Regional Satellite News. Then he pointed the camera at Homer and introduced him. Homer gave the camera a few glances that were almost shy.

People and cameras, thought Goat. *Weird.*

As Goat checked the feed on his laptop, he loaded Foursquare and tried to connect the locator app to a GPS app, but there was no Wi-Fi signal.

"You want this on the Net, right?" he asked.

"Yeah."

"Okay, then once we tape some stuff, we have to get to someplace where I can pick up a signal. Anyplace with free Wi-Fi."

Homer thought about that then nodded. "Sure."

"Are you ready?" asked Goat. Part of his mind seemed to stand at a distance and watch all of this with slack-jawed amazement. They were both flash-burned, filthy, bloody, and on the run from murders and some kind of catastrophic military action, and here he was talking to a Homer like they were ready to talk about the Daffodil Festival or a Little League game. It worried Goat that he could sound so normal, *act* so normal, when normal was something as dead as yesterday's news.

He heard his voice speak with every appearance of calm control as set up the video. "We're on the road—I can't say where. Stebbins County has been—or is in the process of being—destroyed. You've heard some of the field reports by Billy Trout about what happened. All of it is real. However I have a different part of the story to share and it's one everyone is going to want to hear. This is a side of the story that will help everyone understand the man who stands at the center of this storm. A man most people in the world believe was executed two days ago at Rockview Prison here in Pennsylvania. A man who is now beyond death as anyone knows it—and that statement is neither an exaggeration nor a joke. The next voice you'll hear, the next face you'll see, is that of Homer Gibbon."

He turned the camera and switched on the top-mounted light for extra effect. He wanted the image to transform from the murky yellow shadows to something brighter and harsher, something that would show the bright red blood. In the stark light Homer was every bit the true monster. All sharp angles and brutality, but with a bestial intelligence glittering in his dark eyes.

Homer did not speak immediately, and his lack of certainty and clear discomfort kept the dead silence from being empty. This was great theater, thought Goat. This was fucking great.

After a few thoughtful seconds, Homer said, "Everyone thinks I'm a monster."

"What do you think?" asked Goat.

Nearly a mile passed before Homer answered. "Maybe they're right. Maybe that's what I am now. A monster. I guess now more than ever."

Homer shook his head and Goat wondered if there was a flicker of regret in the killer's voice, or was he filtering this through his filmmaker's ear.

"People use that word," Homer went on. "Monster. They like to throw words like that around the way a monkey tosses his shit, hoping it'll stick to the walls. They don't understand anything about what goes on in a person's head, just like they don't understand what it means to be something different. Something bigger." He laughed. "It's like witches."

"I'm sorry . . . witches?"

"Sure. In prison you got nothing to do but read books, and I read this one book, *Witch Hunts: A History of the Burning Times*—it had a lot of pictures in it, like a comic book but it's not superhero stuff. This was about real stuff that happened. What do you call a book like that?"

"A graphic novel?"

"Yeah, that was it. This one was about the history of witches and the things people used to do to them because everyone had some stupid idea that witches were giving blow jobs to the Devil or some shit. Goofy stuff like that. What it really was, was that people—men, mostly—were afraid of the witches because of what the witches knew. And what they called witches were just women who knew some important shit. Medicine and like that. Natural healing and all that sort of thing. Herbs and liniments and potions. There wasn't anything with the Devil. It wasn't about that. You know why those men killed those women?"

"Tell me," said Goat.

"It was because those women knew something the men didn't. They had secret knowledge, and that knowledge didn't *come* from the men. The men didn't own it and they couldn't control it. Those women were out there using this secret knowledge and they didn't need jack squat from the men, and that really scared the men. You only got power if someone needs something from you and you have a leash on it. You understand?"

"Yes, I do."

"Those men . . . they knew that the women weren't fucking around with the Devil or any of that shit. That's not why they got mad. They got mad because the secrets the women had were starting to matter to the people. The common folk. Those men saw their stranglehold over everyone starting to slip, and that meant they'd lose money and they'd lose power. And they couldn't have that. So they said that those women, those witches, were monsters. And since most people are just dumb fucks, they went along with it and soon they were burning chicks at the stake and drowning them and crushing them under rocks. That's how the men kept their power. It's how scared people always keep their power. That's why they killed Jesus. That's why they killed that little Indian guy, Gandhi." He pronounced it Gan-dee. "It's probably why they killed John Lennon, too, 'cause that sonofabitch definitely knew some of the real secrets." Homer nodded to himself. "He sings to me in my head sometimes, did you know that?"

"No. What does he sing?"

"I don't know the names of the songs. New stuff that he wrote after he died."

"Oh," said Goat, and felt vaguely disappointed. He couldn't quite understand why.

"My point," continued Homer, "is that people throw out the word 'monster' before they know what something is. And it's stupid, it's an insult, because that word is so . . . so small, and sometimes what they're trying to describe is way bigger than they know, bigger than they can even imagine."

"And you feel that the way in which they used it to describe you is the same kind of error? The same kind of small thinking? That it's them being—what? Blind or simply unable to understand what they are seeing?"

Homer took a long time with that, and as he drove he kept looking at Goat, as if reappraising him. He nodded a few times to himself.

"Now I'm wondering," he said slowly, "whether you're one of those smart-ass fellows who know how to feed someone enough of a line of bullshit so he can save his own ass."

Goat said nothing.

"Or if maybe you're starting to see what the Black Eye wants you to see. And maybe hear what the Red Mouth is whispering. Tell me, son . . . which is it?"

There was no way to know how to respond, because Goat could imagine how either response might spark something nasty. If he admitted that he was stringing Homer along, then the killer might simply pull over and finish what he almost started back at Starbucks. On the other hand, if Goat came off like a willing convert, would there be a price to pay to join Homer's church?

In the end he told Homer a version of the truth. And he meant every word.

"I don't know what to believe," he admitted, "but I'm sitting here with you and that means I am twenty inches away from the biggest and most important story any reporter has ever heard. This is the kind of story that will change the world. You know that already, Homer. I know it, too. Who knows, maybe I really will start hearing what the Red Mouth says. I probably will, because I think I'm starting to get you, to see things the way you see them. However, right now, at this moment, I'm trying to understand the whole story. That's what I want from you, Homer. I want you to tell me everything so I can report the biggest story in history. That's the truth, Homer. That's the God's honest truth."

It was five whole miles before Homer spoke.

Up ahead, barely visible in the rain, was a 7-Eleven with its lights on. Homer drummed his fingers on the knobbed leather of the steering wheel.

"You want to understand me, son? Fine, that makes sense to me. You saw some of my truth back there at the Starbucks. Now bear witness to more of it."

"What do you mean?"

"I mean that the Red Mouth is hungry and it will not be denied." Homer pulled the Escalade off the road and slid into a slot. There were two cars outside. One was a beat-up old Chevy, the other was a Lexus SUV.

"What? I mean . . . Jesus, are you . . . are you . . . ?"

Homer laughed.

"Yeah," he said, "that's exactly what I'm gonna do. How's *that* for a big news story?"

He got out and took the keys with him, then leaned in through the open door.

"Make sure you film it, too. Every damn bit of it."

Homer slammed the door and headed toward the store.

Goat did not try to run. He never even opened the door. Instead he raised the camera, adjusted the zoom, rolled down the window, and filmed everything as Homer Gibbon opened the front door of the convenience store, strode in, and showed everyone what the Black Eye saw, and let them hear the secrets whispered by the Red Mouth.

CHAPTER SEVENTY-SIX
STEBBINS LITTLE SCHOOL
STEBBINS, PENNSYLVANIA

Dez laid it out for them. The military's withdrawal, the fuel-air bombs, the burned dead, and the vulnerability of the school.

"If we stay, we risk a siege," she concluded. "God only knows how many of these things there are, and I sure as shit don't want to find out. We need to get out now while we still have a chance."

"How do you propose to do it?" asked Piper, following a cue Trout had given him.

Dez pointed over their heads. "Buses. There are more than enough school buses to get us all out of here. We need to clear out any bodies, hose the insides down to prevent infection, and then load the kids and as many supplies as we can take."

"And go where?" asked one of the parents.

"Pittsburgh," said Dez. "Or Philadelphia. Any of the big cities. Anywhere we can get the right kind of help and protection."

"But those *things* are out there," said Clark.

"Sure. Some of them. At last check there were eighteen that we could see. We have enough weapons to take them out."

The crowd murmured at that. Taking them out sounded easy when stated in flat and antiseptic words, but every one of the people outside was a neighbor. Or a relative.

"We can't just . . . kill them," said a thin woman with watery eyes.

Dez walked over and put her hand on the woman's shoulder. "Dottie . . . those people are already dead. You know that. We all know that. The kids in here are alive. *We're* alive, and if we want to stay that way then we have to square this all in our heads. This isn't a bunch of people with the flu. They're dead. They're infected by something that makes them move, but they're dead." She paused. "Besides, considering what's happened to them, putting them down would be a mercy."

"Amen," said Uriah Piper.

A few of the others murmured agreement. Dez patted Dottie and then turned to the rest of the crowd. She explained what she wanted done and separated people into teams. Not everyone liked the idea. The strongest objections came from Clark, the teacher who'd mouthed off earlier. He wanted them all to stay right there in the school. His logic was that if there was a problem like flooded roads or military roadblocks, some might get out rather than all being stopped.

"No," said Dez firmly, "we all go together."

"And what if we don't want to go anywhere?" demanded Clark.

"*You* can stay, Clark," said Dez, leaning on that word. "Doesn't matter to me. But the kids are coming with me and I need enough adults to drive buses and handle guns."

Most of the crowd looked uncertain, but there were murmurs and nods, a few clear votes of support. However, Clark stood his ground.

"Who are you, of all people, to say what happens with the kids?"

She got up in his face. "What's that supposed to mean?"

Clark stood his ground. "Let's face it, *Officer* Fox, you're not ex- actly a role model. How many times have I seen you staggering drunk, coming out of one shithole bar or another? How many times have you been reprimanded for excessive force? Yeah, I know about that stuff. My sister, Bitsy, was on the town council. I know all about you. You're a loudmouth and—what do they call it in the movies? A loose cannon? That's it. Exactly why is it we're supposed to listen to you or follow your orders?"

Trout saw the dangerous red climb up Dez's throat and bloom on her cheeks.

"That's enough, Clark," he said.

Clark wheeled on him. "Oh, right, and we should listen to you, too. Mr. Live From the Apocalypse. Mr. Give Me a Pulitzer Because I Have Innocent Blood on my Polo Shirt. Fuck you. You turned this whole thing into a story because like all reporters if it bleeds it leads, right? I'll bet that when all those bullets were flying and the kids were screaming, you probably had a hard-on just thinking about how big a story this was. Well excuse me all to hell, Billy, but I don't think you have a real stake in this. You don't have any kids here. We do. Or we're charged with taking care of these kids. They're only a story to you. Besides, everyone in town knows that you're been banging Dez Fox since high school, so this is the two of you in cahoots."

Billy Trout snarled like a dog and swung a skull-cracker of a punch at the point of Clark's jaw.

Clark leaned back with the ease of a trained boxer and let the punch pass, then he hooked Trout in the gut with a fist that he buried deep in belly flesh above Trout's belt buckle. Clark pivoted and clopped Trout behind the ear with a right that put him flat on the floor. Trout was so shocked and hurt that he couldn't even break his fall. He fell flat on his chest. And threw up.

There was a click and a blur of movement and then Clark was against the wall with Dez's pistol barrel screwed into the soft pallet under his chin.

"You miserable cocksucker," she hissed, "I'm going to blow your shit all over the—"

"No."

The word was snapped out, sharp and full of cold command.

Then Uriah Piper moved into Dez's peripheral vision. His face was hard as stone. "Put the gun down," he said.

Dez and he locked eyes.

"Now," said Piper.

On the floor, Trout make a sound like a strangling cat.

With great reluctance Dez stepped back and lowered her gun.

"Put it away," suggested Piper. She did. "Now see to your friend there. He doesn't look good."

She slammed her Glock into its holster. Clark, who despite having had a gun pointed at him, managed to sneer with open contempt. Dez sank to her knees and pulled Billy's head onto her lap. His face was the color of an overripe eggplant and he was only able to breathe in small gasps. He made little *yeep* sounds. Dez wiped the vomit from his face and held him. Her eyes never left Clark, and she hoped he could read his future in those eyes.

Uriah Piper, his voice and manner calm, stepped between Dez and Clark as if wanting to break that line of communication. But the action forced Clark to shift his attention to the laconic farmer.

"You handle yourself pretty well, Clark. You box?"

"Sure, so what?"

"So did I," said Piper, and without warning he hit Clark with a short jab that exploded his nose and a right cross that put him on the floor right next to Billy Trout. Both punches were so hard and so fast that they looked and sounded like a single blow.

Everyone stared in sudden, intense shock.

Clark lay there, nose and mouth streaming with bright blood.

Dez Fox gaped. Even Trout focused his bulging eyes on the quiet farmer.

Piper looked at his knuckles, spit on them, rubbed the spit into the calluses, sighed and then seemed to slowly become aware of the crowd. He said nothing to them, but he squatted down next to Clark.

"Here's the thing, my friend," he said mildly. "Some people never want to be part of the solution. All they want to do is bitch and whine and create complications for other people. You've been like that as long as I've known you, and that's going on twenty years. Since, what? Little League? I don't remember you ever once stepping up and helping without running your mouth. Mostly that's okay, that's people being people, and it didn't matter much to anyone. Now it does matter. Now we got to work together or we all get hurt or get killed. Now . . . I'm no fan of Officer Fox and I barely known Mr. Trout outside of what he writes in the papers, so this isn't me sticking up for my friends. This is me, a farmer and a part of this community saying that if you don't shut your mouth and work *with* us, then by the Lord Jesus, when we roll out of here in those buses I will personally tie you to the front grill, cover you with A1 sauce, and use you for bait. Look me in the eye and ask me if I'm joking."

No one said a word. Certainly not Clark, who stared at him with eyes that were filled with fear and strange lights.

Piper dug a clean tissue out of his pocket and held it out. When Clark made no move to take it, the farmer bent and placed it on his chest, patted it flat, then straightened. He turned and looked down at Dez and Trout.

"My guess is that we don't have a whole lot of time," he said. "Probably be best if we got our behinds into gear."

CHAPTER SEVENTY-SEVEN

The Situation Room was crammed with too many people and everyone was shouting. At each other, into phones; some, apparently, at God.

All National Guardsmen in the area had been deployed. Additional troops from joint-use bases were rolling, and the ban on interaction with state and local law enforcement had been lifted. In each of his many phone calls, General Burroughs used the phrase. "This is all boots on the ground."

The Air Force was actively in play now, as were fighters and helicopters from the Marines and Navy.

Scott Blair took or made more calls than he could count. FEMA and all other disaster-response groups were being pressed to their limits. Teams from the CDC were on the ground, but they were being shunted to the side because there was nothing for them to do. Plenty of samples of living and terminated infected had been collected. They had gallons of the black blood, and more samples were being flown to labs all over the country. Everyone with a microscope was studying Lucifer 113. Nobody had an answer.

Then Blair's phone rang and the display told him that it was Sam Imura. Blair snatched it up and cupped his other hand over his ear so he could hear. "Tell me some good goddamn news, Sam. Tell me you have the flash drives in your hand. Tell me what I need to hear."

Sam didn't. Instead he told the truth.

CHAPTER SEVENTY-EIGHT
STEBBINS LITTLE SCHOOL
STEBBINS, PENNSYLVANIA

Billy Trout felt like death.

Since yesterday he had been slapped, punched, shoved, shot at, attacked by zombies, nearly gunned down by helicopters, pulled his back out, and punched some more. There was no part of his body that did not hurt. His stomach felt like it was filled with broken glass and he had a persistent ringing in his ear. Nausea eddied in his gut and his eyes had trouble focusing. He felt ninety years old as he limped slowly after Dez as she trotted down the hall toward the rear exit.

Finally he had to stop and lean against the wall, gulping in ragged lungfuls of air.

When Dez realized he wasn't following her, she stopped and turned. "What are you doing?"

"Watching all the pretty fireflies," he croaked.

He expected a sharp comeback, but instead she came back to where he stood, an expression of concern clouding her pretty face. She smoothed the lank blond hair out of his eyes and placed her palm on his cheek. An act of tenderness that was an echo of a Dez Fox that Trout used to know.

"I should have cut his balls off and fed them to him," she said.

Trout managed a weak grin. "I'd have enjoyed that."

She grunted and smiled. "Piper rang his chimes pretty well, though. Who'da thought?"

"Wish I'd seen it."

"It was sweet."

"Sure."

Trout straightened slowly and then hissed sharply, collapsing back against the wall.

"Jesus Christ, Billy, how fucked up are you?"

"Oh . . . I've had worse."

"No you haven't, you asshole."

"No, I haven't," he agreed weakly. "It's the sort of thing people say."

"Is it bad?"

"It's not terrific," he admitted through clenched teeth.

She shook her head. "We need to get you to a hospital."

He slowly straightened again, face set against pain spikes. He made it to a relatively upright position. "On the list of immediate priorities, Dez, that's right near the bottom."

Dez didn't argue.

"Come on," he said, "we have work to—"

"Officer Fox!" a voice called sharply, and they both looked toward the stairwell as Jenny DeGroot came bursting out. "Something's happening outside."

"We already know about the soldiers leaving—"

"No," said Jenny breathlessly, "it's something else. You'd better come look."

Dez cut a look at Trout, but he waved her away. "Go, I'll catch up."

Dez followed Jenny into the stairwell and Trout could hear their footfalls as they raced up to the second floor. The thought of climbing stairs was intimidating, but Trout forced himself to stagger into the fire tower and climb the stone steps, one at a time. It felt like to took a hundred years and the version of Trout that emerged from the tower was hobbled and hunched and gasping for breath.

Dez Fox nearly ran him down as she tore back toward the stairs.

"What?" he gasped as he flung himself out of her way.

"The soldiers," she said. "They're back."

She took off running with Jenny and a few of the others at her heels.

Trout didn't immediate follow. He couldn't face the steps, not yet. Instead he limped over to one of the classrooms, went inside and peered out the window. Down in the lot a pair of soldiers was walking purposefully toward the school. They wore dark hazmat suits and had guns in their hands. They stopped at the corner of the building and one of them raised a walkie-talkie and spoke into it for a moment, listened, then lowered the device. Then, weapons raised and ready, they began walking slowly along the east side of the building.

Were they walking the perimeter or looking for a way in?

A sudden and alarming thought jolted Trout. Where exactly was Dez hurrying to? He thought he knew the answer and it scared him to death. He set his teeth against the pain and hobbled toward the stairs as fast as he could.

CHAPTER SEVENTY-NINE
THE NORTHERN LEVEE
FAYETTE COUNTY

On the other side of the county from his niece, Jake DeGroot wondered if he was dead.

Everyone else seemed to be.

Jake was a construction worker from Bordentown who volunteered to work all night in Stebbins, and he and his crew had been at it for nearly twenty-four hours.

Until everything went crazy in Stebbins, just over the county line.

Now he lay in a shallow pit, half-drowned, shivering, and terrified; hidden from view beneath the lowered bucket of a yellow front-end loader. His machine, the one he drove every day. Big Bird.

Rain hammered down on the machine. The bucket was half-filled with dirt from the trench in which he lay, and water filled the rest of the steel cup. It spilled over and ran down the sides, dripping onto him, touching him with cold fingertips. Rainwater had filled the pit nearly to the top and the cold was like a thousand knives stabbing over and over again into his flesh. He could barely feel his feet and his fingers felt like they were each being crushed in a vise. Cold was a beast that crouched over him, wrapped around him, bit like a vampire into him and sucked away his warmth.

Jake was afraid to crawl out of the dirty pit of cold water.

He had no idea what time it was. His cell phone was in his pocket and his pocket was under water. The only other clocks were the one in the office—a small travel-trailer parked at the edge of the construction site that might as well have been on the dark side of the moon—and the steel diver's watch strapped to the forearm of Burl Hansard, the shift foreman.

Burl lay thirty feet away.

What was left of him.

His body was mostly hidden by mud and the front wheel of Burl's Expedition. All Jake could see was half of Burl's face, his shoulder, and his right arm.

Or rather what was left of the supervisor's right arm.

Two fingers and a thumb. Some meat on the wrist, part of the upper arm.

Tendons and bone. Visible now that the rain had washed away the blood.

That was it.

And the face.

He had no face at all. All Jake could see were the ends of broken bones and lumps of meat he could not and would not try to identify.

Jake lay there, shivering, staring at his dead friend.

Two hours ago that ruined face had worn a smile. Two hours ago a soggy cigar had been clamped between strong white teeth, and a grin curled the lips. Burl had been that kind of a guy. You couldn't depress the sonofabitch. No matter how bad things were, he could find something to crack a joke about. He'd always get people to laugh at funerals, even the family members. He killed them when he gave a toast at the union Christmas dinners. Tall, but nowhere near as tall as Jake's six-eight, and built like a cannonball on bowed legs. A John Goodman kind of guy, bigger than life in every way. And smiling. Always smiling, no matter how bad the shit was coming down, or how late an emergency shift went, or how tough a job was. Always laughing.

Until three teenage girls came out of the woods and ate the smile off his face.

The thought—the memory—was so insanely vivid, playing in his head in HD with surround sound. All the colors, all the sounds.

They had been out here working the storm because the weather service said this was going to be a nut-buster. A hurricane, or whatever you call a storm like that this far inland. A supercell. Something like that. Torrential rains, hurricane-force winds, and an absolute guarantee of flash flood.

This was the storm, everyone said, that would finally break the levees.

Everyone always said that.

They were always wrong.

Until they were right.

Until today.

Jake and his crew were at it before the sun was even up yesterday morning and they kept at it all the way past midnight, working with bulldozers and front-end loaders, including his own big Caterpillar 950H. The one under which he lay. The crew were hard at it all damn day, pushing hundreds of tons of dirt into berms to reinforce the levees, cutting rain runoff lines, trying to help the town get ready for the storm. They needed five times as many men and machines on the job, but they used what they had. Did some good, too. The levees held north of the town proper, which is where everyone said the water would do the most damage. Jake and the guys saved maybe fifty, sixty farms from being flooded by dirty river water.

Below the town line, though, the National Guard was supposed to be doing the same job. And they had more equipment.

But then Magic Marti on the radio said that the levees had collapsed down there. Jake never got all the details, though. Not on that and not on whatever the Christ else was happening over there in Stebbins. Even with headphones on, between the rain and the engine roars, it was too loud to hear much of the news. And reception was for shit. He lost Magic Marti, whose radio show on WNOW came up from over the Maryland line, and when he had the chance, Jake tried to pick up the network news out of Pittsburgh. Got a little of it, but the news guy seemed to be losing his shit. Typical newspeople, he'd thought at the time. They go ass-wild whenever things get really bad, so instead of reporting the news they act like the news is all about them. Like Anderson Cooper standing in the fucking wind during Katrina. They shout a lot so you know they're taking the big risk, but they don't say much of anything people can use.

Like today.

Nobody seemed to know what in the blue hell was going on.

Certainly no one on the stations Jake listened to when he could get a signal. And no one he talked to. Lots of cars went by, but everyone was driving so fast you'd have thought the devil was after them.

Then those three girls came out of the woods.

Jake saw them and he was so startled that he almost ran his bucket through the berm he was building. He jerked to a stop to watch.

The girls came walking slowly out of the woods like there was no crisis, no storm, no goddamn ocean of water pounding down on them.

And damn if one of them wasn't naked.

These were high school girls, or maybe college.

The one on the left wore jeans and a torn sweatshirt, the flaps of it hanging down to expose a blue sports bra and pale skin. The one on the right had a windbreaker on with the logo of some sports team Jake never heard of. Probably a school team. But the one in the middle was as naked as if she was taking a shower instead of walking through the woods where everyone could see her. She was thin, with tiny breasts and visible ribs.

Jake had two reactions.

The guy in him immediately checked out her body.

The man in him became instantly concerned. She was young, naked, vulnerable, and clearly out of her mind. Drugs? Something else?

All three of the girls had marks on them that looked like cuts, but the distance and the cleansing rain made the marks look blue and bloodless.

The girls came straight across a muddy field, negotiating the uneven terrain where heavy-equipment wheels had created an obstacle course of wheel ruts. One by one the other guys killed their engines. They all stared. A few of the men were smiling, and one clown whistled, but the sound was shrill and it died in the air. And these kids were clearly in trouble. That bullshit about construction crews sitting around whistling and acting like they had dicks instead of brains may be true sometimes, but nearly every man here had a family, kids.

Burl was the first guy to do more than sit there and gape.

"Yo!" he cried as he jumped down from the cab of his Cat D9. "Yo, kids . . . what the hell's going on? You girls okay? What are you doing out here?"

He kept up a string of questions as he jogged heavily through the mud to intercept them. The girls paused for a moment—just a moment—as he drew close, and it seemed to Jake that in the cold and misty rain they'd been unaware of him until he spoke, until he moved.

He thought that then, and knew it now.

The girls all smiled at him, grinning to show white teeth. Then they broke into a run to meet Burl. Arms outstretched, like children running to the safety of their daddy's arms.

Except that wasn't what it was.

Of course it wasn't.

Even with fractured logic, even if things weren't what they were, that wouldn't have been the way it was.

Maybe Burl knew it, too, Jake thought. Knew it a step too late, because as he got close to them his own pace faltered, and his voice trailed away, ending on a rising note of question.

The girls answered that question by leaping at him.

Driving him backward.

Driving him down to the ground.

Climbing all over Burl.

Bending toward him.

In a damaged guy's fantasy world that would have been a *Penthouse* letters page three-on-one. But this was the real world and naked teenage girls didn't walk out of the rain to bang a fat construction worker.

That's not what they did.

For a moment, though, Jake didn't understand what they were doing. From a distance it really did look like they were kissing him. His face, his throat. Their hands were all over him.

And then the screaming started.

So high.

Jake would never have guessed that a man as big as Burl could scream so loud, so high, so shrill. Like a whistle blowing at the end of a shift. A long, sustained blast that went on and on as the girls' mouths bent to him over and over again.

Everyone started screaming then.

All four of the other guys—and Jake—screamed as they started running toward the tangle of white limbs that were now streaked with bright, bright red.

The first one there was Richie, another bulldozer jockey. He ran up like he was going to handle this shit right there, right then. But when he was twenty feet out his nothing-can-stop-me run slowed to a walk as he saw what was actually happening.

His screams went up a notch. From man yell to something younger, higher, and more frightened.

The three girls raised their heads and snarled at him.

Like lionesses around a zebra.

Jake was fifty yards back and he could see strings of meat caught between their teeth, swaying as they looked at Richie.

Then two of them came off the ground and rushed him. It was so unexpected.

Not really fast.

It was awkward and even a little slow.

But there was absolutely no hesitation. One moment they were looking at Richie and the next minute they were at him. Just like that.

Richie skidded to a stop and tried to backpedal, but the mud was too wet. He went down hard and the girls were on him. Once more the screams changed.

Changed into something raw and filled with denial.

The other guys were there. Hank and Tommy and Vic.

Jake was almost there. He'd been farthest away.

They grabbed the girls. Shoved them. Knocked them back.

The girls turned on them. Their faces were smeared with blood that was so thick the downpour couldn't wash it off.

Everyone was wrestling, struggling.

It was crazy. All those big men. Three teenage girls, none of them bigger than one-ten. The blood.

All that blood.

Jake stepped down wrong and sank to mid-shin in watery mud. Pain detonated in his knee and for a terrible moment he thought he'd broken his leg. But it was just jammed straight. Maybe sprained. It stopped him cold, though, and pitched him face-forward into the mud. It went straight up his nose, into his eyes, into his screaming mouth. Down his throat.

He coughed and gagged and blew, pawing at his face, trying to unclog his nostrils and mouth so he could drag in a breath. Swallowed more mud doing that and a worse spasm of coughing nearly tore him apart. His chest convulsed and he vomited mud and coffee and two Egg McMuffins into the storm, and the fierce wind blew it back into his face.

For a long, twisted time he lay there, dripping with mud and puke, trying to breathe. Failing. Trying.

Until black fireworks exploded in his head and the sounds of the rain dwindled into a distant buzz and Jake knew that he was choking to death. Right there. While his friends fought little girls and screamed and bled.

Desperate, terrified, Jake balled his right fist and punched himself in the solar plexus as hard as he could. It felt like being shot, but a ball of something—bread or Canadian bacon or mud or all of that shot from his mouth and vanished into the rain. He dragged in half the air in the world. The flesh around his eyes tingled and the world was incredibly bright but filled with fireflies.

Then the wind brought the screams back to him.

That was how the day started for Jake DeGroot.

It was the best part of his day.

It got so much worse after that.

CHAPTER EIGHTY
STEBBINS LITTLE SCHOOL
STEBBINS, PENNSYLVANIA

Dez Fox made no sound at all as she opened the small door that connected the teacher's lounge to the corner of the schoolyard. The wind screeched through the chain-link fence and rain hit the concrete so steadily it sounded like white noise. Dez took several small, quick steps, her feet barely lifting from the ground as she moved up behind two of the patrolling soldiers. They were twenty feet ahead of her, walking at a measured pace, heading to the turn at the far end. They carried their M4s at an angle to keep rain from filling the barrels. Even though both of them wore gray-green hazmat suits, Dez could tell that one was male and the other female.

Dez stopped behind a decorative outcropping of red brick and racked the slide of her Daewoo shotgun.

Even with the storm it was a loud and distinctive sound, and she'd waited until she was in position so the soldiers could hear it.

She yelled, "Freeze right fucking there."

They froze. Right there.

"Unsling your rifles and stand them against the wall," Dez ordered. "Do it now."

The soldiers hesitated and the woman started to turn.

"Don't make a stupid mistake, girl," warned Dez.

"You're the one making a mistake," said the female soldier.

"And I'll cry about it later. Drop the guns or I'll drop you. Last warning."

The soldiers exchanged a brief look, then they slid the straps from their shoulders and very gingerly stood their weapons against the wall.

"Place your hands on top of your heads, fingers laced. Good, now turn around slowly. Fuck with me and I will kill you."

They did exactly as told and though Dez couldn't see their faces behind the masks they wore, each of them stiffened in surprise. Dez smiled as she stepped away from the wall. Behind her, Uriah Piper and eight other men—each of them experienced deep-woods hunters—knelt in the rain in a shooting line with rifles snugged against their shoulders. A sound made the soldiers look up to see eight more gun barrels—small arms and long guns—pointing at them from half-opened windows.

"Yeah," said Dez to the soldiers, "you're *that* fucked."

For a long moment there was no sound except the dull impact of raindrops on brick and pavement and clothing and skin. Dez lowered her shotgun and walked over to the soldiers.

"Jenny?" she called, and Jenny DeGroot trotted out of the build-ing holding a plastic trash can. Then Dez began stripping weapons and equipment from the soldiers. Grenades, walkie-talkies, knives, IFAK first-aid kits, ammunition, canteens, equipment-belt suspend-ers, gun belts, and the rest until each soldier wore only their hazmat suit and their battle dress uniform beneath it. All of it went into the plastic trash can until Jenny staggered under the weight.

"Take it inside. Uriah, get their rifles."

"Do you have any idea what you're doing, Officer Fox?" asked the female soldier.

Dez wasn't surprised to hear her name. She was the only police officer left alive in Stebbins, and her presence in the school was certainly known to the military. Even so, she didn't like hearing this woman say it. She produced two sets of plastic flex-cuffs, handed her shotgun to Piper, spun the female soldier roughly around, yanked her arms down behind her and quickly fitted the cuffs around the wrists. She repeated this with the man, who had so far kept silent.

"This isn't how you want to play this," warned the woman.

Dez tore off the woman's goggles and yanked down the cowl of her hazmat suit. The woman had olive skin, short black hair, and dark eyes. She did not look even remotely afraid of Dez or the guns pointed at her, which was very strange. The woman was also older than Dez expected, maybe thirty-three, with crow's feet at the cor-ners of her eyes and laugh lines etched around her mouth.

"Listen, sister," said Dez. "You think I'm making a mistake here? Are you really that stupid?"

"You're only making more trouble for yourself. What do you hope to accomplish?"

Dez wiped rainwater from her eyes. "What do I hope to accom-plish," she echoed, "Sure, fair question. I'll tell you and maybe it'll even sink in." She pointed to the school. "There are eight hundred people in there. Most of them are scared little kids. None of them are infected."

The woman nodded. "And?"

Dez almost smiled at how cool this woman was. Cuffed and

captured, she was keeping everything in neutral. Dez wasn't sure whether to be impressed or nervous.

"The other reason is that we need some insurance that General Zetter won't bomb this place. He might be willing to kill civilians, but I don't think he'll pull the trigger on his own people."

"Are you sure about that?"

"No," admitted Dez, "but fuck it. You play the cards you're dealt."

The woman studied her, then nodded. "Fair enough. However, I don't work for General Zetter. He doesn't know my name, or my partner's name, and he has no idea that you and I are having this conversation."

"Bullshit. If you're not with Zetter, what are you? Regular army? Who are you working for?"

"His name is Captain Sam Imura," said the woman. "Hurt either of us and he will blow your head off."

"That's mighty tough fucking talk but I don't—"

"Dez . . . ," said Trout suddenly. "Oh God . . . *Dez*."

She looked at him and then down at her chest. There, between her breasts, right over her heart, was a tiny red dot. It quivered ever so slightly.

A laser sight.

She stood facing the soldier, which meant that someone out there in the storm was aiming a rifle at her. Someone hidden by rain and the humped shapes of buses and cars.

Dez shifted her shotgun so the barrel pointed at the woman's face. She took a breath and yelled loud enough to be heard above the rain. "Take your shot, motherfucker. I'll blow this slut's shit all over the wall before I go down."

"Officer Fox," said the woman calmly. "This isn't about you."

Suddenly two more laser dots appeared. One was on Uriah Piper's chest. The other moved in a slow line up Billy Trout's body, over his chest, across his face, and stopped exactly between his eyebrows. This dot did not quiver at all.

"Captain Imura was one of the top three snipers in U.S. Special Forces. The other two men are superb shots and they are in positions of concealment. They can drop nine of your people in under four seconds, including you."

"I'm not afraid to die," sneered Dez.

"If we wanted you dead, Officer Fox, we'd have taken you as soon as you stepped outside of the building. This isn't about who's brave enough to die. It's about who's smart enough to live."

CHAPTER EIGHTY-ONE
ON THE ROAD
PITTSBURGH SUBURBS

Goat whimpered when he saw what Homer Gibbon did inside the 7-Eleven; however, he kept the camera rolling.

There were five people there. A family of three, a man who dressed like a bartender, and the young man working the cash register.

The store's employee lay where he'd been dropped, his chest on the floor and his feet still hooked on the counter. That's how it had started. Homer walked in, reached over the counter, grabbed the kid, dragged him up, and took a bite out of his throat.

Then Homer dropped him.

The other people in the store screamed and panicked.

The woman pushed her ten-year-old son behind her as she backed into an aisle. Her husband tried to drag Homer off the cashier. Homer wheeled on him and drove a savage kick into the man's crotch that sent him crashing into a display of chips and pretzels. The other man, the bartender, apparently knew some karate, because Goat saw him throw his own kick, catching Homer in the gut. The blow staggered Homer, but the killer folded around the bartender's leg, clutching it to the point of impact. He bent all the way over it and Goat suddenly realized that he was bending to take a bite.

The bartender screamed and pounded on Homer to let go.

Homer did. Abruptly. He whipped the trapped leg up into the air, which caused the bartender to flip backward. He crashed down on the wire rack, scattering brightly colored bags of Utz pretzels, Lay's potato chips, and Snyder barbecue pork rinds. The man lay there, back arched over the twisted wire, writhing and hissing between gritted teeth.

That's when the woman began throwing things at Homer.

Cans of Spam and Campbell's soup struck the killer's back and shoulders. He threw an arm up to protect his face as he waded toward her. He never once stopped grinning. Homer was as dead as the other monsters, but he wasn't like them. Not entirely. Because he was the first infected person in this plague, because the purest form of Dr. Volker's *Lucifer 113* pathogen had been directly injected into his veins, the parasitic reaction was different. His mind did not die along with his flesh. Goat knew this. Understood it. And it terrified him. It made Homer into a kind of monster that was so much greater, so much more dangerous than anything else.

Goat watched Homer grin, heard him laugh, as he swatted the cans out of the air like someone playing a game.

A game.

It was a mercy—for Goat, not for the woman and her child—that Homer tackled them and they vanished between the aisles. Blood shot upward, though, spattering the top rows of canned goods and stacks of plastic-wrapped Stroehmann bread.

Goat never once looked at the door handle.

He never once seriously thought about running.

He understood that he was trapped inside this drama and that there was no exit cue on his script.

After several minutes, Homer rose from between the rows, his face painted with a new coat of red. He wiped his mouth, though he was still chewing something. He looked across the bloody tops of the bread toward the window, and through the glass to where Goat sat behind the dispassionate camera.

And he gave Goat a cheery, buddy-buddy thumbs-up. Like a football jock after a successful play.

The bartender was struggling to rise, but Homer stepped over him and walked in a casual swagger toward the door. Then he paused, turned, went to the cooler and took out two cold bottles of Coke, and plucked a handful of candy bars from the rack. He nodded to himself and left the store.

When he opened the driver's door he held the Coke and candy out to Goat.

"Guess you got to eat, too," he said.

It took a lot for Goat to accept these things. It cost him an expensive chunk of his soul.

Homer got behind the wheel and started the car.

Inside the store, the mother and child, both of whom had been savaged, were on their feet. Her husband was only now struggling to his feet, his hands still cupped around his crotch, face purple with agony. Goat had never seen a man kicked that hard in the groin before, and from the awkward way the man stood it seemed obvious that bones had to have been broken. He raised his head toward his family.

And screamed as they rushed toward him, reaching for him with bloody hands. He fell beneath them and Goat turned away.

"No," barked Homer, hitting him hard on the shoulder, "you don't look away. You fucking well look."

It cost Goat another part of his soul to turn back. To witness another death.

And another resurrection.

The cashier was rising, too, scrambling toward the bartender with the bitten leg.

More blood.

More screams.

"There," said Homer, "there it is."

"W-what . . . ?"

"That's the secret the Red Mouth wants you to know. The Black Eye wants to open in the center of your forehead so you can see. You *can* see it, can't you?"

"I . . . see it."

"Glad to hear it. I was beginning to have my doubts about you, son." He tapped the video camera. "Did you get everything like I asked?"

"Yes."

"You'll put it on the Net?"

"As soon as we get somewhere with a Wi-Fi."

Homer grunted, a note of deep satisfaction, perhaps of relief.

"Good," he said.

He pulled back onto the highway and headed toward Pittsburgh.

CHAPTER EIGHTY-TWO
THE NORTHERN LEVEES
FAYETTE COUNTY

"Please, God . . ."

Jake DeGroot prayed nearly continually, but he prayed under his breath.

He didn't dare make a sound.

In case someone could hear.

He didn't want anyone to hear him. Not the things that had pretended to be teenage girls. The things that had done those awful things to Burl and Richie and the others.

He was sure they were dead.

He just wasn't sure that it mattered.

After the attack had started—if "attack" was even the right word—Jake had been down in the mud for too long. When he'd fallen face-first into the muck and choked on it and on his breakfast, getting his shit together took a long damn time. Lying there, gasping like a gaffed billfish, his leg screaming at him, his chest on fire, he had no strength at all. Not for a long time. Too long. Maybe. Or long enough. It was all a matter of how you looked at it.

Since then, hiding in the ditch under Big Bird, he'd thought about it a lot.

He thought it all the way through as the HDTV in his head played and replayed it. There was no remote to aim at it and surf away to something better and saner. To something that made any kind of sense.

Before Jake could struggle back to his feet the whole thing with Burl and Hank and the others seemed to have changed. To have ended in a way Jake didn't understand.

The other three guys, Hank, Tommy, and Vic, had pulled the girls off of Burl and Richie. Pulled them off, fought with them, fell to the ground wrestling with them, and beaten the shit out of them. Through pain-filled eyes, Jake watched the guys punching and stomping the girls. It was surreal. Like something out of a bad movie. Like snuff porn.

Except that this was real and no matter how many times his friends hit the girls, they couldn't put them down.

Not down so they'd stay.

First one girl would fall, knocked into the mud by a fist or foot, then another, but then they'd get right back up. With faces broken to ugliness by the blows, with teeth sliding out of their mouths on tides of black blood, with the white ends of ribs coming through their skin and broken fingers, they go right after the guys again.

And again.

And again.

Until Tommy knocked one of them down and stomped on her head. But it took five or ten kicks. At first all he did was drive the girl with the torn sweatshirt deeper into the mud. Tommy was bleeding from half a dozen bites on his hands and wrists. Then one of his kicks must have done something worse. Broke her head, maybe. Or her neck. Something. Because she suddenly stopped fighting, stopped trying to get up. Stopped everything.

Tommy staggered back, staring down at her, his face as slack as if he'd been slapped, eyes bugged. Jake could understand that. The craziness of the attack. The bites and the blood. And what he'd just done.

How could they ever explain this?

All these big guys and three teenage girls. One of them naked. Another with her shirt torn open and her bra showing. Beaten to shit so they didn't even look like girls anymore.

What could any of them ever say that would make sense of that?

What?

What?

Tommy stood there and looked down at the girl while the other guys kept rolling around fighting.

Then Tommy spun away, dropped to his knees, and threw up.

Jake was still trying to haul himself out of the mud, still trying to remember how to breathe. He fought to get to his feet, but his knee immediately buckled and he went down again.

That's when Burl got up.

The naked girl had left him in the mud and was fighting Richie. Hank and Vic were taking turns knocking down the girl in the windbreaker and getting bit and knocking her down again. All of them screaming and cursing.

Jake began to crawl through the mud while across the rainy field, behind the five struggling figures, Burl Hansard stood up. It seemed to take a long time for him to do it. He was so badly hurt, maybe so dazed, that he was clumsy, he looked like he was drunk. The rain slashed at him, sending crooked red lines down to the mud, making his skin look white as paper.

"B-Burl . . ." called Jake, but he was too far away and his voice was lost in the sound of the storms and all that yelling.

Burl paused for one moment, his pale face turned toward Jake, eyes locked; and in that fragment of time, Jake knew that everything here was wrong. Worse even than it had been. He didn't know how he knew—it was a reaction born in the deepest, oldest, most primitive part of his brain. It was a knowledge of wrongness without any intellectual interpretation. It was simply wrong.

Burl's eyes were open but Burl was not in there.

Even from that distance, Jake knew.

Somehow Burl was gone.

So who looked at him from his friend's eyes?

Who, or what?

All of this burned through Jake's head in less than a second.

Then Burl took a step. Heavy, lumbering, like he didn't quite remember how to use his feet. He pulled one work boot out of the mud and took a step, but it was more like falling forward than walking forward.

Not toward Jake.

Burl turned toward the knot of struggling figures. A step, another.

He reached out to help pull the naked girl away who kept trying to bite Vic even though he had her by the hair and kept punching her in the face. Burl grabbed the girl and hauled her away, and Jake expected him to start wailing on her. But he didn't. Instead he simply shoved her aside and with a rush and a yell that was as loud as it was meaningless. Then Burl grabbed Vic's face, taking it in both of his hands the way a grandmother does when she's going to kiss a kid on the lips.

Except that's not what was happening.

Of course it wasn't.

Burl pulled Vic forward, tearing him free from the mud, crushing him close, and then he bit down, tearing into Vic's nose, crushing it, ripping it. Blood exploded against Burl's face and it seemed to incense the man. He growled like a dog and began tearing at Vic, worrying at his face the way a dog does. Vic screamed and screamed. He beat at Burl, punching him with the same red, swollen fists he'd been using with similar futility on the naked girl. The fists bounced off of Burl's massive frame. Vic brought his knee up into Burl's balls. Once, again, and again.

Nothing.

And it was then, at that moment, that Jake lost all hope that there was any way to understand this. He'd been in fights. He'd given and taken shots to the groin. Some guys could cowboy through it, biting down on the pain, bulling through it, but even the toughest of them reacted. You had to react. It was your balls.

Burl didn't twitch. All that happened was a jerk of his body with each impact, but there was no more reaction to it than when somebody brushes your shoulder on the subway. Less. It was nothing. Dead meat being hit.

That was it.

That was all.

Burl never stopped biting.

Vic's face.

Vic's cheek.

Vic's throat.

Then Vic stopped screaming; he stopped kicking. Someone turned on a power hose of red in Vic's throat. Blood showered Burl's face and chest.

Jake lost it then.

He could hear past his own screams.

His eyes seemed to switch off for a moment as if they refused to see any of this.

Time punched him senseless and each second was like a brutal fist against his brain. The sounds and sights of what was going on broke apart and flew off into the storm.

Tommy and Richie were still fighting. One each with a girl.

Then Tommy was down and the girl with the windbreaker knelt on his chest. There was one little, final flap of Tommy's hand. After that, nothing.

Richie picked the naked girl up and flung her away from him. Then he looked wildly around as if trying to decide how to react, failed, and then simply ran.

Badly.

The mud and the rain and the damage brought him down within two steps.

"No!"

The cry was torn from Jake. It was not the first time he'd yelled, but this one found a hole in the storm where there was no thunder, no howling wind, no screams. A flash moment of quiet into which his one word stabbed.

Every face turned toward the sound.

Toward him.

Burl and the girls.

Even Vic.

Oh, God. Vic.

He sat up and swiveled his head around on his ruined throat.

Richie saw him, too, and he reached out with a bloodstained hand. "Jake . . . oh, Christ . . . Jake!"

It was a mistake.

The girls, broken and disfigured, crippled into shambling wrecks, turned away from Jake and began limping after Richie. He tried to crawl away from them.

Didn't.

Couldn't.

Burl and Vic did not go after Richie.

Vic got to his feet and, nearly shoulder to shoulder with Burl, began moving toward Jake.

CHAPTER EIGHTY-THREE

"Mr. President," said Scott Blair, "Captain Imura's team is on-site at the Stebbins Little School. I'm waiting now on word about the drives."

"How soon can Imura get those drives to us?"

"He won't need to. He'll upload them to his tactical computer and send them via burst transfer to us. We'll have them five minutes after he has them."

"Thank God," said the president. "Thank God."

Sylvia Ruddy covered the mouthpiece of the phone into which she'd been speaking. "Scott . . . how much stake are we placing on what's on the drives? I reviewed Trout's broadcasts and it seemed clear that Volker regarded his variation of Lucifer as unstoppable. He said as much to his CIA handler. I have transcripts of all of this and there's nothing in anything Volker said to indicate that there's a silver bullet on those drives."

Blair placed his hands flat on the table. "Have you not been following, Sylvia? I never said that there was a cure on the drives. We need them for our people—Dr. McReady, Dick Price at Zabriske Point, the team at the CDC. They are the most talented bioweapons people on earth. It's always been our hope that they'll find a weakness in Volker's variation."

"That's a long damn shot," said Ruddy.

"It's the shot we have."

The president got up and walked over to the big screen on which the satellite images were shown, with the thermal signatures of hundreds of people scattering through the storm. He touched the screen at the outer edge of the dispersal pattern.

"All the science in the world isn't going to help us if we can't contain the outbreak."

No one spoke.

He nodded to General Burroughs. "Amistad, give me the numbers."

Burroughs punched some keys that overlaid a red circle around the troubled area. "The only thing working in our favor right now is that the infected are unable to drive vehicles, and most of them are slow, moving at a fast walk or slower. So, by estimating the potential distance traveled by foot since the quarantine break, we have extended the Q-zone to cover this area." He hit keys and the line jumped outward so that it covered an area with a sixty-four-mile diameter, with Stebbins in the exact center. "Even if an infected person was traveling on foot at a rate of four miles an hour—which is virtually impossible because of terrain, weather, and, er, the nature of the infection, we estimate that the maximum distance from Stebbins would be thirty-two miles. Therefore we need to designate everything inside this extended area to be our new hot zone."

The president nodded very slowly. "How many people live inside that zone?"

"It's mostly farm country . . ."

"How many?"

It was Blair who had those numbers. It hurt him to say it, though. "One hundred seventy thousand people."

The president closed his eyes.

"However, if it continues to spread at this rate, we'll have to expand the zone again," said Blair. "By tomorrow morning Pittsburgh will be inside the hot zone."

He turned. "Ladies and gentlemen, I will take any and all suggestions for how to contain this. As of right now no option is off the table."

CHAPTER EIGHTY-FOUR
STEBBINS LITTLE SCHOOL
STEBBINS, PENNSYLVANIA

Two of the red laser dots vanished and a few seconds later two men came walking slowly and carefully out of the rain. They wore the same dark hazmat suits as the other soldiers, and carried similar gear. The taller of the newcomers had an M4 in his gloved hands; the other had a sniper rifle. Dez recognized it. A .408 Cheyenne Tactical sniper rifle that fired .338 Lapua Magnum supersonic rounds. A rifle bullet like that would result in a kill shot no matter where it struck a person.

The laser dot on Billy Trout remained where it was and Dez's heart hammered in her chest.

The man with the sniper rifle walked past Uriah Piper and the other farmers, showing a total lack of concern that they all held weapons. He walked right up to Dez, slung his rifle barrel down, raised his goggles onto his forehead, and pulled down his hood to reveal a middle-aged Japanese face. A small mouth, crooked nose, and quiet eyes. Lots of old scars.

"Officer Fox?" he asked, his voice mild and surprisingly deep for a man of his size. Thunder boomed like a dramatic counterpoint and lightning glowed along the edges of his face. Imura raised an eyebrow. "Wow. Nice timing, but I promise that I didn't plan the theatrics."

Dez almost smiled. Didn't.

The soldier offered his hand. "Captain Sam Imura."

Dez did not shake hands. "Get that laser sight off of Billy."

"Sure," said Imura, withdrawing his hand. He tapped the electronic bud seated inside his right ear. "Moonshiner, stand down."

The red dot vanished. Trout sagged and almost collapsed, but Piper caught him under the armpit and steadied him. Sam Imura looked amused. A fifth soldier, big and broad-shouldered, stepped down from his hiding place in one of the buses.

Dez stepped very close to Sam. They were the same height and she gave him the full weight of her anger and disapproval in a blue-eyed glared. "Okay, so now that we're done measuring dicks," she growled, "how about you tell me what the fuck is going on."

"I will," said Sam, "but first I need to know if the flash drives are still safe."

"That's why you're here?"

"Mostly," said Sam. He glanced at Trout. "Do you have them?"

"Don't trust him, Billy," said Cletus, one of the farmers. A few others grunted agreement, except for Piper, who stood as silent as a statue.

"Why didn't you shoot first and just take the drives?" Trout asked sourly.

"Three reasons," said Sam. "First, we're not actually barbarians. I know, big surprise, right? It goes against the cliché, but what can I tell you? Second, if we started a gunfight, do you really think either side would win? We'd kill a bunch of you, and you might kill some of my people. That's pretty crappy math."

Trout pointed to the big auditorium windows halfway along the side of the school. That entire section of the school's facade was peppered with thousands of bullet holes, and the windows were totally gone. "You guys seemed happy with that equation a few hours ago."

"That wasn't us," said Sam. "That was Colonel Dietrich of the Pennsylvania National Guard who, as I believe you've been told, has been relieved of his command. He was replaced by Major General Zetter, who did *not* fire on you. He could have, you know. Your 'live from the apocalypse' broadcasts are being jammed, so no one would have known if Zetter razed this school to the ground. The fact that he didn't should say something to you."

Trout and Dez exchanged an uncertain look.

"What was the third reason, Captain?" asked Dez.

"Because if Mr. Trout here is dead and the flash drives are not in his pocket, then I could burn off a lot of time trying to find wherever he hid them." He shrugged. "It's pretty simple, really. The best approach is a straightforward one, so I decided to come and ask."

"Except that you walked into an ambush," said one of the farmers. "How smart was that?"

"They ambushed *us*, dumbass," said Dez. "Now shut up, Cletus, there are grown folks talking."

Even in the cold rain the man's face flushed red.

Sam said, "Mind telling me why you tried to ambush my soldiers? It was my understanding that General Zetter negotiated a truce with you."

"Fuck Zetter and fuck you."

"There's that," conceded Sam.

"We thought he left two assholes behind to keep us penned in. Turns out we don't think it's safe in Stebbins County. Might come as a shock to you."

Sam said nothing.

"So we were going to tie up Zetter's sentries, take their weapons, then clear out as many buses as it'll take to get these kids and the rest of the adults the fuck out of this particular ring of hell."

"And go where?"

"Anywhere but here."

"That was the general plan," agreed Trout, "until you showed up. And I have to say, Captain, that you played a very dangerous hand of cards there. We could have just as easily shot your people."

"That goes both ways, Mr. Trout, and in any armed conflict I rather like our odds."

Dez tried to get up in his face. "You can suck my—"

Trout pushed her back.

"Much as I appreciate you not turning this into the O.K. Corral, Captain," said Trout, "how about the added courtesy of a few answers. Like why'd everybody light out of here like their asses were on fire? What was that about?"

"Well, you've probably already guessed that this *trouble* isn't over," said Sam. "The infection, the outbreak. It's not over. And that's why we need your help and cooperation. That's why I need you to give me the flash drives."

Trout shifted, wincing at the pain in his body. "How bad is it?"

Sam Imura had the kind of face that rarely gave anything away, but Dez and Trout could both see dangerous lights flicker in the man's eyes. Beneath the placid veneer of calm there was real fear there. Deep and intense, barely kept in check.

"It's bad," said Sam. "We may not be able to contain it. Mr. Trout . . . *please* . . . those drives may be our only hope of preventing a nationwide catastrophe."

Trout sighed deeply and closed his eyes.

"What?" asked Sam.

"I don't have the drives," said Billy Trout.

Sam's face went dead pale.

Moonshiner said, "Oh, shit."

CHAPTER EIGHTY-FIVE
SUBURBS OF PITTSBURGH

"Homer," said Goat, after he started the camera again and adjusted the microphone, "why did you attack those people at the Seven-Eleven?"

"I thought you said you understood."

"I do," Goat said quickly, "but this will go out to millions of people who don't yet understand. You want them to understand, right? That's why we're doing this."

"Sure."

"Then tell them."

The rain was intensifying again, so Homer turned up the wiper speed. "What do you want me to say, exactly?"

"You just walked into a Seven-Eleven and killed five people. Talk about why you did that."

Homer shook his head. "Is that what you think I did?"

"Didn't you? You attacked everyone, bit them . . ."

"I didn't bite everyone," Homer said. "And I only killed two of them, and the Red Mouth brought them right back. It's funny, in court they went on and on about how many lives they say I took. Maybe that used to be true, but that's before I understood the real power of the Red Mouth. I wasn't trying to *take* anything from any-one. I was always trying to give them something. That's why I wanted my lawyer to put me on the stand so I could tell everyone that, so I could explain it. But he wouldn't do it. He said that people wouldn't understand and it would go against me in court. Against me? They fucking executed me. How much more against me could it have gone? I think that if he'd let me have my say, if he let me ex-plain what the Black Eye saw and let me speak with the voice of the Red Mouth, then they wouldn't have sentenced me to any frigging lethal injection."

No, thought Goat, *they'd have put you in a tiny padded cell and spent the next forty years experimenting on your brain to see what makes it tick.*

He did not say this to Homer.

The killer kept talking, working it out for the camera. "That's all different now. Thanks to Dr. Volker and the gift he gave me; now I can share that gift with other people. No one's ever going to die. Not really. Not like it used to be. We're all going to live forever."

Goat kept the camera on the killer's profile, capturing the way he nodded in agreement with his own words and thoughts.

"In the Bible Jesus talked about how the meek were going to inherit the earth. I forget where he said it, but it was important, and I think *this* is what he was talking about. The way people are when they wake up after I open the Red Mouths in their flesh. They don't act the way they used to. They don't talk; they don't say stupid shit. I'll bet they don't even know if they're Republican or Democrats. They're just people. All the bullshit is gone."

"They're zombies," suggested Goat.

"Sure, if you want to use that word. But I don't know. Zombies. I always think of black guys with bug eyes in those old movies. Down in Jamaica someplace."

"Haiti."

"Haiti? Okay. Haiti. Wherever. Those are zombies. Is that what they are?"

"Dr. Volker said that he studied zombies in Haiti. The witch doctors there use a chemical compound to—"

"None of that matters. It's what, voodoo? The Red Mouth isn't voodoo and it's not magic."

"Then what is it?"

"If I tell you, you'll laugh."

"Believe me," said Goat, "I won't laugh."

"It's god stuff. I read a word once in a book. Celestial. You know what that means?"

"Yes."

"That's what this is. I know that because it's what Jesus spoke about. It's the meek inheriting the earth. And he knew. Those Romans opened Red Mouths in his flesh and he spoke the real truth.

And he came back from the dead, too." Homer shook his head. "Maybe Jesus was the first zombie. That makes sense to me."

Goat almost asked him if he was serious or if this was some kind of twisted joke.

He didn't.

And therefore Homer did not have a reason to kill him.

CHAPTER EIGHTY-SIX
WHAT THE FINKE THINKS
WTLK LIVE TALK RADIO
PITTSBURGH, PENNSYLVANIA

"We have Solomon from Philadelphia," said Gavin.

"Great to talk with you, Gavin. Love the show, just love it."

"Always great to hear. So, talk to me, Solomon, what do you think's going down in Stebbins?"

"It's UFOs. This is exactly what happened at Roswell."

"How so, Solomon?"

"First they make an official statement and then they recant it right away."

"Sure, but the first statement was about an outbreak of a new kind of virus."

"Which they recanted."

"Viruses are terrestrial."

"Are they, Gavin?"

"You tell me."

"It's all part of the conspiracy. Something *crashed* in Stebbins and that's how the virus was released. It was something in the blood of the aliens. Something normal to their world but not to ours."

"And the government is covering it up?"

"Absolutely. They want to use that virus as a bioweapon. That's where these governments have always gotten their bioweapons. You think HIV came from people having sex with monkeys?"

"No, I don't, but—"

"There you go. HIV, bird flu, swine flu, Ebola . . . the reason they're so dangerous is because we have no natural immunity to that stuff. And why? Because it's *not from here*."

"How does that account for things like the black plague and the Spanish flu of the early twentieth century?"

Solomon laughed. "C'mon, Gav, you of all people have to know that they've been visiting us since before they built the pyramids."

"Ah."

"And this whole cover-up? That fake news story by Billy Trout? The rumors of soldiers shooting people in Stebbins? That's just the military covering up the fact they have a crashed UFO. It's textbook, Gavin. This is Roswell all over again."

CHAPTER EIGHTY-SEVEN
THE SITUATION ROOM
THE WHITE HOUSE, WASHINGTON, D.C.

"Mr. President," cried Sylvia Ruddy, "I think we have something!"

Everyone in the Situation Room whipped around toward her and all conversation died.

"Tell me," said the president in a way that was an order flavored with a plea.

"Dr. Price at Zabriske Point received the Lucifer 113 samples. I have him on video conference." She spoke into the phone. "Dr. Price, I'm putting you on with the president."

A moment later Dr. Price's thin, ascetic face filled the big view screen. His eyes were red-rimmed with fatigue but bright with excitement.

"Tell me something I want to hear," said the president. "Do you have something for us?"

"I—We believe so. My whole team has been tearing apart the 113 variation and we've learned that Dr. Volker used new mutations of *Toxoplasma gondii*, which had always been a key component of Lucifer. Those mutations were part of his process of the neurological control functions of the bioweapon. While the genetically reengineered green jewel wasp larvae drive the aggression of the infected, the toxoplasma control the brain. That's part of the process of shutting down higher function while keeping active those nerves and processes responsible for walking, grabbing, biting, swallowing, and so on."

"Cut to it, Dr. Price," the president said tersely.

"This is context, Mr. President. It explains what I think might work. Using the older form of Lucifer we were experimenting with parasites that would essentially attack the modified parasites. We had a great deal of success with *Neospora caninum*, which is a parasite similar in form to *Toxoplasma gondii*, but one found predominantly in dogs. Under standard microscopic examination, the *N. caninum sporozoite*—which is the body of the parasite—closely resembles the *T. gondii sporozoite*, and both diseases share many of the same symptoms. However—and this is where we may have hit on it—the *N. caninum* infection has a much more severe impact on the neurological and muscular system of test subjects."

"How so?" asked Blair, and once more that dangerous spark of hope flared in his chest.

"The *N. caninum* variations we've been developing as a possible response to Lucifer create a certain set of symptoms—all of them in extreme degrees—that include stiffness of the pelvis and legs, paralysis distinguished by gradual muscle atrophy in which the muscles essentially seize up and can't move. A secondary set of symptoms include severe seizures, tremors, behavioral changes, weakness of the cervical muscles near to the neck, dysphagia—difficulty swallowing—and eventual paralysis of the muscles involved in respiration."

"Which means what, damn it?" snapped the president.

"It means, Mr. President, that we might be able to introduce a hostile parasite to the infected that will make them blind and paralyzed. Quite literally it will stop them in their tracks."

"Good *God*," gasped Ruddy. "You're talking about people."

Dr. Price looked at her with heavily lidded eyes. "No, ma'am," he said slowly, "once a person has been infected by Lucifer—by any version of Lucifer—they are no longer people. They are dead meat driven by a parasite."

"How is this a cure?" demanded General Burroughs.

"No . . . you don't understand," Price said. "There is *no cure*. Maybe there will be one day, I don't know. That would take years of research. You asked me how to stop the infected. That's what this is. A weapon that can stop them."

Blair watched the president's face, saw how this news hurt him. He didn't like the man, but right now he felt deeply sorry for him. And, to a lesser degree, for Price.

"What form would this weapon come in, Doctor?" asked Burroughs. "If it's some kind of parasite . . ."

"Actually," said Price, "the Chinese developed a toxoplasma delivery system in the nineties. We've codenamed it Reaper. Lurid, I know, but it was designed to attack and destroy, so we . . . well, anyway, we acquired it from them and—"

"What's the potential effect of this Reaper on uninfected persons?" asked Blair.

Price paused on that. "We . . . don't know. We've never tested this on people."

"How do we use it?" interrupted the president.

"Airbursts. The modified *N. caninum* are held in stasis inside a dry medium that can be packed into rockets calibrated for low-level detonation over infected areas. How big is your quarantine zone?"

"The zone is a circle sixty-four miles across," said Blair.

Price considered, quickly doing the math in his head. "That's what—twelve-thousand eight hundred and sixty-one square miles?"

"And it could expand," said Burroughs. "How much of this canine stuff do we need?"

"*N. caninum*," corrected Price. "Or just Reaper. That's what we've been calling it, too. Easier to say. Hold on, let me make that calculation."

They watched him as he tapped for several excruciating moments on a laptop. Blair saw a frown carve itself deeply into Price's face.

"Um . . . the required parasitic load would depend on population, terrain, and weather conditions. However, if we work with the prevailing winds, we could put enough of the parasite-rich medium in a standard airburst bomb or rocket to cover several square miles. Less in a high airburst in low winds. More in the current conditions. Call it fifty tons of the medium."

That was ugly news.

"How fast can we get the Reaper material to Pennsylvania?" asked the president.

Price blinked like a bug. "Mr. President . . . we don't have that much of the Reaper stockpiled."

"How much do you have?"

"Between here and one other lab, maybe eight, nine kilos."

"Shit," hissed Blair.

"Can you make more of it?" asked the president.

"We can make a mountain of it, sir. Making it isn't difficult. But it will take time to set up a production process for it, and then there's manufacture time, bonding with the dry medium, payload assembly . . . Mr. President, at the very earliest we could have the first batches ready for you in six days."

Six days.

Those two words hung burning the air.

"Scott," asked the president in a leaden voice, "do we have that kind of time?"

"Without containment, sir?" Blair shook his head. "In six days we'll have lost most of the East Coast and the entire South. In six days, Mr. President, fifty million people will be infected."

Dr. Price had nothing to say. There was no possible response to a statement like that.

CHAPTER EIGHTY-EIGHT
STEBBINS LITTLE SCHOOL
STEBBINS, PENNSYLVANIA

They went inside out of the rain. Sam Imura and his team—their weapons and gear returned to them, the cuffs removed—along with Dez, Trout, Uriah Piper, Mrs. Madison, and a small handful of the more sober and steady adults. Dez picked one of the smaller classrooms in order to limit the size of the crowd, and she closed the door. Several of the adults in the school clearly wanted to object, but none of them got farther than beginning to say something to her, and then clearly thought better of it.

"Where are the drives?" asked Sam as soon as the door was closed.

Trout started to answer, but Dez cut him off. "No. You first. You tell us what's happening."

"We don't have time for that, Officer Fox," said Sam urgently, "we—"

"Fucking *make* time for it."

Sam turned appealing eyes to Trout, but he shook his head. "You heard the lady," said Trout. "And if the clock is ticking, better cut right to it."

Sam glanced at his people, then gave a short sigh. "Okay, in the spirit of us actually getting somewhere, I'm going to shoot straight with you."

"Figuratively speaking," murmured Trout.

"Figuratively speaking. Let me preface it by saying that my boss is Scott Blair, the national security advisor. He was the one who advised the president to drop a fuel-air bomb on Stebbins County."

"Shit," said Dez. "What an asshole."

Sam shook his head. "No, he's not. Put yourself in his place. He didn't invent Lucifer and he wasn't part of any group that kept that plague after it should have been completely eradicated. Blair's only concern is just what his job title says—he advises the president on matters of national security. This plague threatens the entire nation. There was a window—a very small one—last night when it might have been contained. That window closed when Mr. Trout here broadcast his appeal to the world to save the kids here in the school."

"You're saying this is my fault?" demanded Trout.

"No, sir. I'm not in the business of assigning blame. Neither, I might add, is Scott Blair. I'm a response to a threat. Blair is probably the clearest-thinking person in Washington. When Volker first defected and gave Lucifer to our government, a set of response protocols were written that appropriately addressed the level of threat. If you spoke with Dr. Volker, Mr. Trout, then you understand how incredibly dangerous this plague is. Look at what happened to your town because of a single person being infected. Homer Gibbon. The spread was immediate and exponential; however, it reached that moment when the window could have been closed on the spread."

"By killing children?" demanded Mrs. Madison.

Sam gave her a flat stare. "No. By killing everyone in this town. Every single living person. And, ideally, every animal, bird, and cockroach. Anything that could possibly carry the disease beyond these borders."

"That's insane."

"No," said Sam, "creating a doomsday weapon was insane. Using that weapon in an attempt to punish a death row prisoner was insane. That's where the guilt and blame are, ma'am. If Dr. Volker's handler—the CIA operative assigned to oversee his actions—had done his job, then we would not be having this conversation. If Dr. Volker has been properly assessed, he would have been put into a psychiatric facility and kept far away from any materials with which he could do harm. But, as I said, that was yesterday's news. The truth is that the disease was injected into Homer Gibbon and now it's loose."

Mrs. Madison and several of the others were shaking their heads.

"Tell me," said Sam with dwindling patience, "if you were in charge of the military response to this outbreak, tell me how you would have handled it differently. What could you—what could *anyone*— have done once this thing was known to be out?"

"Not killed children."

"Which is what Mr. Trout told the world we were doing, and the president pulled back. The bombs never fell and the kids in this school are alive. Okay, that's a wonderful thing. No one wants to kill kids. Not even the most extreme hawks. I've got a younger brother and a baby stepbrother. It would crush me if anything happened to them. If they were in Stebbins County, I know I would feel exactly the same way you do. It's impossible for a sane and moral person to feel anything other than outrage, shock, and horror."

"If your brothers were in Stebbins and it was on you to order the bombs," asked Trout, "what would you do?"

"The soldier in me would order the drop," said Sam. "But me— Sam Imura—I'd never want those bombs dropped. I'd hesitate and hope for another solution. That's what anyone would do. And that is what they call fatal hesitation. Emphasis on 'fatal.' That human connection skews the logic and in these situations the logic cannot be skewed. That's why we have so many procedures in the military—in everything from basic training to missile launch sequences—that are designed to separate the human element from the necessary action."

"But the *children* . . ." said Mrs. Madison, leaning on it, forcing awareness of the implications.

Sam looked around at the faces. "This is the problem. You don't understand the implications of what you've done. Of what you still think is the right thing. You want to save these children, and that's beautiful, that's so wonderfully human. But if we can't get ahead of Lucifer, then these children are going to die anyway. If not today, then when your food runs out. You'll have to leave the building and all you'll find out there will be more dead. Dead adults and dead children. That's the only other way this works out. If we can't stop Lucifer then everyone will die. Everyone. Everyone's children. Here in Pennsylvania and everywhere else. Listen to me; hear that word. *Everywhere.* There is no way this disease can stop on its own. It will continue to spread exponentially. The most conservative estimates of a global pandemic of this disease is total human annihilation in ten weeks, with the deaths of all three hundred million Americans occurring during the first five to ten days." He looked at Billy Trout. "Tell me . . . how many children are you willing to kill?"

CHAPTER EIGHTY-NINE
THE NORTHERN LEVEES
STEBBINS COUNTY

Burl and Vic lumbered toward Jake and with every step the world tilted further and further off its axis. Nothing here made sense. Not in any way.

Three teenage girls walking in a storm like they couldn't even feel the weather. One of them naked.

Then those same girls attacking Burl and the other guys.

Biting them. Eating them.

Jake's friends—big men—screaming and falling. Dying.

And . . .

And getting the fuck back up.

It was all so wrong that for a broken handful of seconds Jake forgot about everything else. He lay there in the mud and didn't think about the pain in his leg, the ache in his chest from coughing up mud, or the need to flee. He lay on his stomach, hands pushed into the mud to raise his chest and head, and watched things come toward him that used to be his friends.

"No."

He heard the word but for a moment he could not tell who'd spoken it. Jake never felt his lips move to form the word, didn't feel the push of air as it escaped his throat.

No.

The word hung in the air, telling him everything he needed to understand about the moment and about the future. It answered every question he had.

No.

The rain fell in great slanting lines, popping on every surface.

"No," Jake said, trying to explain it to the day, trying to be reasonable about all this. "No."

Burl and Vic opened their mouths. They had nothing to say, though. Instead they shared with Jake the only thing they understood. The only thing that mattered now to each of them. They uttered a deep, resonating, aching moan of appalling hunger. It did not matter that the hunger was new. The sound of their moans made it clear even to Jake's tortured mind that this hunger ran as deep as all the need in the world. A strange and alien hunger that could never be satisfied.

Behind the two men, the girls raised their heads. Then, to his deepening horror, Jake saw that Richie and Tommy—what was left of Richie and Tommy—were climbing to their feet. All those pale faces turned toward the sound of that dreadful moan.

And joined it.

With broken jaws and shattered teeth, with torn throats and dead mouths, every one of them—all of them—raised their voices in a shared expression of that endless hunger.

Jake DeGroot clapped his hands to his ears to stop the noise, but he could hear it all the way down to the pit of his soul. He screamed.

At the sound of his scream, Burl began moving faster. The sticky suction of the mud tried to slow him, but Burl's face became a mask of bestial hunger and he tore his feet free, step by step, and reached with hooked fingers toward Jake.

That's when something in Jake's mind snapped.

The tethers anchoring him to the civilized man he was parted and that part of him floated away like a mask being removed to reveal his true face. It was an older, simpler, far less evolved face, and the eyes of the ultra-primitive saw the oncoming threat and the synapsis of the ancient lizard brain triggered unthinking and immediate reaction.

Jake screamed again, but this time it came out more as a growl, as a snarl of denial and fear and determination. He pushed himself backward, his legs kicking at the mud for purchase, finding it, taking his weight, propelling him into a crouch on fingers and toes. He skittered backward like a dog, hissing at the pain instead of with it, then he slewed around and launched himself away, rising into a sloppy run, falling, getting up again, running. And all the time screaming.

Burl and Vic and the others followed like a pack of rabid dogs.

Jake angled toward his front-end loader, putting it between himself and the pack. The keys were inside the cab. If he could only get to them.

But Burl and Vic split, each one heading toward one end of the machine as if this was something they had rehearsed. On some level Jake knew that they were simply taking the shortest route for each of them, but it felt like a coordinated attack. Jake glanced up at the cab and then to each side.

He wasn't going to make it.

If he got inside, would the reinforced safety glass keep them back? Even if the glass held, the door didn't lock from inside.

He began backing away from the machine. The trailer they were using as a temporary office was forty yards away. Jake spun around, deciding to make for it. If he could get inside, the doors had locks. There were desks he could push in front of the door to block it. The windows were tiny, too small for someone like Burl to climb in through.

All of that flashed through his brain as he took the first step toward the trailer. Burl lunged for him, actually jumping like an animal to try and grab him. Then suddenly Burl's head snapped to one side and his leap turned into a twisted tumble that send him splatting down to the mud, where he slid to a twisted stop.

His face was gone.

Simply gone.

Jake stared at Burl, trying to understand this new mystery, this new insanity. Even his lizard brain didn't know how to process this.

Then something pinged off the bucket of the front-end loader and went whizzing past his ear with a sound like an angry wasp.

There was a second ping. A third.

That's when he heard the sounds.

Distant. Small. Hollow.

Pok-pok-pok.

He whirled and crouched, staring into the rain.

Someone was firing.

Cold hands suddenly grabbed him from behind and Jake was falling. He twisted violently around to see Vic right there, tearing at him with torn fingernails, snapping at him with cracked teeth.

Vic was tall, over six feet, and nearly two hundred pounds. Jake towered over him, though, standing six-eight and packing an extra hundred pounds of muscle and mass on his frame. With power born of fear and desperation, he swung a punch into Vic's face that knocked the man five feet back. Teeth and blood flew. Vic hit the side of the bucket, spun, fell to his knees, and then was abruptly flung sideways as a fusillade of bullets tore into him, punching holes in thigh and hip and ribs and skull. Vic dropped and lay utterly still.

Jake wanted to stand and stare. He needed to take a moment to reset all of the dials in his head. However bullets pinged and whanged off the machine and behind him the other . . . things . . . were still coming. Jake cut them a single quick look and realized they were paying no heed to the bullets that pocked the mud around them. Or to the bullets that tore into their own flesh. Jake saw clothes puff up as rounds struck them. He saw chunks of bloody skin go flying into the rain.

It was insane.

It was like they didn't care. Or couldn't feel.

Or were . . .

His mind teetered on the edge of saying what he thought it was or might be.

Instead he turned and dove for cover as more bullets hammered into the yellow skin of the Caterpillar. The bucket was still low to the ground where he'd paused it when everything started turning to shit. Beneath the bucket was a trench cut by the scoop, and Jake wriggled into that. Big as he was, the trench was deep enough for him to get below ground level, but it was already half-filled with muddy water that was stingingly cold.

Dozens of bullets hit the front-end loader and went ricocheting off into the storm. Jake could hear men shouting.

Richie came splashing through the puddles, still moaning, still hungry, and then he was falling backward, bits of flesh and bone exploding from his chest, his throat, his face, his skull.

Then one of the girls fell with a big hole in her lower back. As soon as she hit the ground she began to crawl, as if the pain she had to be feeling didn't mean a goddamn thing to her. She saw Jake and began crawling toward his hiding place. She made it halfway there before a bullet struck her in the side of the head and blew brain matter five feet across the mud.

Jake saw it all from his hole.

The shouts were louder now. Men calling to each other as they came running across the construction site. Men in white hazmat suits and combat boots. Men with rifles and belts hung with grenades.

Soldiers.

Jake frowned, unable to understand this. Why were the soldiers in hazmat suits like on TV? That was the stuff they wear when there's some kind of toxic spill. Only this was a hurricane, not a spill. Or whatever they call a storm this bad this far inland. Supercell. Something like that. It wasn't any toxic spill. At least not as far as Jake knew.

Unless . . .

He blinked rainwater out of his eyes. Suddenly a lot of things tumbled together into a single pattern. Ugly, but glued together by some kind of logic.

What if there was a toxic spill?

The radio had been crazy all day with weird shit. Something

about a riot out at Doc Hartnup's funeral home. Something else happening at the school.

Jake only caught bits and pieces of it because you can't really listen to the radio while operating heavy equipment. Too much noise.

Now he wondered what he'd missed.

And he wondered what kind of trouble he was in.

He almost called out to the soldiers.

Almost.

It was not his lizard brain that made him hold his tongue. No, it was the civilized part of his brain. The part that believed that if things were this bad—if they were sending in soldiers in germ warfare gear and letting them kill people this randomly—then things were already in the shitter. Those soldiers never called out a warning. They never checked to see if Burl and the others needed help.

They'd simply opened fire.

"Oh, God," he breathed. But he did it very, very quietly.

As the soldiers hunted down the last girl and Jake's other friends, he sank down into the water until just his eyes and nose were out. He breathed as shallowly as he could, and he closed his eyes.

In order to try and stay alive, he did his level best to pretend to already be dead.

CHAPTER NINETY
STEBBINS LITTLE SCHOOL
STEBBINS, PENNSYLVANIA

Dez looked as if she wanted to either throw up or punch Sam Imura's teeth out. Either way, Trout wanted to grab the moment and pull it out of the fire.

"Captain Imura," he said firmly, "I hear what you're saying, and as a newsman I appreciate the urgency of your story, but if this thing is already out, then why does it matter if I have a copy of Volker's research? Go find Volker. He has all of it. Hell, he's the science. Go waterboard him, I'm sure he'd be happy to tell you anything you want to know. Coming after me seems kind of a waste of—"

Sam's eyes were cold. "Herman Volker is dead. He committed suicide."

Trout bowed his head and slumped into a chair. "Christ. Why the fuck didn't you say so? You assholes always have to drag everything out. Shit."

"We just found out about it," said Sam. "Until now he's been MIA and you were the only known source of intel. Now do you understand why those drives are so important? They are the only known record of Volker's work. We have plenty of research on Lucifer but no one has a clue about what Volker did when he modified the disease into Lucifer 113. Initial analysis of the infected indicate that the disease is radically different from the old Cold War version. We don't know if we have the time necessary to deconstruct and analyze Volker's version. Mr. Trout . . . *where are the flash drives?*"

Trout's mouth felt as if it was filled with burned ashes and bile. In a strained whisper he said, "I gave them to my cameraman."

"Who is he and where can we find him?"

"Gregory Weinman. Everyone calls him Goat. He's the one who was taking my standups and streaming them to the Net."

"Where?"

"He walked out of town just as the Guard were setting up the roadblocks. The last time I spoke with him—before you idiots began jamming all calls—he was at the Starbucks in Bordentown."

Sam Imura staggered. He took two or three small, aimless steps and almost collapsed against the blackboard on the wall. He put his face in his hands and said, "Jesus save us all."

"What is it?" snapped Dez. "What's wrong?"

Boxer went over and put his hand on Sam's shoulder. Moonshiner and Shortstop sat down hard on the chairs. Only Gypsy held her ground.

"What's wrong?" demanded Dez.

"Wrong?" mused Gypsy. "What's wrong is that we are all totally and completely fucked."

"I don't—"

"That's where the outbreak is," said Gypsy. "The Air Force dropped fuel-air bombs on the whole area. Bordentown is nothing but a cloud of hot ash."

CHAPTER NINETY-ONE
SUBURBS OF PITTSBURGH

"How we doing, boy?" asked Homer Gibbon.

Goat hoisted a fake smile onto his face. "We're getting some really great stuff here. I can't wait to get this onto the Net."

Homer pursed his lips. In the dark, Goat couldn't see the blood smeared all over the man. What little there was made it look as if the man was painted in tar. But he stank. At first the car had been filled with the sheared-copper smell of fresh blood, but now it was turning sour as the cells thickened and died. It was like being inside a meat locker with the power off. It took great willpower and a fear of reprisal to keep from vomiting.

"You think they'll watch it?" asked Homer, sounding a little insecure about it.

A sharp laugh escaped Goat before he could stop it.

"You think that's funny, boy?" asked Homer in a tone that was abruptly menacing.

"No," Goat said quickly. "Far from it. I'm pretty sure everyone in the world is going to watch these videos. I don't think anyone is going to watch anything else."

Homer looked at him for a long time. "You really think so?"

"Yeah," said Goat with complete honesty, "I absolutely think so."

CHAPTER NINETY-TWO
STEBBINS LITTLE SCHOOL
STEBBINS, PENNSYLVANIA

"That is not a happy-looking man," said Billy Trout.

He and Dez stood together watching Captain Sam Imura as he stood on the far end of the room having a mostly one-sided phone conversation. The news that Goat had the drives and that the Starbucks where he was waiting for Trout's call had been destroyed had hit everyone very hard. Imura stepped aside to call it into his boss—the national security advisor.

Imura had looked pretty defeated at the start of that call, but as the seconds peeled off and fell away, the man's shoulders slumped. Then Imura straightened and cut a sharp, appraising look at Trout.

"Uh oh," said Dez.

"Yeah," agreed Trout.

Imura came hurrying over, still holding the phone in the way people do when the line is still open. "Mr. Trout, do you still have the satellite phone Weinman gave you?"

Trout nodded and produced it.

"Is it charged?"

"Half-charged, but yeah."

"He has it," Imura said into the phone, listened, and added, "Good. We'll try again in five minutes."

He disconnected the call and considered Trout. "Listen, I guess it'll come as no surprise to you that they've been jamming all communications from Stebbins County."

"You don't say," murmured Trout drily.

"I just asked my boss to have all jamming stopped. Satellite interference, cell lines, the works."

"Good," said Dez, "and then maybe we can go around and close all the barn doors 'cause I'm pretty sure the horses have all run off."

Imura gave her a few millimeters of a tight smile. "If there's even the slightest chance that Weinman left the vicinity of the Bordentown Starbucks, then maybe we can reestablish contact."

"His name's Goat," said Trout, "and he didn't have a car. He walked across a field to get to the Starbucks. Or maybe hitchhiked."

"Then there's at least a small chance he hitchhiked again. If he's as tech-savvy as you said, then maybe he realized that service was being jammed and he moved on to someplace outside of the interference zone."

"Which he wouldn't have had to do if you ass-clowns didn't jam him in the first place," snapped Dez. "If he and Billy'd been able to stay in touch you'd already have Volker's notes."

Imura turned to her. "Really, Officer Fox, you want to Monday-morning quarterback this now? Is that the best use of our time?"

"I'm just saying."

"Fine, we fucked up. It's hereby noted."

Dez looked mildly embarrassed; an attitude that Trout found amusing. As he enjoyed having his scrotum remain attached, he declined to say so.

Imura looked at his watch. "The jamming should be down in a couple of minutes. Let's keep our fingers crossed."

Trout glanced from him to the other members of his team. "Who exactly are you guys? You said private contractors? That's the PC phrase for mercenaries, isn't it?"

"In a manner of speaking. We're former U.S. military who do special jobs."

"Like what?"

"Like classified stuff that I'm not going to talk about to a reporter."

Dez sniffed. "I met some of your kind in 'Stan."

Imura smiled. "The contractors in Afghanistan and Iraq were mostly Blackwater, who are, even by the somewhat loose standards of the mercenary community, total dickheads. Not as bad as Blue Diamond, but swimming at the edges of the same cesspool. Personally, I wouldn't piss on any of them if they were on fire."

"Don't sugarcoat it, Captain," said Trout.

"There are all kinds of contractors just like there are all kinds of reporters and all kinds of cops."

"And what kind are you?" asked Dez sharply.

"The kind I can live with," he said. He cocked his head to one side. "You know, Mr. Trout, I was given a pretty free hand for how I wanted to handle this. We could have done a hard infil of the school and taken you."

"You could have tried," growled Dez.

But Imura shook head. "I mean no disrespect when I say this, Officer, but if we wanted to play it that way we would have succeeded."

"I've met plenty of spec-ops jocks and—"

"You've never met operators like us. I'm not saying this to blow my own horn but to give you a perspective check. You have every right to think of anyone in a military uniform as your enemy. I don't blame you. However, if we were your enemies you would be dead, Officer Fox, and Mr. Trout would be having an even worse day than he's already had. It was my choice on how to play this and I set you up to take a run at us outside so we could take you. From all accounts you are a formidable law officer, but we play a different kind of ball. Let's be clear on that."

"Okay, okay," said Trout before Dez could get into gear with the kind of verbal counterattack that would probably end in fisticuffs, "you could have done it the Rambo way and instead you didn't. Why waste time making that point?"

"Because," said Imura, "if we can accept that killing you isn't high on my list of priorities, then maybe we can all put our dicks away and start working together."

Trout smiled thinly. "It's a lovely speech, Captain, but if knowing Dez has taught me anything it's that trust is earned."

"Not killing you doesn't earn trust?"

"It's a good start," said Trout. "Let's see where it takes us."

He lifted the satellite phone and punched Goat's number.

The number rang.

And rang.

And kept on ringing until Trout felt his heart begin to sink. Then someone answered it.

"Billy!" cried Goat. "Oh my God, Billy—"

There was a snarl of a harsh voice, the sound of an open palm on flesh, a cry of pain, and then a different voice growled, "Who the fuck's this?"

It took Trout a couple of stumbling moments to match this new voice to a recent memory and then to fit those awkward pieces into a puzzle shape that made only fractured sense. He felt his heart lurch in his chest.

He said, " Homer?"

CHAPTER NINETY-THREE
THE SITUATION ROOM
THE WHITE HOUSE, WASHINGTON, D.C.

Scott Blair closed his cell and wanted to scream.

Instead he made another call and got the director of the National Security Agency on the line. He explained about Goat Weinman having the flash drives.

"What do you want me to do?" asked the director.

"Hack his phone and email. He's a reporter and he's on the run. There's every chance that he sent the data to himself as a way of keeping it safe. Find out."

The director didn't ask whether Blair had a warrant. That time had already passed.

CHAPTER NINETY-FOUR
ON THE ROAD
FAYETTE COUNTY, PENNSYLVANIA

"Why as I live and breathe, it's Mr. Live From the Apocalypse his ownself," said Homer. "Billy Trout, how do you do?"

Homer grinned into the phone as he spoke. Beside him, Goat cowered back, one hand pressed to the welt on his cheek where the killer had belted him when Goat answered the call.

"Homer?" repeated Billy Trout. "Is this really Homer Gibbon?"

"In the flesh. Can't tell you how much I enjoyed your little speeches on the radio coupla hours ago. Really exciting stuff."

"How . . . how . . . ?"

"You gonna finish that sentence?"

"How are you with Goat? Is he okay? Did you hurt him? Christ, you'd better not have touched him, you sick fuck."

"Hey, mind your manners," warned Homer, "or I will do some particular damage to your friend."

"No, don't!"

"I ain't done shit to him so far, but that could change right quick, so make sure you keep a civil tongue in your head."

"Yes, yes, okay. I'm sorry. I'm just concerned for my friend. May I speak with him, please?"

Homer pulled onto the shoulder, put his hand over the mouthpiece, and turned to Goat. "This thing have a speaker?"

"Yes," said Goat and when Homer held out the device, he flicked the switch. Homer leaned close and very quietly said, "You don't speak unless I give the nod."

"Yes. No problem."

"And if you say the wrong thing, you know what I'll do to make you sorry about it."

"Yes."

"Good." Homer held the sat phone up between them. "We got this on speaker, so Mr. Goat can hear you, too."

"Thank you," said Trout. "Goat . . . you okay there, buddy?"

Goat looked for approval and got a nod. "I'm okay, Billy. He hasn't hurt me."

"Thank God. Can you tell me where you are?"

Homer shook his head.

"No," said Goat. "I can't do that."

"Can you tell me what you're doing?"

Homer thought about it, then nodded.

"Mr. Gibbon wants me to tell his side of the story. The whole story. About the Black Eye and the Red Mouth. You remember those from the trial, Billy?"

"Sure."

"That was only part of the story. A small part." Goat saw Homer give him a small nod of approval and decided to take that script and run with it. "There's so much more to the story, Billy. I know you'd really appreciate it. It's the greatest story anyone's ever told. It's so . . . deep. So big."

Homer looked pleased, but Goat was afraid of overdoing it, so he closed with that.

"I . . . see," said Trout. "Sounds like something I definitely want to hear."

"You really do." An idea occurred to Goat and he hoped Trout would be sharp enough to catch the ball and run with it. "It's like you always told me, Billy. There are layers and layers to Homer Gibbon. No one really knows him. The stuff at the trial was all bullshit. No one ever asked him the right questions. No one ever really wanted to know what he saw and why he does what he does. It's like people didn't think the Red Mouth or the Black Eye were real. You always said there was more to the story. You always said that it was a crime that no one ever let Mr. Gibbon speak to the jury, speak from his heart, and tell the whole truth. You were right, Billy. Absolutely right."

There was only a half beat before Trout said, "Nice to know you were paying attention, Goat. And I'm jealous that you're there to get that story. Will we ever get to hear it?"

Goat waited for Homer to give another nod.

"That's what we have planned. I have some incredible stuff already. Really amazing stuff. As soon as we get somewhere with Wi-Fi I'm going to upload it and blow everyone's minds."

"That's great, that's—ah, I'm so jealous, man. You're going to do more than blow minds, Goat. You're going to open minds."

"I know."

"Goat, make sure you preserve everything. That information is too valuable to lose. You should back it up."

"I have it saved to my hard drive."

"No . . . back it up on those flash drives," said Trout, very clearly and precisely. "That's how the best reporters preserve the *most important* information."

Goat almost asked him what the hell he was talking about when he realized that Billy was spinning the game on him. Telling *him* something.

And he got it.

The flash drives. Important information.

"You're absolutely right, Billy. I'll make sure I protect that information."

"Good," said Trout, and the relief was there to be heard in his voice. "Mr. Gibbon?"

"Call me Homer," said the killer.

"Thank you, that's an honor, sir. Please call me Billy. I want to thank you for what you're doing for Goat. This is the kind of story he's always wanted. Something big, something that will do a lot of good."

"That's what this is, sure enough."

"Is there any way I can be of assistance?"

Homer snorted. "Aren't you stuck in that little school with a buncha kids?"

"I might be able to get out of here. I'd be happy to help Goat with this story. With his camerawork and me doing the interviews we can—"

"No thanks," said Homer. "We got this covered. You have a good day now."

He ended the call and pulled back onto the road, heading north-west.

Goat's heart was hammering with painful insistence and he stared longingly at the satellite phone. His mind, however, was replaying Billy's word.

Preserve the most important information.

He cleared his throat and made his voice sound normal. "Billy's right," he said. "I need to backup everything on flash drives."

"What are they?" asked Homer.

Goat explained, then added, "I always carry some extras. It's a reporter thing."

He dug into his pocket and showed Volker's drives to Homer.

"All the videos you been taken fit onto those little things?"

"Absolutely, and then we need to get it out to the world."

"Wi-Fi, right?"

"Wi-Fi," agreed Goat.

"Okeydokey," said the killer. He stepped on the gas and the Escalade plowed through the storm winds, heading toward Pittsburgh.

Heading toward hope.

CHAPTER NINETY-FIVE
MOBILE COMMAND POST
FAYETTE COUNTY

Major General Zetter and his top aides met in the mobile command post parked three miles from the blast zone. The big vehicle rocked as winds buffeted it. Electronic workstations provided real-time intel from satellites and field observation posts, and one wall of the MCP was covered in a high-res satellite map of Stebbins and Fayette counties.

"Sir," said one of his captains, "we're clocking sustained winds of forty miles per hour with gusts up to seventy. Western Fayette has winds above fifty. We can't keep the birds in the air."

This had been a problem since the start of this campaign. Helicopters do not like high winds, and with storm gusts, high-tension wires, unlighted structures such as grain silos, cellular towers, and trees swaying in the wind, the helos had had a difficult night. Five were down with damage. Two were wrecked, with the loss of one complete crew and two other Guardsmen in the hospital.

Zetter coughed and fished in his pocket for a handkerchief, found one and covered his mouth as the coughs continued. It was the ash from the firebombs. He needed some clean air and maybe a gallon of mouthwash.

"Sir," his aide prompted gently. "Should I recall the birds?"

On the big satellite map there were hundreds of small red dots. People fleeing from the attack on Route 653 and the resulting bombs.

"Keep them flying," he said. Another fit of coughing wracked him, shorter but intense.

"Sir, did you say—"

"I said keep them flying," snapped Zetter, his face bright red from coughing.

The aide nodded and turned away to relay the order.

As Zetter dabbed at his mouth, aware of the eyes that were on him, listening to a couple of other officers coughing. They'd all been out there with him.

It made him remember the respiratory problems from people who'd inhaled the smoke after the collapse of the Towers. Some of those people got sick from what they'd sucked into their lungs. Some died. He fished for the condition caused by breathing in particulate matter. *Pneumonitis?* He thought that was it.

Zetter wondered if he was going to get sick from the smoke. He already had some mild emphysema from all those years he smoked. He didn't smoke anymore, but it was damage done. No cancer, though, so he'd been lucky there, but his wind was for shit. A long flight of stairs could put him on his ass for ten minutes.

Now this.

The dust.

The stress.

The fear.

Another aide, who was hunched over a small desk speaking into a phone, raised his head and pointed to the western edge of the map. On it several larger dots were moving in opposition to the outer wave of fleeing people.

"General, the additional units have reached the Outbreak Zone. I have their commanding officer on the line."

Zetter hauled himself out of the chair and lumbered over to the desk, snatched the phone and identified himself. "With whom am I speaking?"

"Sir," said a woman's voice, "this is Colonel Ruiz."

"Give me a sit-rep, Colonel."

"We are tracking a large number of individuals heading west through farmlands. Estimate four hundred plus. They appear to be civilians."

"Colonel, have you been briefed on Lucifer?"

"I have, sir."

"Are you able to determine if these people are infected?"

"No, sir. Though a large number of them appear to be injured. We are seeing torn clothing, what appear to be flash-burns, and—"

"Colonel, can you contain the civilians and examine them for bites? We need to make certain that—"

Before the colonel could answer, Zetter could hear sounds from her end of the line. Military personnel yelling to the oncoming wave of people. Zetter turned and looked at the satellite map and saw the outer edge of the wave of lights closing very fast on the line of larger dots—military vehicles and their crews. He heard the shouts turn to yells.

And then there was the rattle of gunfire.

A few sporadic shots at first.

Then sustained gunfire.

And screams.

Colonel Ruiz never came back on the line.

CHAPTER NINETY-SIX
LAUREL RIDGE STATE PARK
FAYETTE COUNTY

Demolitions specialist Mike Chrusciel liked blowing things up. After getting caught once rigging cherry bombs to the tailpipe of his high school disciplinarian, Mike was given the first of what became a series of lectures. Half the lecture focused on not playing with dangerous items and the dangers to himself and others. Once during that half of the lecture Mike had made the mistake of saying "Yeah, blah, blah, blah" out loud. He spent the next month in detention and got his ass hammered flat at home. That was ninth grade.

The second half of the lecture took a different direction. It was filled with suggestions for how he could turn his "hobby" into something useful. The military. Nobody loves blowing things up more than the army. That was the gist. Not in those words, of course, but that's the message Mike took away with him.

Occasionally there was a third part of the lecture. More of a warning, really. The only really likely alternative for someone like him was a different institution. One with bars.

After high school, and with no adult criminal record at all and his juvie offenses sealed, he rode an administrative recommendation from the school vice principal into the National Guard. During screenings and training it became clear to everyone that Mike Chrusciel liked to blow things up. And when it became clear that he wasn't going to be a danger to his fellow Americans, they put him into the right classes and taught him everything he ever wanted to know about explosives, IEDs, mines, grenades, satchel charges, and all of those other wonderful toys. He discovered that his connection to explosives went beyond the simple pleasure of seeing things go *bang*— he had a real talent for it. And working in the field, being *allowed* to play with explosives, gradually erased the immature thrill seeker part of him in favor of a more focused and intellectual aspect. Bombs of various kinds became like puzzles. Selecting the right device for each situation, purpose, or goal. He'd earned another stripe in Afghanistan and there was already some talk about him going higher. There was talk about OCS and maybe a career in the army rather than a short hitch to keep out of jail.

In the world of military ordnance, Mike Chrusciel had found himself.

He never expected to be planting mines here on American soil. Not outside of a test range. But the orders from General Zetter had been crystal clear. The infected were breaking through the lines. There were several chokepoints, where the landscape and the presence of rivers and streams would funnel anyone on foot to routes of least resistance. He and his partner, Cyrus, were assigned to mine one of those routes. Two miles farther down the road, a checkpoint was being reinforced in case any infected got through.

Mike smiled at that thought.

Get through?

Not once he was done. No, sir.

The orders were to disable any infected. Killing them, Mike was told, was more difficult in that it required very specific damage to the brain and brain stem. Fair enough. He could rig the paths so that anything dumb or unlucky enough to step onto that path would be crippled in a hot second. That would allow Mike and his partner to finish them off with headshots, or they could be left for the roving patrols that were scheduled to check all of these hot spots.

He studied geodetic survey maps and then walked the landscape to make his own determinations about likely routes. The infected were supposed to be as close to brain dead as made no difference. Aggressive but stupid, that's how one of the guys described them. Mike had to make some important decisions and he took a little extra time to do it, fighting the clock to get it all right.

Mike concentrated on blast mines that would be triggered by someone stepping on them. He set the tension so that anyone over sixty pounds would trigger it. A deer's footstep wasn't heavy enough because its weight was distributed between four legs. But a human? When a person stepped on a blast mine, the device's charge detonated, creating a blast shock wave composed of very hot gases traveling at extremely high velocity. When the blast wave hits breaks the ground surface, it results in a massive compression force that blows a victim's foot off.

Infected or not, they were going down.

In areas where a larger group might pass, Mike planted the bigger and heavier fragmentation mines. These were crammed with several kilograms of shrapnel. A real party pleaser.

And for narrow areas where a single infected might pursue one of the patrolling soldiers, Mike positioned more than a dozen M86 Pursuit Deterrent Munitions. These PDMS were small U.S. antipersonnel mines generally used by Special Forces to deter pursuit. In function they were like small hand grenades, and each had a pin and fly-off lever. Once the pin is pulled and the lever has been ejected, a timer starts and after twenty-five seconds it launches seven tripwires with a maximum range of six meters. That creates a spiderweb effect; anyone pursuing the user trips a wire that activates the mine and a liquid propellant charge launches the mine a couple of meters into the air. The fragmentation warhead detonates, breaking the mine into six hundred flesh-rending fragments. Normally these devices deactivated themselves after a few hours, but Mike disabled the timers. To warn other soldiers, however, he tied plastic tags to tree branches. Yellow for land mines, orange for devices mounted in the trees. The tags had tiny sensors that would alert troops to their presence. Modern warfare, baby. Mike loved it.

Elsewhere, in spots where the infected were closing in on fields, Mike heard that planes were going to be dropping cluster bombs. Part of the GATOR land mine system. The Navy would drop five-hundred-pound CBU-78/Bs and the Air Force would lay down some thousand-pound CBU-89/Bs. Very heavy shit, and Mike wished he could be there to see it. Not the drop . . . he wanted to see what happened when a bunch of infected tried waltzing across a field of those puppies.

Ka-boom.

Once Mike had everything just so, he carefully retreated to where his partner waited. The guy they paired him with was a moonfaced kid from Monroeville named Cyrus who never said two words when no words would do. Mike knew chattier rocks. But that was okay. It was better when Cyrus said nothing because when he did say something it was dumb shit like, "Look, a deer." Like it was a thing of wonder.

A deer.

In the woods?

How amazing.

This was the ass-end of Pennsylvania, deep in farm country, and both Stebbins and Fayette counties overlapped with state forests. Deer were as thick as mosquitoes out here, and just as annoying.

Big brown rats, in Mike's view.

In the dark, though, and with all this rain, deer were a real problem. You could hear them and not know what was moving in the woods. You could see them and not know what they were, because they blended in so well, and moved so quietly. And they could just as easily trip a mine as one of the infected.

Mike explained this to Cyrus, who didn't so much nod or say he understood as simply look marginally less vacant for a moment.

"We need an elevated shooting position," suggested Mike. "That way if we see any deer coming along the path we can put them down, keep the network of devices intact. Okay?"

Cyrus made a grunting sound that Mike took as assent.

He put Cyrus in the crotch of an elm. For all his apparent vacuity, the kid could climb like a monkey. He was also a good shot, a safe weapons-handler. He wasn't rewarding company but Mike didn't expect to take any friendly fire.

With Cyrus in place, Mike drifted down a game trail, stepping around or over tripwires, double-checking that everything was just so.

Then he froze.

It wasn't exactly that Mike heard or saw anything, but instead had a sense that something moved out there in the storm-filled, shadowy woods. He turned very slowly, surveying the landscape. The boughs of the trees swayed like the arms of drunks fighting for balance. Rain fell between the trees, gathered into fat dollops, and dropped from branches and leaves. Winds howled through the forest at ground level, slapping the bushes and shrubs this way and that.

There was so much movement that Mike couldn't tell if there was *nothing* out there or an entire herd of deer.

Command had warned of packs of infected crossing farm fields after the bombs in Bordentown, but so far Mike hadn't seen a single one of them. He hard the chatter on the radio and knew that there were some real problems out there, but it all seemed to be happening elsewhere. Sure as hell not here. So far the most they'd seen was a red fox, a bunch of squirrels, and not much of anything else.

The forest kept moving, but as far as Mike could tell it was just Superstorm Zelda being a total bitch.

He found his own tree and climbed up onto the lowest limb, relieved to have the dense canopy of leaves shield him from the heaviest of the rain.

And then he saw something that was neither wind nor squirrel.

The leaves trembled on the far side of a slope, and Mike put his rifle to his shoulder and aimed at the center of a wall of rustling shrubs. If it was a deer, he was going to shoot its Bambi-ass before it could trip one of the mines.

Then the shrubs parted and something stepped through.

It wasn't a deer.

It wasn't a fleeing civilian.

It was a soldier.

It was a soldier, in fact, that Mike knew. It was a good friend of his. "Teddy?"

Sergeant Teddy Polk staggered out of the dense line of shrubs and nearly lost his footing at the top of the rise. His white hazmat suit was covered in mud and torn in several places, the hood hanging down behind his back. Polk had no rifle and he walked uncertainly, weakly, with one hand clamped to his left bicep. Polk's foot came down wrong and he pitched forward, staggering down the slope toward the pressure mine hidden halfway down.

"Teddy! No!" bellowed Mike as he dropped from the tree and began to run toward his friend. He knew the pattern of his traps; Teddy was walking right toward a blast mine.

"*Stop!*" screamed Mike. "*For God's sake, Teddy, freeze. Don't move. Land mines!*"

Teddy stopped. He looked around but his face was clouded by pain and confusion. He blinked and his mouth worked for a moment, trying to form a word.

"M-Mike?"

"Yeah, it's me. Shit, man, don't move. There's a mine five feet in front of you. Stay right there. Let me come to you."

Teddy Polk nodded, but it was a vague movement and Mike couldn't be sure if his friend really heard him.

"Stay right there, okay, buddy? Don't move."

Teddy swayed like a drunken man, but he didn't take another step.

Mike began creeping through the deadly landscape he'd created. He knew where he'd planted everything, and the yellow and orange tags were there, the colors glowing with luminescent paint even in the darkness, and pulsing when the lightning flashed. Mike was almost to the safe zone when he heard a sound behind him, and he pivoted, expecting to see that idiot Cyrus.

It wasn't.

A woman stood directly behind him.

Middle-aged, dressed in jeans and a sweater covered in flower appliqués and blood. A woman with ragged bite marks on her cheeks and eyebrows. Black blood dribbled from between her lips.

"Shit!" cried Mike as he reached for his side arm.

The woman spit right into his face. Into his eyes and mouth. A big, wet gob of black blood.

Mike screamed and backpedaled, dropping the gun that was halfway out of its holster. The black muck was as thick as molasses and it tasted like copper and bile. He gagged, but he could feel it in his mouth. Itching. Burning. He pawed it out of his eyes as he reeled. He could see, but only a smeared swatch of the world. The woman hissed and reached for him, but Mike backhanded her away.

Then Teddy Polk caught him, kept him from falling.

Teddy called his name.

Except that wasn't what Teddy said.

It wasn't his name. It was just a meaningless moan. Not his name, not even a word.

A moan.

Like the sound the woman made.

Mike screamed.

He tore free from Teddy Polk and shoved his friend—or whatever this thing now was—and watched the wounded soldier stumble backward. Two steps. Three.

And Teddy's foot came down on a pressure mine.

Mike tried to run.

He really tried.

He pivoted in the mud, spun the woman behind him—trying to put her between his body and the blast—and Mike bolted for the steep upslope that was free of mines. He got four good steps away from Teddy before the blast.

The shockwave picked him up and punched him hard into the slope. He felt something hit him in the lower back. He felt it stab him.

Stab all the way through him.

He half-lay, half-stood against the sharp canted slope, his chin resting on the knurled curve of an exposed tree root, his arms dangling at his sides. Thunder echoed in his ears and he could feel warmth running in lines down the insides of his clothes, front and back. It was the only warmth he could feel; everything else was strangely cold.

Off somewhere to the north he could hear someone call his name.

Was it Cyrus?

Was it his mother?

He couldn't tell. His eardrums were ruptured and his head hurt so badly he couldn't think.

He didn't even remember pushing off from the slope. It happened somehow and now he stood on the path, looking down at the red things that had been Teddy and the woman with the sweater. They had been right there when the mine exploded, and it had exploded them. Torn them from humanity into—what? Parts? Pieces?

Mike didn't like putting the right word to it.

Teddy had no legs at all. He couldn't even see the pieces of them.

His back hurt.

And his stomach.

He touched the front of his hazmat suit and tried to understand what he was touching. His eyes stung from the black blood the woman had spat at him. The itching in his mouth and throat was really bad.

But Mike wasn't sure if he cared about that or if he was just aware of it.

He ran his fingers over his stomach, and over the thing that stood straight out from the white material of the hazmat suit. When he raised his fingers he saw that they were smeared with red.

Yeah, he thought. *That's right.*

He knew on some detached level that he was hurt. Maybe hurt bad.

He heard his name again. It floated to him on the wind.

Definitely not his mother.

Mike took a few small steps away from the red carnage on the ground. The rain jabbed at the skin of his face. It washed more of the black goo from his eyes.

After a while, Mike looked down at his stomach. Just to see.

It took him a long time to understand what he was seeing, to construct an explanation for the long, slender white thing that seemed to be growing out of him. It was jagged and heavy.

Like polished ivory.

Except that it wasn't ivory.

He knew what it was.

He knew where it had come from.

The woman's legs had been totally blown away.

But not all of the parts were lost. Mike tried a word, one he thought made sense of this.

296 | JONATHAN MABERRY

"Femur," he said. He heard how rational his voice sounded. That was okay.

The itching in his mouth was now deeper. Inside his nose, behind his sinuses, down in his stomach. His lungs.

Itching.

Hurting.

Aching.

Mike felt something moving on his lips. Drops of blood. He touched them, looked at them. Red. Sure. But threaded through the red were lines of black. And inside the black were twisting little white things.

He said the only word that really mattered. The word that made a statement about this whole farce, from the time his unit was rolled out until now. And maybe it was a statement about how this thing would continue to unfold.

He said, "Fuck."

He heard Cyrus call his name, and hearing the voice provoked two immediate and intense reactions in him.

The first was that he wanted Cyrus to find him. To get him the hell out of here. To get him to an aid station because, fuck it, he had a piece of thigh bone shoved all the way through his body. Shit. Shit. Shit.

The other reaction was totally different, totally alien, totally terrifying.

When he heard his partner's voice it made him so goddamn hungry.

Hungry.

Hungry.

Oh God, he thought.

He could hear Cyrus coming, crashing through the wet brush, circling wide around the area marked by the yellow and orange tags. Coming close, coming fast. Coming soon.

Mike Chrusciel tried to yell, to warn his partner, to tell him to get the fuck out of here. But his voice was barely his anymore. It was thick, filled with wrongness, and his warning cry sounded more like the moan of someone in pain.

But not physical pain. Not thigh bone through the stomach pain.

No, it was a different kind of pain.

The pain of a terrible, bottomless hunger.

Cyrus would be here in a few seconds. He'd come running up to help. And then what?

The officers had been pretty damn graphic in the briefings. They pulled no punches when they explained what happened to the infected.

People who were like him.

Jesus.

As Cyrus came running, calling Mike's name, Mike turned and used the last little bit of him that was his left to own. He made his legs move. It was just a few steps.

He heard Cyrus yell, "No!"

Then Mike stepped onto one of the mines.

He loved explosions. Always had. They made him feel powerful. They always comforted him.

Take me home, he thought as he raised his foot, releasing the trigger.

He rode the blast all the way out of the world.

CHAPTER NINETY-SEVEN
ROUTE 26
SOUTHWESTERN PENNSYLVANIA

"Put something on it," screamed the man.

"I'm trying," his wife yelled back.

In the backseat the baby was crying. The woman knelt on her seat and tried to cram a folded baby blanket against the hole in her husband's shoulder. It was not a torrent, there was no artery there, but it pulsed with his heartbeat, and his heart was hammering. His whole right side was slick with red.

"I don't have anything to tie it with," she said, trying to hold it in place with one hand as she tried to unbuckled her belt with the other.

"How bad is it?" he demanded in a terrified voice.

"It's not bad, it's not bad," she said, knowing it was a lie.

"Did you *see* that? That cop just fucking *bit* me."

"I know, I know. He must have been . . ."

She let that go because she didn't know what the cop could have been. The radio was saying wild things, and the whole world behind them seemed to be on fire.

"We need to find a hospital."

"No," he barked. "No way. Keep the pressure on. I'll be okay."

"But you're bleeding!"

"No way I'm stopping anywhere near here. Everyone's nuts around here."

She worked the belt off and managed to cinch it around his arm.

"Not too tight," he cautioned, feeling a little calmer, a little more in control as the miles fell away behind him.

The baby was crying so loud that they both had to shout.

"I'm okay," he said. "I'm good. See to Lucy. I'll be fine."

"We need to stop."

But he shook his head. "No way. No damn way."

The car shot down the road and vanished into the storm. They crossed the state line into West Virginia at nearly eighty miles an hour.

CHAPTER NINETY-EIGHT
BEYOND THE QUARANTINE ZONE
THE HEARTS AND ARMOR MEDIEVAL FAIRE
NORMALVILLE, PENNSYLVANIA

Rob Meyer and his friends sat around a small foldout table in the singlewide trailer used as a greenroom for the performers on the fairground. None of them were in armor, having shucked the heavy chain and plate mail hours ago, after the pig roast that ended each day of swordplay, bawdy songs, medieval crafts, heavy drinking, and choreographed jousting. Since most of the events were under tents, the show had gone on yesterday—although in abbreviated form.

The guys were all in sweats and T-shirts, their hair and beards glistening from rainwater. Rob had gone around the camp, banging on trailer doors, rousing the staff, telling them what was going on.

Some of them already knew. Night owls who'd been glued to their portable TVs or laptops since last night, watching storm-soaked reporters do standups outside of the Stebbins County line. Others had slept through it, dropping off to exhausted sleep after shucking their weapons and armor.

Now everyone was watching. Some there in the greenroom, others in their own trailers. No one was sleeping anymore.

Not on the fairgrounds, and probably not anywhere.

"Is this shit real?" asked one of the roustabouts. It was the sixth or seventh time he'd asked the same question.

"It's real," said Rob.

"Yeah, okay, but what *is* it?"

"It's a riot," said one of the grooms.

"I don't think so," said Rob. Before the groom could ask him to explain, the CBS affiliate out of Pittsburgh cut in with breaking news. They managed to get one of their news trucks close to a section of Route 653 in Fayette County. The reporter stood in the rain and shouted impossible things. Behind the reporter something was burning. Police vehicles whipped red and blue lights through the night.

"This is a scene of total chaos," said the reporter. "You can see the fires that are still burning. Witnesses claim that military aircraft dropped bombs on the western edge of Bordentown. We can't get any closer than two miles, but even from here the heat is incredible. An unnamed source in Washington says that these measures are being taken to prevent an outbreak of an as-yet unknown disease. This source claims that the disease is highly contagious and causes anyone who becomes infected to act in a violent and irrational way. Local police departments throughout the region, including many in northwestern Maryland, are reporting a shocking increase in violent crimes."

Behind the reporter a man and woman, both bleeding from several wounds, were shoving their children into their car. The children were screaming, and the woman clutched a small, limp child to her breast. The husband slammed the doors and hit the gas so hard the rear tires showered a dozen people with mud. A moment later there was a heavy crunch and then the reporter was running with the cameraman following. On the road a woman in a waitress uniform lay sprawled in the road as the taillights of the car dwindled in the rain.

"Are you seeing this?" cried the reporter. "That car just ran over a woman."

"Is this shit real?" asked the roustabout again.

"It's real," said Rob.

"This is crazy," said one of the jousters. "That's close. That's like fifteen miles from here."

"I know," Rob said and cast a troubled eye toward the door.

The groom said, "It doesn't make any sense. What kind of virus makes people do this kind of thing?"

"Maybe it's a—" but that was as far as Rob got. There was a series of loud pops and they all whirled toward the door. "What the hell?"

There was another wave of them. Sharper now, closer.

"Someone's shooting."

But it was more than that. Beneath and between the shots, wrapped inside the fist of the storm, there were screams.

Suddenly the whole bunch of them were scrambling up from the table and crowding through the door into the rainy darkness.

The shots were louder but sporadic. A handgun, thought Rob. Not a rifle. Not automatic gunfire.

They peered through the rain, trying to orient themselves.

"There!" cried the groom, pointing down the long, wide avenue of the jousting field. The colored banners whipped and popped in the gusting wind. The field was turning into a muddy lake. On the far side of the field the horses neighed and whinnied with anxiety.

Rob took a few tentative steps onto the field and for a few seconds he couldn't see anything.

Then there were three more shots. Three muzzle flashes that created a brief strobe-effect that revealed struggling, staggering figures. The screams came from there, and Rob's mouth opened in horror as he saw staff members from the fair fighting with dozens of people. Strangers. Someone was firing, but there was only one last hollow crack and the gun fell silent.

The screams increased.

Some of the men—the groom, the roustabout, and a few others—immediately began running toward the melee. They all had friends there.

But Rob caught the arm of the jouster.

"No," he said urgently. "There's too many."

"Christ, we have to do something . . ."

"I know. Come on."

Rob dragged him toward the prop shed, which was bolted to the side of the greenroom trailer. Rob fished the key from his pocket, jammed it into the padlock, threw the lock and chain into the mud, and yanked the doors open. With only a quick worried glance at the jouster, Rob began pulling items from the shed. He pressed a broad-sword into the jouster's hands and then, almost as an afterthought, pulled a rondache shield from the rack and handed it to him.

"The fuck, man," growled the jouster, holding up the sword, "it's not even sharp."

"Yeah, but it's fucking heavy." He grabbed his own long-sword—an exquisite replica of the ninth-century Viking Sæbø sword—and another of the round shields. Then he and the jouster turned and began running.

Some of the strangers were sprinting or staggering across the field toward them. They howled like animals. Their bodies were pale and wrong, and some of them had terrible wounds on their faces and arms and throats.

"Jesus Christ!" cried the jouster as two of them closed on him, racing forward with waxy white fingers.

The jouster was frozen in shock and indecision, so Rob shouldered him out of the way. He smashed one of the strangers in the face with the shield and struck the other one across the face with the flat of his sword.

The blows were heavy, backed by a lot of muscle and mass, powered by fear and a surge of adrenaline. The strangers staggered, slipped in the mud, and fell.

And then they got back up again.

Rob blinked in confusion.

The strangers snarled, revealing teeth that were smeared with blood so dark it was almost black. Then they launched themselves at him.

Once more Rob swung the rondache at one of the strangers. The shield was made of leather-covered wood with plates of metal studded with nails. Although the swords were unsharpened, the shields had to be fully functional or the performers would be crippled if they failed to block. Rob drove the metal edge of the rondache into the biting mouth of the closest attacker, and suddenly black blood and pieces of teeth filled the air. The man went down, but he writhed in the mud, trying to get back to his feet. Rob pivoted and brought his sword around in an overhand cut that packed muscle and gravity into the blow. Even without a sharpened edge, the second man's head burst apart, showering Rob and the jouster with brain matter and more of the black blood.

They reeled back, spitting out the blood, gagging at the horror of what had just happened.

Then they heard feet slopping in the mud and they turned to see a dozen of the strangers running toward them.

Rob and the jouster exchanged a brief look.

For years they'd played the roles of warriors—swordsmen and knights, Viking raiders, Roman soldiers, even pirates. They'd each fought in thousands of duels, and on their off days they fenced with their peers. They were superb swordsmen and each of them held weapons with which their hands and reflexes and minds were perfectly attuned.

So despite the absolute madness and unreality of this moment, deep in the hearts of each of them some ancient voice cried out a challenge. A warrior's call to arms. A bellow that would not have been out of place on the medieval battlefields of feudal Europe. As they yelled, their mouths began to curl into fierce smiles as if remembering those ancient days of bloodshed and glory.

With swords in hand, thy rushed forward to meet the charge, hacking and smashing.

The crowd of zombies swept over them in seconds.

But oh, how glorious those seconds were.

CHAPTER NINETY-NINE
STEBBINS LITTLE SCHOOL
STEBBINS, PENNSYLVANIA

Dez said, "What in the big green fuck was that all about?"

"Goat has the drives and I just told him that he needs to upload the contents and get them out."

"I didn't hear that," said Dez.

"I did," said Sam Imura. "And it was mighty damn clever. You think your friend understood what you were saying?"

"Positive."

"Good." He took the phone from Trout and removed the cable he'd jammed into it as soon as he realized who was on the other end of the call. The cable was plugged into a small computer strapped to Imura's forearm, and the captain spent a few seconds tapping keys.

"What's that?" asked Dez. "You running a trace?"

"Trying to. We already pinged the satellite Goat used earlier when he broadcast Billy's messages from here. And . . ." His voice trailed off as he read the display. Then he snapped his fingers and one of his people hurried over with a different sat phone connected to a portable battery pack. Sam snatched the phone and made a call, which was answered immediately. "Sir . . . we may have caught a break. Goat Weinman is still alive and we're reasonably sure he has the flash drives in his possession. The call was too short to get an exact fix on him. He's in Pennsylvania, closing in on the suburbs of Pittsburgh. We need a team monitoring the frequency of his sat phone, and we need people watching the Net. Goat is going to upload videos of Homer Gibbon. Interviews. They should be large files, which means fairly long upload times. Once the first is up we need to capture his computer signature and backtrack him. He may try to upload the Volker files at the same time, so we have to put together a pattern search that includes as many keywords as we think might be in the Volker files. I suggest the Latin names of the parasites. They're not likely to be in any other uploads tonight. Search on those and then feed that to the ground forces. We'll need all local and state police in on that, too." Sam listened for a few seconds, and then said, "No, sir, I don't think that's an option. The storm's getting worse. There's no way a chopper's going up in this, which means that my team is too far away. I'm handing the football back to you." He listened again. "That's not how I see it, Scott. I do have my priorities straight. I'm not in a position to be of use in the manhunt, but there are other fights worth fighting."

Trout thought he heard Blair yelling as Sam ended the call. The captain handed the sat phone back to his soldier.

"Well," he said, "you've actually been a big help."

"If it works out," said Trout.

"Sure, if it works out."

"Now what?" asked Dez bitterly. "You and your goon squad waltz off and leave us ass-deep in the alligator swamp?"

Sam smiled. He had a lot of very white teeth. "Actually, Officer Fox, I was rather hoping that I could help you get a few hundred kids the hell out of this particular ring of hell."

Dez and Trout stared at him.

"What?" they asked in unison.

"You said that you wanted to load the buses and take the kids somewhere safe? Well, if you could use five very well-armed body-guards, consider us part of *your* team."

CHAPTER ONE HUNDRED
THE NORTHERN LEVEES
FAYETTE COUNTY

Jake DeGroot realized that he couldn't hide in a wet hole all night.

They might find him.

The soldiers. And the . . .

He had no word for the other things. Things like the girls. Like his friends. Like Burl.

Just because they hadn't found him so far didn't meant they wouldn't.

Or couldn't.

He had no real idea what they could or couldn't do.

He had to move. To get out of the hole.

Before that.

And before he froze to death.

Jake knew that it wasn't really cold enough for that, but the water was cold enough to numb him. He remembered seeing something about hypothermia on an old episode of *Survivorman*. His teeth chattered constantly, shivers swept over him in waves, and he didn't like the way his heart was beating. No, he didn't like that one bit. He was a big man, and the last thing he needed now was a heart attack. Or slow feet because his nerves were in some kind of shock.

But leaving the pit . . . That was so scary. It made his balls want to climb up inside his body. It made him want to cry. Or scream.

Or go to sleep.

That was the other problem.

Between working hard all day yesterday and last night, and then lying here for hours in the cold, he was getting weirdly drowsy. He kept nodding off and then jerking awake when his face fell into the water.

"Got to get out of here."

He didn't know he was going to say it out loud until he'd said it. His voice sounded ridiculously loud and very strange. There was a sharp note of panic in his voice. A whine that was almost a sob.

He didn't like that, either.

"I'm losing my shit here," he told himself, trying to make his voice sound normal and reasonable. It didn't.

The rain was heavy, relentless. The ditch was so completely filled that the whole area was becoming a small lake.

"You're going to drown here, you dumb fuck."

There was anger in his voice now. That was better.

Better.

Even so it took Jake another three minutes to will his right arm to rise out of the water. Not because it was so numb with cold—which it was—but because he was numb with terror. There was no light except what flashed across the sky, and all that showed him was water, mud, and the bodies left behind by the soldiers.

Burl.

"Move, goddamn it. Move, move, move, move."

His right arm came up slowly, rising to the surface, then above it, and finally out toward the mud beyond the ditch. The rain immediately washed the mud from his hand, and when the next lightning flashed he was horrified to see how pale he was. Blue-white. Corpselike.

Like one of them.

"It's the cold, asshole," he told himself. "It's just the cold."

He reached for higher ground at the edge of the pit, but his fingers sank into the mud and found nothing to hold. He tried again and did nothing more than splash and stir the water in which he lay.

"No," he said, and that note of panic was back in his voice, stronger and sharper than before. Jake tried it with both hands. Nothing. He tried to kick against the near edge of the ditch, but his feet sank to the ankles. It took real effort to pull his feet out again. The right one came first, plopping free of the mud, but as he pulled the left one out he felt his shoe slide over the bulb of his heel.

Then he heard the sound.

Off to his right, on the other side of Big Bird, his yellow front-end loader.

It was a splash, but it was too heavy to be rainwater.

He froze and listened.

Another splash.

And another.

Each one just a little louder and more distinct than the last. Coming closer to where he wallowed in the mud.

"Oh, Jesus . . ."

At the sound of his voice the sounds of splashing paused for one moment and then began again. Not faster, but faster. Coming around the end of Big Bird. Coming in his direction.

He heard the other sound then.

The moan.

Jake almost screamed, knowing it for what it was.

One of *them*.

Stay or go, stay or go? He was trapped inside a bubble of indecision for a terrible long moment. Then the splashes got even louder, and suddenly Jake was moving. His whole body thrashed and twisted like a beached dolphin. He pawed at the mud and kicked and wormed his way up the edge of the pit.

Closer and closer. The moan louder. A single voice raised in a plaintive cry.

Jake was halfway out of the pit when he saw it.

It was a man. A stranger. Dressed in a business suit, jacket torn, tie askew to expose a ravaged throat.

For an awful moment their eyes met. The man in the mud and the thing in the rain. Then with a cry like a wild animal, the creature rushed at him, hands outstretched. Jake screamed and tried to scramble away, got halfway to his feet, and then it was on him, slamming into him, knocking them both down so they slid back into the muddy pit under the front-end loader. It clawed at Jake, trying to grab him, trying to pull him toward teeth that snapped and clacked.

Jake punched it, hitting the infected man in the face, in the throat, in the chest, but it was hard to find the balance and resistance to throw a solid punch. Jake was six-eight and more than three hundred pounds and this man couldn't have been more than two hundred, but in the mud and water they were evenly matched.

Except that the thing did not react to any of Jake's punches. Jake felt cartilage collapse beneath his knuckles as he hammered at its nose and throat. He felt bones crack in the face and temple and ribs. And he felt pain explode in his fingers and knuckles and wrists as the impacts took their toll while the struggle reawakened shocked nerve endings.

But the thing kept fighting as if pain was not even connected to its existence.

And maybe it wasn't.

This thing was like Burl and those girls. It couldn't have been alive. Not with the injuries it had. And yet it was fighting. It was a monster.

A monster.

He rammed his forearm under its chin and pressed the damned thing down into the mud. Inch by inch he pulled himself atop until finally he straddled it, pinning its arms down, battering its head deeper and deeper into the mud.

"Die you motherfucker!" he shouted, then choked on spit and snot and mud.

Jake kept shoving it down, using his massive body to try and smother it, bury it. Mud filled its mouth. The bones of its throat crumbled to nothing. And yet . . . those hands kept flailing beneath Jake's shins. Buried in mud and drowned, battered to a wreck, it kept flailing.

Jake sobbed with helpless terror. He fought a thing that could not be whipped and his own understanding of the world began warping at the edges, pieces flying off it until everything seemed distorted and surreal.

Something inside Jake's head broke.

Not a bone, not anything physical.

Something much deeper.

Something in his mind that was stretched to its farthest limit could not stretch any further and it snapped.

The blackness became blacker still as his eyes filled with dark poppies that blossomed like fireworks. He heard a weird tearing sound in his ears and an animal growl that he could feel coming from his own throat. The growl turned into a roar as Jake reared back and tore the dead thing out of the mud, then grabbed its chin and a fist-ful of hair and with more raw power than he had ever put into a single action ever in his life, he wrenched the head around. Bones exploded inside the savaged throat and still Jake turned. The body stopped struggling, and still Jake turned. His mind began falling into a dark, red well and still Jake turned.

And then he was pitching sideways, all resistance gone, the hair and chin locked inside his hands, but the creature's torso flopping the other way.

Jake plunged into the waters, still holding the head.

He lay there for a moment and in that moment he heard, saw, felt, and tasted nothing. There was nothing. Only a vast blackness.

Then . . .

Water seeped past the spasm in his throat and he inhaled it.

With a wracking, aching, gargling cry he came awake again. Light-ning flashed and its reflection lit the underside of the front-end load-er's bucket. Jake saw what he held in his hands and with a choking cry of disgust he flung it away, and then he was scrambling again, thrashing his way out of the pit, away from the headless thing, away from the reality of what he'd just done.

The screams that made it through the coughs were high and shrill and inhuman.

He got sloppily to his knees and tried to run, but gravity and balance were at war and all he could manage was a sloppy lope on all fours. He fell, got up, fell again, and finally managed to get to his feet, and there he stood, wide-legged, wide-armed, letting the rain assault him as he screamed.

CHAPTER ONE HUNDRED ONE
THE SITUATION ROOM
THE WHITE HOUSE, WASHINGTON, D.C.

"Where the hell is General Zetter?" thundered the president.

General Burroughs had a phone to his ear, but he said, "There's no technical problem, Mr. President. We pinged the lines and everything's working. However no one is picking up."

"Get some-damn-body on the phone," the president insisted. "I want to know what the hell is happening."

Aides scrambled to call secondary contacts.

"Sir—*sir*—" yelled one. "I have one of the helicopter pilots on the line. Lieutenant Mills. Putting the call on the speaker."

"*. . . ah, Christ this hurts . . . Jesus . . .*"

"Lieutenant Mills," said the president loudly, "this is the president. I need you to give me a sit rep."

"Sir? Sir . . . ?"

The pilot's voice was filled with panic and pain.

"Listen to me, son," said the president, "I need you to take a breath and tell me what is happening. Can you do that?"

They heard the man take a long, hissing inhalation. Then in a voice that was a fraction steadier, the pilot said, "It's . . . it's all falling apart."

"Are you injured, son? Can you tell me that much?"

"The bites . . . damn, you never think they could hurt this bad."

The president closed his eyes. "Son . . . do you know what happened to General Zetter?"

There was a very long pause filled only with rapid breathing that was close to hyperventilation. Then in a substantially weaker voice, the pilot said, "He wasn't bitten. I'm sure about that. None of them were."

"Who wasn't bitten?"

"The general. Everyone in the command truck. I was with them. I was on the ground by then. We weren't anywhere near the fighting. Nobody was bitten. But . . . but . . . oh God. We thought he was sick, you know? From the dust cloud after we dropped the fuel-air bombs. We thought it was just from breathing the ash. But, damn it, nobody was bit. Not until . . . not until it all went to shit. General Zetter, Captain Rice. All of them. They went apeshit. Ah, jeez . . . I think they clipped the artery. The tourniquet's not doing shit. Oh God, oh God."

"Where is General Zetter?" asked the president.

But there was no answer.

None at all.

Which was too much answer for everyone in the Situation Room.

CHAPTER ONE HUNDRED TWO
STEBBINS LITTLE SCHOOL
STEBBINS, PENNSYLVANIA

Billy Trout was no damn use at all to anyone. He knew it and everyone else knew it. Too much of him was bruised or strained, which meant he couldn't drag bodies—and body parts—out of the buses, and he couldn't work the janitor's power-hose to wash away the black blood. It was gruesome work and he was not sorry that he couldn't help.

Instead he set up his camera and began filming it. That and everything else.

With the jamming off, he put together a new field report, explaining the facts as he knew it, with many of the blanks filled in by Sam Imura.

It surprised Trout how forthcoming Sam was, and he pulled him aside for a moment to ask about that. They stood by a window that looked down on the parking lot and the rows of big yellow school buses.

"I've interviewed a lot of cops, soldiers, and federal types in the past," Trout said, "but I don't think I've ever had one actually spill the goods without either going off the record or prosecuting a personal agenda. In a nutshell, what gives?"

Sam shook his head. "I come from a long line of realists. My dad's one. He's a cop in California, in a small town out near Yosemite. He was never the kind to pad the truth or get behind an 'official' story. Dad believes that the truth is the truth."

"No one I ever met in Washington agrees."

"They can't," said Sam. "They're politicians, and politics is about leverage, not about the truth. Not sure I ever heard a politician ever give a straight answer to anything. Everything's agenda-based with them."

"Okay, but you work for a bureaucrat."

"Sure, but Scott Blair's a lot like my dad. He's not very well liked in D.C. because he always wants to cut to the bottom line."

"He's the one who wanted the president to bomb us back to the Stone Age?"

Sam met his eyes and nodded. "Yes, he was."

"Nice."

"Tell me something, Billy. Considering what's happened and how things might be if POTUS followed Scott's recommendation . . . do you think he made a bad call? Or do you think the president was right to cave and send the bombers back to the barn?"

"That's unfair. You're asking me to say whether it's right or wrong to kill six hundred kids."

"Take fairness out of the equation. Look at it for exactly what it is, a problem of survival. Not of a few, but survival of the species. Take a step back and look at the real problem, the big picture, Billy, and tell me what we should have done?"

"First, tell me the absolute truth . . . is it really that bad out there?"

"Yes." Sam said it without hesitation.

"Are we in danger of losing control of this whole thing?"

Sam's face turned to stone. "Billy, we may have already lost control of this thing. The math is so bad. There are so many ways this can go bad on us, and almost no way that we can put this genie back into the bottle."

"You're saying we've lost? Christ, Sam, is that what you're saying?"

"I . . . don't know. There are still some cards we can play. And the spread will hit some natural barriers. Rivers, mountains, lakes, bridges. All of those are potential chokepoints or they can act as firebreaks. Can we get ahead of it? I don't know. Not unless we up the game."

"Up it from fuel-air bombs? Shit, what's the next upgrade after that?"

Sam said nothing.

Billy looked down at his hands. "Oh, man . . ."

"So, again I ask you, Billy, last night, what should we have done last night?"

It hurt so much for Trout to say it, but he managed to get the words past the stricture in his throat. "You should have killed us."

"Yes," said Sam, "we should have killed you. And God help my soul for saying and believing that."

They sat in silence for a moment, each of them looking at the world through that lens.

"Then why are you helping us now?" Billy asked again.

Sam nodded to the buses down in the lot and the dozens of people scrambling to prepare them for an escape. "For me and my guys it's like being cut off behind enemy lines. Sure, we could make it back to the front, but I have a feeling that this is going to change from a gunfight—which is what we do—to a war we're only going to be able to fight from the air. Providing the storm ever stops. In a mechanized war, we're not much better than five extra sets of hands. It's a waste of our specialized skill sets." He gave Trout a rueful grin.

"And here?"

"You kidding me? Six hundred kids, two hundred civilians, and a horde of flesh-eating monsters? We might actually get to be bona fide heroes. And wouldn't that make a nice change."

"You're joking."

Sam held up his thumb and forefinger an inch apart. "Only a little."

Down in the lot the four members of the Boy Scouts were helping with the preparations. Trout had been introduced to them only by their combat call signs and what little he could deduce about their personalities. The woman, Gypsy, was a problem solver and apparently the second in command. Moonshiner was gruff and lacked obvious warmth, unlike Boxer who seemed to wear his heart on his sleeve. Shortstop was the most detached of the bunch, very pragmatic but aloof.

"What about your team?" asked Trout, nodding out the window. "Are they on the same page as you?"

Sam nodded. "They usually are. We tend to think like a pack of . . ."

He stopped speaking and leaned close to the window as lightning flashed and flashed again. The soldier's body went suddenly rigid with tension. Then he tapped his earbud.

"Team Alert, this is Ronin. I have eyes on the street beyond the north fence. We have potential hostiles. Repeat, potential hostiles."

It was Boxer who turned first, snatching his rifle from where it lay under a jacket and out of the rain. He brought it up and snapped on the top-mounted light. The beam cut through the rain and the openings in the chain-link fence, and there, filling the street, were silent figures who moved with slow, implacable steps.

"Give me numbers," ordered Sam.

"Christ, boss, I got forty of them. Shit, no, there's more coming."

Gypsy's voice cut in. "We got more coming in from the west and . . ." Her words trailed away.

Boxer turned, saw what she saw, and said what Sam and Trout were only now just beginning to see.

"They're soldiers," said Boxer. "Oh, goddamn, it's the National Guard. They're all . . . they're all . . . ah, shit."

"Got to be fifty of them," said Moonshiner.

Moonshiner popped a flare and sent it high into the air.

There were not fifty.

There were hundreds of them.

Torn, bleeding, shambling, and hungry.

CHAPTER ONE HUNDRED THREE

THE SITUATION ROOM
THE WHITE HOUSE, WASHINGTON, D.C.

The experts did one threat assessment after another, each time rebuilding both outbreak and response models to fit new data.

With each new assessment the president felt the world slip away from him. He sat in his chair, fingers balled into fists on the tabletop, staring at speaking mouths and screens filled with data.

Scott Blair looked every bit as bad. He hung up from a call and rubbed his eyes. Or was he wiping at tears? The president couldn't tell.

Blair held up a trembling hand and the room fell into a flawed and troubled silence.

"That was Dr. McReady. She's with the NBACC field team in Fayette County. They reached General Zetter's command post. It was deserted except for several infected. The, um, infected were all members of the Guard command staff."

"How the hell is that even possible?" demanded General Burroughs. "If they'd been overrun we'd have known about it."

"That's why Dr. McReady called. Her team was able to subdue and examine the infected at the command center. A few had been bitten, but most showed no signs of violence. No bites, nothing."

"Then what in hell happened?" asked the president.

Tears broke from the corners of Blair's eyes. "Dr. McReady thinks that the bombs reduced many of the infected to particulate matter and ash. Those particles still contain parasitic larvae, and the storm winds are spreading them throughout the region."

There was a beat and for a moment some of the people around the table seemed unable to comprehend the implications.

The president wiped at his own tears. "Say the rest, Scott. Tell them."

Blair placed his palms on the table and leaned heavily on them, his head hanging down between hunched shoulders.

"Lucifer 113 has gone airborne," he said.

CHAPTER ONE HUNDRED FOUR

THE NORTHERN LEVEES
FAYETTE COUNTY

Jake DeGroot came back to himself slowly.

So slowly.

With pain and realization and horror.

He stood in the rain and slowly looked around, trying to remember what world this was. Fifty feet away the yellow bulk of Big Bird stood like an anchor that held him to the world.

He gasped and spat out the awful tastes in his mouth, and wiped his face with the back of one big hand.

His first clear and cogent thought was that this was not an isolated event. It couldn't be. The girls had been hurt—*Killed? Was that the word?*—somewhere else and had walked onto the construction site. That meant whatever this was didn't start here. This wasn't some old Indian burial ground or any of that horror movie stuff. This was something else, and whatever it was, it was happening out there.

Out . . . where, exactly?

The second thing he thought was that they knew about it.

They.

The government, or at least the National Guard. Those were soldiers who shot Burl and the others. Soldiers.

That meant that this thing was really damn big.

"Oh, shit," he said.

He listened to his voice. There should be panic there, that desperate whine, but it wasn't there. He sounded like himself. The way he should.

It was the second thing that anchored Jake DeGroot.

It helped him take a real breath.

"Think it through," he told himself, liking the sound of his voice.

He didn't have much family in the area. Only a niece, Jenny, who lived in Bordentown.

He could go there.

But no. Jenny was a single woman and a teacher.

With the storm, the single teachers volunteered to work at the region's emergency shelter. The Stebbins Little School. The kids would have all been picked up, but the cops would have moved the old folks to the school. And some families from the flooded areas. The school had cots and food and a generator.

That's where Jenny would be.

And suddenly he was very afraid. Not for himself this time. Jake thought about Jenny. She was a tiny little thing. It took everything Jake had to stop that one guy.

Jenny?

She could never . . .

Before Jake even realized he was doing it he began running for his car, slapping his pockets for his car keys.

And not finding them.

They'd been in his jeans pocket.

He looked back at the pit under Big Bird.

They must have fallen out. Down in the water. Down in the mud.

Jake swallowed a lump the size of a fist.

"No fucking way."

Even if he could work up the nerve to crawl down there where the dead man was, what were the chances he would find those keys in all that mud and water. After all that fighting and thrashing. His car was useless to him. Even if he knew how to hotwire it, there was no time and no tools.

His heart started to sink, but then he raised his eyes. Just a few feet.

And stared at the big metal monster.

Big Bird.

"No," he told himself. It was too clumsy, too slow. And the school was too far.

Then he was running through the mud toward the machine.

The key for Big Bird was still where he'd left it, right in the ignition. He twisted it and the big diesel engine roared to life with a growl so loud that it sounded like a dragon rousing from a troubled slumber. He pulled the door shut, sealing himself inside the Plexiglas cab. He turned the heat to high, shifted hard, and began moving through the mud. The Cat's top blacktop speed was forty, and the mud cut that down to less than half.

The school was eleven miles away, almost due south.

"I'm coming, Jenny," he said aloud, and the fact of having a purpose, of having someone else to fight for, made his whole body feel as hard and powerful as the steel of the machine in which he rode.

He did not hear the crunch as the left rear tire rolled over the corpse in the mud. Nor when the right rolled across the nearly submerged body of Burl.

Or, if he did, Jake refused to allow himself to acknowledge it.

"I'm coming, Jenny."

CHAPTER ONE HUNDRED FIVE
STEBBINS LITTLE SCHOOL
STEBBINS, PENNSYLVANIA

"Everyone back to the school!" screamed Dez, but the adults were already dropping hoses and running. She ran behind them, shoving the slower ones, chasing them all to safety. "Check the doors. Keep the kids away from the windows. Move . . . *move*."

Moonshiner and Shortstop laid their rifles atop the front and rear hoods of a burned-out police car. Boxer climbed atop one of the buses and Gypsy went into another one and pointed her gun out the window. Only Sam and Trout stood their ground.

"We'd better get inside," warned Trout, but Sam didn't move.

"There are so many of them," he said softly.

Dez ran back to join them, her Glock in a two-handed grip, face set and hard.

"You want to fight them here?" she asked incredulously. "There are too many ways they can come at us."

The dead were closing in. The nearest ones were fifty feet beyond the fence.

"It's your house," said Sam. "It's your call."

"There's more coming across the yards," called Boxer, pointing.

They turned and saw more of the infected staggering through the lines of connected yards to the east.

"Dez," said Trout, taking her by the arm, "this is stupid. There are too many of them. Let's get inside."

But Dez pulled her arm free. "No." She turned to them. "Listen, Billy, Sam—we can reinforce the building and hole up, but for how long? The supplies we have won't last. Sam, can you guarantee that the army's coming back for us?"

The answer was on Sam's face. "This is falling apart. I don't think anyone can make promises right now."

"What are you saying?" asked Trout. "That we could be stuck here for weeks?"

"Billy . . . I'm saying if this keeps going the way it's going, then no one will be coming for us."

"Until when?"

Sam shook his head. "We could lose this war."

"War? It's an outbreak . . ."

Sam pointed to the dead soldiers who were approaching the fence. "Not anymore."

Trout felt his blood turn to ice. He cut a look at Dez, who looked horrified, but she was nodding to herself.

"How long can your team hold them on the other side of the fence?" she breathed. "How much time can you buy us?"

The soldier's mouth tightened. "How much time do you need?"

"An hour," she said. "Maybe less."

"To do what?" demanded Trout.

"To do what we started out to do. Get all the supplies and everyone in the school onto the buses."

"And then what?"

"We get the fuck out of here."

"And go *where*?"

"I don't know," she said. "Philly? New York?"

"No," said Sam. "Go south. Go to Asheville."

"North Carolina?" asked Dez. "Why there?"

"Because the storm is heading east. Roads will be bad and they'll be blocked. Because everyone running from this will be going east. And we can't go west because when we pinged Goat Weinman's satellite phone it was clear he was heading northwest. Maybe to Pittsburgh. We should go south and get into the mountains."

"Sure, but why Asheville?" asked Trout. "Why there specifically?"

Sam hesitated for a moment. "There is a government installation there."

"Since when?" Dez asked skeptically. "I never heard of it."

"You wouldn't have. It was built during the Cold War. The mountains there are honeycombed with miles and miles of labs, living quarters, the works."

"That's just an urban legend," said Trout. "I read about that. It's not real."

"It's real. In the event of a nuclear exchange it was deemed a save zone because it's outside of the prevailing drift patterns for likely nukes."

"Hey," called Gypsy, "somebody out there want to make a fucking decision? We're going to be dancing with these things pretty soon."

Sam touched Dez's sleeve. "It's there. Trust me."

Dez met his eyes, searching them for truth and trust. Then she nodded. "Okay."

"Good," said Sam, looking relieved. "We'll hold them as long as we can. You better get your asses in gear. Hurry!"

Dez spun and ran for the building. They could hear her shouting orders before she was even inside.

CHAPTER ONE HUNDRED SIX
THE SITUATION ROOM
THE WHITE HOUSE, WASHINGTON, D.C.

The president stood up slowly and walked the length of the room until he stood in front of the big screen. He stood, hands clasped behind his back, head bowed, appearing to stare into the middle distance.

"Mr. President," said Scott Blair, "we're starting to get reports of random attacks in other places. Harrisburg, Gettysburg . . ."

"How?" asked Sylvia Ruddy. "How is that possible? None of the infected could walk those distances, and the winds can't have reached there yet."

"Survivors," said Blair. "People in cars or trucks. Either bitten or people who breathed in the ash. We know that some escaped the containment. We have to shut down the highways and the airports. Trains and buses, too. We need roadblocks. If we have to, we can blow the tunnels and bridges on the major highways."

The president nodded, and phones were snatched up to make those calls.

"Sir," said Ruddy, "I think we need to initiate the Emergency Broadcast Network."

Another nod.

"I'll draft a speech to the nation," she said, and hurried out.

After she was gone, the president turned slowly to face his tableful of generals.

"Talk to me about nuclear alternatives," he said.

CHAPTER ONE HUNDRED SEVEN
BESSEMER COURT
WEST STATION SQUARE DRIVE
PITTSBURGH, PENNSYLVANIA

"You said you need to connect to the Net, right?" asked Homer.

Goat looked up from his laptop. He was cutting Homer's diatribes into video bites that would be short enough to be watch in their entirety.

"Yes. I have several bits ready to go up on YouTube. Why?"

Homer tapped the windshield, and Goat peered through the whisking wipers to see the words "FREE WI-FI" glowing in blue neon on the front of a redbrick building.

"How long's this gonna take?" asked the killer.

Goat hedged. "Video files are big," he said slowly. "Takes a while for them to upload and—"

"You need both hands to do that shit?"

Goat immediately flinched back, pulling his hands back as far as he could get them from the murderous madman. But Homer laughed. A deep, creaking bray.

"I ain't gonna eat your hands, you dumb shit," he guffawed. "Jesus. You're fucking hilarious sometimes."

"Why—why did you ask?"

"'Cause I want to go inside for a minute and I want you here where I get back."

"I don't—"

Homer reached into the backseat and produced a coil of heavy, hairy twine. It was brown and the spiky hairs made it look like a vast, coiled centipede. "Took this out of that last place. Useful shit. Gimme your left hand. C'mon, give it here unless you want me to take it."

With great reluctance, Goat slowly extended his trembling hand. Homer caught his wrist with fingers that were as cold and damp as worms but as strong as steel. He jerked Goat's arm toward the steering wheel and then began looping the hairy twine around wrist, steering column, and between the spokes if the wheel. He tied sophisticated knots in the twine, looped more twine, tied additional knots, and then pulled on the ends until the bulb of each knot was compressed into a tiny, rock-hard nugget.

"That ought to do 'er," he said, admiring his work. He gave Goat a friendly grin. "You only need one hand to jerk off with, right, boy?"

"I—"

"You set about putting my story out there for people to see and hear. You do that while I go see some folks about something I need."

"What is it? What are you going to do? What is this place? Why are we here?"

Homer's friendly grin became lupine. "You ain't figured it out yet?"

"Figured what out?"

"What I am."

"I . . . know what you are. I mean I understand what Dr. Volker did to you. I know about Lucifer 113."

"I ain't talking about no zombie bullshit, boy. Try again."

Goat licked his lips. "I understand about the Black Eye and the Red Mouth. Is that what you mean?"

The killer sat there for a long moment, his eyes flicking back and forth between Goat's as if looking for something first in the left, then the right, and over again. It was like the flickering of a candle. "You listened to everything I said and you sat as a witness to everything I done tonight, and you still don't understand. That's a damn shame, boy, 'cause I thought you were going to be my apostle. I thought you were like Luke and John and all those holy men who wrote the Bible. I thought I could use you to tell the truth. The real and gospel truth."

The shift in Homer's voice and phrasing was immediately chilling. Instead of the faux homespun shit-kicker lingo, these few sentences were spoken in a slow, more precise manner. Goat had noted it only once before, when Homer discussed the way the Red Mouth spoke through him to tell the truth. He wanted to replay that clip, to listen once more to what the man said then because now he felt—no, he was absolutely certain—that it was far more important that the pseudoreligious rant of a psychopathic killer. He saw the dangerous look of cold disappointment in Homer's eyes and knew that he needed to do something right now.

He said, "I'm trying to understand," he said, making his words come out with equally slow and sober gravitas. "I *want* to understand. But the apostles—how many of them understood right away? They had to think about it, to witness it, to let it speak through them, right?"

Goat was Jewish but he'd seen enough movies to know the basic New Testament story. He'd even watched parts of that old *Jesus of Nazareth* miniseries during a filmmaking class. He grabbed for every detail he could snatch out of memory.

"Peter . . . the one who was Jesus's right-hand man. He didn't get it at first, but look what happened. He's the role model for the pope, right? He was a fisherman and don't they say that the pope wears the shoes of the fisherman?"

He wasn't sure if this was exactly true or if it was something else from another movie. It sounded more or less right.

"And all the others," Goat continued, keeping the rhythm of it going, "they *became* true believers. And Paul, what about Paul, remember him? He was kind of a prick and a bad guy and then something happened to him on the road to Damascus and suddenly he's writing most of the New Testament." He paused, giving the moment a dramatic beat, choreographing it, directing his own performance. "You want me to tell your story, and I agreed to do that. If you need me to understand the secrets and mysteries of it, then you have to give me time to process it. To think it through. To let it speak inside my head and heart."

Those were lines from an old movie, an art film about socialism in Paris, but he was pretty sure it was one Homer would never have seen. Goat twisted them to fit, pitching his tone to have a smoldering passion waiting to bloom. Or at least that's how he imagined it if he was directing someone for this scene. He hoped he was actor enough to pull it off.

Homer Gibbon said nothing as the slow seconds ticked by. Then he reached out and touched Goat over the heart with the tip of his index finger.

"If you open your heart to the Red Mouth, you will see with the Black Eye."

Goat swallowed. "I-I want to. Just give me time."

The killer gave him a single, slow nod and let his finger trail down Goat's body, over his stomach and groin, along his thigh and up cover the edge of the laptop. "You better use this thing to tell my truth, or I will—"

"Homer," said Goat quickly, taking a terrible risk, "don't. Look at me. Use the Black Eye to look into my eyes. *See* me. You don't need to threaten me anymore. We've crossed a line, Homer. We're somewhere else now."

The moment stretched and stretched, and then Homer withdrew his hand. He reached for the door handle, but paused to pat Goat's bound left wrist. "The rope stays on. Trust, like faith, is earned."

Then he got out of the car and began walking, bare-chested and erect, through the rain to the building with the Free Wi-Fi sign.

Goat sagged back and had to fight to keep from hyperventilating. It was an even harder struggle to keep from pissing in his pants.

Then he was in motion. Even one-handed he was fast on a laptop. He accessed the system preferences and found the Wi-Fi, connected to it, and began uploading the files. But as he did so a small window popped up telling him that his email was sent.

Email?

It was only then that he remembered the message he'd composed way back at Starbucks.

In Bordentown. Homer Gibbon.
Quarantine failed.
It's here . . .

"Oh my God," he breathed, realizing that no one knew.

Then he thought back to the violence on the road, the helicopters, the explosions.

People knew.

But they didn't know that Homer was loose, that he was on the road.

That he was free.

Goat used the webcam on his laptop to record a quick and desperate video message. He had no idea how much time he had—or had left—so he made it short. He gave their location, and explained what Homer had already done. He emphasized that Homer had killed people, and had wounded others. He referenced Lucifer 113 and that Homer was, for all intents and purposes, the patient zero of this plague. He ended it with a statement that was both a call to arms for the authorities and a desperate cry for help.

It took several agonizingly slow seconds for the video file to upload to his media listservs, including the one that had all of Goat's White House correspondent colleagues. Then he posted it on YouTube and immediate deleted the file from his computer.

He kept glancing out the window at the building into which Homer had disappeared. It was a club of some kind.

What could Homer want in there?

He checked the video files of the interviews with Homer. Most were so big that they were still uploading, but many of the shorter ones were already up. He sent the same batch of them to his listserv using DropBox and WeTransfer, dumping all of the raw footage into the media cauldron, praying someone would watch it, understand its reality and importance, and act on it.

With all of that done, Goat scrolled through the video clips until he found the one in which Homer used the same eerie tone of voice. He watched it all the way through. It wasn't long, but it hit him like a punch to the throat.

He watched it again.

And again.

It was on the third viewing that the whole truth broke through.

The awful truth.

He suddenly knew why Homer was here.

Just as he knew why Homer had stopped those other times. He knew why Homer killed, and he knew why Homer sometimes spared lives. It wasn't mercy and it wasn't any of his humanity connecting with individuals.

It was something else.

Something horrible.

Something far worse than anything Homer had ever done, before or after he'd become the monster that he now was.

Homer wasn't on any vengeance kick. He wasn't hunting for his former foster parents. No, that was too mundane and cliché a motive for a person who was hearing the kinds of voices Homer heard.

No, what Goat realized with perfect clarity was that Homer, knowing and accepting what he was, what Volker had done to him, had embraced it. He hadn't killed everyone at the 7-Eleven, but now that made sense. He hadn't killed them all, but he'd infected them all.

The same with the people back at Starbucks. He killed some and fed on some, but his real agenda was spreading the infection. Like some kind of nightmare blend of John the Baptist and Johnny Appleseed, Homer was on the road to spread the word of his god. To spread the gospel of the Red Mouth and the Black Eye.

To create the paradise that he'd envisioned, that he'd spoken of. A world inherited by the meek. By the mindless dead. By those raised up, as Jesus had been.

At least according to Homer's view of the cosmos.

It was a horrible plan, but a very practical one. A workable one.

Behind them, at the 7-Eleven and the traffic jam on the road, the infection was probably already spreading. Outside of the quarantine zone.

Goat snatched up his camera and babbled all of this into a live stream. He saved it and posted it on Facebook.

Then he logged onto Foursquare, the social media app for sharing your location.

"Find us," he begged. "Find us."

CHAPTER ONE HUNDRED EIGHT
STEBBINS LITTLE SCHOOL
STEBBINS, PENNSYLVANIA

"Okay, listen up," said Sam into the team channel. "This is a holding action. We don't fire until and unless there's a danger of a breach. Watch the fences. If they start putting pressure on it, we use selective fire to drive them back, or we drop enough to block access. This is a target-rich environment but that's also a good way to burn through too much ammo. Check your targets. Headshots only. Unless you're pressed, take time for accuracy. Make 'em count."

Behind them Dez and Uriah Piper had set up chains of people to bring out the hundreds of boxes of food, water, and supplies. The chains split off to feed the stuff into a dozen Type C Blue Bird school buses. Uriah Piper was running from bus to bus to start engines and check fuel levels. A couple of teachers were busy siphoning gas from buses that were too low in fuel to make a long run or too badly damaged. Each bus had a standard capacity of seventy-seven passengers and the driver, which meant that a dozen of them would easily transport the eight hundred survivors of Stebbins County with room for boxed supplies.

Jenny DeGroot had found a can of spray paint and was writing a message on the outside wall of the school, but Trout couldn't read it at that distance. Probably a note about where the buses were going. Smart, he thought.

Trout, too dinged up to help, was recording everything and, he hoped, streaming it out to the Net. He wanted people to know. Unfortunately, he had no laptop, so he couldn't check to see if anything was showing up on the Web.

Sam came over and looked Trout up and down. "Do you have a gun?"

"No. I'm not very good with one."

"You're worse without one." He bent and removed a small automatic from an ankle holster and held it out to Trout. "Beretta 3032 Tomcat. Seven-round box magazine. Less than a pound and fits into any pocket." He showed Trout how to use the thumb safety. "Better to have it and not need than need it and not have it."

"One of Dez's favorite lines."

Sam smiled. "Dez . . . is she your lady? Girlfriend? Wife? Something?"

"Something. We've been a couple more often than you've had hot dinners, but recently we've been on a break."

"A 'break'?"

"As in she keeps threatening to break parts of me I don't want broken."

"I joined the army because war is easier than love," said Sam.

"Very wise words." Trout glanced over at Dez. "She's a foul-mouthed redneck who is, politically speaking, to the extreme right of Glenn Beck, but even with all that I love her. Always have."

"That street go both ways?"

Trout sighed. "Not lately."

"Ah."

"I mean . . . apocalypse and all. Not a hearts-and-flowers sort of thing."

"I hear ya."

"Tell you what, though," said Trout. "For all of her rough edges—she has the biggest heart. She'd die for any one of those kids, and for most of the adults, too. No, that's not quite right. She'd happily and mercilessly kill for those kids."

Sam nodded. "A warrior rather a soldier."

Trout cocked an eyebrow. "There's a difference?"

"Soldiers are called to serve and when their service is done they go home. A warrior lives on the battlefield. It *is* home."

Trout studied him. "Yeah . . . that's Dez." He weighed the gun in his palm, nodded thanks, and put it into the pocket of his stained and torn sportscoat.

"Listen, Billy, I think I'd better tell you some things. I heard from my boss, Scott Blair."

"Good news, I hope."

"I wish . . . but, no. Lucifer has become an airborne pathogen now."

"Ah . . . jeez . . ."

"Our bioweapons people are scrambling to mass-produce a different parasite that might render the infected inert. Not sure if it'll kill them or not. I don't think they're sure."

"How soon will they try that?"

Sam shook his head. "Not soon enough. I told Scott that we're heading to Asheville. He said he'll call ahead to make sure we get an open door."

"Can we trust him?"

"People should have trusted Scott from the jump."

Trout took his point, and nodded. "They still want me dead?"

Sam gave a half-smile. "No, just the opposite. They want you to get out any information you can. Scott thinks it might help some people, especially if things keep going the way they're going."

"Sam . . ." Trout said tentatively, "how *bad* are things? No bullshit, how bad?"

"I wasn't joking before when I said that we were losing this war. They may have to drop nukes to stop this."

"Are you fucking crazy? Are *they*?"

"It's being looked at as the scenario resulting in the lowest number of casualties."

And it was then that the full enormity of it hit Billy Trout. Until then, despite everything he'd seen and all that he knew, it had been a local issue. It had been a Stebbins County thing.

Now he understood.

Now his own words came back to pummel him, to lash at him.

Reporting live from the apocalypse.

"Boss!" yelled Boxer. "They're coming!"

They spun around and saw that a mass of them were at the fence, and the chain links and piping were starting to bow inward under the combined weight of more than fifty bodies.

"Can you really hold them?" begged Trout.

Sam unslung his rifle. "Tell your girlfriend to hurry."

The Boy Scouts took careful aim, and fired.

CHAPTER ONE HUNDRED NINE
PITTSBURGH INTERNATIONAL AIRPORT

"Did you hear?"

Captain James Yakima looked up from the flight log at his copilot for the nonstop to Paris.

"Hear what? The riots or the storm?"

"Both, I think," said Beecher, the copilot. "They're shutting us down."

"Shutting who down? Our flight?"

"The airport," said Beecher. "At least that's the rumor."

"Goddamn it," growled Yakima as he dug in his pocket for his cell. He punched in the number for his boss at Delta and had to wait six rings before the call was answered. "Carol, what's this crap I'm hearing about the airport getting shut down?"

Beecher stood and waited while Yakima listened.

"Okay, with any luck I'll be eating a nice piece of veal at the Restaurant du Palais-Royal before they pull the plug. Thanks, Carol. Keep me posted."

He disconnected and placed the phone on the table.

"So—what's the verdict?" asked Beecher.

"Carol says they're going to do it, but the official order hasn't come through yet."

"The storm's going the other way. Local winds are below twenty and—"

"It's not the storm. Carol said they were going to impose martial law on western Pennsylvania and maybe parts of Maryland and West Virginia, too."

"For a *riot*?"

"She says it's not a riot. Carol said her brother-in-law works for MSNBC and they're still running the virus story."

"I thought they shot that down."

Yakima spread his hands. "What can I tell you? The good news is that it doesn't affect us. We're wheels up in sixty-six minutes. C'mon, let's get a coffee before we go aboard."

He closed the flight log and stood up. As they headed toward the door to the crew lounge a short fit of coughing stopped Yakima in his tracks. He coughed for twenty seconds, then waited, listening inside his body for more, and gradually felt the spasms stop.

"You okay?" asked Beecher.

"Yeah. It's nothing. Tickle in the back of my throat."

"I have some lozenges," said Beecher. "In my bag. Want me to dig 'em out? Won't take a sec."

"Nah," said Yakima. "It's nothing. I have four days off in Paris. If it's a cold, where better for a little R and R?"

They headed out of the lounge, got their coffee, and proceeded directly to their plane. In a little over an hour they were in the air, flying high over the storms of Pennsylvania, skirting the edge of the worst of it, crossing into New Jersey and then far out over the Atlantic.

CHAPTER ONE HUNDRED TEN
TRICKSTER'S COMEDY CLUB
PITTSBURGH, PENNSYLVANIA

The comedian's name was Jeremy Essig and he felt like there should be sirens blaring and dogs hunting him. Not just there at Trickster's, but at a lot of comedy clubs. After all, the image the audience saw was a sketchy-looking character looking nervous in a spotlight splashed against an unpainted brick wall. It screamed "escaped prisoner." If not from a prison than definitely from a facility for people with dangerous social disorders.

And the audience was a lot like a posse. They seemed like nice people, but they could turn mean and dangerous in a heartbeat.

He'd seen it. All comics have seen it. One minute you have a crowd hanging on your every word, laughing in anticipation of what you'll say before you even begin the joke, willing to follow you through twists and turns of skewed logic and occasionally clinical observation, believing that you'll steer the boat into port in some magical lands. That's when it's working right, when the rhythm is like jazz and the words tumble out with the kind of timing that opens minds and unlocks the muscles so that smiling and laughing is the easiest thing to do. Those are the times when the comic and the audience are all together, sharing the ride, understanding each other on a level you can't really describe.

But then there are those times when everything on the other side of the spotlight looks alien and hostile. Pale faces in the dark, staring with dead eyes, their mouths unsmiling, hands on tables or in laps as if they're too damn heavy to light for even a token clap. There are times when the joke's rhythm is off, like a discordant note that paints itself in the air and no matter what else is played that's the thing everyone can't look away from. Like that. What sucked most was that there was no pattern to it. Sure, sometimes it's hitting the wrong note or forgetting to take a look at the demographic. Like busting on the Tea Party in South Carolina, or skewering Obama in Chicago. Like being the first comic to make a joke after a crisis and really seeing firsthand what "too soon" actually means. Rookie mistakes that even the pros make, and Jeremy could remember too many of those moments in his own career.

On the upside, after you survive the moment and crawl out of a dead gig like that, you can take the experience and spin it into material for another date.

Tonight, though, the audience was right there with him. The mojo was red hot and despite the late hour they were all coconspirators in a mad scheme.

Plus, everybody was hammered. Even the waitstaff at Trickster's was in the bag. And the emcee for the event, Lydia Rose, was smiling the kind of smile only a very happy, very drunk person can manage during that last hour before falling over becomes a gravitational imperative.

Jeremy walked back and forth on the tiny stage, letting movement and the shifting of the travel spot kept any moment from getting stale. He wore an ancient Flaming Moe's T-shirt and scruffy jeans and looked as comfortable as he felt.

The gig was largely impromptu. What had started with a standard double-bill with him and Tom Segura, and a handful of raw up-and-comers, had become something else. The original show should have ended at midnight, but then word started coming in about how Superstorm Zelda had pretty much wiped a small town off the Pennsylvania map. A lot of people were believed dead. And there was a bunch of wild conspiracy theory crap thumbtacked to the story. Viruses, something about the National Guard trying to kill a bunch of kids, some asshole ranting about the apocalypse, and—this was the best part, as Jeremy saw it—zombies.

Fucking zombies.

They all had a good laugh about that during the break, but then they started hearing more and more about the number of expected casualties and it stopped being funny. Jeremy couldn't remember who suggested doing a fund-raiser. Maybe him, maybe Tom. Maybe Lydia. Or maybe it was one of those things that just evolved. At first it was something they thought would be good if someone else did it. Then it was something they thought they should do. Then it became something they needed to do. Then it became what was actually happening tonight.

Alcohol and some serious weed were involved in every stage of the process. Smoke your way to the right level and everything seems incredibly doable, even logical. The basic pitch was a comedy marathon for the duration of the storm, with Tom Segura and Jeremy Essig as ongoing headliners. Calls went out to other comics within driving distance.

Finding a name for it took the longest. Tom wanted to call it Blow Me, Zelda. Jeremy liked Comic Relief: Redneck Edition, but Lydia thought they'd get sued for that. After another blunt they settled on Laugh at the Storm, and bullied a friend who had a 501(c)(3) to accept donations via PayPal.

Now they were into the second hour of it.

They streamed the show live to the Net and put clips on You-

Tube, reposting those to Twitter and Facebook. Some friends of Jeremy and Tom Skyped in and did bits that were flashed onto the wall. While the comics were doing their bits, Lydia put the event on Foursquare, then pulled photos from the video stream and posted them on Pinterest, Tumblr, and InstaGram. Suddenly it was real. It was an actual charity fund-raiser for the victims of Superstorm Zelda.

The crowd at Trickster's were totally into it, and within forty minutes carloads of people showed up from all over Pittsburgh, fighting their way through storm winds and rain hard enough to swell all three of the city's big rivers. It was standing-room only, and the bartenders were mixing drinks and pulling pints as fast as they could.

Jeremy did several twenty-minute sets, cycling through old material and some new stuff, and also improvising on what was happening.

"According to the Internet news," he said, half-smiling as he paced in front of the audience, "there are monsters out in the sticks around Stebbins. Slack-faced, empty-eyed, unthinking, shambling hulks who will kill anything that moves. And aside from the locals, they also have zombies."

The audience loved that. It was a running joke that the entire length of the state between Philadelphia and Pittsburgh was an even more redneck version of Mississippi. A red state with blue bookends. Certified gold for observational comics like Jeremy Essig and Tom Segura.

"It's not really surprising that they have a zombie outbreak in farm country. All those graaaiiiiins."

A smaller laugh that time, but they were still with him. Jeremy took a beat to comment on the lack of laughs, and that got a laugh. One of the golden rules of his kind of comedy was to own the bad moments so they were part of a shared experience, rather than simply try to limp away from a wounded joke.

He switched gears a bit and drove his routine onto safer ground by talking about how people on the Net were saying that the government was trying to cover up the zombie thing. No matter which lever the audience pulled, it was usually safe ground to attack the government as a whole. Not necessarily taking potshots at specific politicians but at the huge, self-destructive, creaking machine that was national politics. He saw Tom and Lydia watching from offstage, grinning and nodding encouragement.

Jeremy took some of his old jokes about FEMA's failure after Katrina and gave them a Superstorm Zelda spin.

"If you wait until the zombies eat most of the people, then you only have to save a few. And since the survivors will be the ones fast enough to outrun the living dead, you have people who look better on TV."

From there he cruised into the vagaries of pop culture.

"Tell me there won't be a reality show in six months. *Real Zombies of Stebbins County*. Strap on a lie detector and tell me we won't be watching that."

And he was casting the show with redneck subtypes when someone in the audience screamed.

It wasn't a scream of laughter or even a shout of inarticulate drunken mirth.

It was a real scream.

A stop the show scream.

The kind of scream where the entire crowd is jerked out of the moment, the spell instantly broken, and they focus on a single spot in the room.

In the back of the small club, standing framed in the pale rectangle of light from the lobby, stood a tall figure. A man. Bare-chested and wild-looking. Grinning. The woman who'd screamed sat at the table closest to the exit, and she and everyone at her table were frozen in a tableau of horrified recoil.

And . . .

Here Jeremy's mind began stumbling over the details.

The man was wrong.

His whole body was wrong.

It was red.

Bright, glistening red.

Like he'd been splashed by red paint. Or . . .

A *Carrie* joke started forming in his head in the split second before the red-splashed man turned, grabbed the woman who'd screamed, hauled her to her feet, and . . .

And he dug his teeth into the hollow of her throat.

CHAPTER ONE HUNDRED ELEVEN
STEBBINS LITTLE SCHOOL
STEBBINS, PENNSYLVANIA

"Forget the supplies," growled Sam. "Get the kids on the damn buses."

He didn't wait for Dez to respond. He laid his rifle atop a car hood and began firing slow, spaced shots. With each shot Trout could see the head of one of the infected fly apart and splash those around it with black blood. The other soldiers were nearly as good, and soon the bodies were piling up, clogging access to the fence.

But that was one attack point.

Dez vanished into the building but was back a moment later leading a line of children. The kids were all holding hands. Most of them were screaming as they ran. Adults ran with them, shepherding the kids toward the buses. It started as an orderly evacuation, but with each second it began to disintegrate.

Boxer yelled, "Hostiles at nine o'clock. Count seventy plus."

He peered through a bus window and saw several tattered figures climbing awkwardly over the low chain-link fence. Boxer opened fire on them, but the wind was whipping up leaves and debris, spoiling his aim and warping the flight path of his rounds.

"Close on them," bellowed Sam.

Boxer shot him a despairing look, then climbed down from the bus and began running across the playground toward that part of the fence. At twenty feet he knelt, put his rifle to his shoulder, and began firing. Now one after another of the dead pitched backward. The other Boy Scouts closed on other sections of the fence and began firing from closer range.

The children kept screaming, and the sound tore at Trout's heart. It was a steady, unbearably shrill wail of total terror and total hopelessness.

"We're losing the fence," cried Gypsy, and even as she said it a fifteen-foot section of the chain link collapsed into the schoolyard.

Infected spilled forward, falling over each other, piling up, writhing and scrambling to keep moving forward toward their prey.

Moonshiner and Gypsy began shuffling backward, yard by yard, while still firing.

"Reloading," called Moonshiner. "Last mag."

"Dez, hurry up goddamn it!" roared Sam.

Trout limped over to try and help, but there were already enough people. There simply wasn't enough time. Six hundred children, many of whom were too scared to leave the school. Many of whom had to be dragged or carried out. Some of them broke away and ran back into the school, with teachers and parents chasing them.

There was no order left in the exodus.

Against all sanity, one of the children tore free from Mrs. Madison and went running directly toward the zombies who were getting to their feet. Trout could not understand it until he heard one awful, heart-wrenching word.

"Mommy!"

In the midst of the living dead, a woman with half her hair torn away and fingers missing from her left hand, reached for the child, her mouth splitting into a mockery of a mother's smile, teeth bared to bite.

Trout realized that he was running. Pain shot up his back and down his legs. Cracked ribs grated beneath his skin. His breath burned in his lungs, but he was running, angling away from the bus, racing to intercept the little girl.

He reached her four paces before the zombie did.

With a cry of agony he snatched her up and tried to run with her.

But his legs buckled and he went down hard on his kneecaps. He twisted as he fell, hitting the ground on his back instead of crushing the girl under him. Then cold fingers were tearing at him, trying to rip the child from his arms. Black drool fell from ragged lips as the infected thing bent close to try and bite the child who had been her daughter when the world was a different world.

Trout rolled sideways and kicked out, felt his foot hit something, heard a bone break, and then the zombie fell next to him. It did not react at all to its broken leg, but immediately buried cracked teeth in Billy Trout's shoulder.

CHAPTER ONE HUNDRED TWELVE
TRICKSTER'S COMEDY CLUB
PITTSBURGH, PENNSYLVANIA

Tom Segura sat on a stool with Lydia, the short, curvy, brunette emcee. The two of them were having a great night, riding the wave of excitement that was their impromptu fund-raiser comedy marathon. Tom was sipping a Redbull and covertly trying to count Lydia's tattoos every time she moved. Some of them were in really interesting places. Onstage, his friend Jeremy Essig was killing them with an on-the-spot series of jokes about a zombie reality show.

Then everything changed.

Just like that. From one side of a moment to the other.

The audience was laughing their balls off about Billy Bob and Bubba the zombies and their monster truck when suddenly a woman's scream knocked the whole night off its wheels.

"What the hell?" cried Lydia as she launched herself from her stool. Tom was a half-second slower, and he tried to see what was going on, but there was a waitress with a tray of drinks between him and the woman who'd screamed.

"Great fucking timing," Tom muttered as he tried to edge around to get a better look. On the stage, Jeremy looked like he was frozen into the moment, eyes and mouth wide.

The whole club went silent for a heartbeat, but as Tom stepped around the waitress to see what was up, the entire club erupted into mad panic.

Utter.

Mad.

Panic.

Suddenly everyone was screaming. Women. Men. Everyone.

On stage, Jeremy screamed, too. The part of Tom Segura's mind that was a regular guy felt twin pangs of fear and confusion. The part of him that was a professional comic actually provided commentary.

You scream like Chloë Moretz, dude.

But then the crowd split apart as people panicked and scattered, revealing an image that Tom knew was being burned onto the front of his brain as he looked at it. A bare-chested, bloody man, viciously tearing at the skin and muscle of a woman's throat.

Right in front of him.

This wasn't movie special effects and it sure as shit wasn't someone's idea of a practical joke. What Tom was seeing fifteen feet in front of him was real. Real blood, real flesh, real madness, real pain.

And he screamed, too.

He did not remember picking anything up, and even when he threw the beer bottle he was surprised that it was his hand that winged it at the attacker's head. Tom was not a fighter. He didn't know many comics who were. Words had always been both his sword and shield. Sarcasm was his left hook and insight was his right cross.

He saw the bottle leave his hand, saw it close the distance in what appeared to be ultra-slow motion. Saw it strike the killer right on the temple.

As good a throw as anyone in the Major Leagues ever hurled.

Dead on. A hundred-mile-an-hour ball that burned across the plate fast enough to make a fool out of a .300 batter.

Tom expected the killer to go down.

That would have been the button on this routine. That should have been the logical end, or maybe the opening act of a new phase of his career. Tom Segura, hero comedian. The stocky kid from Cincinnati who dropped a psycho with a bottle of Coors Lite.

That was the script he was already writing in his head. That was the lead for the Breaking News.

Except . . .

Except that's not how the scene played out.

The bottle hit hard, hit with real force, hit hard enough to make a *clunk* that Tom could hear over the woman's gurgling screams. Then it ricocheted off of the killer and hit the woman square in the right eye.

The bottle fell to the floor.

The killer dropped the woman right on top of it.

He turned to Tom.

And smiled with bloody teeth.

Tom thought, "Oh . . . shit."

Or maybe he said it aloud. He wasn't sure, because after that he was screaming louder and more shrilly than Jeremy.

CHAPTER ONE HUNDRED THIRTEEN
THE SITUATION ROOM
THE WHITE HOUSE, WASHINGTON, D.C.

"Mr. Blair!" yelled a young officer, one of the sharpshooters from the military intelligence group. "You need to see this."

Blair hurried over and bent to look at something on the officer's laptop.

"What is it?"

"We were able to pick the IP address of Gregory Weinman's computer from the files he uploaded to the Net. Well, sir, he just uploaded a new batch."

"Is it more of Trout's ramblings?"

"No, sir. There are several files, including what appears to be interviews with Homer Gibbon. The autodating on the video files say that the interviews were all done in the last few hours."

"Christ!"

"And there's more. Weinman posted a message, a plea that appears to be directed to us. To the military. He's asking us to find him because he is with Homer Gibbon and Gibbon is spreading Lucifer."

"Did he provide an exact location?"

The officer smiled. So strange a thing under the circumstances.

"Yes, sir, he did."

CHAPTER ONE HUNDRED FOURTEEN
STEBBINS LITTLE SCHOOL
STEBBINS, PENNSYLVANIA

The pain was immediate and excruciating, and Billy Trout screamed. He thrashed and beat at the woman, trying to shake her loose. The little girl shrieked, too, her voice as shrill as a seagull's, and she began beating her tiny fists all over Trout's face. She smashed his nose and hit him in the eye.

And then another screaming, howling thing plowed into them. It hit the zombie with so much force that teeth snapped off at the gum-line and the creature fell away. Trout instantly rolled the other way, shoving the child from him. He flopped onto his stomach and saw Dez Fox sitting astride the infected woman, fingers knotted in what was left of the woman's hair, lifting her head and slamming it down on the concrete over and over again until the back of her skull exploded and sprayed the wet ground with brain tissue and black blood.

The little girl shrieked again and tried to rush to her mother's defense, but Trout caught her wrist and pulled her kicking and screaming down to where he lay.

Trout was screaming, too, trying to determine how bad the bite was, trying to wriggle out of his jacket to see how soon he was going to die. The hysterical little girl kept hitting him, making it impossible to do anything. Then suddenly Dez pivoted off of the dead zombie, plucked the little girl off of him and then started tearing at Billy's sportscoat. She yanked it down and tore his arm from the sleeve, then pawed at his shirt to find the bite.

"Am I dead?" Trout cried. "Oh, God, Dez . . . am I dead?"

And she kept saying, "Don't you leave me, Billy Trout, don't you dare. Don't you fucking leave me, too. I'll fucking kill you if you leave me . . ."

The lightning flashed and Dez used its brief light to bend close.

"God, please don't let me be dead," he wailed.

Dez straightened, glared at him and slapped him across the face as hard as she could. It rocked his head sideways and he snorted blood from his broken nose. Then she grabbed two fistfuls of his shirt and half-hauled him off the ground.

"It didn't break the skin you stupid motherfucker." She shook him hard enough to rattle his teeth. "I could fucking kill you, you stupid son of a bitch."

Then people were crowding around them, pulling her back, lifting him to his feet, taking the little girl away from the horror that lay on the ground. Trout saw Sam there, firing a pistol instead of his sniper rifle. Moonshiner was with him, too. Firing, firing, firing.

There was an awful sound behind them and Trout turned to see another section of fence collapse and a wave of the dead come rushing into the lot. At least a hundred of them. Some fell with the fence, but the others climbed over them, shambling or running. Screaming their hunger, moaning louder than the storm. Sam fired and fired. There was no time to aim now.

Moonshiner yelled for them to get back. He dropped a spent magazine and reached for a replacement.

Which he did not have.

There was one terrible moment when his questing fingers spider-walked across his belt and harness and found nothing.

"Shit!" he said. He reversed his rifle in his hands and swung it like a baseball bat as the mass of zombies came swarming at them over the fence. Another section fell. And another. Hundreds of the dead were closing in on them.

The bus engines roared and fists pounded on the horns. Children screamed somewhere behind them. Trout kept swimming in and out of consciousness, aware that he was being half-carried, half-dragged along, but with no idea who was helping him. He saw Dez and Sam standing shoulder to shoulder, firing into the onrushing sea of the infected, trying to buy Moonshiner time to retreat.

And then the dead were on him.

"*Noooooo!*" howled Sam.

The big soldier swung the rifle once more and two zombies staggered back with shattered faces, but a dozen more launched themselves at him. Sam fired over and over again, killing an infected with every shot. So did Dez.

It did not matter at all.

Moonshiner vanished beneath a tidal surge of the dead.

"Get onto the bus!"

Someone was yelling that over and over again, but Trout couldn't tell who it was. It might even have been him.

Hands reached out and grabbed Trout, pulled him, lifted him, and then he was out of the rain, inside the bus.

But where was Dez? He began thrashing, fighting the hands, struggling to get to the window to see if he could find Dez. Guns were still firing. The dead moaned like demons.

"Go, go, go!" yelled a voice.

Sam Imura.

Where was Dez?

God, thought Trout as the darkness began to drag him down, *where was my Dez?*

CHAPTER ONE HUNDRED FIFTEEN
TRICKSTER'S COMEDY CLUB
PITTSBURGH, PENNSYLVANIA

Lydia Rose was too short to see over the milling crowd.

She saw the bloody man enter the club and saw Tom throw a bottle at him, but then everything went totally to hell. People screamed and screamed as they ran for the exits. They collided with one another and tripped over tables and chairs. Lydia was buffeted back by the crowd and fell hard against the corner of the stage. Five feet in front of her a frat boy in a Pitt sweatshirt lay sprawled like a starfish, eyes open, mouth slack, as at least forty people ran over his body. Not leaping across it, but stepping on the college kid's stomach and legs and chest. Then a skinny white woman with beaded dreads hooked a foot in the frat boy's armpit and pitched face forward to the ground. A dozen others fell atop her, wrenching a terrible scream from her collapsing lungs.

Lydia crawled onto the stage, where Jeremy was yelling at the crowd to get out, which they were already trying to do, and alternately yelling at the bloody man to stop biting the woman.

It seemed to Lydia to be such a strange thing to yell.

If the guy was biting someone, then how likely was it that he'd be reasonable enough to take Jeremy's suggestion to heart? What was he supposed to do? Let her go, spit out what was left of her throat, give a rueful apology and buy a round for the house?

She got to her feet and from the stage platform was able to see what was actually happening there at Trickster's.

She saw.

She screamed.

Beside her, Jeremy was still yelling at the crowd. Across the club, Tom Segura was running from the bloody man and throwing chairs at him. Most of the chairs were hitting the guys who were trying to throw punches at the intruder.

The bloody man snatched one of the chairs out of the air and swung it into the face of a burly football player who was winding up a haymaker. The football player went down hard.

Two other guys piled atop the bloody man, punching him with both fists. Lydia lost sight of the killer for a moment, then she heard a piercing shriek, and one of the guys reeled back clutching a hand from which blood spurted from the stumps of two fingers that were now missing beyond the first knuckles. The second guy rolled off, clutching his throat, and Lydia couldn't tell what the bloody man had done to him. Punched him?

Tom waded in as the killer was rising to his feet, swinging yet another chair, but someone stepped into the path of the swing, and for a moment Lydia couldn't understand what she was seeing.

It was the woman who'd been bitten.

Her face and clothes were splashed with her own blood and there was a black, ragged hole in the front of her throat, but she bared her teeth and leapt at Tom like a cat. They both went down and Lydia lost sight of her friend.

Then she was moving. She snatched the microphone stand from in front of Jeremy and leaped off the stage. She was only five-one and the mike stand was taller than she was, but Lydia took it in a two-handed grip and swung it with all the force and focus of a Major League ballplayer. The chrome shaft made a glittering arc and the heavy black base hit the woman who was atop Tom right in the side

344 | JONATHAN MABERRY

of the head. There was a meaty crunch that sent such a shockwave up the length of the stand that it shivered it right out of Lydia's hands. She staggered backward and collided with someone. She felt hands on her shoulders, trying to pull her backward. Lydia pivoted and swung her right arm as hard as she could to dislodge the grabbing hands. She didn't need any Galahad to pull her to safety. Lydia knew how to fight, mean and dirty, and she wasn't about to let some psycho bastard hurt Tom.

But as she spun she looked up into the face of the man who'd grabbed her.

A tall man.

Bare-chested.

Ugly and powerful.

Covered in blood from eyes to knees.

A man who smiled at her. A man whose dark eyes looked her up and down.

"Nice," he said. "Juicy."

And they he lunged at her, teeth snapping.

It's not funny, she thought. *This isn't funny.*

Those were her last thoughts and then all she saw was a big, black nothing.

CHAPTER ONE HUNDRED SIXTEEN
DOLL FACTORY ROAD
STEBBINS COUNTY, PENNSYLVANIA

It was too dark down in the hole and there were too many monsters, so Billy Trout fought his way back to the surface. He came awake with a cry.

For a moment he did not know where he was. The world seemed to be moving.

The ceiling was low and curved and seemed to be made out of metal.

He heard voices.

Prayers and whispers.

People crying with dry, broken sobs that seemed to cling to the ragged edge of sanity. Other voices, younger and more plaintive, called for mothers and fathers and were not answered. One voice kept repeating the word "no" in a relentless monotone.

Pain was the next thing Trout became aware of. Intense pain, and in many places. His nose, his chest, his ribs. His shoulder.

Oddly, his back no longer hurt, as if somehow whatever had been dislocated before had slid back into place. What a small and random mercy that was. It felt cheap and out of place when so many others were so badly hurt and needed comfort more than he did.

A shape moved above him and it took Trout several seconds to focus his eyes.

Woman shape. Blond, haggard, filthy.

Beautiful.

"Dez . . ." he breathed.

Dez Fox bent and kissed his forehead, and his eyes, and his lips. Then she bent and whispered into his ears. "Don't ever leave me, Billy Trout. Don't you dare."

He constructed what he hoped was a smile. "Not a chance."

The bus—for that's now what he realized it was—jounced and bounced as it rolled. Trout tried to sit up and nearly passed out again. He took a ragged breath and tried it again, this time with her help.

"Where are we?"

"Center of town," she said. "Doll Factory."

Trout saw Sam Imura sitting with Gypsy near the front of the bus. They sat in identical postures, forearms on knees, heads bent. In weariness or defeat?

No, he realized. In grief.

"Moonshiner?" Trout asked quietly.

Dez shook her head. "No."

"Damn."

"We . . . we lost Uriah Piper, too. And Mrs. Madison. Ten others."

He closed his eyes, not wanting to see the way those words twisted her mouth. "Any of the kids?"

"No," she said. Tears cut silvery scars through the grime on her face. "We saved the kids, Billy. We saved them."

CHAPTER ONE HUNDRED SEVENTEEN
PITTSBURGH, PENNSYLVANIA

Homer Gibbon said, "You get it all done? You upload all the film we did? The interviews and such?"

"Everything," said Goat weakly. "Everything's out there."

It was true. All of the video files had been uploaded to YouTube, with crosslinks on Twitter, Facebook, and other social media. Goat could only imagine the feeding frenzy.

He'd also sent Volker's notes out. By now it had been received by thousands and thousands of news sources. He even sent it to the White House, the CDC, and the Department of Homeland Security. Maybe it would do some good.

But he had his doubts.

While he waited for Homer, Goat checked the online news services. Lucifer 113 was already spreading beyond Stebbins. The president was set to address the nation, and the Emergency Broadcast Network had replaced most of the regular stations.

This was it. This was the actual end.

Volker had called it a doomsday weapon, and tonight was the first night of the end of the world. Goat was sure of it.

He was certain for two reasons.

First, because of the news stories of the infection spreading. He didn't know—nor, apparently did the reporters—whether the "viral outbreak" as they were calling it, could be contained and eradicated. Maybe it could. There were some pretty extreme measures the government could take.

The other reason Goat believed that the doors to hell were swinging open—the reason that filled him with true despair—was the insight he'd had while waiting for Homer to come out of the comedy club. It was a process. It was an analysis of character motivation, and Goat dissected it the way he would with actors playing roles in a movie. His training, after all, was movie direction.

"I think I understand now," said Goat.

Homer grunted. "What?"

"I understand. I get it."

The killer glanced at him. "What is it you think you get?"

"Your plan."

"My plan? I don't have a plan."

"Okay, let me put it another way," said Goat. "I think I understand what the Red Mouth is telling you to do. I think I can envision what the Black Eye wants everyone to see."

Homer smiled. It looked like a genuine smile, too. "You had a vision?"

"Not exactly."

"Then what? Did the Red Mouth start whispering in your ear?"

"Maybe," said Goat, "it sort of came to me."

"What do you mean? What are you seeing?"

"You're just going to drive across country, stopping every once in a while for a bite, and then keep going. You want to spread this thing as far and as wide as possible. You want to kill the whole fucking world, don't you?"

Homer thought about it for a while as they drove on through the rain. "Yeah, that about says it."

"Is any of that stuff about the meek inheriting the earth true? Was any of that what you believe or was it all bullshit for the camera?"

Homer's smile was slow and sly. "Does it really matter, boy?"

"I need to know."

The lights of the big rigs in the opposite lane illuminated Homer Gibbon as he smiled again and shrugged.

"Wait . . . that's it?" demanded Goat. "You put me through all this shit and then you brush me off with a fucking shrug?"

"What's it matter to you?" asked the killer. "It's all going to work out the same whether it's true or not."

Goat made a disgusted sound low in his throat.

"Dr. Volker told me what I am and you know what that is, don't you, boy?"

Goat said nothing.

"I'm a fucking zombie. I'm already dead. You ever wonder why I move like I got arthritis? You don't know your basic medicine? I got rigor mortis. That means I'm already rotting. I may hear the Red

Mouth speak to me, but when I look into the future with the Black Eye, you know what I see? I see me fucking dead and gone, mother-fucker." Homer suddenly struck the steering wheel with the heel of his palm. "That's what I fucking see. Me. Dead. So I figured what the fuck. I might as well turn this into a party town. If I got to go then everybody's got to come with me. Every-fucking-body. And, yeah, to answer your question, I *do* believe. And what I believe is that life's a bitch and then we all fucking die. But not alone, boy. Not alone."

Homer punctuated his remarks with a brutal laugh. Totally without mirth or humanity. A dead man's laugh. A killer's laugh.

"It's the end of the world, boy. Just like the song says. And you know what? I feel just fine."

Goat stared at him and something in his head seemed to break. To snap. To tear open. Maybe it was the Black Eye opening so he could see his own future. Maybe it was that. If so, the future that Goat saw was that of a desolated world. It was a wasteland of disease and rot, and there, standing amid an endless crowd of unmoving, un-thinking, undying dead, was his own body. Robbed of life, of hope, of any possibility of anything. It was the ugliest thing he could imagine. Bleak and pointless.

He leaned closer to Homer Gibbon, wanting to see the killer's face clearly in the whitewash of headlines. As each of the big inter-state truckers whisked by he saw that evil face in a stark strobe. Each blink, each flash image, was identical. Inert, eternal, irredeemable.

He said, "Fuck you."

Then he grabbed the steering wheel in both hands, shoved it to the left with all his strength, and sent the Escalade careening into the headlights of a monstrous eighteen-wheel Freightliner pulling a full load of steel I-beams. Right into eighty thousand pounds driving at eighty-two miles an hour.

Although the impact opened a thousand red mouths in the flesh of Homer Gibbon, they whispered no secrets; and the Black Eye went forever blind.

PART FOUR

FIRST NIGHT

". . . So, when the last and dreadful hour
This crumbling pageant shall devour,
The trumpet shall be heard on high,
The dead shall live, the living die,
And Music shall untune the sky."

—John Dryden, "A Song for St. Cecilia's Day"

CHAPTER ONE HUNDRED EIGHTEEN
ATLANTA, GEORGIA

No one at the bar knew his last name. When asked he said that his name was John. It wasn't exactly true, but true enough.

John sat at the end of the bar, drinking red wine, making it last, paying for it with money he'd taken from the biker he'd killed. He would have more money when he sold the motorcycle. John was not a biker type. He disliked machines and especially loud ones. Noise irritated him. It was hard enough to listen to all of the voices in his head without those kinds of distractions.

The bar was quiet, especially this early in the day. The bartender, two other early-bird customers, and John. He'd come in as soon as it opened, found his favorite stool, and sat down to watch the news. So many wonderful things were happening in the world.

Pennsylvania, Maryland, West Virginia, and Ohio had all clearly been touched by the hand of God.

He wondered if that meant that *it* was starting.

The Fall.

The collapse of the false world of idolatry and sin.

It was something for which he'd prayed every day of his adult life.

It was something he always believed would happen one day.

The Fall.

Then the news station interrupted its own broadcast to play another video clip from a reporter named Gregory Weinman. The reporter, who was somewhere in the affected area, had been sending videos all night, and at first the press had dismissed them as elaborate fakes and the worst kind of practical jokes.

As the night burned away and the morning dawned with fear and promise, the reaction to those reports changed. Now they were being trotted out as hard news. News that terrified everyone at the bar.

Except John, who found them so incredibly comforting.

The TV reporter warned that the footage they were about to show was disturbing and contained images not suitable for children.

John saw the predatory gleam in the reporter's eyes. Then the footage began, showing a man that John immediately recognized as the supposedly executed serial killer Homer Gibbon as he went into a 7-Eleven and began attacking people.

It was all very messy and crude. John did not like biting. He always preferred knives.

Knives held within them a purity of purpose. They were instruments of God's will. John had several of them in special pockets he'd sewn inside his clothes. He was never without his knives.

The video played out and then it cut to the interior of a car as Homer Gibbon spoke about why he was doing what he did.

He spoke about seeing with the Black Eye.

He spoke about hearing the secrets of the Red Mouth.

The Red Mouth.

That was something John understood, though he had never used the exact phrase before. Red Mouth. How perfect. How apt.

He mouthed the words, and they felt like ambrosia on his tongue and lips.

He knew right then that he would forever use those words to describe what he, in his holy purpose, had done so many times and would continue to do if God willed it.

Then Homer said something else that struck to the very core of John's personal faith.

"In the Bible Jesus talked about how the meek were going to inherit the earth. I forget where he said it, but it was important, and I think this is what he was talking about. The way people are when they wake up after I open the Red Mouths in their flesh . . ."

"Yes," said John.

He said it a little too loud, a bit too emphatically, and the two other patrons turned to him.

"What?" asked one of them. "You agree with that bullshit?"

John said nothing.

"I asked you a question," demanded the man, sliding off his stool. "I have friends in Pennsylvania. I have some family there."

John considered how to play this. He could construct a response that would dial the man's outrage down to a simple misunderstanding. He could do that because he'd done that sort of thing many times before, and with sharper people than this. He'd managed conversations with psychiatrists and parole review panels.

And yet . . .

On the screen Homer Gibbon continued to talk about the meek inheriting the earth, and about how he was helping them have eternal life. About how it was God's will for a peaceful planet. A world without war, without hate. A world of the silent, mindless, meek. A world of people emptied of everything except the grace of a loving and generous God.

John understood and agreed with everything Homer Gibbon said.

"Yo, asshole," said the loudmouth, moving down the bar toward John. "I'm talking to—"

His last words were gone, trapped inside the man's chest, unable to get past the blood that now filled his throat. The man stared in uncomprehending horror at the glittering steel that seemed to have appeared as if by magic in John's hand.

The other patron and the bartender gaped at what was happening, their incomprehension every bit as great as the dying loudmouth.

"John?" asked the bartender. "What the hell did you just do?"

Explaining would take too much time, and John did not believe either of these men would truly understand.

He killed them both.

They tried to make a fight of it. As if that mattered.

As they lay bleeding, with red mouths opened in their flesh, John watched the face of Homer Gibbon.

This was the face of the chosen of God, the rock upon which a new church was being born in the farmlands of Pennsylvania.

"You are my god," he told the killer on the TV. "And I will be a saint of your church."

Smiling, filled with great joy, Saint John wiped his knives clean and stepped out into the morning sunlight, knowing with total certainty that the noisy, cluttered, sinful world was about to fall. It was all going to become quiet.

As God so clearly intended.

CHAPTER ONE HUNDRED NINETEEN
ROUTE 40
FAYETTE COUNTY, PENNSYLVANIA

The buses painted a long line of yellow through the gray of the pre-dawn morning. Dez, Trout, and Sam sat in a huddle in the front of the lead bus. They passed a few cars, but they were all driving too fast. Panic speed, thought Trout. A UPS truck lay on its side at a cross-roads and several figures were hunkered down around a ragged red thing that twitched even as it was consumed. Off in the distance, on the far side of a massive cornfield, a farmhouse burned, flickering its souls to the winds.

They found an armoured personnel carrier standing alone and empty on the shoulder of the road. Sam and the remaining members of the Boy Scouts got out to check it. Dez went with them and Trout, weak and trembling, stood in the open doorway of the bus. There was no blood on the APC, no scattering of shell casings, nothing to indi-cate a battle. However, it was completely empty. No crew, no bodies, no traces of how it came to be abandoned there. Boxer, Shortstop, and Gypsy came back with armloads of ammunition and extra guns. Sam tottered back carrying a heavy metal case of fragmentation grenades.

They stripped the APC of everything of use, and all of it done in a hasty silence. Then they piled back into the buses and the convoy began rolling.

The landscape that whipped by seemed murky and deserted to Trout, though his gut told him otherwise. Twice he saw figures in the woods, pale and silent, watching the buses as they passed.

Inside the bus things quieted down. Many of the children were asleep, dragged into troubled dreams by shock and exhaustion. Others sat and watched the forest with the fixity of attention of a bunch of plastic mannequins. Dez followed the line of Trout's stare and took his hand to give it a gentle squeeze.

Sam sat nearby thumbing bullets into a stack of empty maga-zines. His eyes were shuttered windows.

Jenny DeGroot came and squatted down in the aisle. She had somehow conjured hot coffee. "It's instant," she apologized, handing out steaming Styrofoam cups.

Trout took his with a greedy sigh. "I don't care if it's boiled gutter water."

He burned his tongue on the first sip, didn't care, blew on the surface and took another sip.

Sam Imura sat with his head cradled between his palms, eyes unfocused as he stared into his own thoughts.

"I was sorry to hear about your friend," said Trout.

"Moonshiner," murmured Sam, nodding his thanks.

"What was his real name?" asked Dez.

"Staff Sergeant Bud Hollister. Good ol' boy from Alabama."

Dez nodded. "He had biker tats. He used to ride?"

A memory put a faint smile on Sam's hard mouth. "He rode with the Outlaws before he moved from 'Bama."

"Rough boys," said Dez.

"Very. He rolled out with them when he was sixteen lying about being nineteen. He was with them until just before his eighteenth birthday, then got arrested for some petty stuff. Judge offered him a choice of jail or enlistment. Not that he stopped kicking ass and taking names as a soldier. Running joke was that he had Velcro on his stripes because he kept losing them."

Trout cleared his throat and cut a look at Dez. "Lots of that going around."

"Bite me," muttered Dez. "You can live small and boring or you can go and tear a piece off for yourself."

Sam grinned. "You and Moonshiner would have gotten along fine."

"He wasn't half bad-looking."

"Hey, I'm sitting right here you know," Trout reminded her.

Dez ignored him. She held out her cup. "To Bud 'Moonshiner' Hollister. A true American ass-kicker."

"And a good man," added Sam, touching his cup. Trout did the same and they drank in silence for a while.

"After we get to Asheville," asked Trout, "what will you do? Stay there or go back?"

"Back is a relative term. I'm not part of the regular army, so I don't have to report back. I'll stay in touch with Scott Blair and if he needs me to do anything special, something that could help, then I'll do that."

"And if there's nothing you can do?"

Sam shrugged. "My family is in central California. Dad and step-mom. Brother who's twenty and in the police academy, and a step-brother who's eighteen months old. Dad's a cop, too, but he's getting up there. Been driving a desk for the last ten years. Mom's an E.R. nurse. If this thing continues to spread, then I'm going to want to get to them and help keep them safe."

"I hope it doesn't come to that," said Trout, and Dez nodded. Sam made no comment. The conversation dwindled down to a shared, moody silence.

Trout stared out the window as he sipped the last of his coffee, then he frowned. "Hey," he said, "I thought we were going to North Carolina."

"We are," said Dez.

"Then why did we just pass a sign for Fort Necessity? You planning on visit a historic battlefield during a flight to safety? I don't know, Dez, I doubt the gift shop is open this early."

"We're not going to the fort," said Dez irritably. "We're going to Sapphire Foods. It's a mile past the fort on Route 40. I told you about it. The big food distribution warehouse."

"Ah yes, the one where your ex-boyfriend works. If he's still an *ex*-boyfriend."

"Don't start, Billy."

"It's a good call," said Sam. "We got less than half the supplies out of the school."

Trout knew that it was a good idea but he didn't want to admit it. He fished for an objection. "What if they won't let us take any-thing."

"We'll ask nicely," Sam suggested.

"Charlie will give me what I want," said Dez.

"Charlie? Charlie who? And why would he give you anything? Would that be a matter of him committing a crime?"

"We're in a state of emergency."

"Uh-huh."

"And Charlie likes kids. He always has. He coaches the boxing and wrestling teams at the PAL in—"

"Whoa, wait, are you talking about *that* Charlie?"

Dez colored and said nothing.

"Are you freaking serious, Desdemona Fox? *Him?*"

"Who?" asked Sam, but he was ignored.

"He's a scumbag, a thug, and very likely an actual criminal," said Trout.

"He's not that bad."

"Your nose grew six inches when you said that." Trout shook his head in genuine disbelief. "I know you've dated some lowlifes over the years, Dez, but how drunk were you when you thought dating Charlie Pink-eye was a good idea?"

"He doesn't like to be called that."

"I don't care what he likes or doesn't like. Charlie's a psychopath. So's his brother and so's his dad. Didn't his old man kill Charlie's mother?"

"It was never proved. Might have been suicide. But what does that matter, Billy? We're not going there so I can give him a blow job. We need supplies and I know that if I explain the situation, he'll help us. And if we need to, he'll let us stay there."

Trout began to fire back a crushing reply, but the driver called out, "We're coming up on it."

The bus rounded a curve in the road and there it was. A tall double fence encircled a plot of land that had to be a mile per side. The heavy-gauge rolling gate was peeled back on its hinges, the pipe frame twisted into a useless curl. The vehicle that had hit it, a Staples delivery truck, was still wrapped inside the gate like a spider caught in a web. The driver's door was open and splashed with black blood.

"No . . . no . . . no . . ." said Dez under her breath.

In the middle of the property was a massive one-story building made from dull gray stone blocks. As Dez had said there were no windows at all, but along one side there were bays for fifty trucks. A dozen trucks were backed into bays. There were a dozen cars parked haphazardly in the lot, some crumpled together. One sat there burning in the dying drizzle.

"Oh . . . shit . . ." breathed Trout.

There were zombies everywhere.

Dozens of them.

CHAPTER ONE HUNDRED TWENTY
151 FIRST SIDE
FORT PITT BOULEVARD
PITTSBURGH, PENNSYLVANIA

Alex Jay Berman stood on the balcony of his high-rise apartment and watched Pittsburgh burn. His wife held his hand and her grip was like a vise. So tight that he knew she would never let go.

Never.

Screams rose up from below, and Alex bent forward to look down. Twenty-three stories below, moving through patches of sunlight and shadow, the crowds surged. From up here it was impossible to tell who was infected and who was not.

Or at least not yet.

Everyone was in motion.

Cars and trucks moved through the crowds and from up here they looked like leaves buffeted along atop a moving stream. Alex wondered how many of those people the vehicles rolled over. Up hear you couldn't hear the sound of breaking bones.

Only the screams.

And the gunfire.

And the explosions.

Those were continual.

The rains had dwindled to nothing and then faded as the sun burned through the clouds. The sky above was pretty and blue. A bright blue. Like the summer skies of his boyhood. Pretty. Birds fly up there, far above the sounds of dying from below.

Behind him, on the other side of the closed French doors, fists beat on the glass. Small sounds made by small fists.

Alex did not turn to look. He had done many things in his life, some brave, some crazy, but he was absolutely sure it would take a greater insanity and far more courage than he possessed to turn and look through that glass. He could not do that.

His wife sobbed.

Once, a deep sound that was filled with everything either of them ever needed to say.

Except for one more thing.

Alex turned to his wife and smiled at her.

"I love you," he said. "And I always will."

Her tears glittered like jewels in the sunlight.

Still holding hands they stepped off the balcony ledge.

CHAPTER ONE HUNDRED TWENTY-ONE

SAPPHIRE FOODS
ROUTE 40
FAYETTE COUNTY, PENNSYLVANIA

"What do we do?" asked the driver of the bus.

The lead bus idled in the short curving driveway, the others were still around the bend. So far the infected in the parking lot had not reacted to the bus. They were all close to the building, which was hundreds of yards away.

"We have three choices," Sam said quickly when Dez joined them. "First choice is we bug out now and take our chances with the supplies we have. It's less than a day to Asheville."

"Sure," said Dez bitterly, "if the roads are clear. If people are going apeshit—and you know damn well they are—then those roads could be jammed and those buses can't exactly go off-road. It could take a day or it could take a week. And we don't have a week's worth of food and water. Nothing close to it. Most of that stuff got left behind at the school."

"Okay . . . second choice is my team draws the dead off to one side, away from the building while you park the buses and off-load everyone through the loading bays. Then we make this home base."

"Good call," said Trout. "Right, Dez? You said this place has plenty of food and water and their own generators."

Dez chewed her lip as she considered it. "There's probably enough fuel in the generators for maybe a week. Ten days at the outside. After that the lights and heat and everything else shuts down. There are also no windows. Good for security, but once the lights are out it's a big, black box. And there are two bathrooms but no showers. If it was a week, maybe, but since we don't know how long . . . and since we have no way of telling how many of those *things* are going come sniffing around, we could be well and truly fucked if we get trapped in there."

"Agreed." Sam sighed and nodded. "Then that leaves the third choice. Plan A, I guess. We load as much as we can and we get back on the road."

They watched the zombies in the parking lot.

"Can we actually *do* that with them hanging around?" asked Trout.

"No. We'd need to take them out. I count—what? Thirty, thirty-two? They're spaced out . . . we can take them down."

"And how many more will come looking to see what all the shooting's about?"

Sam nodded. "Which means we need to work mighty damn fast."

"Hey," said Trout, snapping his fingers. "You black ops guys do assassinations and stuff, right? Don't you have silencers?"

"First," said Dez impatiently, "they're called sound suppressors."

"And second," said Sam, "we didn't bring them because this wasn't that kind of job."

"Oh." Trout felt foolish, but then something else occurred to him. "Don't we have to check the building first before we go in? Who's going to do that while you clear out the yard?"

"My team gets to do both," said Sam wearily. Then he brightened. "And I think I know a way to speed the process."

He outlined it to Dez, who approved. Then Sam touched his ear-bud and explained the situation and the plan to his remaining team members. Trout couldn't hear their replies, but he doubted they were any happier about this than he was.

But it all began happening very fast.

Dez told the driver of the first bus to go into the lot. The other buses followed. Sam jumped out and began walking alongside the bus, which proceeded at a pace slow enough to keep pace with him. Boxer, Shortstop, and Gypsy did the same.

The plan was simple. The buses would enter, cut right, and follow the inside of the fence all the way around the building, staying so close that none of the infected could get between the fence and the buses. The engine sound drew the infected like a bright light draws moths, and soon the dead were shambling across the lot toward the lead bus. Sam and the Boy Scouts walked without haste toward them and as each zombie came within twenty feet, one of the soldiers put it down with a single shot to the head. It quickly became a rhythm. Easy and mechanical. Though to Trout, watching from the lead bus, there was a different kind of horror to this. The zombies closed in, they were shot, the convoy inched along, over and over again. Aboard the buses, people started cheering with each kill. As if this was a game and the number counter jumped up with each death. As if the infected were no more real than animated monsters in a video game. As if each of those infected had not been a person hours ago.

It shocked and repulsed Trout.

Lucifer 113 had stolen the life from these people. And this . . . the necessary killing took away their posthumous sham of being alive. But the reaction of the people on the bus, the cheers like spectators at the Roman circus, seemed to strip away the humanity of each infected. It reduced them to things rather than people.

Somehow this indifference, or detachment or madness or whatever it was, frightened Trout every bit as much as the plague itself. As each cheer went up, louder than the first, Trout thought he could glimpse a future where the survivors of this placed no value whatsoever on human life.

He knew that this was shock, that this was a shared traumatic stress reaction. He knew that. But he feared it, too.

It took over an hour to clear the parking lot.

It seemed like a year to Trout.

When it was over, Shortstop peeled off and headed to the open gate to stand guard.

At Dez's direction the entire convoy of buses circled the huge building. Dez and Sam pressed their faces against the windows so they could examine the building. Along one section of wall were slots for employee cars. First in the line was a mint-condition 1967 fire-engine red Pontiac Le Mans convertible. Trout knew that car all too well. It belonged to Charlie Matthias.

The other cars and pickup trucks were unknown to him.

"Looks intact," she said after they finished appraising the building. Then she reached out and tapped the bus driver on the shoulder. "Think you can back this into one of those bays?"

"Drove a tractor my whole life," said the man. "I can park this in a phone booth."

He was as good as his word, turning in a good angle, spinning the wheel before shifting, watching the mirrors, and sliding down the slope to a gentle stop against the heavy rubber fender covering the base of the load bay. Dez went back to make sure the door would open, and found there was a half-inch of clearance. She closed the door, though, and made sure it was locked, then hurried back to rejoin Trout. The other buses began imitating the process of backing into the bays. Most were able to manage it, but after a couple of them failed to do it, the driver of Dez's bus went trotting out to help them.

Dez exited the bus and waited on the deserted loading bay until Sam, Boxer, and Gypsy joined her. Trout lingered in the open doorway, feeling enormously useless.

Dez had six extra magazines for her Glock, and thanks to the APC they'd looted, she had a second nine millimeter tucked into the back of her belt. Sam had switched from his sniper rifle to a more practical M4, and he had magazines tucked into every pouch and pocket. Six grenades were clipped to his harness.

"What's the call, boss?" asked Gypsy.

Sam nodded to the service door at the far end of the bay. "We knock and let Dez negotiate with her friend, Charlie Matthias, if he's still alive. She believes he'll allow us to stock up, given the situation."

"And if he doesn't?" asked Gypsy.

Dez shrugged. "I like the guy," she said, "but I'm not married to him. One way or another we're rolling out of here with food and water. Not really interested in taking fuck you for an answer."

Boxer held out his fist and took the bump.

"Gypsy," said Sam, "watch our backs."

They moved away from the buses, running lightly, weapons up and out. Trout noticed how smoothly Dez fit in with the Boy Scouts. Like she belonged more to their world than to any other. In a moment of irrational jealousy he wondered what would happen if Sam Imura and Dez had to work together for any length of time. Trout did not like his chances in a competition with that man. Not in combat and not in romance. Sam was everything Dez liked. He was strong, confident, capable, and decent.

"Fuck," Trout murmured. Then he added, "Billy Trout you are a total damn fool."

CHAPTER ONE HUNDRED TWENTY-TWO
TOWN OF STEBBINS
STEBBINS COUNTY, PENNSYLVANIA

Jake DeGroot drove through hell.

That was the only way he could describe what he was seeing.

The whole town of Stebbins was in ruins. There was death everywhere, but not enough of it was lying down. People—as torn and vacant as the three girls that had attacked Burl and the others—wandered through the streets. Many of them turned toward the sound of the front-end loader. Some even ran at it and tried to attack it.

At first Jake tried to avoid them, but the machine wasn't fast or nimble enough to zigzag through the crowd.

He understood more about what they were now. On the slow ride here he'd put on headphones and turned the radio all the way up and listened to someone from the government say crazy things about a plague.

A plague.

A disease that made people murder each other.

It sounded plausible, though Jake knew it was much worse than that.

Even so, he didn't want to hurt anyone. Not unless he had to. Not unless there was no other choice.

He ran out of choices on the way to the Stebbins Little School. By the time Big Bird was rolling down the road that lead to the front gate, the way was clogged by victims of the plague.

Unable to go around them or evade them, he took a breath, cursed God, and drove over them. The only mercy he received was that the engine noise was so loud he couldn't hear the crunching of bones.

So many bones.

He turned away from the biggest mass of them and plowed right through an open stretch of fence, rolled across the parking lot past empty school buses, looking for some sign, some proof that Jenny and the others were still safe inside the school.

Then he rolled to a stop, idling, staring.

At two things.

The first was the open doorway of the school. The infected wandered in and out, and Jake recognized some of the teachers among them. It came close to breaking his heart.

Then he saw the second thing. Words written in brown spray paint on the red bricks of the school wall.

It was a message about who had been here at the school, about how they'd left, and about where they were going. As he read it the infected began climbing onto his machine.

With a growl, Jake put the loader in gear, turned, and with some of the dead still clinging on, headed for the road that led out of town.

CHAPTER ONE HUNDRED TWENTY-THREE

SAPPHIRE FOODS
ROUTE 40
FAYETTE COUNTY, PENNSYLVANIA

They were twenty feet from the service door when Sam froze, one fist raised. Then he waved the others up so they could see what he was looking at. The door to the building was not, as they first supposed, shut. It was slightly ajar, about a half inch from a tight fit. That wasn't what jolted Sam, though. There was a partial handprint on the frame, just the palm and a thumb, the rest hidden by the door.

The handprint still glistened with red blood.

"Shit," whispered Dez. "Can God give us one fucking break?"

Gypsy and Boxer shifted to take clear lines-of-sight once the door was opened. "Dez," said Sam, "you open the door. I go in first, then my team, then you. Keep all lines clear. Nobody fires until and unless I do."

He shifted to allow Dez to grip the door handle.

Sam finger-counted down from three, and she pulled the door open quickly, blocked it with her leg and took her gun in a two-handed grip.

Sam went in first, moving silently on cat-feet. The others followed, moving smoothly, weapons moving from corner to corner, covering everything. Dez went in last, and stepping inside wasn't like stepping into a warehouse.

It was like stepping into an abattoir.

The place was massive, with hundreds of tall rows of steel shelves that stretched off into darkness. Most of the lights were out except for small emergency lights bolted every dozen yards. There was not enough light to see into the building. But there was enough illumination so that Dez could see that the walls to either side of the door and floor in front of her were splashed with blood.

There were bodies everywhere. A dozen at least, and they lay in disjointed tangles, with arms and legs missing, heads crushed, necks chopped through. Trails of blood—shoes and bare feet—led off into the main warehouse and vanished down shadowy rows.

Only one figure still stood.

He was massive, with chest and shoulders so heavily packed with corded muscle that it made him look like a great, pale ape. His skin was the color of milk and there were dreadful scars covering his arms and face. Old scars, barely visible through the blood—both red and black—that covered him from scalp to boots.

He glared at them with mad eyes. One bright blue, the other as red as a subway rat.

He held a crowbar in one fist and a meat cleaver in the other, and he stood there, panting, wild and thoroughly savage.

Sam, Boxer, and Gypsy immediately pointed their guns at him.

Dez pushed her way past the soldiers.

"Charlie?" she said softly.

The wild eyes flared and for a moment it seemed as if this monstrous man would attack.

"Don't," murmured Sam Imura. He said it very quietly.

Charlie's eyes flicked to him for a moment and the thick lips curled back from uneven teeth. Maybe it was a sneer, maybe it was a smile. In either case it was unpleasant and feral.

"Charlie . . ." Dez repeated. She lowered her gun, holding it in one hand and reaching out toward him with the other.

The mad eyes blinked.

And blinked again, and each time there was a fraction less of the frenzied look and a fraction more of sanity. Of realization of self.

Of recognition.

"D-Dez . . . ?"

"It's me, Charlie," she said. "It's okay."

"Okay?" echoed Charlie Matthias as if that was the strangest word he'd ever heard. "Okay? Jesus Christ, Dez, what's happening to the world? Nothing's okay."

He let out a breath and lowered the weapons.

Sam and his team held their ground, though.

"What happened here, Charlie? Who are these people?"

The bodies on the floor were so badly mangled that it was impossible to tell who or what they had been.

"They're . . . they're my boys."

Dez frowned. "Your—?"

"My crew. The guys I fucking run with." He looked around in confusion. "Rico, and Tyrone. Tony Dale and Fez Zimmio. Christ, Dez, what the fuck's going on? We were playing cards and Rico went outside to take a piss. Then he comes in all crazy and fucked up. Comes back with a whole shitload of people I don't know and suddenly everything went to shit. Rico . . . *bit* Fez. Bit his throat right the fuck out. Christ, Dez, he started eating him. How's that not fucked up?"

Charlie's voice was rising to a dangerous hysterical note, and as he ranted he began waving around his weapons. Sam shifted to stand between Dez and the big man.

"Mr. Matthias, I am going to need you to calm down. Put down your weapons and put your hands on your head. Do it now."

Charlie stared at him with total incomprehension.

"Who the fuck are you? What's happening? Somebody better fucking tell me what's going on."

"Charlie—*Charlie*!" yelled Dez and her voice was so loud and sharp that Charlie flinched as if he'd been slapped. "Haven't you listened to the news? Don't you understand what's happening? It's a plague. It's spreading out of control and it makes people want to kill each other."

"W-what?"

"Stebbins County is gone. Everyone's dead. Everyone, Charlie, except a bunch of kids and some other folks, some adults. We have twelve school buses outside and we're trying to get out of here. We're heading down south, but we need supplies. I came here because I knew you'd help us. I knew I could count on you, Charlie."

With each sentence she changed her voice from sharpness to soft appeal. It worked on Charlie, drawing him back from the edge.

"Is this real? Are you bullshitting me, Dez?"

"It's real. We're in trouble and we need your help."

He looked down at the weapons he held, considered them for a moment, then let them fall. The clangs they made echoed through the building.

"Boxer, Gypsy," said Sam, "do a sweep. Stay together and make it fast."

They moved off, each of them throwing Charlie ugly looks.

"Mr. Matthias," said Sam, "were you bitten?"

"Huh? Me? No. Not that they didn't try. Christ, Fez chewed on my boot trying to bite my ankle, and that was after I busted his knees and broke his damn back. How's that make sense?"

Dez quickly explained the situation, compressing it into a few terse lines. Lucifer, Homer Gibbon, the outbreak, the parasites. When she got to that last part, Charlie bolted and ran for the men's room. They followed and stood in the doorway while Charlie stripped out of his bloody clothes and scrubbed his skin with hot water and soap, and then rubbed himself down with nearly a full bottle of Purell. Charlie was almost an albino, but he had some splotches of color. He rinsed his jeans and put them back on. The shirt was a total loss.

"Clock's ticking," said Sam. "We need to—"

And then Shortstop cut in via the team microphone. Sam held up a hand and used the other to touch his earbud.

"What've you got?"

"We got incoming, boss."

"How many?"

"Too many."

CHAPTER ONE HUNDRED TWENTY-FOUR
COLDWATER CANYON DRIVE
LOS ANGELES, CALIFORNIA

Albert Godown tied his running shoes, stood, and stretched slowly, feeling the muscles come undone, the cramps from the long flight gradually releasing their hold on him. His wife, Mary, was by the park, holding a deep lunge. She coughed a few times, but she controlled her reaction to it, keeping it small.

"You okay?" he asked.

Mary nodded, then shrugged. "It's good."

He waited for more, but that was all she said. So he nudged it a bit. "You still sick to your stomach?"

"Not really."

Albert walked over to her. "C'mon," he said, "you were sick as a dog last night."

"Just airsickness. It was like a rodeo up there."

"Are you sure? They're still talking about some kind of flu on the news."

She shook her head. "It's better than it was. Might have been allergies. Did you smell the air on the plane? Until they closed the doors it smelled like we were parked right next to an open sewer. Burned my eyes."

He nodded, though it hadn't bothered him as much. "It was worse by that hotel."

Because of the first wave of Superstorm Zelda, the flights the day before had been canceled and the airline had put them up at a hotel near the Pittsburgh airport. The kind of hotel you only ever stay in if your flight is canceled and it's that or sleep in the terminal. They'd worked out in the little gym and when the rain let up for an hour they jogged around the property for an estimated five miles. That, at least, had been the plan, but halfway through it the humidity turned the air into a cold soup more conducive to swimming than running, so they bagged it and went inside. That humid air stank, too, and that's when Mary's cough started. A tickle, at first, and then worse as the evening went on. It came and went, and didn't really settle down until this morning, when they got a 6:45 flight out of there. They changed planes in Chicago after a three-hour layover, and Mary's cough sparked up again, but settled down once they were on the plane. Now it was back to being an infrequent thing. Still there, though, and he thought she should have it checked out. He told her so.

"It's just allergies," she said. "Or whatever. I bet if we get a good run now it'll just go away. It's so nice and dry here." To prove her point she took a deep breath and let it out. "See? No cough."

He shrugged and they set off.

They each wore headphones. Mary had her iPod set to one of her playlists. Albert could never imagine jogging to classical music. It seemed so counterintuitive to cardio. He usually listened to classic rock or, as with today's run, the BBC news station. Better and less biased coverage than any of the domestic stations.

But before they'd gone half a mile he began frowning, and soon his run slowed to a walk and then he stopped, touching an earbud to make sure he could hear everything. Mary ran on for half a block before she realized she was alone, then she circled back.

"What is it?"

He pulled one earbud and gave it to her. They listened together as the BBC reporter talked about an outbreak of a disease that was so dangerous that the military was using force to stop those infected from leaving the quarantine zone. Albert saw Mary mouth the word "military."

The reporter said that the quarantine zone included large parts of Pennsylvania, Maryland, West Virginia, and Ohio.

They stared at each other, stunned by this. Not believing it. Unable to not believe it.

They looked around them. The California sun was still shining. Birds coasted on the thermals high above them. Children played in front yards.

The reporter said that the estimated death toll might reach half a million.

Mary said, "What?"

All Albert could do was shake his head.

This happened while they slept in an airport hotel. While they were in the air. But it must have started while they were still in Pittsburgh. It had to have been mere miles from them.

How did they not know about it?

How could something this big have spread so fast?

Mary coughed again and wiped at her mouth.

Albert didn't much notice it this time. His mind was reeling.

Then Mary coughed again. Much harder. Much louder. It doubled her over, and Albert lunged to catch her.

"Jesus Christ," he cried as she sagged against him. "Are you all right?"

She wiped her mouth with the back of one trembling hand.

And the moment froze for both of them as they stared with abject horror at the wetness smeared across her hand.

It was not the colorless wetness of spit.

Nor was it blood.

It was black.

And in the black wetness, small white shapes wriggled.

Mary screamed.

Albert screamed, too.

CHAPTER ONE HUNDRED TWENTY-FIVE

SAPPHIRE FOODS
ROUTE 40
FAYETTE COUNTY, PENNSYLVANIA

They hurried outside and stood on the dock, watching with sagging hearts and growing horror at the roads beyond the fence. Dez felt like she was caught in an endless loop. This was the schoolyard all over again except there was a forty-foot-wide gap in the fence.

Sam turned to his team. "We need to secure that fence right now."

Charlie stared at the approaching wall of the dead. "Hope you don't expect me to—"

"No," said Sam tightly, "you can go back inside and help Dez find what she needs. Do it fast and do it now."

Charlie cut a look at Dez and straightened as if realizing how bad his remark sounded. "Hey, don't get me wrong, I'd hold the line but I don't got a gun."

Sam's eyes were cold. "You won't need one to carry boxes. We'll hold the line."

With that he turned away and began running toward the open gate with Boxer and Gypsy at his heels. Dez lingered for a moment, then spun and raced for the building, shouting for all the adults to gather on the dock.

Charlie's pale face had turned beet red. He caught Trout smiling.

"The fuck you grinning at?"

"Nothing at all," said Trout. He began limping toward the loading bay, determined to be of some use, however small.

Charlie shoved him roughly aside and jogged heavily after Dez.

He didn't see Trout shoot him the finger.

Trout just reached the loading bay when the gunfire began. He looked back and saw that the road was crowded with the dead.

CHAPTER ONE HUNDRED TWENTY-SIX
MARIPOSA COUNTY, CALIFORNIA

The cadets came in from a long run, all of them panting and sweating, some of them laughing, a few too exhausted for trash talk and chatter. One young man trailed the group, walking slowly while stretching his arms. He had been among the first group to complete the ten-kilometer run through the hills, but he'd stopped for a long yoga cooldown. The other cadets nodded to him as they passed. Although he was a quiet and introspective man, he was well-liked and respected.

The day was beautiful and even when the last stragglers had gone inside, he lingered to consider the fleet of white clouds sailing high above the mountains toward the eastern horizon. The birds of autumn sang in the trees and the gentle breeze carried the scent of dogwood and California lilies.

The young man smiled at the day. As he mounted the steps to the front door he thought of his little brother, who was a year and a half old. Maybe he'd take him for a bike ride to a hummingbird garden. The kid would like that.

His fingers were inches from the door when it suddenly swung outward so fast it nearly smashed his hand. The young cadet jerked his hand back as his friend Jerry Buckley came bursting out of the building. The men collided, but the young cadet was always fast on his feet and he grabbed his friend and spun him, keeping them both from falling.

"Damn, Jer!" he barked. "What the hell—?"

Jerry grabbed the front of his sweatshirt with both hands. "Christ, Tom, I got to get home. It's all going to shit."

"What is?"

"That thing back east. That plague. Holy shit, man, they're saying that they lost control of it. It's showing up everywhere."

Jerry tried to pull away, but the young cadet, Tom, held him, kept him right there. "Who said this? The news?"

"No," said Jerry, "they made an announcement as soon as we got in from the run. Everyone's getting changed and getting their shit. They're sending us all home. You should get your gear and get to your folks' place, man. This is all falling apart."

"Slow down, Jer," said the young cadet, "that's the other side of the country."

But Jerry was already shaking his head. "No, aren't you hearing me? It's everywhere."

"I don't—"

"It's in L.A.!" yelled Jerry, pulling away. "At the airport. Jesus, Tom, it's already here."

As if to punctuate his words, the air above them was torn by the grinding of helicopter rotors and they looked up to see a wave of Apaches heading south. Four big Chinooks followed behind them. Higher still, the contrails of jet fighters gouged white scars in the beautiful morning.

Tom stared at them and inside his chest, in the core of his heart, ice began to form.

"God almighty . . ." he breathed.

Jerry began backing away. "This shit is really going south, man," he said. "Get to your folks' place. They live in that gated place a couple hours from here, right?"

Tom nodded. "Sunset Hollow, up north . . ."

"Well, tell everyone there to close the damn gates," said Jerry. He took an abrupt step forward and took Tom's hand. "Listen, brother, you take care of yourself, you hear? From what they're saying this is going to get really bad. You do what you have to do to keep your family safe. You hear me? You do what you have to do."

Then Jerry pulled Tom into a fierce, brief hug. He pushed him back spun, and ran for his parked car. Soon other cadets were pushing their way out of the building, running, running.

Then Tom was running, too. Into the building, down to his locker where his clothes and weapons and keys were. Then back out of the building, catching only seconds of the TV broadcast in the muster room.

". . . I can see the city. Oh my God . . . Pittsburgh is burning . . ."

He had no memory of reaching his car, of starting it or driving it. But the radio . . . that he remembered.

". . . LAX is under siege. SWAT and TSA agents have been over-run . . ."

Every account was hysterical.

Every account was worse.

Another wave of helicopters thundered overhead.

As he drove, Tom tried to call his parents.

No one answered the phone.

Not the house phone, not their cells.

"Please," he begged as he slammed the pedal all the way down, pounding the horn, tearing along the shoulder of the road, running red lights, spinning the wheel to avoid collisions with a handbreadth to spare, forcing other drivers to career into each other to avoid him.

"Please."

Tom was not a deeply religious man.

Not until then.

All the way from the police academy to the gates of Sunset Hollow he prayed with his whole heart and every shred of need, begging whatever powers there were to take this back, to make it not real.

Los Angeles was three hundred miles away from where his parents lived in their quiet home behind high walls in Mariposa County.

CHAPTER ONE HUNDRED TWENTY-SEVEN

SAPPHIRE FOODS
ROUTE 40
FAYETTE COUNTY, PENNSYLVANIA

They worked in frenzied silence.

The bodies of the infected Charlie had killed had been dragged into a corner and covered with a tarp. Big rolls of plastic had been spread over the bloodstains so that nobody tracked black blood onto the buses.

Charlie went up and down the aisles with Dez, with Trout limping along behind. It irritated him that Charlie was suddenly so helpful and conciliatory. Trout knew that the big man was trying to make up for his moment of weakness outside, and maybe for being crazed out of his mind when they arrived. Trout could easily forgive Charlie for that part of it—under the circumstances anyone who had the good sense to go completely mad was doing themselves a favor. What Trout didn't like was Charlie being Mr. Friendly.

He knew about the man, and about the whole Matthias family. Some folks liked them because they were funny and, in their own strange way, charismatic. A lot of people feared the Matthias clan because they were every bit as dangerous and unpredictable as they appeared. Trout detested them and always had. He'd done too many news stories in which one or another of that family were suspected of a crime, and those crimes ranged from domestic violence to grand larceny to murder. Lots of arrests but never a single conviction.

And yet Dez not only liked Charlie, she used to *date* him—if one can actually date a simian subhuman. Other, less polite, words occurred to Trout than "date."

Even with that, Trout had to admit—however grudgingly—that Charlie was a big help. His knowledge of the warehouse and its contents shortened the process tremendously.

Then Jenny DeGroot came running to find them.

"Dez!" she cried as she tore along one of the rows.

"What's wrong?" asked Dez, hurrying to meet her.

"That soldier, Captain Imura . . . he's in trouble. You'd better come quick."

Dez blew past Trout and raced for the door. Charlie was right with her.

By the time Trout managed to hobble to the loading bay the sun was above the horizon and the long night was over.

But the nightmare was not.

The dead were inside the parking lot.

And there were so many of them.

Far too many.

Boxer, Shortstop, Gypsy, and Sam were walking backward, firing as they retreated. They killed a lot of the dead, but it wasn't even making a dent in the seething mass of infected.

"Oh my God," whispered Jenny, her hand covering her mouth, "where are they all coming from?"

Trout shook his head.

Jenny asked another, even more destructive question. "How bad *is* this?"

Trout whirled. "Jenny, get everyone on the bus. Tell them to drop whatever they're carrying and get on the damn buses. We need to get out of here *right now*."

Then he was yelling and grabbing teachers and parents who were standing and watching with slack jaws and horror in their eyes. He shoved them toward the buses.

"Get the engines started," he bellowed. "Pull out of the bays and get into a line. Check all the windows. Come on—*move!*"

The gunfire was louder but more sparse, and when he turned he saw that the soldiers were no longer backing away. They were running. It was a full rout. Sections of the fence were bowing inward, but that mattered less than the steady stream of zombies who crowded in through the big open gateway. Trout's orderly mind kept wanting to quantify them, to put a number to the horde.

A thousand?

No, that was too small a number.

Two or three thousand at the very least.

Coming from where?

He tried to remember how many towns were nearby. There were a number of them, but not enough to account for these numbers.

Then Trout remembered the highway. All those cars, all those travelers.

Had something happened to block the highway?

And had the lines of stopped cars become a feeding frenzy?

He didn't know and probably never would, but it was the only thing that could account for there being so many people here. So many dead people.

Not all of them were slow. Some of them ran like sprinters, cutting ahead of the slower zombies, racing to try and tackle the soldiers. They ran so fast that it sometimes took two or three shots to bring them down. That gave the slower ones more time to stagger forward, and it wasted bullets.

We're all going to die, thought Billy Trout.

The last of the adults were piling onto the buses.

"Dez!" screamed Trout. "Come on!"

Dez Fox stood halfway between the loading docks and the front rank of the living dead, firing her Glock, dropping empty magazines, swapping in new ones, firing, reloading, firing. All the time she did this she screamed. Rage and terror.

Charlie Matthias had a length of black pipe in his hands. Eight feet long and bent in two places. He'd run up to a gap between Sam Imura and Gypsy and swing the pipe with incredible power and ferocity. Infected were hurled aside like broken dolls. He hit and hit and hit, the massive muscles flexing under his milky skin.

He, too, screamed.

The bus engines roared to life and the first of the convoy pulled out of the bay. The others woke up with terrible slowness and crept into line. All too slow, thought Trout. Too slow.

He thought, in all the confusion, that he heard another engine roar over to his right. A different engine, but it vanished again. A hallucination, thought Trout, and he wasn't surprised that his mind was fracturing.

He hobbled forward to where Dez was reloading.

"Get into the bus," he shouted.

She ignored him and slapped the new magazine into place, raised her weapon, but didn't pull the trigger. Instead her eyes went as wide as saucers and she said, "What the fuck . . . ?"

Trout heard that strange engine roar again and as he turned he saw something moving beyond the throng of dead at the gate. It was big and yellow and for a moment he thought it was another bus. Had they lost one on the way here? Had someone else come up with the same plan?

But then the front of the vehicle seemed to lift.

No, it *did* lift.

With a sharp whine of hydraulics it raised up as the machine smashed into the packed dead. The impact sent bodies flying, but some seemed to hang in the air. Then Trout realized they weren't hanging, they were clinging to something. To the part of the machine that had raised up. His mind fought to make sense of it.

Then the machine turned and he understood.

It was a massive piece of construction equipment. Bright yellow, washed clean by the rains, and wearing a writhing coat of moaning infected, it was a front-end loader.

Monstrous and bulky, improbably heavy, riding on eight huge wheels, the machine crashed into the dead, rolled over them, ground them into bloody paste. The bucket rose and Trout could see that it was completely filled with struggling dead. The driver tilted the bucket to let them fall then brought the steel bucket down on top of them.

The dead in the parking lot seemed to be caught in a moment of indecision. Fresh meat was in front of them, but their instinct to pursue noise and movement compelled them to react to the machine. Some of them left the chase and began shuffling toward the loader; the rest turned stiffly back and continued to chase Sam and his team.

In that instant of indecision, though, Sam turned and ran, yelling to the others to move, to abandon the fight. Some of the faster zombies tore through the crowds in close pursuit. Dez moved up to offer covering fire, and Charlie Matthias shifted into the path of two running infected. He swung his pipe at the knees of the first one, sending it crashing to the ground. The second tripped over it and fell, and before it could climb back to its feet Charlie smashed its skull.

Then five more of the fast ones broke from the pack and ran straight at Charlie. They were between Dez and him; he was in her direct line of fire.

Charlie flung his pipe at the leading zombie, pivoted like a dancer and sprinted for the line of parked cars. Trout lost sight of him, and a moment later he saw Dez turn away. Charlie had either made it to safety or not.

The big front-end loader was still by the gate. The entire cab was covered in zombies like bees on a honeycomb, but the driver kept rolling forward, kept raising and lowering the heavy bucket. The movements were so erratic, though, that Trout couldn't tell if he could ever see out of the control cab.

Dez fired at the front rank of zombies as the soldiers reached her. Then the others turned and suddenly they had a shooting line. They fired as they walked backward. The dead kept coming, and the gap between the soldiers and the infected was rapidly closing. Fifty feet.

Forty.

Thirty.

Trout could see from the looks on their faces that they knew they weren't going to make it.

That's when the first of the buses came hurtling past the line of shooters and plowed into the dead.

It was a wonderful, heroic, desperate move.

And it was absolutely the wrong thing to do.

School buses are tough, but they are not built for head-on collisions with masses of people. The bus struck the wall of zombies and slammed to a stop. Everyone inside was thrown forward. The driver's airbag burst out and slammed the driver backward. The windshield cracked in a thousand places.

"Shit!" yelled Trout and he began running toward the bus.

Running hurt.

Every step was screaming agony.

He took that pain and ate it. He fed on it. He devoured it whole and used its fiery heat to drive his legs and propel him off the dock and around the back of the bus to come up on the side farthest from the zombies. He jerked the door open and saw that the driver—the farmer who'd driven tractors all his life—was out cold. The airbag, designed to deflate after impact, was sagging. Trout grabbed the driver, hauled him out of the seat, shot the handle to close the door, and slid behind the wheel. Kids and adults were both screaming. Zombies were pounding on the cracked windshield. It was not going to last. He backed the bus up to get a better angle to go around the swarm.

There was a series of loud thumps on the side and then on top of the bus, and to his horror Trout realized that bodies were scaling the side of the bus. He started accelerating and was about to jam on the brakes to try and jolt the dead off the roof when he heard a fresh barrage of shots.

From above.

He looked to where Dez and the solders had been but they were gone. Then he understood. When the bus crashed, Dez and Sam and the Boy Scouts had clambered atop the bus, out of reach of the dead.

Could the dead climb, too? He had no idea.

He began moving forward again, but the dead were closing in and forming an impenetrable wall. With every few feet he had to slow down or risk another collision. The windows would never withstand another hit.

Then there was that engine roar again and the front-end loader came smashing through the wall of dead. The digging teeth of the big bucket crunched into the backs of the zombies, shattering spines, snapping their bodies backward. The dead still swarmed over the cab, but one by one they pitched off. Almost as an after echo Trout heard gunshots from above. Dez and the others were clearing the dead off the cab so that the driver could see what he was doing.

Trout felt movement beside him and Jenny DeGroot was there, staring out the window in astonishment, pointing at the driver.

"Uncle Jake?" she gasped.

Trout understood. The big, burly man in the loader's cab was Jake DeGroot. He wore a fierce, strange grin as he worked the levers that brought the bucket up and down, up and down. From above Trout heard Dez screaming two words.

"Turn around! Turn around!"

Jake either heard it despite the din of gunfire, moans, and engine roars, or he simply grasped the need of the moment. He began backing and filling, backing and filling, making a big, bloody, bone-breaking, meat-burst turn amid and atop the milling dead. They were legion, but the diesel monster with the hydraulic bucket was unstoppable. It completed its turn and began rolling toward the front gate, crushing everything in its path. As more of the dead swarmed up onto the cab, Dez and the soldiers shot them down.

The gunfire from above was continuous.

The front-end loader roared out with a voice like a dragon; Jake lowered the bucket so that it scraped along the surface of the ground as the tons of unfeeling yellow-painted steel, splashed now with red and black, hit the wall of unfeeling flesh and bone. The front-end loader paused but for a moment as it pushed through tons of slack meat, then the bodies fell to either side, creating a chute through which twelve yellow buses passed.

When the loader reached the road it turned right, and Trout followed.

Trout caught a flash of red off to the far side of the lot and saw Charlie Matthias's red Le Mans go rocketing out of the gate, turn left and head west. Within seconds the vehicle was dwindling into the distance.

In rumbling convoy, they left the warehouse behind. The dead followed in their hundreds, but even at the slow speed of the loader, the shambling mass of infected fell farther and farther behind.

Soon they were not following at all.

CHAPTER ONE HUNDRED TWENTY-EIGHT
THE SITUATION ROOM
THE WHITE HOUSE, WASHINGTON, D.C.

Scott Blair and the president stood side by side in front of the big screen. There were now dozens of smaller windows open to show live streams of ongoing battles, of troops moving into position, of swarms of the dead moving through towns and cities, of the mass exodus of whole populations trying to flee the outbreak.

The reports were coming in from all over.

The latest incidents were in Oregon and New Hampshire. Anywhere a car could drive or a plane could fly.

Which was everywhere.

There was even an unconfirmed report of an attack in Charles De Gaulle Airport in Paris. A Delta flight from Pittsburgh touched down there. The news reports were erratic, wild. And probably true. England, Italy, Germany, and Russia had fighter-bombers on deck, waiting for go orders to make preemptive strikes.

Blair had no doubts that those orders would be given.

Just as new stories went viral on the Internet, infecting the world at the speed of social networking, so now could a biological threat spread globally at the speed of modern travel. Planes, trains, and automobiles.

And wind.

The devil was in the wind now, and the earth itself was exhaling the parasites into the global weather pattern.

Soon Lucifer would be everywhere.

An aide came hurrying over and handed the president a paper, which he read, sighed, and handed to Blair. It was from Dr. Price. The Reaper counterparasite was in full development now. The first batches were being loaded into rockets for deployment over Pittsburgh.

"We're going to use a monster to fight a monster," said the president. "How wrong does that sound to you, Scott?"

"We have to try something. We have to try everything."

"Yes, I suppose we do."

One of the small windows showed an aerial surveillance feed of a line of yellow buses rolling through the forested hills of West Virginia. The president touched the image, brushing the vehicles with the tips of his fingers.

"All those children," he said. "The children of Stebbins and the children everywhere . . ."

"Sir?"

"They will never forgive us for this," said the president.

Blair's mouth was a tight and bitter line. "Maybe they shouldn't."

The door burst open and Sylvia Ruddy came running in, her face flushed, eyes wide with a fierce excitement.

"Mr. President! Oh my God, Mr. President!"

CHAPTER ONE HUNDRED TWENTY-NINE
ZABRISKE POINT BIOLOGICAL EVALUATION AND PRODUCTION STATION
DEATH VALLEY, CALIFORNIA

All of Z-point had become a hive, filled with techs and aides and support staff who ran everywhere in a mad scramble to prepare all samples of Reaper, and to kick the manufacturing process into high gear.

Dick Price was the only person who stood still and silent.

There was a big glass window separating him from the main production floor of the station. Everyone on the far side of that three-inch-thick glass wore hazmat suits. He was in his immaculate white lab coat. To his right was a bank of security monitors and three of them showed exterior views of the helipad carved high onto a mountain far away from any possibility of civilian ground or air traffic. A powerful Chinook was lifting ponderously from the pad. In the air beyond it were three more. Waiting to land. Waiting to off-load viable organic vectors.

A nice name for people who had been transformed by Lucifer into something else.

The military kept bringing more of them here to Z-point in the hopes that among the samples would be evidence of mutation or variation. Within mutation lay potential. Mutation suggested that Volker's monster was not unchangeable. Anything that could, in time, be changed could, in time, be understood and defeated.

In time.

Price felt icy lines of sweat trickle down his spine.

Three of the monitors had been switched to live news feeds.

Pittsburgh was in flames.

The whole city. Burning.

There were outbreaks in Philadelphia, New York, D.C., Atlan A dozen other cities. And now there were reports in Paris, Londo and Madrid.

The experts the press trotted out decried these reports on the grounds that no disease could spread that fast. And that was true enough if this was the beginning of the twentieth century instead of well into the twenty-first. Any disease could spread at the speed of transportation.

A lot of planes flew out of Pittsburgh in the hours after the fuel-air bombs shot the parasites into the atmosphere and transformed Lucifer from a serum-transfer pathogen to an airborne pathogen.

A whole lot of planes.

Beyond the glass wall his people worked like crazed ants to produce and pack the Reaper mutagen.

Price was too numb to pray that Reaper would work.

The tests on the Volker infected were ongoing, but it would be months before any reliable conclusions could be drawn. He'd told the president that. He'd told the generals that.

It *might* work was a million miles away from it *will* work.

It was even farther from *we should try it.*

If only they had Volker's notes . . .

He prayed to a God he'd long ago ceased to believe in. He prayed with every fiber of his being that there was still time to find that research and to study it for a doorway out of this hell.

On the monitor the second Chinook was now landing on the pad and the first was already dwindling in the distance.

His cell rang and it jolted Price out of his horrified daze. He fished it out of his pocket and saw that the scramble alert was active. He punched that button and held the phone to his ear.

"Th-this is Price."

"We have it," said a breathless Scott Blair.

"What?"

"The reporter who had them gave them to his cameraman and he sent it all via DropBox to his email accounts. The cybercrimes team cracked it and downloaded everything. I'm sending it to you now."

Price closed his eyes and swayed. He murmured three words he would have mocked anyone else for saying.

"Thank you, God . . ."

CHAPTER ONE HUNDRED THIRTY
ROUTE 80
FAYETTE COUNTY, PENNSYLVANIA

When they were sure it was safe, the convoy stopped in the middle of the road.

Trout nearly collapsed over the wheel. Strange, bad lights were bursting all around him and he saw darkness trying to close in around the edges of his vision. He took several long breaths and gradually—gradually—reclaimed himself.

Jenny jerked the door open and went running toward the front-end loader. Big Jake DeGroot climbed down, snatched her up and swung her around. She was like a toy in his massive arms. Their simple joy seemed to put a tiny swatch of color into the day.

Behind him, children were snuffling and crying. With fear and perhaps with relief.

Thumps atop the bus told Trout that Dez and the soldiers were climbing down. He hauled himself out of the seat and staggered outside to find Dez.

She was the first to come down and she ran to him and wrapped her strong arms around him. She was stained with gunpowder residue and sweat, and Trout could not help kissing her lips and her face over and over again. Then he held her as Gypsy and Boxer climbed down.

Trout looked up, waiting for Shortstop and Sam.

Waiting.

"No," said Dez, and there were tears in her eyes. Gypsy leaned her head on Boxer's shoulders and they sobbed quietly together.

He stared at her without understanding what she meant.

"What—wait, Dez, where are they? What happened?"

"Didn't you see? Back at the loading bay?"

"See what?"

"They *died*, Billy," she said wretchedly. "Both of them. We climbed up onto the bus, but they didn't have time. Those bastards were all over us. God, Billy. I tried to pull Sam up. I tried . . ."

She sobbed brokenly and beat on his chest. It hurt, but he did not care.

Sam Imura?

Gone?

Trout didn't know how to process that. Imura was so tough, so capable. Trout was sure that he was the leading man in this drama, the hero that would save everyone.

Gone. Off screen.

Simply edited out of the story.

Shortstop, too, and Trout realized that he didn't even know the man's name. But Sam . . . even though the soldier had only been with them for a few hours, he'd become a friend. They trusted him. They knew him.

Now he was gone, and Sam was gone.

The heroes of the story were gone and Trout had not even seen it. Somehow that was worse than if he'd witnessed it. These men was simply gone from the world. Dragged down. Consumed.

No . . . worse . . .

Even now the thing that had been Sam Imura would have risen. What was left of him would have risen and maybe it had been part of that horde of things that had pursued the convoy.

It was too horrible to imagine.

It was all too horrible.

Who would be the heroes now?

He held on to Dez, who was frayed and worn and nearly spent.

Who was going to ride to the rescue now?

While the sun burned through the last of the clouds and painted the landscape with yellow light, Dez and Billy clung to each other and wept.

CHAPTER ONE HUNDRED THIRTY-ONE
ZABRISKE POINT BIOLOGICAL EVALUATION AND
PRODUCTION STATION
DEATH VALLEY, CALIFORNIA

Dick Price and his senior staff sat in a silent line, each of them bent forward, their faces washed to a pale blue by the lights of computer monitors. On each computer pages of data flashed by. Research notes. Developmental procedure records. Laboratory tests on animals. Formulae. Data on the transgenesis of a dozen parasites. Dosage tables. Biological warfare applications. Modifications for use on death row prisoners. A complete medical history of condemned serial murderer Homer Gibbon.

It was all there.

All of it.

One hundred and ninety-two thousand pages of information.

Some of it was in Russian. Some in Lithuanian. Some in Polish. Some in Latin.

Some in English.

Some written in the hieroglyphics of molecular chemistry.

Parts of the data were old, scans of handwritten documents dating back to the early 1970s. Other parts were very recent, as new as five days ago, which meant that it was one day before Homer Gibbon had been given Lucifer 113 instead of the drugs meant to kill him during the court-mandated lethal injection.

Two days before Homer Gibbon woke up in the mortician's suite at Hartnup's Transition Estate.

Three days before the army dropped their fuel-air bombs.

Four days before Pittsburgh was overrun and subsequently burned.

Five days before the mass outbreaks that turned Manhattan into a war zone. Before Paris was carpet-bombed by the French Air Force.

Before the prime minister of Great Britain ordered all of the bridges spanning the Thames to be blown.

Five days before the Air Force began exploding missiles packed with payloads of raw Reaper over Philadelphia, St. Louis, Detroit, and a dozen other cities. Each bomb was precisely timed to detonate in the path of prevailing winds that would carry it over large portions of the most densely populated areas.

That was today. The Reaper mutagen was in the wind now and soon they'd all know if it would slow Lucifer's spread. Or, if God had any mercy left for His children, stop it.

Price's team had worked without sleep for days. Reading Volker's information, making sense of what was clearly the work of a man who was both brilliant and insane.

An actual mad scientist.

Price had tried to laugh at that, to find one moment of comic relief in which the irony would vent some of the crushing tension. But he couldn't. When he'd tried to laugh he cried instead.

Scott Blair kept calling. Over and over and over again, demanding answers.

Demanding hope.

Price's cell rang again and Price snatched it up with a snarl and very nearly smashed it on the floor. Instead he pushed the green button with a trembling thumb.

"P-Price . . ."

There was no immediate reply.

"Hello?"

The only thing he heard from the other end of the all was the sound of someone quietly weeping.

"Mr. Blair?" said Price gently. "Scott . . . ?"

He heard a sniff and then Scott Blair's voice. "Price . . . Jesus Christ, what have you done?"

"What is it? What's wrong?"

Before Blair could answer someone screamed. Price and everyone turned away from their line of computers and saw one of the techs—a woman whose name Price couldn't remember in that moment—standing before the bank of TV monitors on the far wall.

She wrapped her arms over her head and sank slowly to her knees. She kept screaming.

Each of the monitors was set to local news in Philadelphia, St. Louis, Detroit, Los Angeles, Las Vegas, Minneapolis, Newark, Omaha, Chicago, and Miami. The cities with the largest populations where there were outbreaks. The cities most heavily hit by Lucifer. The cities over which Reaper missiles had been detonated a handful of hours ago.

Until now there had been a pattern to the outbreaks. A predictable speed.

Until now there had been a splinter of hope buried in Dick Price's soul.

Until now.

In those areas where Reaper was interacting with Lucifer, the rate of infection had shot up. The degree of murderous ferocity had doubled. Tripled. The reporters on the ground were letting the pictures tell the story that they were no longer able—or perhaps willing—to report.

The cycle of bite to infection to death to reanimation was now so much faster.

Too fast.

Way too fast.

The infection was out of all control.

Out of any possibility of control.

Reaper, inadequately tested, not at all ready for deployment, had been used by the military in a desperate gamble to introduce mutation to a perfect weapon. If something was perfect then any change would, by definition, create flaws in that perfection. That was the logic, and it was as flawed as the science.

Dick Price stared at the screen and now he understood the last secret in Volker's science. The most important secret.

Lucifer, for all its power and aggression, had not been perfect.

Better than all generations before it, but far from perfect.

Until now.

Until something allowed—even encouraged it—to mutate further. That one step further until it was, without doubt, perfect.

Until Reaper.

The phone fell from Price's fingers and shattered on the floor.

The woman kept screaming.

Everyone else began screaming.

It seemed like the only possible response. The only appropriate response. So Dick Price screamed, too.

CHAPTER ONE HUNDRED THIRTY-TWO
ROUTE 81
NEAR HUNGRY MOTHER STATE PARK
SOUTHWESTERN VIRGINIA

The traffic on the highway started off as bad, became worse, became impossible. Dez and Trout crouched in the exit well and studied the road through the big windshield. Jake DeGroot was behind the wheel of the first bus, and Dez touched his arm and pointed to a small side road blocked by a chain and a sign saying that it was reserved for forestry service vehicles only.

"There," she said. "Let's get out of this shit. Pull off."

"What about the chain?" asked Trout.

"Fuck the chain," she said. "Jake, get us out of this shit and I'll deal with the chain."

Jake edged the bus that way, but the traffic was jammed tight and moved forward an inch at a time. He hit the horn, got nothing, then jammed his hand down on it in a continuous blare. Still got nothing.

Jake shook his head. "It's too tight, there's not enough room."

Dez snarled and jerked the handle that worked the door, snatched up a combat shotgun and jumped out.

There was a big Tundra to the right of the bus, blocking their way. Dez used her scuffed knuckles to rap on the driver's window.

"Hey, buddy, how about pull off so we can get through?"

The driver, a big man with a John Deere cap, refused to even look at her. He had snow-white hair and a mean-looking face. The man riding shotgun was equally muscular and twice as ugly. He felt for the pistol in his pocket.

Dez tapped again, much harder. "Yo! Dickhead, you deaf or something?"

The driver raised one hand, forefinger extended and still didn't look at her.

"Dez," called Trout as he stepped down from the bus, "be careful."

Dez ignored him. With a grunt of angry effort, she slammed the shotgun's stock into the driver's window. It imploded, showering the driver and the man in the passenger seat with safety glass.

That did it.

Both doors opened and the two men got out.

"The fuck you think you're doing, you cu—"

That was as far as he got before Dez Fox hit him across the face with the rifle stock. The blow ripped a bloody gash in the man's jaw and whipped his head around so hard that he spun into the side of the Tundra. His forehead hit the open doorframe and he dropped right onto his kneecaps.

The other man came running around the car, fists raised to smash Dez.

Billy Trout shoved the barrel of his borrowed pistol into the man's ear.

"Touch her and I'll blow your fucking head off," he said.

He heard himself speak the words, felt his mouth say them, and he did not recognize the voice. It was him and it wasn't. There was such cold honesty there and in that moment he knew that he would, if he had to, shoot this man.

It sickened him to realize that he'd come to this point.

But it made him feel stronger, too.

For maybe the first time since this thing started.

His arm was out straight, the gun in his fist, and it was rock steady.

Dez turned and saw the gun and then looked at him. Into his eyes. A tiny smile flickered across her lips. There and gone.

To the passenger, Dez said, "You're going to help your butt-buddy into your car, and then you're going to pull off and let us pass. That's not a request. We got a couple hundred kids in those buses."

The man with the gun to his head looked terrified. He licked his lips. "We have to get out, too. I got a kid at home. Barney has three kids. We're just trying to get home."

Dez's eyes stayed hard. "All you had to do was pull over and let us pass. The fuck's wrong with you?"

"God . . . don't touch me," begged the man, shrinking back from her. "Please. Don't touch me."

That's when Trout noticed that no one else had gotten out of their cars. With all of the traffic stalled for so long, somebody should have gotten out. There were always people who viewed traffic jams like this as impromptu tailgate parties. But everywhere he looked, everywhere Dez looked, the people were hunched inside their cars, the windows up, eyes wide with fear, faces locked into expressions of desperation. Trout almost laughed at the absurdity of it. These people were fleeing in slow motion. Unwilling to get out of their cars, they sat there, waiting for the traffic to move, maybe praying for it to inch forward, and every single one of them terrified at the thought of contact with the people around them. Who was infected? Was the thing on the radio here?

Slow motion panic.

It was a brand-new concept, and it kept turning over and over in Trout's mind until he couldn't help but laugh.

Dez shot him an angry, worried look. So did the frightened passenger, and the people in the closest cars.

The only sound on the whole road was the sound of that laugh.

And, without support to prop it up, Trout's laughter slowly collapsed. Almost into sobs, but he coughed his throat clear and stepped back until he sat down hard on the entrance step of the bus, the pistol hanging limply from his hand.

"Billy?" ventured Dez. "You okay?"

He wanted to explain it to her, to see if she'd laugh, too; but he didn't. It would be too much like telling a dirty joke in church.

"Don't hurt him" was all he said.

The passenger looked from Trout to Dez.

"Move the car," said Dez quietly.

The man nodded. He picked up his friend and helped him around to the passenger side, belted him in, closed the door, and came around to the driver's side. While he was doing all of that, Dez leaned in and used her palm to brush the glass off the seat. She stepped back to the let the man slide in behind the wheel.

"I'll lose my place in line," he said.

Dez shook her head. "No, you won't."

She backed away from the car and turned in a slow circle to look through windshields at the other drivers. The shotgun was in her hands, barrel sweeping along at the level of headlights and grills.

"We're getting off this road," she said, pitching her voice very loud. "This car is going to pull off to let the buses out. Anyone else in the way needs to do the same. Once we're out of here, you can all fill in, but the cars that move get their places back."

Trout thought it was one of the most surreal things he'd ever heard. It was like Dez was announcing the rules before a school-yard game of dodgeball. It was all done in an otherwise absolute silence.

Dez seemed also to realize how absurd it was and Trout saw different expressions war on her face. Dez took a breath and in her best cop voice, her voice of officialdom and authority, said, "This thing isn't here. No one in these cars is infected. If they were we'd know it already. You're safe. Your families are safe. Stay in your cars and when the road clears out keep heading south. There's a big safety camp in Asheville, North Carolina. Head there. You hear me? Head there."

No one said a thing. The windows stayed up. Hands gripped steering wheels. Eyes were fixed on her.

"You'll be okay," shouted Dez. "Everyone will be okay."

Nothing. Not a word, not a toot of a horn, not even a nod from the watching people.

In a quiet voice, Trout said, "Come on, Dez. You did what you could."

Behind her the Tundra revved its engines and began a turn between the tightly packed cars. At first it looked impossible in the nearly bumper-to-bumper crush. Then the car in front of it rolled forward a couple of feet; and the car behind it did the same. Even with that it was still tight, but the Tundra began the turn. Dez walked past it to the forest service road. She swung the shotgun up, aimed it at the lock and blew it to shiny metal splinters. The chain fell away and the sound of the blast echoed along the road.

Trout watched people flinch, but otherwise they sat in their eerie, watchful stillness.

The shoulder was blocked with cars, too, but with Dez calling directions and banging on hoods with the shotgun, the cars shifted by slow, painful inches forward and at angles until after ten excruciating minutes there was a lane just big enough for the bus. She waved to

Jake, who put it in gear and crept with infinite slowness around the wall of cars on his right. At one point his bumper scraped the trunk of a VW, but if the driver of the car cared about it, he kept it to himself.

"Come on, come on," Dez said between her teeth as she walked backward, guiding Jake's turn. Trout had gotten out of the bus to watch the other side.

The stillness of everything else except the big yellow bus continued to gnaw at his nerves. As the first bus finally cleared the road and rambled through onto the access lane, he realized what it was. Nothing about this fit into any workable scenario for a world he understood. This slow-motion panic, the absolute fear of human contact, the weight of the disaster that pressed down on them, the terror of what might be behind them—all of that was new. Sure, there were corollaries to different elements of it, but as a whole this was a new thing. A new pattern. And he greatly feared that it was part of a new world.

Or, perhaps, a new world order.

A new age of the world. He was sure it was something like that, though his mind rebelled at a specific definition because it all felt too big, too grandiose.

Except that it wasn't.

It was unprecedented.

This was no longer the world he and Dez and the children on the bus and the people in these cars knew.

Since the release of Lucifer 113 it had become a different world. And in every bad way that mattered, it seemed to him that this new world did not belong to these people. Or to any people. This world now belonged to the Devil.

Maybe it wasn't the biblical Devil, he told himself, but he wasn't sure if that distinction even mattered.

Lucifer, by any definition, in any form, owned this world now.

"God help us," he murmured as the line of buses moved slowly past. He saw the pale faces of terrified children, and the blank and vacant eyes of those for whom terror was a minor milestone left behind in a distant country. "God help us."

But if anyone listened to that prayer, no voice offered even the ghost of a promise to Billy Trout.

CHAPTER ONE HUNDRED THIRTY-THREE
HUNGRY MOTHER STATE PARK
SOUTHWESTERN VIRGINIA

They bumped and thumped along the access road for nearly five miles until they came to a forest service station near the crest of the mountain. There was a small building and a large parking lot with various pieces of heavy equipment. A road grader, flatbeds for hauling downed trees, a dump truck piled with gravel.

There were no people and no personal cars.

Dez, Boxer, and Gypsy approached the building, guns up and out, but they found nothing. The door was open, the lights were on, but the station was deserted. Jake led the way and the buses pulled into the lot and lined up in a row. Somehow Trout found it disturbing that the row was so neat. Each of the adults driving the buses parked in a precise line with the other vehicles. There was something wrong about that, but he couldn't decide what it was.

A disconnection from reality, perhaps. He kept it to himself.

The last vehicle in the convoy was a flatbed truck they'd stolen from a construction site a few miles from Sapphire Foods. Jake had loaded his Big Bird onto it and one of the parents helped him and drove the big rig. He parked the rig with the same precision.

Maybe they're trying to impose order on chaos, thought Trout. That was probably it, though it felt a bit like tidying the furniture and vacuuming the rugs during a house fire.

Trout got off the bus and waited for Dez to come out. He watched the parents and teachers begin lining up the kids for trips to the bathroom in the station. Some—those that couldn't wait—were escorted to the tall grass on the far side of the parking lot. Jake, his niece Jenny, and a few of the adults who had guns, began fanning out to stand perimeter watch. As if that was something they'd always done. As if that was somehow normal.

It is now, he told himself. And that wrenched the knife in his heart another quarter turn.

Dez came out of the station, looked around for him, then came over, her shoulders slumped, face haggard.

"Anything?" he asked. "You were in there a while."

"There's a radio," she said.

"And?"

She simply shook her head.

They walked together to the edge of the drop-off. He could barely walk and needed to lean on her for the seventy paces to the bench that offered a beautiful view of the mountains and the sky. On any other day it would be breathtaking.

Down below, the traffic on the highway crawled.

"At least it's moving," said Dez.

"Yeah, there's that."

Neither of them could manufacture any convincing optimism.

"What did the radio say?"

From where they sat they could hear the sobs of the children and the constant murmur of adult voices as the parents and teachers did everything they could to convince the kids that it was all going to be all right.

Trout marveled at how similar a promise sounded to a lie. Or was it all just wishful thinking?

"Dez?"

She removed the walkie-talkie from her belt and turned up the gain. It babbled at them in a dozen overlapping voices. Military and civilian authorities, and even some militia groups whose shortwave signals were breaking into the flow. It was all hysterical and most of the voices were asking for backup, for relief, for medical attention, for emergency services, for help.

For answers.

"The radio's the same. No one has any answers," she said. "Most people don't know about Homer or Volker or any of that. All they know is that there's a plague and nobody seems to be able to stop it. There's a lot of bullshit, too. People saying it's the Rapture, shit like that."

"Maybe it's true."

"Don't start, Billy."

"Sorry."

He bent forward and put his head in his hands. Some of the glass cuts on his scalp and arms hadn't yet been seen to, and he didn't care. Dez sat beside him, hollow-eyed and hollow-cheeked, her arms mottled with powder burns, her knuckles as raw and red as her eyes as she methodically reloaded her pistol and shotgun.

Slowly, painfully, Trout raised his head as a flight of six fighter jets screamed overhead into the northeast.

"Thunderbolts," said Dez automatically.

"Where do you think they're headed?"

"I don't know." She thought about it. "Charleston, maybe."

He nodded.

There were more than a hundred thousand people in Charleston. *Maybe*, he corrected himself. He didn't really know if that was true anymore.

Dez got up and went back to the bus, then returned with a bottle of water, his camera bag, and a map. She set the bag down in front of him.

"What's that for?" he asked.

"In case you want to use it."

He shook his head.

They left it there as she opened the map and spread it out over their laps.

He studied her blue eyes for a few moments. He saw so many things in those eyes. A fear so deep that it looked like it was cracking the hinges of her sanity. He saw ghosts in her eyes. JT, the dead children, her colleagues and neighbors in Stebbins, the people who had died on the buses. Each of them had left its specter in her mind, polluting her, driving fissures into her. Trout knew with absolute certainty that if Dez had to live on this edge for much longer, she was going to break. Those qualities that made her so strong—compassion, her love for the children, her need to save as many as she could—they were each failures waiting to happen. A person cannot be sustained on a diet of their own failure, even if that failure is not their fault. This thing was so big, so vast that it even consumed people like Sam Imura. What hope did Dez really have?

He almost took her in his arms, almost made the unforgiveable error of offering comfort and a shoulder to someone who was right there at the edge of her control.

Billy Trout almost made that mistake, but he didn't.

Some instinct stopped him even as he began to raise his hands. It was as if JT Hammond stood behind him and bent to whisper advice in his ear. JT, who was more of a father to Dez than her real one had been. JT, who was, very likely, the best person either of them had ever known.

She needs to be strong, Trout imagined he heard JT say. *She needs to take these kids home.*

Trout took a breath and let it out.

"Asheville, huh?"

"That's what Sam said."

"Okay," said Trout, "then it's Asheville."

He did not dare ask what they would do if the infection had reached Asheville. That was a war they could fight on another day. If they had the chance.

For now, Asheville was a direction.

It was far away from Pittsburgh.

It was in the mountains, so maybe that would be something.

Trout didn't know and really couldn't make any guesses. It was a direction, a place to head to. And that felt much better than having a place to run from. So much better.

They heard a sound like thunder and looked up to see more aircraft. Helicopters this time. Dozens of them.

Maybe hundreds.

Black Hawks and Apaches. And the big cargo choppers, the Chinooks. An armada of the air. Powerful, threatening. They filled the sky, flying in waves, heading north, and the clouds seemed to fall back before them, revealing blues skies that offered at least the illusion of promise.

Trout wanted to feel hope when he looked at them, but it was slow in coming.

"The storm's over," he said, hoping it meant more than a weather report.

Dez watched the helicopters fly across the clearing sky.

"Will it be enough?" Trout asked.

Dez shook her head. "I don't know."

After a thoughtful moment, Dez nudged the camera bag toward him.

"I told you, I don't—"

"You need to file a report," she interrupted.

"Why? What's the point?"

Dez bent and unzipped the case, removed the camera, studied it, and found the record button. She rested a finger over it. "This isn't everywhere yet," she said. "It's spreading, but it isn't everywhere yet."

"I know, but—"

"You need to tell people, Billy. You need to *keep* telling people. You need to tell them everything we know. What it is. How it spreads. How to fight them. Everything."

"Who's going to listen?"

Dez shrugged. The drone of the helicopters was fading to a rumor in the sky. "What does it matter? Somebody will. Maybe if all we do is get the word out to a few, that'll matter. Maybe we'll help some people get through this."

"*We'll* get through it."

Dez smiled faintly and nodded. "Then it's on us to help whoever we can. However we can. Everything's going to shit, Billy. We can't be a part of that. We can't be a part of the end. We have to be a part of whatever survives. We have to help people so they know how to fight back. Am I . . . am I making sense?"

He stared at her for several seconds, watching her eyes, seeing the lights deep inside the blue. Loving her for this.

"Yes," he said, "you're making sense."

After a while Dez took his hand. Then Billy Trout reached out and pulled her gently into his arms. Not to comfort her.

He kissed her with all the heat and hope and love that he had left inside.

The kiss she gave back was scalding.

When they stopped, gasping and flushed, Trout murmured, "I love you."

She said, "Now, Billy? Really? God, you're such a girl."

Laughing out loud, she walked back to the bus.

CHAPTER ONE-HUNDRED THIRTY-FOUR

SUNSET HOLLOW GATED COMMUNITY
MARIPOSA COUNTY, CALIFORNIA

Tom Imura ran and the night burned around him.

The darkness pulsed with the red and blue of police lights; the banshee wail of sirens tore apart the shadows of the California night.

The child in his arms screamed and screamed and screamed.

Tom clutched little Benny to his chest. He could feel his brother's tiny heart beating like the flutter of dragonfly wings. His own felt like a bass drum being pounded by a madman. Sweat ran down his chest and mixed with the toddler's tears.

Tom turned once and saw them.

He saw her first.

Standing in the window, her arms reaching toward him. She was so pale, so beautiful. Like a ghost in a dream. Her dark eyes were wide with terror, her mouth shaped words that were lost in all the noise. He knew what those words were, though. Just one word really, said over and over again.

"Go!"

Tom ran. He felt like a coward.

Tom Imura, the police cadet. Tough, top of his class. Tom, the martial artist, with black belts and trophies and certificates. Tom, the fighter.

Tom, the coward.

Running.

"I'm sorry!" he yelled, but he was sure Mom didn't hear him.

And then he saw the other figure. Paler, larger, infinitely stranger, coming out of the shadows of the bedroom, reaching as Mom had reached, but not reaching for Tom and Benny. Those pale hands reached for her. For Mom. Reached for her, and dragged her back into darkness.

With all of the sirens and gunfire and the pounding of his own heart, Tom could not have heard her screams. He could not have.

And yet they echoed in his head. In his arms, Benny kept screaming.

Tom screamed, too.

Pale shapes lurched toward him from the shadows. Some of them were victims—bleeding, eyes wide with shock and incomprehension. Others were them. The things. The monsters. Whatever they were.

Tom had weapons in his car. His pistol—which he wasn't even allowed to carry yet because he didn't graduate from the police academy until tomorrow—and his stuff from the dojo. His sword, some fighting sticks.

Should he risk it? Could he risk it?

The car was at the end of the block. He had the keys, but the streets were clogged with emergency vehicles. Even if he got his gear, could he find a way to drive out?

No. Buildings were on fire. Fire trucks and crashed cars were like a wall.

But the weapons.

The weapons.

Benny screamed. The monsters shambled after him.

"Go!" his mother had said. "Take Benny . . . keep him safe. Go!"

Just . . . go.

He ran to the parked car. Benny was struggling in his arms, hitting him, fighting to try and get free.

Tom held him with one arm—an arm that already ached from carrying his brother—and fished in his pocket for the keys. Found them. Found the lock. Opened the door, popped the trunk.

Gun in the glove compartment. Ammunition in the trunk. Sword in the trunk.

Shapes moved toward him. He could hear their moans.

He turned a wild eye toward one as it reached for the child Tom carried.

Tom shouted in terror. He lashed out with a kick, driving the thing back, splintering its leg. It fell, but it was not hurt. Not in any real sense of being hurt. As soon as it crashed down it began to crawl toward him.

It was unreal. Tom understood that this thing was dead. It was Mr. Harrison from three doors down and it was also a dead thing. A monster.

Benny kept screaming.

Tom lifted the trunk hood and shoved Benny inside. Then he grabbed his sword. There was no time to remove the trigger lock on the gun. They were coming. They were here.

He slammed the hood, trapping the screaming Benny inside the trunk even as Tom ripped the sword from its sheath.

Three terrible minutes later, Tom unlocked the trunk and opened it.

Benny was cowering in the back of the trunk, huddled against Tom's gym bag. Tears and snot were pasted on his face. Benny opened his mouth to scream again, but he stopped. When he saw Tom, he stopped.

Tom stood there, the sword held loosely in one hand, the keys in the other.

Tom was covered with blood. The sword was covered with blood.

The bodies around the car . . . more than a dozen of them were covered with blood.

Benny screamed.

Not because he understood—he was far too young for that—but because the smell of blood reminded him of Dad. Of home. Benny wanted his mom.

He screamed and Tom stood there, trembling from head to toe. Tears broke from his eyes and fell in burning silver lines down his face.

"I'm sorry, Benny," he said in a voice that was as broken as the world.

Tom tore off his blood-splattered shirt. The T-shirt he wore underneath was stained but not as badly. Tom shivered as he lifted Benny and held him close. Benny beat at him with tiny fists.

"I'm sorry," Tom said again.

He gathered up what he could carry, turned, and with Benny in one arm and his sword in his other hand, Tom ran into the night as the world burned around him.

CHAPTER ONE-HUNDRED THIRTY-FIVE

EAST COMPTON
LOS ANGELES, CALIFORNIA

"This is Billy Trout, reporting live from the apocalypse . . ."

The car sat in the middle of the street with the radio playing at full blast.

All four doors were open.

The voice on the radio was saying that this was the end of the world.

There was no one in the car, no one in the streets. No one in any of the houses or stores. There wasn't a single living soul to hear the reporter's message.

It didn't matter, though.

They already knew.